"Sam." Elizabeth whispered his name and felt the electricity surge through her body as his mouth moved. He raised up a little so that he could look down at her. The pain and confusion were plainly written on Elizabeth's face. She spoke, but her voice was only a tiny, frail whisper. "Sam, please tell me, what's going to happen to us?"

The question pierced through him again and again. He had asked himself that many times, but to hear it on her lips gave it a power he didn't want to acknowledge. Sam stared at her eyes, and then her mouth, and with great effort the answer finally came from his lips. "I wish I knew, Elizabeth. I wish to God I knew...."

ABOUT THE AUTHOR

Andrea Davidson was born in Oklahoma and attended the University of Missouri where she received her B.A. in English. She began her writing career with the American Medical Association while living in Chicago. After the birth of her first child she became a free-lance writer for magazines and medical journals, as well as a free-lance editor for several Chicago publishers.

After moving to Houston, Texas, where she now resides with her husband and family, Andrea started her romance-writing career. She also writes under the pseudonym of Elise Randolph.

Andrea has written three American Romances: #16, *Music in the Night;* #21, *Untamed Possession;* and #45, *Treasures of the Heart.*

THE GOLDEN CAGE

ANDREA DAVIDSON

Harlequin Books

TORONTO • NEW YORK • LONDON
AMSTERDAM • PARIS • SYDNEY • HAMBURG
STOCKHOLM • ATHENS • TOKYO • MILAN

Published April 1984

ISBN 0-373-65001-9

The sea and the earth are unfaithful to their children:
a truth, a faith, a generation of men goes —
and is forgotten, and it does not matter!
Except, perhaps, to the few of those
who believed the truth, confessed the faith —
or loved the men.

Joseph Conrad
Nigger of the Narcissus

Chapter One

The shrill screech of metal wheels against metal track pierced the stagnant air with ruthless intensity as the elevated train rounded the curve on its route into downtown Chicago. Below the track on Blackhawk Street, in the tired, run-down area near the Turning Basin, a ceiling of brown hung like a heavy tarp over the late morning, a dull half-light that clung in brooding shadows to the withered facades of old buildings. Superfluous human forms loitered, aimless and apathetic, between the paint-chipped frames of doorways. All were indifferent to the passing commuter train.

Harry Finklemann, the pug-faced owner and operator of The Windy City Pawn Shop, was too busy bilking people out of their most treasured possessions to notice. If a sheep had fleece, it was a sure bet slippery Harry would find a way to shear it, and that was all that concerned him on this cool October morning.

Alvaro Eugenio-Montes-Ciruti Rodriguez, on the other hand, was too drunk to acknowledge much of anything. He was leaning against the side wall of the liquor store, his brown felt hat pulled down so low, it pushed his ears straight out to the sides like flaps. The neck of a bottle of Thunderbird protruded from the brown paper sack in his hand, and a silly grin plastered itself across his face.

Across the street, Maggie Moon was busy searching for treasures. Mumbling aloud to herself, she bent over and picked up an abandoned brown left boot, examining it closely. She stood it next to her own left foot and decided it would do quite nicely. Arguing loudly with herself on whether to house it in her green shopping bag or in her purple, she finally decided on the purple, then shuffled on down the street, rounding the corner where two skinny teen-agers huddled together and exchanged a thick wad of bills for a tiny packet of fine white powder.

None of them paid any attention to the train screaming along the tracks above them. Only Sam Winslow observed it, and he was trying to suppress a twinge of corrosive resentment for the apathy that was aboard the train.

He was walking down the sidewalk on his way to the Blackhawk mission as the train passed. Neighbors, leaning over the pigeon-mottled sills of second floor windows, greeted him with a smile and the dust from their flapping rugs. Those on the sidewalk nodded as they swept away the nightly accumulation of debris in front of their wilting shops.

Everyone on Blackhawk Street knew Sam Winslow.

He had a muscular build, an easy gait, a sturdy, handsome quality about him. His sandy-brown hair was carelessly groomed, his corduroy jeans faded, and his tan poplin jacket sported a couple of unfashionable iron-on patches. But it was his eyes that were most often remembered. A soft autumn brown, they radiated both self-confidence and an optimism rarely seen in this part of the city.

Although at this moment the optimism was hidden behind his annoyance as he stared up at the train. All eyes behind its windows were buried in the newspaper headlines, sheltered from the harshness of life below the tracks, divorced from its grim reality. Not one face had turned to the windows to take note of the disintegrating neighborhood below. Not one.

He knew that within minutes the train would ease into the downtown Loop, where the city crackled with the electricity of life and prosperity. There, newspapers would be folded and slipped into briefcases and the passengers would emerge from their iron-gray cocoon, safe at last from the threatening world only two miles to the northwest.

Sam took a shortcut across a vacant lot, but he stopped when he saw three young boys clamber up the tall steel supports to the tracks. A sense of panic began to rise within him as a vision of the tiny lifeless body he helped carry down from the tracks only a month ago flashed across his mind's eye.

He ran toward the boys, trying to catch them before they reached the top, but they were too far ahead of him. He yelled, but his warning was lost in the deafening clamor of wheels rattling against the metal rail.

Now in position, holding tight to the top of the iron posts, they hurled empty bottles at the train and hollered with delight at the sound of splintering glass. Then quickly they scrambled back down the supports, shrieking deliriously at their own bravado.

Sam caught up with them as they reached the bottom. He grabbed one of the boy's arms, but the other two got away. His heart was pounding with the memory of the little boy who had not been so lucky a month ago, and it filled him with impotent fury.

His eyes wide with mutinous protest, the captured boy stared at him, daring Sam to make the first move. The deadlock lasted only a moment before Sam loosened his hold and dropped his hands to his side. For a second the boy stood still and then, with a triumphant laugh, disappeared behind a rusty heap of abandoned cars and battered washing machines.

Sam let out a slow breath and shook his head in frustration. Here, every day was an uphill climb, but surely he would eventually reach some plateau where life would level off and become a little easier. He knew he had made some progress in this neighborhood since he came here a few years ago; but he also knew he still had a hell of a long way to go.

He lifted his eyes toward the tracks. The fading squall of the train as it hurried on its journey to downtown was like the cry of a child, carried on the wind in a long, lost sob.

Elizabeth drew open the heavy drapes with a flourish and clasped her hands together in anticipation of the response. To the delight of her guests, the strategically lighted lawn with its kidney-shaped pool and brick patio was revealed in all its splendor. The new waterfall had finally been completed and everyone at the party was just dying to see it.

Amidst the expected "ooohs" and "aahhs," Elizabeth mingled like the perfect hostess she was, shimmering blond hair swinging across her shoulders as she laughed gaily at one of the guest's not-so-witty remarks, and long emerald-green silk skirt swishing as she moved gracefully through the crowd.

If a prize were given to the loveliest hostess on Chicago's North Shore, it would surely have gone to Elizabeth Parkins. She was tall and willowy, with a pale softness that triggered a soaring pulse in any man around her.

The men adored her. The women envied her. And everyone fell all over themselves in attempts to be noticed by her. She was indeed a lucky woman.

Elizabeth yawned, then quickly scanned the room, hoping no one had observed the breach of etiquette. It was the typical crowd in their latest Paris creations. The same old stories, the same old faces. The same old sameness. She raised her glass to one of the handsome men across the room, and the playful smile she flashed at him could have dazzled the heavens.

Despite the indistinct tuggings of boredom, the sounds of the party were reassuring ones to her, familiar and reliable—the clinking of fine-cut crystal, the sonorous drone of inane small talk, even the low hum of careless elitist remarks. "Of course, my dear," she heard a woman say. "Our organization has donated a small fortune to those poor little colored people over there in the Sudan." The woman was rewarded with one of Elizabeth's prettiest smiles as she walked by.

Platters heaped with untouched but now tepid delicacies were carried by the help to the kitchen, where their contents were dumped unceremoniously down the disposal. Every now and then one of the maids with the catering service would dip a tiny shrimp in its sauce or spread a wafer with pâté before it was thrown away, but even they had grown used to excess and its tendency toward extravagant waste.

Adrienne Stebbins walked over to Elizabeth and studied her hostess and best friend with a mixture of admiration and jealousy. "Liz darling, you've been holding out on me. Wherever did you get that divine dress?"

"I had it made." Elizabeth smiled. "Do you really like it?"

"I love it."

"You look lovely too, Adrienne."

Adrienne picked at her dress. "Hmmm, thanks." She laughed. "God, would you listen to us. We sound like the mutual admiration society. But speaking of dressmakers, do you remember Janette Brenner? Don't you remember, she was at Vassar with us and she was studying to become a designer?"

Elizabeth laughed as the recollection came back to her. "Oh, sure. How could I forget her? She was the one who always had fifty pins stuck in her mouth and bolts of cloth following her down the hallways. Did she make it?"

"Amazingly enough, yes," Adrienne answered smugly. "And she's going to be here next month, showing at Saks. Let's go see what kind of rags she is designing, want to?"

"I'd love to. It sounds like fun."

"And don't forget that project on the west side you volunteered us for."

"What project?" Elizabeth asked.

"Uh-oh," Adrienne groaned, "here comes Melanie Hearndon. I don't think I can handle a conversation with her right now. We'll talk later," she whispered conspiratorially.

Elizabeth watched Melanie moving toward her, so she readied her smile. "Melanie dear, so glad you could make it."

"Liz, you always throw such marvelous parties. Have you met my cousin, Thomas Benson?" The auburn-haired woman linked her arm through the man's as she introduced him to her hostess.

Elizabeth held out a jeweled hand, and he lifted it to his lips, his eyes locking with hers for a glittering moment. He was quite handsome, elegant one would say, with almost-black hair that was styled to perfection. And those blue eyes! The way they followed her curves as if he would devour her.

She had heard all about Thomas Benson. In fact, she had heard of almost nothing else since he had come to town. Extraordinarily wealthy, dashing, debonair, and on and on and on. She had been positive that the man would turn out to be a terrible disappointment in person. However. . . maybe she should ask him to stay for a drink after the party.

Her sweeping glance took in the other men at the party. Since none of those in her social circle needed to work, very few of them did. Mostly they just hung around the club every day, riding horses as a prelude to rounds of drinks—that being the main event of the day—playing cards as an adjunct to rounds of drinks, and attempting halfhearted business deals as a finale to too many rounds of drinks.

The image made her uncommonly weary.

She slipped her hand from Thomas Benson's grasp, dodging with perfect ease any implied invitation his eyes might have held. "So glad you could make it tonight. I do hope you will be able to come with Melanie to my dinner party next Friday."

"If I'm still in town, I would love to come," he replied with just the right touch of aplomb.

Relieved that the more amorous moment had passed, she turned toward her other guests, her smile generous and irresistible. But the smile faded when she was faced with the disapproving frown of her mother, Louise Parkins Banning—Banning being the latest in a long line of husbands.

"He appeared to be a charming young man, Liz. Who was he?"

"I don't know. Benson something or other."

"Really, dear, you must try to remember names better. It's a reflection of your breeding, you know." Louise sloshed her drink over the rim of her glass. "Ooops."

Elizabeth's smile was restrained. "Yes, Mother, breeding."

Her mother, as well as all of her friends, were always pushing one eligible bachelor after another at her. They simply could not get it through their heads that she had no desire to marry. "Liz, you're thirty years old," her mother would whisper in incriminatingly hushed tones, relegating her daughter to the status of one who has some unmentionable social disease.

It was true that she was a curiosity among her set. Though there were other single men and women around, they were most often the products of divorce. None of them had never been married! Why, it was unheard of. That sort of thing was supposed to be reserved for feminists, gays, or—worse yet—working women.

But, then, perhaps it was her single status that enhanced the intriguing aura around Elizabeth. After all, it gave the men someone about whom to fantasize, and it gave the women someone to secretly pick to pieces.

Louise pursed her lips. "You're frowning, Liz. I hope that doesn't mean you're getting petulant. It does not become you, love. Did I remind you about the committee that's being set up? No, I didn't, did I? The members of the Guild are expecting you to head up their new fund-raising drive, so you mustn't disappoint them."

Elizabeth reached out to steady her mother's glass, but Louise continued without missing a beat. "You have such a flair for those types of things. Besides, you know how important this fund-raising is to your grandmother, not to mention what it will do to enhance your own standing. Liz, are you listening to me?"

Elizabeth's bright green eyes were scanning the room, making sure with inbred efficiency that each of her guest's needs were being assuaged. But she forced her attention to swing back to her mother. "I'm listening, I'm listening."

"Well, will you do it?"

"Yes, Mother, of course." Her tone was that of the dutiful daughter she had been taught to be.

"Good." The older woman nodded in satisfaction, grabbing her sixth glass of champagne off a passing tray. "And don't forget, on Wednesday your grandmother is giving her report at the Book Review Club and she expects you to be there. She says this book is *the* definitive work on societal decline in this country. You will be there?''

''Wouldn't miss it for the world,'' Elizabeth mumbled dryly. ''Oh, Joan!'' She waved to a woman she absolutely abhorred. ''Sorry, Mother, but I've been dying to hear about Joan's trip to Spain.''

''Well, all right,'' Louise said. ''Do you want me to stay after the party to help clean up? You know how these hired maids are. They never put anything where it belongs.''

Elizabeth watched her mother closely. Louise's expression was as sober as a judge, but she held her glass at a sharp angle and a steady trickle of champagne poured to the carpet.

''No, thank you, Mother. I can handle it.'' Elizabeth sighed and turned toward her guests. She lifted her shoulders, adjusted her smile, and moved through the crowd with grace and beauty, the regal princess at home among her adoring subjects.

Mama Vinzetti handed Sam another dish to dry. ''Sam, it's nearly seven o'clock. You've done more than enough. Why don't you go on home.''

''I'll help you finish up here. There certainly was a crowd out there today.''

Mama Vinzetti plunged her hands into the hot soapy water. ''Lots of hungry people.''

The mission's staff of eager volunteers was irregular—their rotation determined by the lunar cycle or perhaps only by whims of conscience. For whatever reason, the soup kitchen was often shorthanded, and when it was, Sam pitched in.

He stacked the unmatched plates and bowls in the cupboard above the sink and wiped a few beads of sweat from his forehead with the sleeve of his plaid shirt.

Though the stove had been turned off for some time, the heat from it was still almost overwhelming.

"Come on now, Sam, you've done enough. I've got Anna here with me, and you know how good she is in a kitchen." She turned a sly eye on him. "Maybe she will come cook for you someday, yes?"

Sam cleared his throat and looked away, but he found himself staring straight into the hot, hungry stare of Anna Vinzetti.

From Chicago Avenue to North Avenue and from Ashland to Halsted, everyone knew of Mama Vinzetti's crusade in life. She carried it out with the inexhaustible vitality of her Italian heritage and with the dogged perseverance of a zealous crusader in a savage land. Her well-intentioned campaign? To find a man for her nineteen-year-old daughter, Anna.

This might not have been such a difficult task, except for the fact that Anna was five feet eleven inches tall, weighed two hundred pounds, and had a sexual appetite that could debilitate the entire infield of the Chicago White Sox.

And Sam, being no fool, was fully aware that he was the latest target for which Mama Vinzetti and Anna's passionate cupid bow was aimed.

Swallowing certain emasculating feelings of being outweighed and outnumbered by these two very determined, confident women, Sam grabbed his jacket from the back of a chair and stepped out the door.

"See you tomorrow, Sam." Anna's low slur stroked the back of his neck, sending unwanted prickles all the way down his spine.

"Sure, Anna. Sure." He shoved his hands into the pockets of his jacket and hurried out into the evening.

From his pocket he extracted an apple he had tucked away and raised it to his mouth. But before he could take the first bite, his eyes landed on Billy Hawkins, better known on the street as "The Mole."

The grizzled, arthritic old man, who always wore the same long, tattered brown coat, was, with single-mindedly determination, rummaging through an overflowing trash can.

After finding a discarded can of red beans, Billy scraped the remains with his finger and poked it in his mouth. He smiled broadly, his unshaven face framing a toothless grin, as Sam walked up to him.

"Come with me, Billy," he said. "Let's go get something to eat." As expected, Billy shook his head vehemently, his eyes darting about in agitation, and Sam tried to hide his impatience with the old man. Billy had his ways, just as the street did, and nothing or nobody was going to change them.

Sam thought of some of the arguments he had used in the past, but decided against all of them. Instead, he offered the apple. Without a moment's hesitation Billy nodded his thanks and greedily accepted it, then dropped down to the sidewalk and beat the fruit against the pavement, splitting and smashing it into manageable bites.

He looked up, grinning, and Sam smiled. "You're welcome, Billy." A few harrowed lines appeared at the corner of Sam's mouth as he moved on down the sidewalk toward home.

He walked up the precarious stoop of his Victorian house, sidestepping the wood rot and loose boards on the steps. There were lots of things he would like to do to fix up the old house, but those things took time and money, two commodities he didn't have right now.

Sam unlocked the front door and noticed that the crack in its beveled glass pane had lengthened at least half an inch since last week.

Once inside, he emptied the pockets of his jacket and

tossed his keys and several scraps of paper onto the table by the coat rack. He unfolded one of the pieces of paper and frowned as he tried to decipher his own handwriting. Elizabeth Parkins, it said. Who was she and why had he written down her name?

He was always jotting reminders to himself and then stuffing them into pockets where he promptly forgot all about them. But he did recall now that he had written down this name several days ago. Elizabeth Parkins was the chairman of a select coterie of wealthy North Shore socialites who had volunteered to come look over the hospital tomorrow.

Sam wadded up the piece of paper and tossed it back onto the table. He had seen too many of these self-proclaimed philanthropists come and go in the last five years to get his hopes up with this group.

He hung his jacket on the coat rack, then grabbed his White Sox baseball cap off a hook and put it on. He flipped on the radio to the Monday night football game and stared into the near-empty refrigerator. He had forgotten, as usual, to stop at the market, so he was short on food as well as everything else. But, nothing new about that.

He ended up with a grilled cheese sandwich and a soda while he listened for the score of the game. One of these days he was going to scrape up enough money to go to Soldier Field and watch the Bears play. Someday.

He switched stations on the radio when he heard how bad his team was playing and tuned in some classical music. After cleaning up his dishes, he poured a glass of wine, carried it into the small living room, and set it on a lopsided table by the faded, overstuffed chair where he sat each night to read.

He crossed the room to the window and looked out, watching the night emerge. The street imparted a different texture after the sun went down, a frenetic, almost desperate energy of lonely people playing the only roles they knew. He rested his knuckles on the windowsill as he watched the electricity charge the night.

His thoughts filtered back to a night fourteen years ago, when he stood at the window in his fraternity house, much as he was now with his hands resting on the sill. Another form of reckless energy galvanized the air as the Chi O's invaded the Kappa Alpha house next door. It was a reverse panty raid, an oddity in itself, but especially so in those troubled days of rage.

That morning, word was out that United States and South Vietnamese troops had invaded Cambodia. The demonstrations on the Wisconsin campus had been particularly riotous and bitter all day, with overwrought students responding to rabid leaders of the Students for a Democratic Society. It had seemed to Sam on that day that the world had come unhinged. Nothing was as it should be; maybe nothing ever would be again. And, in the midst of all of this, here were these fair-haired girls from the Chi Omega house, with their creamy thighs and uptight virtue, out on the lawn in their short nightgowns, expending their own form of mindless energy.

Funny that he should think of that night now, that inadvertent turning point in his life. It had all happened so long ago.

He moved away from the window. There were thin cotton chintz curtains hanging there, but he didn't bother to close them. Life on the street was a part of him and he a part of it, so it had never seemed necessary to shut himself off from it. This was where he lived.

He sat down in his old chair and picked up *The Fratricides* by Nikos Kazantzakis. On the radio Mozart's Concerto in F Major was playing. He opened the novel and continued reading. As was often the case, Sam was alone. He would prefer that it not be so, but it was okay. He was a man who had given up expecting a lot out of life, so he was rarely disappointed.

And tomorrow would just be another day. He would probably help out at the mission again. He needed to find a building to hold the counseling sessions for juvenile parolees. That committee of North Shore debutantes would come to the hospital and might or might not decide to donate time or money. Just another day.

In the yellow glow of the lamp he read. And the window lay bare to the cool October night on Blackhawk Street.

The party was over, the guests had departed, and Elizabeth deflated. Like a punctured plastic blow-up doll, she lost her air. Her smiling exterior caved in upon her, stifling, squeezing.

It wasn't the first time she had experienced the feeling. But she had no idea what to do about it. Maybe her mother was right. Maybe she should get married. At least then she wouldn't have to face the long nights alone.

It was so quiet in the house, except for the soft chatter of the maids as they emptied ashtrays and carried glasses and plates to the kitchen to be washed.

Elizabeth walked to the bare window and stared out into the dark at the flawlessly manicured back lawn. Tomorrow a crew was supposed to come and empty the pool to ready it for winter. She opened the French doors and listened to the waterfall as it trickled and gurgled over the skillfully aligned rocks. It had impressed her guests as she had anticipated. But now the sound that reached her ears was lonely in its repetitiveness. Lonely and sad.

She closed the door and latched it tightly, wondering with a bubble of apprehension if perhaps she should have asked Thomas Benson to stay. At least it would have been company, someone with whom to talk, perhaps even to hold through the night.

She shrugged, picked up a pillow from the couch, and then distractedly tossed it back. But then, what could they possibly have talked about that would have been new and different?

And as for anything more intimate, it was far too much trouble anyway. She would have had to be charming and sexy. He probably would have expected champagne tonight and breakfast in bed tomorrow.

Too much trouble.

Wouldn't it be nice if she could wake up in the morning to some new and wondrous adventure? Her bitter laugh followed the weak moment of irrational fantasy. No, tomorrow would bring nothing more exciting than a few tennis tips from that handsome new pro at the club.

A wave of fatigue swept over her. She turned to her maid, who was cleaning away the debris. "Letti," she said, "let the caterers out when they're finished and turn out the lights, will you?"

"Yes, Miss Elizabeth."

Closing the heavy drapes to shut out the dark, lonely night, Elizabeth walked through the living room to the foyer and slowly climbed the sweeping staircase, following the gilded hallway to the white frills and flounces of her exquisitely furnished bedroom.

Chapter Two

"Would you please stop shouting, Adrienne! For God's sake, I have the phone a foot from my ear and I can still hear you bellowing."

"If you were here, Liz, I wouldn't be yelling."

"Where?" Elizabeth frowned. "You sound so far away."

"I am far away," Adrienne hissed through the wires. "About as far away from civilization as you can get. The question is, why the hell aren't you here too?"

Elizabeth sighed and glanced over at the peach tennis outfit lying on her bed. Five more minutes and she would have been out of here. She just hated that puffed-up drawl Adrienne used when she was in one of her little snits.

"Start at the beginning." She plopped down on the edge of her bed and waited for the explanation.

"I'm talking about this west side hospital thing you roped me into. Dammit, Liz, you're chairwoman of this stupid committee. Why I ever volunteered to help out with this . . ."

Elizabeth blanched. "It's today!" She frantically started flipping through her date book on the bedside table, searching for the reminder. "Oh, damn, I forgot to write it down. I had forgotten all about it."

"Well, it is today," Adrienne snipped. "And I for

one am not going to sit around here all day twiddling my thumbs.''

"Are you at the hospital now?"

"If you want to call it that. You won't believe this place, Liz. God, it smells like dirty sweat socks.''

"You're really making me want to rush right over there, I guess you know. What about Millie and Kate?"

"They're here. And Judith Bartlett too. But, believe me, dear, if you think I'm in a tiff, you ought to see the three of them sitting across the lobby like a firing squad. Hope you're planning on wearing a heavy suit of armor when you come, because you're going to need it.''

"Thanks for warning me. And try to spread some cheer around until I get there.''

"I'll feel a lot more cheery and charitable when I see you walk through these doors.''

"I'll hurry, Adrienne. I promise. It shouldn't take me more than an hour.''

"I'm not sure I can wait that long.'' She hung up the phone with a slam, and Elizabeth was left holding both a dead receiver and a growing sense of irritation. Only five more minutes! That's all it would have taken, and then she would have been out of the house, heading for the country club and her tennis lesson. She certainly didn't need lessons, but it was such fun letting that new young pro help her with her swing. Certainly more fun than hanging around a hospital that smelled like dirty socks.

Oh, what a disagreeable way to start the day this was! It was such a long drive over to the west side, she might even have to cancel her manicure. She glanced again at the outfit and her tennis bag on the bed.

Elizabeth walked over to the window and stared out at the glorious, but now wasted, autumn day. She could see boats on the lake, their bright sails glistening under the morning sun. She had a direct view across the deep expanse of front lawn and sweeping drive, down the block to the small shady park that perched atop the bluff overlooking Lake Michigan. Below the jagged cliff where the water converged with the land, there was no beach, only large bleached rocks that broke any lapping waves the infamous Chicago wind blew in. From her vantage point she could not see the rocks. There was only a sharp, horizontal line where green park ended and blue water began.

She turned away from the window and walked into her large dressing room and closet, searching for something to wear. Having no suit of armor, she tried to find some appropriate outfit for performing good deeds in one of the sleaziest neighborhoods in the city. But what did one wear to a place like that? A Halloween costume, perhaps?

The Women's Guild and its do-good projects were a necessary part of a woman's life—or so Grandmother Eva continuously insisted. She and Louise had been cramming this good works mentality down Elizabeth's throat ever since she graduated from college, and she had finally come to view it the way, she supposed, the middle class looked upon taxes—as just one of those necessary evils in life.

It wasn't so much that Elizabeth disliked fundraisers, benefits, and philanthropic drives. Actually, she was quite good at it. If there was anyone who could raise a hundred and fifty thousand dollars for the new church wing or throw a lavish two-hundred-dollar-a-plate dinner for the Lumis Orphanage, it was Liz Parkins.

Without a doubt, Elizabeth had an inborn flair for such activities. A natural leader, she had always been called. At the same time she had cultivated a flamboyant knack for overseeing the work rather than actually doing it. The real work was usually delegated to the junior members of the Guild, who were more than eager enough to do anything that would insure their acceptance by the more prominent members.

For Elizabeth the basic problem with all of this was that she didn't seem to have any choice in the matter. Her grandmother had, it seemed, invented charity work; her mother had made it—along with numerous marriages—a way of life. And now Elizabeth was expected to follow suit. Breeding, that's what her mother called it. It was the catalytic enzyme within her genes, and it was the vital fluid in the very rich blue blood that traveled along her veins.

Because *fund-raiser* was the buzz word to describe the well-endowed woman of the eighties, Elizabeth and her friends dutifully went about spreading kindness and goodwill to those recipients deemed worthy enough by club members to receive their blessings.

But this project went way beyond the call of duty, and she had no one to blame but herself. The new minister of her church had contacted her about this hospital on the west side. He told her it was in need of new equipment and basic refurbishing. And she had felt...well, obligated.

She shook her head as she pulled the peach scarf from her ponytail, letting her hair fall free about her shoulders, then grabbed a skirt and a blouse from the closet. Well, next time she would simply have to be more careful for what little projects she volunteered.

She picked up a brush from her white marble dressing table and ran it through her hair. And, out of habit, she dabbed a bit of perfume on her throat and wrists. Looking into the mirror, she could see the reflection of the room behind her. The room that had been designed especially for her when she was only six years old. It was a gift from her grandmother Eva.

Families with histories were not uncommon in Chicago. Elizabeth's had not originally been the most powerful by any means, but they were connected to power by symbiosis. Mutual need. An intimate relationship much like that of ants and aphids. The less powerful families needed the more powerful to give measure to their lives. A certain dignity, definition, and most definitely a goal for which to strive. The more powerful, on the other hand, needed those with less to give them the stature in the first place and then to help them keep it.

Eva Marguerite Rowen née Calhoun had grown up as one of the less powerful. Still, if she were to have written her autobiography, most certainly entitled *Coming of Age on the Gold Coast*, it would have been littered with such eminent Chicago names as Palmer and Field, Gregory and Hibbard. Her parents had been neighbors of the Marshall Fields, but then they had followed Potter Palmer in his move from "The Avenues" to Lake Shore Drive. In a classical Greek mansion with elms, lindens, and cottonwoods shading the yard and with a spectacular view of the lake, Eva grew to womanhood along the fringes of wealth. Later, it was her husband's decision to build the house in Winnetka when a move north became fashionable.

Elizabeth was the only child born to Louise and Joseph Parkins, and Eva's only grandchild upon whom to dote. And dote upon her she most certainly had. Nothing was ever too good for Eva's little princess.

Even this house, in which her grandmother resided for many years before aging into the security of high-rise condominium living, was given to Louise after her divorce and then to Elizabeth when Louise decided to tackle life with a new husband and house.

Elizabeth knew that her grandmother could have sold the house for a considerable sum, but she didn't. Instead, it stood as an offering, one of Eva's magnanimous gestures of love for her only grandchild.

Elizabeth pulled a red cardigan from the large chest of drawers and slipped it on her arms as she headed downstairs. Stopping in the doorway of a small study, she planted her hands on her waist in a pose of exasperation. As usual, her housekeeper, Letti, was sitting on the couch with her bare feet propped up on the coffee table in front of her. A morning soap opera whined with pathos and drama on the television set only four feet away. A box of Frango Mints from Marshall Field lay open and half-eaten on the table and a bottle of Coke sat next to it.

Letti Hasselbrock had been with the family for thirty-five years, since before Elizabeth was born. She had worked for Eva, then Louise, and had stayed on when Elizabeth took over this house. Like that gaudy gold statue in the living room, Letti just sort of came with the house. A fixture, unnecessary but immovable. She dabbled in housekeeping and helped with parties, but she hardly did enough to warrant her salary. For years Louise had threatened to get rid of both the statue and Letti, but both were still here. Elizabeth wouldn't dream of trying to remove them.

She huffed loudly to get the housekeeper's attention. "Letti, how many times have I told you not to sit so close to the television. You're going to ruin your eyes."

Letti waved her hand distractedly. "Don't you worry about me none, Miss Elizabeth honey. You just run along and have a good time. No, sir"— she shook her head —"don't you worry about Letti."

Elizabeth hid her exasperated smile. "I'll be back sometime this afternoon. But listen, if I haven't returned by two o'clock, would you call The Windsor and cancel my manicure appointment?"

"I surely will," Letti answered, but every fiber of her being was honed in on the love scene now taking place on the color screen in front of her.

Elizabeth nodded her head. "Right."

Sam tried to keep the amusement out of his voice as he talked to Father Stanislavski, but the old parish priest's hangdog expression and antiquated opinions made it extremely difficult to keep a straight face. "I know what you're saying, Andrew." Sam nodded. "The lack of community spirit is a real problem, all right. But... well, I just don't think a block party is quite the right solution."

"It worked in the old neighborhood, Samuel. Everyone brought a dish from their homeland. Even the Italians brought some of that garlic-and-tomato concoction they eat over there. It was great fun, Samuel. It brought everyone together."

"I understand what you're saying, Andrew. I really do. But you've got to understand, this isn't the old neighborhood. And as far as ethnic dishes go, everybody on this street is American."

Father Stanislavski looked aghast. "But... but there are Poles, Negroes, Puerto Ricans, and—"

"Of course there are several different races and nationalities represented here," Sam patiently replied. "But they were born here, Andrew. They're Americans. They don't know as much about their ancestral homes as you and I probably do. How many of the Polish kids on this street do you think have any idea what's going on in Warsaw? If you mentioned the word *Solidarity*, I'll bet nine out of ten of them would think you were talking about some new-wave rock group."

The priest's face fell. "But it worked so well in the old neighborhood."

"I'm sure it did," Sam said, placing his hand on the old man's shoulder. "But that was the old neighborhood. That was forty years ago. This is Blackhawk, 1984. There is a way to reach these kids, Andrew, but a block party just won't do it."

"I suppose you're right," Father Stanislavski said as

he turned to walk away. "But it worked in the old neighborhood. Those were the days...."

Sam shook his head as he watched the old man slowly walk away, and then he too moved on down the sidewalk. He checked his watch for the time, but the hands were on the same hour and second they had been stuck on for the last two days. He held up his wrist and tapped the face of the watch with his finger. Nothing. Well, what did he expect from a twelve-dollar watch?

He knew he was probably late to meet those ladies at the hospital, so he quickened his step and took a shortcut, crossing an empty lot that sparkled with the shards of thousands of smashed bottles and windows. In every block there were vacant tracts, desolate and weedridden, intersected at all angles by narrow dark alleys, like stationary spokes of a wheel.

He slipped through a narrow passageway between two buildings. A few yards ahead a girl no more than sixteen years old huddled in a shadowy doorway.

"Mary?" Sam called as he drew nearer. "Is that you?"

When she heard the voice, she straightened up and sniffed loudly. She nervously patted her black wig and ran a hand across the slim hip of her gold skintight pants. "Oh...Mr. Sam. It's...it's you."

"Yeah, it's me, Mary. Are you okay?"

Her eyes shifted about in agitation and she wiped the back of her hand across her cheekbone. "Sure...fine."

Sam's eyes gradually adjusted to the shadows that hung between the buildings and he frowned. "What happened to your face?"

She angled away from him. "It ain't nothing."

"Mary?"

"It ain't nothing, Mr. Sam." Everybody on the street called him by his first name, but for some reason it just didn't seem right to her to call him just Sam.

"Let me see." He reached for her chin and turned her toward him. Her lip was split in two places and there was a dark blue contusion beneath her left eye. His voice turned hard and cold. "Who did it, Mary?"

"Weren't nobody...some john...I dunno..."

"It was your pimp, wasn't it?"

"It was an accident, Mr. Sam. I promise! You know my man would never hurt me."

His jaw snapped and his palms balled into fists inside his coat pocket. "I know Sly, Mary. How many times are you going to let him hurt you?"

The fear and pain in her eyes turned to raw panic. "Oh, Mr. Sam, please! I know you ain't afraid of Sly. I know you ain't afraid of nobody. But you can't go after him. You just can't, Mr. Sam. He'll kill me! You just can't..." The tears broke loose from her eyes and rolled down her cheeks.

Sam clenched his teeth but he forced his fingers to relax and unwind. "Okay, Mary. I won't...I won't do anything if you don't want me to."

"Promise?"

"I promise. But you have to give me your word that you'll go to the clinic and get that cut checked."

She sniffled and nodded.

"Can you tell me why he did it, Mary? Why he hit you?"

She placed a protective hand over her enlarging stomach and hung her head, shaking it back and forth. Sam's eyes followed her hand, and he nodded. Whether he liked it or not, the street had its codes of ethics. Loyalty was one of them.

"You know, Mary, I still need someone to clean my house once a week. You hear of anyone who might want the job?"

The girl shifted self-consciously. "Maybe...maybe not." She shrugged with a touch of insolence and stared at Sam. "A clean place—that all you really want?"

"That's all."

An impertinent twist sneaked back into the curve of her bruised lips and she slinked away from the doorway and toward him with her hips swiveling provocatively. "I can offer you more, you know. How come you never look at me the way most men do? Ain't I got what you're looking for?"

The quick lift of an eyebrow was the only sign of his surprise. He watched her carefully, studying the rich brown face, the soft, full lips that were painted a harsh red, dark eyes that shone with life even under the somber shades of colored powder that caked the lids.

Despite her brassy tone of voice, he knew the question was wrought from somewhere deep inside of her. He wished he had the answer she sought.

"Sometimes a man needs a woman who will be his friend more than anything else."

Mary looked through the shadows toward the street beyond as if it held some undeniable truth. "Ain't never had no man for a friend."

When her gaze switched back to him again, it was wary and belligerent once more. "Mama says I ain't never gonna have no man be my friend, 'cause I'm bad, she says."

Sam shook his head. "Not bad, Mary. We all do what we have to do."

She looked down at the pavement, then back at him. "I gonna think about that job."

"Fine, whatever you decide. You get that cut checked now."

Mary watched his receding figure as he walked into the grayish-white haze of sunlight. She was aware of that same gut reaction she had every time he was around. She wasn't sure exactly what it was—her mama called it gas—but it wasn't like anything she'd ever felt for any other man.

She looked down at the slight swell of her stomach and clutched it protectively. She didn't know exactly what was going on inside of her, but she knew that wasn't gas, either. Sly knew it too, and that was why he had felt obliged to teach her a lesson. But the only thing she learned from it was to stay out of his way from now on. She didn't want any more problems with her man.

With a fatalistic shrug she moved back out to the sidewalk, shifting her hip to the side. Here she waited for another man, another body, another hour of urgent intimacy.

Elizabeth drove too fast, as she always did. But being out on the freeway in her Mercedes did that to her. The hum of the engine, the easy piano jazz on the tape in the cassette deck, the flat, smooth plane of the road all gave her an impression of flight, of freedom from some invisible chain that anchored her to the ground and to the overly nurturing hand of the neighborhood in which she lived.

This dissatisfaction was not something she could pinpoint. If anyone had asked her to describe her life, it would have to be said that it was one long golden ride on a carousel. Her pedigree was flawless, her behavior above reproach, and to most eyes she was an extraordinarily beautiful woman. Why, all one had to do was ask her grandmother to know that Elizabeth Parkins was perfect in every way. And yet...

And yet, somehow, it was when she was driving alone, away from the North Shore, away from her family and friends, that she felt most alive.

She watched for signs to indicate her exit, and in two more miles she eased her car around the sloping curve. Down here, below the level of the freeway, the city assumed a different pose. Funny how you never noticed it when you were humming along the highway at fifty-five miles an hour. From up above, this remote, alien territory simply did not exist. One passed over it and around it to go to the theater or restaurants, but never passed through it.

The streets were cracked and rutted, and the buildings that lined it were all in various stages of decay. Elizabeth swerved her car around a large pothole and stopped next to a crumbling curb. After first checking to make sure that her doors were locked, she opened up her map to plan the most direct route. She still had several blocks to go, but she would have to start watching carefully for the street signs.

Out of habit, she checked her hair in the rearview mirror, tested the locks on the doors once more, then pulled slowly away from the curb.

She made several wrong turns and once even ended up going the wrong way on a one-way street. Her nerves on the frazzled side, she finally located the hospital, a dirty brick building that was as sickly as were, no doubt, the patients within.

She slowed the car, searching for a place along the curb to park. She didn't want to have to walk anywhere in this neighborhood. *What on earth am I doing here! Curse Adrienne and her phone call! I could be on the courts right now with that gorgeous Ştefan Vorga.*

She finally found a vacant spot in which to park, but it was half a block away from the hospital. The idea of walking even that far on this wretched street caused gooseflesh to erupt on the back of her neck. As she parked next to the curb she became acutely aware of the curious and somewhat hostile stares from people who wandered aimlessly about on the street or who hung, like unwashed laundry, over second-story windowsills.

The fronts of the buildings near the hospital were

defaced with clumsy and crude graffiti, words hastily scratched against the gray surfaces, reflecting an anger she could never understand. A side wall of the hospital sported a large hand-painted mural that depicted the complex ethnic texture of this central Chicago community.

She took a deep breath. *Well, here you go, kiddo. You got into this mess; now let's see how quickly you can get out of it.* She opened the car door and set a slim Charles Jourdan-covered foot onto the pavement. She stepped out of the car and smoothed the wrinkles in her beige raw silk skirt and tried to ignore the sensation she was causing on the street. She was familiar with some of the words that were mumbled around her. Some she had never heard before. But she had watched enough police shows on television to know how these people talked. All she had to do was show a little tough bravado of her own.

Elizabeth walked around the car toward the sidewalk only a split second before a white Cadillac Eldorado with a leopard-skin top and huge white sidewall tires snaked into the curb in front of her, missing her car by a fraction.

He almost hit her car! She wondered if he had any idea how close he came to her car and to her. Well, no matter where she was, she wasn't going to let that pass; that type of behavior was just totally unacceptable.

A black man, sporting a goatee, a turban wrapped tightly around his head, jumped from behind the wheel and sauntered toward the sidewalk. He was wearing maroon harem pants tucked into black patent boots, and a silver sequined shawl.

She cleared her throat. "Sir, you almost hit my car...and me, I might add." The man passed a casual eye over her, but the only response she received was "Whoa, mama," as he strolled on down the sidewalk.

She tightened her mouth and glared after him, totally at a loss as to what she should do. If someone had done that to her in Winnetka, she would never have let it pass. But here. . . well, she just didn't know.

A couple of ugly snickers greeted her as she stepped onto the sidewalk, and in her flustered state, she lost control of her purse. It dropped to the ground and the entire contents spilled out onto the sidewalk. She watched in mute desperation as a tube of lipstick rolled off the edge of the curb and down into the muck of the litter-filled street.

"Dammit!" She stooped down, keeping her skirt tucked primly beneath her thighs, and grabbed for the spilled contents, shoving them back into her purse before anyone decided to take advantage of the moment and steal her wallet.

She was working as quickly as possible, but she became aware that a man had squatted down beside her. He reached for her wallet, but she grabbed it first, swinging it upward in an arc and smacking him hard on the cheek.

"Just try it, you son of a bitch, and I'll scream my head off!" She glared at him and wondered from where inside of her that gutsy remark had germinated.

Sam Winslow's expression was nothing short of shock as he rubbed the red spot on his cheek. "I was only trying to help."

Elizabeth crammed the wallet into her purse, holding back tears of frustration that wanted to escape. "I just bet you were," she snarled, clutching her bag against her chest. Her gaze took in a group of young men leaning against the building, and in an uncontrollable race of adrenaline, she raised her voice so that it would carry to them. "If anyone so much as lays a hand on my car, there will be hell to pay."

A couple of boys backed against the wall in mock

submission, laughing and ridiculing her as she hurried down the sidewalk to the hospital.

For a minute Sam was too stunned to move. His eyes narrowed on her back and hips as she scurried away from him. She had a nice walk. An expensive red sweater and a very nice walk. Gutsy too. He had to give her credit for that. But one thing he had learned early here is that you didn't go around making too many rash threats in this neighborhood. He could warn her, but then she probably wouldn't be around long enough for it to matter. He already knew who she was, or at least he had a pretty good idea. And she would no doubt make her obligatory appearance and then be on her merry way.

Sam caught up and fell easily into step beside her. There was a subtle tightening of her body as she tried to buttress herself against him and all that he must represent to her. She hated being here, that was obvious, and for a brief moment he felt almost sorry for her.

If Elizabeth had been able to read the man's thoughts, she would not have been able to agree with him more. She did not want to be here. How could anyone actually stand to live in a neighborhood like this! One thing this mercy mission was making very clear was the fact that she would never, ever volunteer for something like this again. Never!

Aside from everything else, she could not for the life of her figure out why this irritating man seemed bent on following her to the hospital. Wasn't it enough that he tried to steal her purse? "Why don't you people go get jobs instead of hanging around the streets all day? This is disgusting."

She climbed the stoop and opened the front door of the hospital, but a prickly sensation on the back of her neck forced her to turn around and look at the man below. He was standing with one foot on the bottom step, staring up at her, disbelief and amusement warring with each other on his face. She quickly turned away and hurried into the sanctity of the building.

Standing at the foot of the steps, Sam shook his head and released a short cynical breath. He glanced back at the curb where her purse had spilled and, instead of following her into the hospital, walked back in the direction of her car.

Inside, Elizabeth was greeted by the snap of Adrienne's peevish whine. "There you are...finally." She pushed off the torn vinyl couch in the lobby and walked over to her, the other three women volunteers in tow. "Do you have any idea how long we've been waiting for you? You said an hour, but it has been exactly sixty-eight minutes."

Elizabeth glanced from Adrienne to the gaggle of women behind her, each with identical ill-humored scowls. Sighing, she shrugged. "I came as quickly as I could. Why didn't you call me earlier this morning and remind me? We could have ridden together." And I could have avoided that horrible experience out there, she wanted to add.

"I was at I. Magnin this morning." Adrienne pirouetted in a frivolous display of her new outfit. "The new collection by Saint-Laurent is in, and I didn't want to miss out on anything."

"Oh, I like it." Elizabeth smiled. "That color is great on you. Hi, Millie. When did you and Bill get back from Hawaii?"

"Last Tuesday," she answered coolly, not yet ready to absolve Elizabeth of her crimes.

Elizabeth saw the look and tried hard not to roll her eyes. Tardiness in the first degree and felonious forgetfulness. So hang me!

Millie had turned toward the other women. "But it's just awful, my tan is already fading."

"Go see them at The Windsor," Kate Lyons suggested. "They have those tanning lights that are marvelous."

Sam had walked through the door, but no one noticed. He leaned back against the wall for a minute and listened. Tans, trips, Saint-Laurent. If it wasn't so pathetic, he might laugh.

"Liz darling, I can't stay much longer," Kate said. "I've been here since ten, and Ginny has her piano recital at one, so. . ."

"Okay. Where is the minister who's supposed to meet us here?"

"That's another thing." Adrienne's snit was back. "He hasn't shown up, either."

"Well, how are we supposed to take a tour of the hospital if he isn't here? Presumably, he's the only one who knows what's going on in this place."

Sam pushed away from the wall. "Sorry I'm late, ladies."

Elizabeth turned to greet the man who had spoken to them. Her eyes widened in a split second of shock, then blinked slowly in despair as she watched him walk toward them and introduce himself.

"Sam Winslow." He extended his hand to each of the women.

"Re-Reverend Winslow?" Elizabeth asked, her face doing a perfect imitation of a ripe tomato.

"Guilty as charged." He smiled and held out the lost tube of lipstick. "You forgot this."

She stared at it blankly. Rio Rum. Ten dollars a tube. "Thank you," she mumbled. A preacher. She had called a preacher a son of a bitch! Oh, heavens! She chanced a quick look at his eyes to see if there was any condemnation in them. They were a warm russet color, but whatever thoughts they held were closed to her. Her quick appraisal discovered hair that was thick and wheat-colored and in desperate need of a professional styling. But his face was strong and open and very handsome. He had removed his jacket and held it with one hooked finger over his shoulder. His khaki pants and striped shirt fit his body nicely, but she couldn't help but notice that they were threadbare in spots.

"I'm Elizabeth Parkins," she said, recovering quickly from her horrendous faux pas. "We are at your service, Reverend. What would you like us to look at?"

Sam had been watching her too, ever since she stepped out of that Mercedes 450 SL. His gaze flicked to her hands. No wedding ring. Not that he cared. It was just passing interest, sizing up the person to see what fit where. And everything with this woman fit. Sun-yellow hair that danced about prettily with each gesture of her head, brilliant green eyes that were rimmed in long lashes.

He forced himself to include the other women in his appraisal. All comely, all wealthy—the rich, sweet cream that floated on top of society. Milk-white skin, smoothly manicured hands, every hair conditioned and in place, their clothes the height of designer skill and style. Yawn. Four little Miss America clones all in a row. He supposed if a man were looking for blue-chip stock issue in a woman, he couldn't go wrong with any of these four.

He shifted his gaze back to Elizabeth. "As I told the minister of your church, Miss Parkins, this is a small hospital that is in need of much repair. The children's wing is probably in the worst shape, although all of the hospital needs massive amounts of refurbishing."

His eyes swept across the women's faces, but their features had relaxed and settled in a complacent blur of civic duty. He sighed. "Come on, I'll show you the wing."

They walked down the gray plastered hallway to the

children's section, and, as always, the smell of mold clogged Sam's nose and the oppressive humidity that permeated the building clung to his skin. He wondered with a flash of uncustomary anger if any of these women behind him had an inkling of what it was like to suffer. To be alone, to be sick, to be poor.

Elizabeth's pragmatic gaze scanned the hall as they walked. She noticed large cracks in the plaster and wrinkled her nose at the strong odor of mold and mildew.

A stretcher, with a little boy lying on it, rounded the corner, and the women stepped aside for it to pass. Elizabeth jumped when she heard Reverend Winslow bark at the two orderlies who were pushing the gurney. "Where are you going with him?"

"He's going to have a liver biopsy."

"Daniel?" Sam leaned over the tiny body lying inert on the stretcher and took the small, frail hand in his own. "Hey, buddy, you get back to your room in time for me to finish that story for you, okay?"

The boy blinked rapidly in response. Elizabeth knew he couldn't be more than five or six, but his head was overly large for his tiny body. Tubes extended from his nose and mouth and two bottles of clear liquid, traveling through needles into his arms, hung on each side of the gurney. The skin on his hands was loose and tinged with blue, but the groping fingers curled around the older man's hand with an almost desperate plea.

Elizabeth stared at the minister, so calm and controlled. But she noticed a thin trickle of sweat that rolled down his temple and suspected that it had to be due to something more than the heat in the corridor.

"I love you," Sam whispered, and the boy responded with a weak smile. Sam watched silently as the gurney rolled down the hallway and disappeared behind a couple of swinging doors before he turned back to the women. He tried to temper the hostility he felt toward them, but it took a supreme effort. They represented everything that children like Daniel could never have. He cleared his throat, but the catch in it was still there. "We need so many things here, ladies. A dialysis machine, a dehumidifier. We need to have these walls replastered and painted, bright curtains hung on the windows, a few toys for these kids, something to give a little hope. We need so much."

"In other words," Elizabeth said, "after we take a look around, we can decide if we want to contribute to the wing."

Cool as beautiful crystal, he thought, without a trace of kindness. "That's right."

Judith Bartlett, a tall, thin bleached blonde, had volunteered for this project for the same reason she volunteered for any committee—she wanted out of the house and away from her immeasurably wealthy seventy-five-year-old invalid husband. She now hiccuped with a nervous laugh. "Of course, we can't do everything that needs doing." Her throat fluttered with that same uneasy laugh again.

Sam held back any comment.

"True," Adrienne piped in, reflecting the eagerness all of them felt to be away from here. "I'm sure we can talk about it more tomorrow. Right, Liz?"

Elizabeth smiled and nodded. "Oh, that's right, we meet for lunch tomorrow, don't we?"

Sam rolled his eyes.

"Yes," Adrienne chirped. "But listen, love. Right now I really have to run." She checked her watch for emphasis. "I have to get my hair done, and you know how Giovanni is if you're late for an appointment. The man's a tyrant!"

Elizabeth's gaze flicked up to Adrienne's black cap of

shiny curls. It looked exactly the same as it always did. Perfect.

"Besides, dear," she continued, "you did say this would only take an hour, and I was here at least that much before you."

Elizabeth wished she would stay. She didn't want to have to walk back out to her car alone. But, of course, if she had an appointment... "No problem, Adrienne. You run along. I'll see you for lunch tomorrow."

Watching from the perimeter to make sure Elizabeth wasn't upset over Adrienne's defection, the other women each sidled up with their excuses to leave. And Elizabeth accepted them all with calm resignation. After all, they had their own schedules to keep, their own lives to worry about.

Sam watched remotely and felt nothing but disgust for all of them. He should have known. He had known. It had been a stupid idea to ask them here in the first place. But he had to try. *Okay, Sam, you fool, you tried and it didn't work. You'll just have to find another way.*

He smiled politely at each of the women as they left, then waited patiently to hear Elizabeth's measly excuse for leaving.

But what she actually said surprised him. "I'd like to see the rest of this wing and some of the others."

For the next half hour he led her through the children's wing, into the obstetrics and nursery area, and finally down the hallway filled with patients who fell under the category of general illness.

She walked slowly back down the corridor toward the lobby, making mental notes of all the things that could and should be done to make this hospital more habitable. But the list was far too long to be filled by her organization alone. Perhaps she could contact some of the other women's clubs in the North Shore area, the medical auxiliaries.... Goodness, Elizabeth, you are crazy! Don't get involved in this mess. Do your duty and then get on to something else, something more palatable.

"Well, Reverend Winslow, I think we have a fairly good idea of what needs to be done here, so..."

"Please call me Sam."

She blushed and shifted uneasily.

He frowned. "Did I say something wrong?"

"No, no! It's just that... well, I was raised to call a—a man of the cloth by his title."

"A man of the cloth?" He chuckled lightly and looked behind him to see if she was referring to someone else. Surely she wasn't talking about him. "I've been called lots of different things in my life, but that's probably the most proper and definitely the most quaint."

The color in Elizabeth's cheeks heightened. "I just can't imagine walking up to my minister in Winnetka and calling him... Ralph."

"Hmm, I see what you mean." He smiled. "That doesn't have much of a gospel ring to it, does it?"

Elizabeth laughed in spite of herself, noticing how attractive this man was when he smiled. "You are not exactly a stereotypical minister, are you?"

"I'm not sure what a stereotypical minister is."

She shrugged in dismissal and ran her hand along the wall. "Well, it seems to me the first thing that should be done is to have these walls replastered. A coat of yellow paint might be nice. And if there was some way to keep this mold down... I would think a cleaning crew in here once a week would take care of that...." The rapid-fire words trailed off as she looked up at Sam. "Why did you choose my organization for this project?"

He adjusted his jacket over his arm and pushed one hand into the back pocket of his pants. "There is a network of organizations that indulge in charitable projects. I wanted one from a well-to-do suburb, so I called the minister of the richest church in the area and your name came up."

"Indulge in charitable projects?" Elizabeth's eyes widened in innocent affront. "I'm afraid I don't know what you mean by that, Reverend Winslow."

"Sam, and what I see is what I see."

Her voice was now brittle. "Oh, and what may I ask is that?"

For a brief moment he regretted the remark, but then he had never been one to mince words or to hold back his feelings on an issue. "What I see is a group of women who want to wash away some of their societal guilt with a sweeping gesture of philanthropy."

"Guilt!" Her hand flew to her throat. "That is the most outrageous thing I have ever heard." She spoke softly, but her voice was filled with righteous indignation. "I have absolutely nothing to feel guilty about."

His eyes narrowed on her and moved across her beautifully sculptured face and down her expensive, stylish sweater and skirt in studied appraisal. "That's good, Miss Parkins. I'd hate for you to ever question why it is that you have so much when there are so many who have so little."

Elizabeth stared at him for a long moment, too shocked to speak. What kind of minister would say such a thing to her? To anyone? She looked at the wall and ran her hand along it simply for something to do. This man, minister, sociologist, con artist, or whatever he was, made her feel more uneasy than she had ever felt in her life.

She cleared her throat, wanting to finish up this unsavory business and be gone. She felt a sudden urge to be away from him and this hospital as quickly as possible. "Well," she said, "my organization will be in touch with you next week after we decide what can be done."

He nodded. "Thank you for coming. I'll wait to hear from you. This hospital, this neighborhood, needs your help." *Stop it, Sam! Stop wasting your breath. Save it for someone who can really make a difference.*

Elizabeth smiled weakly and walked back through the front lobby, placing a hand on the door to push it open. She stopped and turned around to face Sam. "Tell me, Reverend, the little boy in the hallway on the stretcher...what was the matter with him?"

"Starvation." He watched the shock move across her face in disbelieving waves, and for a fleeting moment he almost wished he hadn't told her. She was a beautiful, innocent butterfly. Maybe it was better to let her simply light for a brief instant, then fly on in blissfully ignorant freedom. But something drove him to wedge the reality into her. "Hard to believe, isn't it? The land of plenty and that little boy was found a week ago in an abandoned building...battered and emaciated."

"Is he going to live?"

Let the butterfly go, Sam. Let her go. "It's doubtful," he said.

Elizabeth nodded slowly and turned toward the door. She knew instinctively, without knowing all the reasons, that she had to get away from here. Fast! "Good-bye, Reverend Winslow." She pushed open the glass doors and stepped out into the dying autumn afternoon.

Sam stood at the door and watched her go. Watched the butterfly float on the wind and fly away.

Chapter Three

"So I worked with her for a month on her colors and her address and things like that," said Jennifer Morgan to the other three women at the table. "And I was so nervous the whole time they were testing her."

"You mean they have to know all of that before they start preschool?" Elizabeth asked, lifting her glass of white wine to her lips.

"Elizabeth dear, you have no idea what is involved in the raising of children," Adrienne said in her typically callous fashion. "If you want them to get into St. Francis, which, of course, we all do, you have to pass the entrance exams."

"But Sarah is only three," Elizabeth argued, though she knew she was fighting a losing battle with these women.

"Competition, Liz," said Paula Ayers. "The competition in these places is fierce."

"When do you hear if she made it in, Jenny?" Adrienne asked.

"Next week sometime. And I swear I'll just die if she doesn't get into that school!"

Paula patted her arm. "She'll make it. She has to."

The four women had been meeting for lunch every month for three years now. They were all Vassar graduates, all lived on Chicago's North Shore, all enjoyed each other's company, and of the four, only Elizabeth was unmarried and childless. It had become a ritual to meet each month and none of them would have dreamed of suspending the function.

"Did I tell you who I heard from the other day?" Jennifer asked.

"Who?" they all responded together.

"Angela Flanders."

"You're kidding!" Elizabeth cried. "I thought she had dropped off the face of the earth."

"Well, she did practically. She married that professor from Northwestern and then he took a job with some podunk college in Arkansas. Can you imagine that? Angela in Arkansas!"

"So why did she call you?"

"She's back in town, divorced, and obviously wanting to get back into the swing of things. What do you think, should I ask her to my Halloween party?"

"Sure," said Paula. "I always liked her."

"I did too," agreed Elizabeth.

"I don't know, Jenny," Adrienne hedged. "She couldn't possibly be the same. Not after living down there in the boonies and running around with school-teachers' wives. It might be embarrassing, you know."

Jennifer sighed. "Well, I just don't know. I'll have to think about it a bit more. Oh, by the way, what are you two going to do about raising funds for the new Allen Women's Hospital?"

"We were there this morning," Elizabeth said. "We talked to the chairman and the chief surgeon about what is needed for the new wing. I think we'll have a dinner and dance sometime around Christmas. What do you think, Adrienne, a hundred and fifty dollars a plate?"

"Sounds fine to me. You ought to see the plans that Liz and I saw this morning. Beautiful, just beautiful. They're cutting no corners on this one. And the decorating...well, it's just high time they started making these hospitals more attractive.''

Elizabeth took a bite of quiche and lowered her fork slowly. It suddenly struck her how different this hospital was from the one they had seen yesterday. The planners of this new wing were worried about the type of stereo system for the rooms and where to install each color television; the west side hospital was wondering how to get the cracks in the walls replastered and the hallways cleaned.

She took a drink of water to wash down the lump in her throat. Why did she have to think about that place now, today? It was such an enjoyable day; she didn't want to ruin it.

Her mind pushed away the ugly scene, but the image of Sam Winslow was left in its place. She saw him as he looked standing in the lobby of the hospital before she left. She remembered details she didn't even realize she had noticed yesterday. The way the light through the glass doors touched his hair, the fluctuating rays of optimism and disgust in his eyes, the low voice that said ''I love you'' to a little boy, the straight white teeth that were revealed when he smiled, his hand sliding down into his hip pocket...

''You know that's why we keep inviting you to these luncheons, Paula.'' Adrienne laughed. ''It's cheaper than paying my accountant to come along and figure out the tab.''

Elizabeth laughed gaily with the others, pushing all thoughts of the west side hospital, only a couple of miles from this restaurant, out of her mind.

Paula donned her glasses and pulled her calculator from her purse, setting it in front of her on the table. She picked up the bill and scanned the list. ''Okay, who had the crepe?''

''I did,'' Adrienne said.

"Yes, but I had a couple of bites of it," Jennifer pointed out.

Paula looked over the tops of her glasses, her fingers poised on the calculator keys. "Okay, okay. Did anybody else eat any of Adrienne's crepe?"

Sam leaned against the doorway to his living room and crossed his arms. "I'm not very particular, Mary. Just so the place is reasonably clean. You know, sheets changed on the bed, dishes washed, furniture dusted, that sort of thing."

Mary walked about the old house, feeling incongruous in her tight red slacks. She didn't say much, just looked everything over, not sure she should even be there. "How much you gonna pay me?"

"One day a week, fifteen dollars."

"I can get more than that in an hour on the street."

"Yes, I know. But I think you'll find this sort of work a little easier."

She looked away, embarrassed by such talk with Sam. She had made the mistake once of telling her mama that she liked Mr. Sam a lot. But her mama had just laughed and said no respectable man like Mr. Sam would think twice about a girl who had done the things she'd done. Now here he was talking about it like he could actually see her doing those things. She wondered what it would be like with him, wondered if he even thought about those things.

"Sly ain't gonna like it," she said.

"He doesn't have to know."

"Oh, he'll know all right. He knows everything I do."

"You can't work the streets much longer, Mary. Not in your condition."

She turned around sharply, upsetting the lamp on the table. It wobbled precariously for a few seconds before settling back into place. "What...what...I don't know what you're talking about."

"You're pregnant, aren't you?"

Her eyes shifted about nervously and then she started to cry. "I don't know, Mr. Sam. I just don't know. I feel so...funny, and I'm getting so fat!"

"You could go to the clinic, you know. Talk to one of the nurses. They could tell you all the different signs, give you a test to see if you are. There are ways to know."

"You mean like my monthly," she mumbled in embarrassment.

"That's one."

She shifted again, uncomfortable with such talk. "It don't come around more than every six months or so, so that don't seem much of a sign. But I got this funny feeling here. And several months back I was sick all the time and now I'm so tired. Missed two days work last week."

"Is that why Sly hit you?"

"I ain't talking about that, Mr. Sam. I gots to go anyways."

"What day is good for you to work here?" he asked.

She thought for a moment. "Wednesday ain't bad."

"You'll be here then?"

"I'll be here."

Sam closed the door after she left, went to the refrigerator, and snapped the aluminum top on a can of strawberry soda. He leaned back against the counter, taking long sips while he thought about Mary and what was happening to her. She was probably at least five or six months pregnant already. There wasn't a whole hell of a lot of hope for a girl like that. And if she were to have a baby...well, maybe one of the nurses at the clinic would have some answers for her.

He glanced up at the clock on the wall. Three o'clock.

He had to get over to the hospital for the afternoon visiting hours. As it had several times since yesterday, his mind flitted to thoughts of those women from the North Shore and what they might do to help the hospital. It had been a long shot and it was doubtful that much would come of it, but he could always hope.

He remembered each of them as they stood there with those magnanimous pocketbooks and blank stares. But it was Elizabeth Parkins on whom most of his thoughts centered. Probably only because she was their leader; that was why she stuck in his mind so. Whatever it was, he remembered exactly how she looked when she dropped her purse and then, in her frightened state, lashed out at him with what was probably the worst insult she had in her vocabulary.

He saw her pale, manicured hand slide along the wall of the hospital corridor. And he remembered the flash of emerald in her eyes. But he especially remembered that look of hers when he told her that Daniel was dying of starvation. That look of a young bird when it first learns that there is danger out in the world, that all is not as safe and warm as it was in the nest. He saw that look in Elizabeth Parkins's face and he couldn't seem to get it out of his mind.

He crushed the can in his hand and tossed it into his sack full of empty ones, waiting for their trip to the recycling center.

"I don't see what the problem is," Judith Bartlett was saying. "All we're suggesting, Liz, is that we find another project. One that we can really sink our teeth into."

Elizabeth was not used to having dissension in her committees, and she did not like it one little bit. "Why is it that we can't sink our teeth into this one?" Her question was directed at all three women who had been with her at the west side hospital.

The entire Women's Guild was meeting for their regular monthly luncheon at the country club, and the colors were flying as usual. Plum and amber, jade and burnt umber, all in fashionable fall fabrics of textured silk, polished cotton, and suede. There was no middle or lower crust at this luncheon; all of these women were sliced from the top—rich and flavorful and corpulent with their own importance to society.

Elizabeth was standing before the group, relating the status of her committee's project on the west side, and, only a moment ago, Adrienne decided to drop her bombshell.

"We talked it over, Liz darling, and we decided we couldn't go ahead with this one." Not only had the remark come as a complete surprise to Elizabeth, but it was also a humiliating experience to have her own committee drop out on her in front of the whole club.

Grandmother Eva was sitting silent and watchful in her front-and-center position as always, right next to Elizabeth's mother, who was already in a fog from her fourth martini. The more Elizabeth argued, the tighter Eva's face grew.

"I just don't understand why you want out," she said to the other three women. "You saw what the conditions were like in that hospital. You could smell the mold, feel the dampness, see the dirt that clung to every corner. And you saw as well as I did that sick little boy whose skin was practically falling off his bones...."

"Elizabeth Adele!" Grandmother Eva's autocratic voice resounded in the room, and every tinkling of glass and silverware, every whisper-soft voice full of gossip, was immediately stilled.

Elizabeth stopped also, her hand poised in the air where she had used it to abet her in the argument. Her eyes were trained on Eva, the powerful matriarch of this organization and the grandmother who had given her everything her little heart had ever desired. A tremor of anxiety rippled through her.

"We are here for a luncheon, Elizabeth. We are all aware that there are those in the world who are less fortunate than we, but please, dear, let us not hear of the dreadful details while we dine on chicken divan. I am sure that everyone's appetite is thoroughly abated by now. I know that mine certainly is."

"I'm sorry," Elizabeth said to everyone in general.

"You also know," Eva continued, "that if your committee members do not wish to continue with a particular project, that project is to be dropped. Those are the rules of the North Shore Women's Guild and have been since I joined this organization forty years ago. I for one have no intention of allowing those time-proven rules to be abolished."

Elizabeth felt every eye in the room upon her. They were waiting for her response; silently embarrassed for her and at the same time glowing with their own superiority and relief that it was not they who were chastised by the powerful Eva Rowen.

"You are absolutely right, Grandmother Eva, as usual." Elizabeth let loose her own sigh of relief when she noticed Eva's shoulders relax and a thin, dry smile curve her lips upward. She turned to the members of her committee. "And, of course, if you want to do something else, we'll just find another project."

A nagging doubt wormed its way down her throat as she walked back to her table amidst the speculative stares. But she refused to think about it right now. After that public wrist-slapping, it was going to be hard enough to digest her food without letting any other worries intrude.

When on earth had life become so complicated!

At her dinner party the following Friday the tangled web became even more convoluted. Everything was going beautifully. If Adrienne would just keep her big mouth shut, things would be perfect. But she was in one of her moods tonight and stupidity poured like gravy from her mouth. At Adrienne's insistence, Elizabeth had invited a well-known astronomer who was lecturing for a month at Northwestern University, but now the unfortunate man was being lambasted by the most idiotic questions.

"You mean shooting stars aren't really stars that are falling?" Adrienne asked, wide-eyed.

"No, no," Dr. Dubon answered politely. "They are simply tiny meteor fluff that blaze as they enter the Earth's atmosphere."

"Oooh, how sad," Adrienne crooned. Everyone stared at her for a long moment, until she squirmed under their scrutiny. "Well, what I mean is, it's another myth that is shattered. When I was little, I used to make a wish upon each falling star and I'd imagine all those little worlds suddenly losing their grip and falling through space. I imagined the people on them and what they thought at that moment and..."

There was a substantial round of silence until Thomas Benson astutely filled in the gap. "I was wondering, Dr. Dubon, what you've found to be the general attitude of the students at the universities where you've lectured recently. Do they seem to think we should concentrate more on the Shuttle missions or the search for extraterrestrial intelligence or interception of comets, or do they think we've spent too much already on space exploration?"

"Actually, I've been very pleased with the various responses and suggestions I've received from some of these students. I definitely notice a turnaround from a few years ago. These young kids now see the need for expanded space exploration, and..."

Elizabeth was watching Thomas Benson at the other end of the table. He was the most handsome man who had graced her dining table in a long time. Dark hair, classically sharp features. She had asked him to come to the dinner when she met him last week at her party. And since he was still staying with his cousin, Melanie, they had come together tonight. But the surprise to Elizabeth had been how witty and charming and intelligent he was. He was truly a man with style.

He glanced up and caught her stare and smiled, his blue eyes filled with sensual intimations. Elizabeth watched fascinated as he slid a slow finger up the stem of his wineglass. But he prudently shifted his attention back to Dr. Dubon and listened closely to everything the man was saying, inserting pertinent questions and comments as they were called for.

"Liz? Liz?"

Elizabeth's attention snapped to the woman next to her. "I'm terribly sorry, Margaret, what did you say?"

"I was wondering how that book sale went the other day."

"It went fine. We ended up with eight thousand dollars. I must say, I was never so glad to get rid of anything in my life. Those cartons of books had been sitting in my den for three weeks. Heaven forbid what my housekeeper found growing beneath them when they were finally moved."

"What sold the best?"

"Mostly the art books. We had a Doré gallery of Bible illustrations, a Bosch, a Dali. We also sold quite a few collection sets of the classics like Milton and Shakespeare. Some of them were very old."

"How much more do you need before the library can be finished?"

"We're hoping an additional twenty-five thousand dollars will be enough to get started."

"Liz, you're a genius. Where would we be without you?"

Elizabeth's smile was humble. Friends of the Library, Friends of the Zoo, friends of this, friends of that. I must be the friendliest person in the world, she decided. "I suppose if I were smart"—she laughed —"I'd hand a few of these projects over to someone else for a change."

Margaret took a bite of Roumalade and spoke without thinking. "Everyone else is busy with their husbands and children, dear. And if you didn't have all of these causes, what on earth would you do with yourself?"

Elizabeth picked up her fork, then set it down again. What indeed? It was the health club on Monday and Thursday mornings, cards and a hair appointment on Tuesday, tennis on Wednesday and Friday mornings, committee work two afternoons a week, parties, church on Sunday and lunch at the club. Her life had become enmeshed with committees, luncheons, raising money for the symphony and the ballet and the theater and... on and on and on. Without those things, what was she?

An empty shell.

"You just wouldn't believe it!" Adrienne laughed at the other end of the table. "Here was this pathetic little hospital...if you want to call it that. And this preacher. My Lord if he wasn't a bleeding heart!"

Elizabeth felt the skin tightening along her arms and chest as she listened to Adrienne's nasal prattle. "Then he does this tear-jerker act with this sick kid in the hallway. The man is definitely a con artist, and Liz... Liz dear, why in God's name did you try to insist the Guild get involved with that place? I just cannot understand it."

Elizabeth suddenly had the irrational urge to scream at Adrienne, at all these people sitting around her rosewood table, drinking her Montrachet '69, and eating her exquisitely prepared duckling with Grand Marnier sauce. But she didn't. "The hospital needs help," she said quietly.

"Of course it does, dear." Adrienne giggled. "But please, not us. Of what possible benefit could it be to the Guild to do something there?"

"If you'll excuse me, I need to check on our dessert." Elizabeth's voice was a thin croak as she thrust her chair back and walked into the kitchen. Once behind the closed kitchen door, she leaned against the counter and grasped the edge of the ceramic tile with her hands.

Letti and Clara, her part-time cook, were busy dishing up the dessert on the other side of the kitchen, so they hardly took notice of her presence. They were used to her coming in to check the progress of meals anyway.

Elizabeth turned on the water at the sink and washed her hands, gently slapping her damp fingers against her cheeks. What was the matter with her!

"Are you all right?"

She pivoted sharply and stared into the concerned blue eyes of Thomas Benson.

"Yes," she nodded, embarrassed to have been caught like this. "I was...just feeling a little faint all of a sudden."

"You've worked too hard. Maybe you'd better sit down." Without waiting for her response, he led her to the small glass-enclosed breakfast room and set her in a chair at the table. "I'll get you some water."

"No, really, I'm fine. Please. It's nothing."

He brought her a glass of water anyway and insisted that she drink it. "Feeling better?"

"Much. Thank you." She looked into his eyes and

noticed the same fiery suggestions that had blazed from them all evening. He was a very handsome man, and she was entranced by the subtle fragrance of his cologne.

"I'm sure you are aware that I'm very attracted to you, Liz. You're a beautiful woman."

Her gaze remained on his face and she wondered why she was hesitating in her response to him. He was gorgeous and she should be running her hands up the front of his tan suede jacket right now, curving herself into his embrace.

"Yes, I'm aware of that." She had never wasted her breath on coquettish repartee with men and she had no intention of using it with this one. She knew what he wanted. And she knew what she should want too. *Ask him, Elizabeth. Ask him to stay for a drink after the party.* "Would you like to stay for a drink. . .after the others have gone?"

"Yes."

She was relieved that he was going to be direct with her as well. That was what she needed. A straightforward, intimate relationship. Nothing with a carnival atmosphere. Nothing enduring.

"I'm feeling better now. Maybe we should go back and join my guests."

"I think you're right."

Taking Thomas's arm, she walked back into the dining room, her smile once again radiant and her light wordplay perfectly tuned to the evening and the guests.

It was an hour and a half later when the last of her guests finally departed and she was alone with Thomas Benson. He had removed his jacket and was draping it over the back of the couch as if it belonged there. As if he did this every night.

"Would you like a drink?" she asked, wishing with a sudden spasm of anxiety that she had not asked him to stay after all.

"Yes, a little Cognac if you have it. Want some help?"

"No, I can manage." Her bar was enclosed, like a large closet or a very small room. Private and quiet. She opened the Cognac and thought about the man in her living room. She couldn't understand her resistance to him. He had everything. He was successful, handsome, incredibly wealthy, interesting. A perfect specimen, Adrienne would call him. Elizabeth frowned as she poured a healthy dose of Cognac into each glass. Insipidly, unrelentingly perfect.

Without warning, she saw another face before her. Warm brown eyes that were slightly disdainful, but a smile that was genuine and full. Hair the color of a summer afternoon. Her hands started to tremble and she set the glasses down on the counter to keep from sloshing amber liquid onto the front of her oyster crepe de chine dress.

When the trembling passed, she hurried out of the bar and handed Thomas his drink. He smiled up at her and patted the couch, inviting her to sit down beside him. His eyes were full of admiration for the way she looked, all soft and feminine, every square inch of her a lady.

She sat, leaving a space of two feet between them, and smiled at him, wanting more than anything to feel something for him besides this raw emptiness.

"How long will you be in Chicago?" she asked, trying to sound casual, not too interested, but her voice had a slight catch to it.

"I'll be here a couple more weeks on this trip. But I'm looking for a condominium in town. It seems I'm going to be spending a considerable amount of time here over the next year or two."

Her mother had called her two days ago with the "scoop" on Thomas Benson. Born with a silver spoon in his mouth, he was given control of several of the family's companies after he graduated with an MBA from Stanford. And, according to her mother, it was very clear that he was due to inherit an absolute—*absolute* being her mother's term to indicate that he and anyone who latched on to him would have it made—fortune.

"You were talking earlier about what your company does...some sort of sound equipment...but I'm afraid I didn't quite understand it."

He laughed easily and the sound struck her as quite pleasant. "White noise."

It was her turn to laugh. "What on earth is that?"

"We install systems in businesses...something like a stereo system, except that the sound emitted is not music, but a kind of rushing noise."

"You are kidding, aren't you?" Elizabeth was smiling at him in disbelief as she kicked off her heels and curled her legs beneath her.

"Not at all." He chuckled, used to such reactions. "It's called white noise and it helps to muffle conversations and typewriter and other machine noises in offices. Soothes tension as well."

"Did you invent this system?"

"No, it's just one of the many products I manufacture and market. I'm going to be working with several corporations in town this year, setting up the systems for them. Anyway, I'll be in and out of the city a lot in the future."

She couldn't help but notice the shift in his tone, as if he were silently questioning her about what she thought of that last bit of information.

"I'd like to spend much of my time with you, Liz."

Direct and to the point. She liked him very much and the thought of seeing him on a regular basis was an attractive one. "That would be nice, Thomas. I'd like that too."

"But?" he asked. "I detected a note of hesitation in your voice."

She smiled. He was certainly no fool.

He set his glass on the coffee table and reached across the couch, wrapping his fingers around her upper arm. "Is there someone else, Liz?" He hoped not. He really would be disappointed. He had been incredibly attracted to her from the moment they met. She was a real lady, and there weren't too many of those around anymore.

"No *but*'s, really. I just wanted you to stay for a drink tonight so that we could talk. I'm not sure I'm ready for anything else yet."

Thomas puffed out his cheeks and expelled a shaky breath. He shrugged one shoulder and tried to smile. "I do admit that I was hoping for more. I must have been reading the vibrations wrong earlier." He brought his palm up to her cheek. "But if that's the way you want it...may I at least take you to dinner tomorrow night?"

"I would love that." Elizabeth laughed at her own quick response. "I guess I should have played a little harder to get. Checked my social calendar or something."

"You're delightful, Liz. I like you just the way you are." Thomas stood and reached for his jacket. "You've had a busy evening and are probably exhausted, so I'm going to go and let you get some rest."

Elizabeth walked him through the living room and foyer to the front door. He laid both hands on the tops of her shoulders. "It was a lovely evening." He bent down and kissed her lightly on the lips. A gentle kiss. Not particularly stirring, but nice all the same. "Is eight o'clock tomorrow night okay?"

"Perfect."

"Good night, then." The door closed with a sigh, and Elizabeth walked back through the grand foyer and living room in an aimless meander. Perfect, that's what she had said. That's what she had thought about him, about the evening, about the prospects for tomorrow night. Perfect.

She sighed. Perfectly lifeless.

She flopped down on the couch, hugging a pillow next to her chest. The insistent image of critical brown eyes wandered up before her once again. Reverend Sam Winslow. Do-gooder of the west side. How crazy that she was thinking of him. . .a minister, a man so unlike Thomas Benson. But she did think of him, and she couldn't stop the strange progression of those thoughts. In her mind he was no longer just a preacher. He was also a man. A man with hands that could touch, with a mouth that could give and take. . .

She jumped from the couch and raked her fingers through her hair in agitation. A shame and embarrassment washed over her. What would make her think of such things about him, about a man she didn't even know, and a minister, at that! For all she knew, he was probably married to some dowdy hausfrau who spent her days happily sewing patches on his worn clothes. Besides, who cared? It didn't matter one way or another.

It was just guilt, anyway. She felt bad because the committee had rejected the project in the hospital. Why did that bother her so much? There were thousands of needy people, and her organization couldn't help them all. But there was something about this one that stuck with her, cried out to her.

She was climbing the stairs to her room and stopped halfway up. What if she were to do something on her own? Not with the committee, just her. A contribution or. . .or something! But how would that look to the Guild if they found out? It wouldn't look right at all, not after they had turned down the project.

She continued the ascent and walked down the long hallway to her bedroom. With each step, the question volleyed back and forth. She wanted to help, to do something. But . . . well, it just wouldn't look right.

Sam walked out of the school building where the drug rehabilitation program was held each Friday night. The air was chilly but clear and the sky was illuminated with the glow of the city lights. He buttoned his jacket and glanced at the angry boy walking beside him.

"Sure would be nice to see a star up there once in a while," he said, but the boy only snorted in reply. "What did you think of the session tonight, Chaco?"

"Same as always," he muttered.

"You were very quiet in there. Something bothering you?"

Chaco shoved his hands into the pockets of his black leather jacket. "What ain't bothering me, man?"

"Want to talk about it?"

"I'm sick of talking about it," he grumbled. "And I'm sick of sittin' in there night after night, listenin' to all those other asses crying around. Bull, that's all it is. Bull."

"Maybe it would help if you ever showed some anger yourself."

He looked at Sam with frightening intensity. "Man, if I was to show my anger, the damn walls would come tumbling down."

"So?" Sam watched the young man closely, trying to reach through the thick shell that surrounded him. "What are you afraid of?"

With the speed of lightning, Chaco grasped the collar of Sam's coat and thrust him violently against the front of The Windy City Pawn Shop. "I ain't afraid of nothin', man. You got that? Nothin'!"

"Take it easy, Chaco." Sam clasped his hands

around Chaco's wrists. He knew all the moves. He could physically outmaneuver the kid, but he didn't. He simply said, "Take it easy." No warning, no threat, no fear, nothing but a reassuring tone that cut through to the rational sector of the boy's mind.

He finally loosened his hold on Sam and stepped back. Once again he shoved his hands in his pockets, but his arms were beginning to twitch and he licked his lips continuously. "I didn't mean to do that."

"It's okay." Sam straightened his jacket and watched the physical dependency that took over the boy's body.

Chaco shifted from one foot to the other. "My old man...every time I get mad at home...he hits me. Then he hits my old lady. For nothin'. Every time I get angry, somebody gets hurt." His shoulders began to lift erratically as the nerves jumped like live wires. "I got to get out of here, man. Gotta go."

"Why don't you let me buy you a beer, Chaco?"

"No, man, I...no." He turned and walked back in the direction they had come, and Sam knew there was nothing more he could do tonight.

He called out to him. "Will you be at the meeting next week?" There was no answer as the boy continued walking. "Be there, Chaco."

The boy finally stopped and turned around. "Yeah, and if I ain't?"

Sam watched the skittish figure, heard the belligerence in his voice, and felt utter defeat wash through his own body. "Then I'll miss seeing you and talking with you," he said.

The boy said nothing more, but turned and walked away, losing himself in the frenzied night life.

Sam leaned against the brick building for a minute and closed his eyes. For all the work, where was the end product? What did he have to show for all of this?

He flipped his palms over and stared at the backs of

his hands. Was he really only thirty-five? He felt so much older right now. How many years had he been swimming upstream? Five? Fifty? Forever?

And when had it all started? Was it the war...the night Jonas dropped acid while he was supposed to guard the perimeter? Hell, he probably didn't even see the V.C. who crawled on his belly up to his side and blew half his face off. His only brother. The one who had known all his secrets, who first taught him how to score with the girls, who had been his sparring partner when Sam was struggling to make it as a boxer to the Olympics, who got drunk and cried with him when he didn't make it that far. His best friend.

But it was more than that. Maybe it was those damn Chi Omegas and their panty raid that provided the ultimate in absurd backdrops as his parents called to tell him about Jonas. Maybe it was the sticks of dynamite someone threw into the ROTC and chemistry buildings on campus. Maybe it was India and the two years he spent in the Peace Corps, feeding and immunizing starving brown children. Maybe it was too much freedom, too little freedom, caring too much, caring not nearly enough.

He pushed away from the wall and walked home, but his shoulders sagged with the weight of uncertainties, with the needs that were unfulfilled.

He let out a slow breath. Not all of those needs had to do with this neighborhood, either.

His mind once again conjured up a picture of Elizabeth Parkins, with that yellow-gold hair sweeping across her shoulders. Eyes like a sea of emerald a man could drown in.

But as he climbed the stoop to his house he tried to force all that she represented from his mind. Just as she had not wanted his social afflictions invading her conscience, he did not want her stagnant apathy in his home.

Upstairs in his bedroom, he undressed slowly, too tired to move any faster. A minor skirmish between two young men broke out down below his bedroom window on the sidewalk, but it was settled before Sam could open the window to intervene. Crawling between the sheets, he lay there quietly, examining the forces that would give him enough strength to carry on tomorrow. It was his own personal form of prayer, a product of a unique faith that helped him over life's rough spots. He was asleep within minutes.

The shrill ring of the telephone shattered the quiet bliss. Sam sat up in bed and tried to shake the fog of sleep from his mind. He climbed out of bed and hurried downstairs to the kitchen to answer the insistent call.

"Yeah." He leaned against the wall with his eyes closed and scratched his chest.

"Reverend Winslow? Hello?"

His eyes flew open as he assimilated the voice at the other end of the line.

"Reverend Winslow? This is Elizabeth Parkins."

"Yes?" He blinked his eyes several times, trying to figure if he was awake or if this was some bizarre dream he was having.

"I'm just calling to tell you that my organization is hiring someone to replaster the walls in the children's wing. And a cleaning crew will come once a week." There was a flutter of excitement in her voice. "And... and the committee members are going to paint the walls."

Sam glanced up at the time. One o'clock. One o'clock in the morning! Why was she calling to tell him this now? "That's...well, that's great, Miss Parkins. Frankly, I'm surprised."

A long moment of silence hissed loudly through the phone wires. Elizabeth cleared her throat. "The plasterer will be there on Monday. And I was wondering

if there were any children in the neighborhood who
might want to help paint.''

"I'll see if I can round up some. What about the
needed equipment, the dialysis, the dehumidifier..."
What was he doing? Give the lady a break!

Elizabeth breathed in deeply. Why was he pushing
her? What did he want? Wasn't it enough that she was
willing to do something, anything? "We thought we'd
start with the walls," she said.

"Okay. Thank you for calling." He shook his head
and smiled. *Even if it is the middle of the night.* "You'll
let me know when the committee is coming to paint,
won't you?"

"Yes, I'll let you know." Elizabeth spoke so softly,
she had to repeat her answer so that he could hear. So
many strange emotions were tangled up inside of her.
Too many conflicts that she couldn't reconcile and
wasn't even sure she wanted to think about. Not tonight, anyway.

"Good night, Miss Parkins."

"Good night, Reverend Winslow."

Sam replaced the receiver and leaned his back against
the wall, one foot raised to the lower rung of the stool
that sat by the counter. He frowned and looked at the
clock once again. One in the morning. Maybe she was
one of those late-night people who assumed that everyone else kept the same crazy hours she did.

He walked back to the bedroom, slowly, his mind
trained on Elizabeth Parkins and what she was doing
right this minute. Had she telephoned him from her own
in-house office, a blue room with a feminine rosewood
writing desk in the middle facing the fireplace, a
cloisonné vase holding the fragile stems of orchids set
just to the left of the French-styled telephone? For some
reason he couldn't quite see that.

It was easier to see her calling from her bedroom,

propped up against fluffy white pillows, her body covered by a thin sheath of satin, one hand resting on a book that lay open on her lap while the other hand held the phone receiver.

He lay back against his own pillows, his arms folded behind his head, and he exhaled a slow, uneven breath. White satin... sliding across her skin as his hand moved up her thigh... his mouth on her breast...

He tried to sleep, tried to forget her. But it was a long, uneasy time before he stopped thinking of Elizabeth Parkins lying only a few miles north but a lifetime away in a big warm bed, draped in white satin.

Call anytime, Miss Parkins. I'll be home... as late as you like.

Chapter Four

There were three things about her on this overcast Wednesday that affected Sam immediately. First, she walked into the hospital alone, without her cortege of silk-stockinged co-philanthropists.

The second thing he noticed was how pretty she looked; totally inappropriate for the job at hand, but lovely still. The one bright light amidst the gray gloom. She was dressed in freshly pressed khaki slacks and a bright yellow blouse that matched the golden lights in her hair. And her eyes, like two exquisite jewels, shone even more brightly than the last time he saw her.

But the third thing that struck him was the most startling of all. It was the realization that just as he had been waiting for her call to tell him when she would come, he had also been waiting like a kid at Christmas for her to show up today. Waiting for a glimpse of her red Mercedes easing into the curb along the street. Waiting for a chance to hear her voice, see her smile, and breathe in the freshness that she brought with her. He suddenly wanted to suck in that freshness until his lungs were filled.

"Hello, Reverend Winslow." Elizabeth stretched her hand out to him, but her smile was more tentative than usual. He was even more handsome than she had remembered—sunlight lifting the lighter streaks in his hair, a lazy smile that conjured up an image of long, erotic afternoons, and in the center of his brown eyes was a warm, inviting glow that was almost...intimate.

"Hi." He shifted his jacket to the other arm so that he could shake her hand. "Please, it's Sam." Her hand inside of his was small and soft, and he breathed in sharply to avoid the overpowering urge to enclose it tightly in his grasp. It was the urge one has to capture a small bird, hold it in the palm of the hand, wanting to make it your own. He released her hand very suddenly.

"All right...Sam." She smiled.

"Reverend Winslow is a little stiff and formal for a fellow painter." He smiled back.

"You're going to be helping?"

"Yes, along with several more little helpers." He pointed to the seating area where two boys and three girls were clambering over the furniture, laughing and swatting each other on the heads with old magazines. When Sam saw Elizabeth's look, he shrugged. "When you're working with volunteers, you take what you can get."

"I know exactly what you mean." She grinned and walked over to the seating area. She rested her hands on the back of the couch and began speaking. Her voice was so soft, he knew the kids wouldn't even hear her, but miraculously enough, they stopped, stared, and listened with rapt attention. "I need the two strongest and calmest assistants to help me get the paint out of my car." It was so quiet, Sam could hear the nurses at the far station whispering back and forth.

"All right," she said. "You two can help Rev—Sam get the paint from my trunk." She handed one of the boys the keys. "Now, I need one quiet helper to hold the door open while the paint is carried in. Yes, you... What is your name?"

"Lela."

"Okay, Lela, hold it wide for them so they can get through there with the paint cans." She looked at the two standing there waiting for instructions. "Now, you two I saved for the last for a very important reason." She rummaged around in her large purse until she came up with a couple of rolls of masking tape. "I can tell you are very careful assistants, so you will get to tape along the ceiling and floor and around the windows."

After a few minutes Sam and the two boys walked back in, lugging a cardboard box full of paint cans, brushes, rollers, pans, drop cloths, and rags. He looked impressed. "You thought of everything."

"Well, don't look so surprised. I do know how to do something more than just play bridge."

"You also know how to control these kids. I think it must be your soft tone of voice. About all they ever know and hear is yelling and screaming."

"I'm like Teddy Roosevelt," she whispered. "I speak softly, but I carry a big stick."

He laughed. "Knowing this group, before the day is out you'll probably have to use it."

The kids dragged the box of supplies down the hallway, and Sam and Elizabeth followed. "They emptied out the children's wing this weekend," he said, "before the plasterer arrived. They're all wedged in with the patients upstairs."

"Well, if we work straight through, we should have most of this finished up by this afternoon and the children can be moved back in tomorrow."

She reached for a drop cloth from the box the boys set down and shook it out to spread along the floor. The linoleum was worn and mottled already, but the cloth would at least protect it from further discoloration.

"Where are the others?" Sam asked while he helped her spread the cloth to the baseboards.

"Others?"

"The women from your club. Adrienne, wasn't it? And Judith, and—"

She answered hurriedly. "Oh, they had some conflicts today. Adrienne had a doctor's appointment, and, let's see, Judith had to take her son somewhere, and..."

"No one else is coming, right?" He stood up and watched her as she smoothed her hand across the tarp.

She tried to remain nonchalant. "No, like I said, they all had things to do and couldn't make it today." She lifted her eyes finally to look at him.

"They're not coming because they're not interested in helping this hospital, isn't that right?"

Her gaze moved to the floor, then to the children lined up against the wall like small sentries, capturing every word that was said. She looked back at Sam. "They felt they could be more effective somewhere else," she offered lamely.

"I see."

"I don't think you do."

"Why are you here?" The words were uttered almost without breath. For some reason he couldn't seem to find it.

"I don't know."

"Did you pay for the replastering yourself? And for the weekly cleaning service? And for the paint?"

She glanced at the children as if they might offer a response for her. They were silent, watchful, waiting. "Yes."

"Why?"

"Sam, please don't try to psychoanalyze my reasons for being here. I'm just here, okay?" Not waiting for an answer, she reached into her purse, pulled out a print scarf, and tied her hair back into a ponytail.

He watched each of her movements as if she were a

phenomenon he had never seen before, a thing of grace
and beauty to behold. She touched him in a way he had
not been touched in years. She was an innocence that he
had lost somewhere along the way.

She was also a temptation he had to resist.

He watched her as she used a screwdriver to pry off
the lid of one can and handed one of the kids a flat
wooden stick.

"Dip the stick all the way to the bottom of the can,"
she explained. "And slowly, very slowly, lift the thicker
paint to the top. Keep stirring for a few minutes." She
held out a paintbrush to Sam.

"Don't I get instructions too?" he asked.

She looked up at him. "Hold, dip, swipe."

He nodded slowly, his eyes narrowed in pensive
study. "Hold, dip, swipe. Okay, I think I've got
it."

The morning passed quickly as they all worked together on the walls. The children laughed and talked
and ended up with so much paint on them, they looked
like speckled canaries. One of the boys had brought his
radio and insisted on listening to rock music at full
volume.

Sam and Elizabeth were busy painting in different
rooms, so there was little conversation other than "Pass
the paint...pass the roller...need more paint...quick,
a paper towel!"

At noon, Raul was sent to the Deli on the corner for
pastrami sandwiches and by four o'clock that afternoon, the short hallway and three double-occupancy
rooms were finished.

They sat on the floor of the corridor and stared in a
tired daze at the walls around them.

"Wow!" one of the kids said, stupefied by the bright
color.

"Wow is right," Sam said. "It's so...yellow."

"It's supposed to be cheery," Elizabeth argued, wiping the paint from her hands with a paper towel.

"Oh, it is that," he agreed. "But it's just so... yellow."

"Yellow is a very up color, great for perking up the spirits."

His gaze dropped to her bright cotton blouse. "Is that why you wore yellow?" Was that what she wore on all of her mercy missions? he wanted to ask.

She stared back at him. "I suppose." Her gaze switched to the children. "You were all great helpers." She fished a couple of dollars from her purse. "After we leave, why don't you go have some Cokes or something."

The oldest boy took the money and mumbled a quick thanks.

"You're welcome," she said. "It's the least I can do for the fastest painters I've ever worked with."

They rolled up the tarps and carried all of the painting equipment to a supply room and left it in case the hospital needed to do some touch-up painting later on. As soon as they left the building the five children scattered like dandelion seeds in the wind.

Sam and Elizabeth stood for a minute watching them disperse and then started down the sidewalk in the direction of her car. The sky was still overcast and the late October air was hinting at a winter that was just around the next bend.

Uninspired people took up space between the frames of shop doors and little children darted across the street and down the sidewalks without any adult supervision. A rat scuttled beneath a pile of trash that graced the side of one building, but Elizabeth swallowed her revulsion and made no comment.

She was noticing all of the little details that made up this world that was so different from her own, when she felt the tug of Sam's hand on her upper arm. She stopped and looked at him, but he was staring straight ahead. She followed his line of vision to her car...now a foot closer to the ground than when she left it. Every wheel on it had been removed, and it now squatted like a roosting chicken, undignified and helpless.

She didn't know what to say. She could only stare, disbelief robbing her of all words. It was only when she heard Sam's muttered curse that she broke through the shock that enveloped her.

"My God! What has happened to my car?"

Sam expelled a slow breath. "Damn." He pushed one hand into the pocket of his jacket and raked the fingers of his other hand through his hair.

"We have to call the police!" she said, shifting nervously about on her feet.

He shook his head. "Wouldn't do any good." He glanced around at the interested bystanders, but most of the people wouldn't meet his eyes or else they simply stared back with bold insolence. "Ramos? Juan? You guys see any of this?"

They yawned and shook their heads. Sam walked over to the group of boys that leaned like impertinent cigar store Indians against the building. "You sure? Stripes, what about you?"

Stripes, the physical, intellectual, and psychological leader of this gang of misfits, was leaning against the wall with a superior grin on his face. "Like my colleagues said here, Re...ve...rend...we didn't see a thing."

Sam's look was a mixture of disgust and fatalistic resignation. "Right. You and your boys weren't even around when it happened."

"Actually, we were." Stripes crossed his arms and ankles and smiled cockily. "But we were so involved in a discussion about the existential isolation and responsibility of being a white-slaver, the irreducible unique-ness of such a profession, and—''

"I don't want to hear it, Stripes." Sam turned away and walked over to Elizabeth.

"Maybe the lady would like to hear," Stripes called out. "Maybe she'd like to know what we decided about that. There's a real market for lily-white flesh in some sectors.''

"They didn't see anything," Sam said, ignoring the boys behind him. "Let's go."

"I don't believe that for a minute," she hissed. "They had to have seen something.''

"Let it go, Elizabeth.''

"No!'' She turned around and started to walk back up to the guys, but Sam grabbed her arm before she could get very far.

"It's not worth it over a set of wheels.''

She pulled her arm free of his grasp. "It's the princi-ple of the thing.''

"Principle! Are you kidding me? Do you really ex-pect them to understand principle?''

"I know what they'll understand," she said, march-ing up to the three young men and standing before them without a trace of fear. "Look, I'm willing to pay you for information.''

"Really?'' The two underlings snapped to attention, highly interested in this new possibility for easy money. Stripes never altered his casual stance against the wall.

Sam reached for Elizabeth's elbow at the same mo-ment a flash of metal snapped in the air in front of them. Stripes didn't change his position, but he had flipped open his blade and was now cleaning beneath his fingernails with it.

"How much money?'' he asked without looking at her.

Elizabeth hadn't even considered that he would have

a weapon. What had she gotten involved in! She glanced at Sam. His body was relaxed but alert, and his jaw was tight, but his eyes held no fear. They showed more benign annoyance than anything else.

"Okay, Stripes," he finally said. "You've flexed your muscles and now the lady knows how tough you are, so we'll just be on our way."

Elizabeth's surprised gaze traveled from Sam to Stripes, who was now closing up the knife and stuffing it back into his groin-gripping jeans. But he glared at her with a hatred she had never seen before.

"Why don't you get your tight ass out of this part of town, gringa."

Sam gave her a gentle push, moving her a few yards away. He now stood halfway between Stripes and Elizabeth. His own hard glare was directed at the young gang leader. "She's done nothing to you."

"Yeah?" he snarled. "Just her being here does something to me, man. She makes me want to puke. What are you doing with a broad like that anyway? Getting a little high-class tail?"

Juan and Ramos backed up as Sam's body tensed. They had seen him in action before. He might not have been raised on the street, but he sure knew how to deal with it. And he was one hell of a fighter.

Sam stood two inches from Stripes. He was taller and larger, but he didn't have a knife. Still, his eyes squared off with the young man and his voice was menacingly low. "I'm going to forget you said that. This time."

Stripes glared up at Sam for a full ten seconds before finally loosening his shoulders and leaning back against the wall. The impertinence returned to his face. Sam too relaxed and backed up, turning around to join Elizabeth, who had watched the exchange with macabre fascination. She had seen movies like this, sure. But never had she seen anything like it in real life! And Sam

Winslow was the biggest surprise of all. He radiated such confidence and toughness, and yet he never once used any display of physical force. It was more like an undercurrent of hot steam that bubbled just under the surface. Only his own control kept it from spewing forth like a geyser.

He led her down the street with his hand on her lower back and he felt the trembling in her body. "Are you okay?"

She nodded. "I'm...sorry. I had no idea he would have...I..."

"It's okay. You just have to be careful. Nothing wrong with courage, but there's a fine line between being brave and being foolish."

"Where are we going?"

"We'll go to my house and you can call a tow truck from there." He smiled at her, hoping to relieve some of her tension. "Welcome to Blackhawk."

"Great neighborhood," she said, smirking.

He looked away, scanning the street in one sweep. "It is a good neighborhood. I know you probably won't believe it, but things like this don't really happen every day."

"You're right, I don't believe it."

A young boy ran down the sidewalk, kicking viciously at a tin can. "Hi, Jackson." Sam smiled.

"Hey, Sam," the little boy mumbled as he gave the can another punt.

Sam watched him hurry down the sidewalk. "That kid is going to take on the world someday."

"With Molotov cocktails?" Elizabeth mumbled dryly.

He glanced at her as they walked. There was a substantial pause before he spoke. "If that's the only way he can be heard."

"Aren't there any normal people around here?"

His gaze once again swept down the street. "Sometimes this seems like a place where people can't develop normally." He shrugged. "I guess that's part of the reason I'm here. I want to help change that."

"But how can you stand living here?" she asked. "There is so much hostility. So much... anger."

"What's the solution, ignore it? Not even try to find the reasons for the anger? Close your eyes to what these people have to deal with on a daily basis, all their lives?"

He could see the total lack of understanding in her face. She had no idea what was involved here.

"Elizabeth, there are children in here who will never speak English, will never be able to read a book, never visit a museum, never have a birthday party or a Christmas tree."

"But how can you put up with ones like those boys who have nothing better to do than terrorize innocent people and steal from them?"

"How do you know they stole your wheels?"

"Well... I..."

"It's a mistake to jump to conclusions or fall back on stereotypes around here. Everybody has a story."

"You can't tell me they are as pure as the driven snow," she argued.

"I didn't say that. But it's not as easy for those boys as you might imagine."

"Seems pretty easy to me. All that boy has to do is flip open his switchblade and he probably gets anything he wants."

Sam smiled wistfully. "You want to know why he's called Stripes?" At Elizabeth's nod, he explained. "Because his back and chest are covered with long scars from the beatings his father used to give him. That problem ended when he was ten, because his father shot and killed both himself and the boy's mother. He did it right before Stripes's eyes."

Elizabeth was pale and silent as she walked beside Sam. "What happened—" She cleared her throat. "What happened to him then?"

"He's been on his own since then. The boy is a genius. He never went to school, but he taught himself to read. And he reads everything he can get his hands on. But he doesn't know how to deal with society, and society certainly doesn't know how to deal with him. So, he struts about like a banty rooster, flashing a knife because he wants to feel important and it's the only way he knows how. No one has ever...ever cared about him. And he'll probably die before he finds someone who does."

Elizabeth tried to understand, tried to put herself in the boy's shoes. But a lifetime of social structuring made it an impossible fit. She felt sorry for these people, but she couldn't help but feel that they could change if they wanted to. "Why doesn't he get a job instead of hanging around on the streets all day?"

"What for? What good would that do him?"

"Well, he could make some money, leave this neighborhood, have some self-esteem."

"He doesn't need that. What people don't realize is that the ghetto is like a hothouse, breeding a new form of man. Stripes is that kind of man. Dangerous, hard, impenetrable. He's a power factor here now. He has the only kind of respect he knows. If he left, he would be a nobody, a mutant in society. Here he's a supreme being. As far as money is concerned, he finds or steals enough to get by. That's all that matters here. The bottom line in this neighborhood isn't profit, it's survival."

Sam turned left onto a narrow, uneven sidewalk, and Elizabeth followed. He had long since removed his hand from her back, and they both kept a tangible distance between their bodies as they walked. "This is it," he said, leading the way toward a narrow Victorian house, very similar to the ones on each side of it. It was full of old-world character, but it was in sad need of repair.

He chuckled at her expression. "If you squint your eyes, you can imagine what it could look like. Watch out for these steps. They're pretty treacherous." He took her elbow and led her up the safe side of the front steps.

While he unlocked the door Elizabeth looked back down the block. "Where is your church?"

He looked at her, then swept his hand toward the street. "You're looking at it."

"What do you mean?"

"The street is my church," he said. "Oh, officially, I assist the minister of a little storefront church a few blocks from here. But I'm not needed as much there as here. It gives me a salary, though, something to live on."

He opened the door for her to enter. She walked into the small foyer and was met by a pretty, young black girl coming down the stairs, carrying a broom.

"Elizabeth, I'd like you to meet Mary Jackson. Mary, this is Elizabeth Parkins."

"Hello, Mary," Elizabeth said.

"Hey," Mary mumbled, eyeing Elizabeth with suspicion. "Think I'm through for the day, Mr. Sam."

"Okay, let me run upstairs and get your money." He left the two women alone while he went in search of some cash, and Mary and Elizabeth stared at each other as if each thought the other was an alien being from another planet.

"Have you worked a long time for Reverend Winslow?" Elizabeth asked politely.

"Nah."

"Do you live around here?"

"Yep."

"Do you go to school?"

"Nah."

With great relief to them both, Sam came back down the stairs with the money for Mary. "Here you go, fifteen dollars."

She held out her hand for the money, but didn't say anything.

"Isn't that what we agreed upon?"

"I s'pose. Sly ain't gonna like it, though."

"Don't tell him, Mary."

"Yeah, and what am I supposed to say I did all day? Pulled one trick and this is all I got? He ain't gonna be happy."

"Well, if you have any problems with him, you let me know, okay?"

"Yeah." Mary cast another suspicious look at Elizabeth, then walked out the door and down to the sidewalk below.

"Is Sly her father?" she asked as Sam removed his jacket and hung it on the hat tree near the door.

"Sort of. He's her pimp." His outstretched arm indicated the living room, but it was several seconds before Elizabeth could make her feet move.

"What...oh...you mean she was here for... What exactly was she here for...in your house?"

He leaned against the doorframe that divided the foyer from the living room, crossed his arms, and smiled. "She cleans my house."

"Oh."

"Yes, oh." He grinned, then waited for her to enter the living room. "The phone is in the kitchen if you want to call a tow truck. I've got a phone book around here somewhere." He started searching through a cabinet in the living room.

"It's not necessary. I know the number." She walked slowly through the living room, taking note of every detail. The house was run-down, but it had been built by true craftsmen. The ceilings were high and carved moldings bordered the walls at the top. The room was sparsely furnished and what few pieces he had were inexpensive. Two old, unmatched stuffed chairs sat on each side of a small table. These were facing the fireplace about six feet away. A large bookshelf covered one whole wall and books and magazines were crammed haphazardly on the shelves. There wasn't an inch of empty space. A stereo component system rested on a low cabinet and a stack of old jazz recordings by George Shearing, Oscar Peterson, and Dorothy Donegan sat beside it. A pair of boxing gloves hung on a hook by the kitchen door.

"Are you a boxer?" she asked.

"I was. . . a long time ago."

She smiled self-consciously at him and picked up the telephone receiver. She dialed her grandmother's number, and the housekeeper answered.

"Madelene? This is Elizabeth. Is Grandmother there? Well, is Walter free? No, you don't have to call him to the phone. Just tell him that I need to have my car picked up. All of my wheels were stolen. Yes, all."

Sam washed his hands, then opened a cold can of soda. He listened to the disgusted tone creeping back into her voice as she gave directions to the hospital on Blackhawk. "Make sure he sends someone to get it soon. I don't want it to disappear piece by piece." She glanced up at the clock on the wall. "Yes, send Walter to get me. I'm on the same street at— Hold on. What's your address here?"

"Six forty-two."

"Six forty-two Blackhawk. It's a grayish-blue Victorian house. I'm fine. . . No, Madelene, I'm at the home of a very nice man." She rolled her eyes at Sam and covered the mouthpiece with her hand. "You are a nice man, aren't you?"

He slipped on his White Sox baseball cap and grinned at her funny expression. "I've got to be. I was an Eagle Scout; totally above reproach."

"Hmmm." She glanced again at the cap and suppressed a smile. She spoke back into the phone. "Thanks, Madelene. Bye."

She hung up and faced Sam. "Well, that's all taken care of."

He nodded and took a sip of his strawberry soda. "That's nice. You just dial a number and all of your problems are taken care of. Would you like something to drink?"

She stared at him for several seconds, weighing his remark in her mind. "You don't like me, do you?"

He looked away quickly. He didn't know what he felt for her and he didn't want to have to think about it right now. He had thought about her incessantly since last week, thought about things, intimate things that would never be and that he'd never know with her. But like her? She represented everything he had turned away from, everything he was fighting against.

"Would you like some wine?" he asked instead.

Okay, she thought. So he wasn't going to answer the question. Maybe she really didn't want to know what he thought about her anyway. After all, it didn't matter one way or another. "That would be nice," she nodded, but glanced at the can of strawberry soda in his hands and hesitated.

"Oh, I'm addicted to this stuff." He shrugged. "But I don't expect anyone else to like it. I've got some white, or a red, if you prefer. Have a seat."

Elizabeth pulled out a chair at the round wooden table. "White would be fine, if you don't mind. But may I wash some of this paint off my hands first?"

"Sure." He pulled the bottle from the refrigerator while she washed in the kitchen sink. She sat down at the table and he poured the wine into a small jelly glass and set it before her. "One of these days I'm going to get some regular wineglasses. Shopping for crystal is just one of the things I can't find the time for. So you will have to make do with Welches."

"I'll just close my eyes and pretend it's Waterford." She smiled, and they both suddenly began to laugh.

"If you've got a real good imagination, maybe you can pretend the wine is a Moët et Chandon instead of Mogen David White Concord."

She lifted her glass to the light and toasted Sam, who was still standing at the counter. "Ahh, Mogen David 1984. A very good year."

They laughed again, and Sam sat down in the chair opposite her.

"I really want to thank you for your help at the hospital. It looks great."

"You're welcome. I enjoyed it."

There were several minutes of awkward silence between them as they watched each other with new interest. "I hope I'm not keeping you from something you need to do," Elizabeth said.

"No. This is a nice change in the routine."

She took a slow sip of her wine and lowered the glass. "Yes, it is a nice change."

His grip on the aluminum can tightened. The single bulb above the table cast a glow of warm light down on her head and the contrast of light and shadow on her face was accentuated. Here she was, sitting in his kitchen, at his old claw-foot table, drinking his wine out of a jelly glass. He thought he had never seen any woman look as good as she did right now. He smiled. "What are you giggling about?"

She touched the back of her hand to her mouth to remove a drop of wine, and giggled again. "I was just thinking what my grandmother would say if she saw me here.''

''What would she say?''

Elizabeth cleared her throat and sucked in her cheeks. ''Why, Elizabeth Adele! How on earth could you get yourself in that position. I mean, the west side, really, dear! Such a jungle over there. And Mogen David... well, that is just going too, too far.''

Sam laughed good-naturedly. ''You've very good at that.''

''I've had years of listening to it. You have to understand Grandmother Eva. She's very fastidious and she would never, ever find herself in such a compromising position.''

''Do you feel compromised?'' he asked her seriously.

She met his eyes directly. ''No.''

''I'm glad.''

Elizabeth looked down at her glass, feeling self-conscious all of a sudden. They were no longer on neutral territory, and she wasn't sure she wanted to diverge too much from the straight-and-narrow path with this man. ''How long have you lived here?'' she asked, hoping to straighten the course.

''Three years.''

''And before that?''

''Born and raised in Oak Park, college in Madison, two years in India, two years of graduate school at the University of Chicago, three years of seminary after that.''

She was very surprised. Why would someone who had all of that education choose to live here? ''What were your degrees?''

He leaned back in his chair, raising the front legs off the floor. ''Well, let's see. Undergraduate work in economics, master's in sociology, and doctorate in theology.''

"It seems that with all of that education, you'd have the solutions to most of the problems around here."

He nodded slowly. "It seems that way, I know. But it's kind of ironic the way it actually works. The more education you have, the more you realize how difficult the problems are. With a little bit of education, the problems and their solutions seem simple. But the more you learn, the more you question the accepted practices. One thing I learned in seminary was that there are no answers—only questions...and beliefs."

She studied him closely, searching for the clues that made up this man across from her. She wanted to know everything about him. And at the same time, she didn't want to know him at all.

"What was in India?"

"The Peace Corps."

"Oh."

"What about you?" he asked. "College?"

"Yes, but just undergraduate," she said. "English lit."

"Ah, yes. More commonly known as the rich-girl's degree."

Elizabeth shrugged. "I suppose."

He placed his index finger against his temple. "Let me guess...Radcliffe. No? Smith. No? Then it must be Vassar."

"It's where my mother went."

They were quiet for a while as she sat there drinking her wine and he his soda. Looking at her across the table was like turning the clock back to a simpler time. He had seen so much, too much it seemed sometimes. It would be very nice to wrap himself in this woman's innocence—just for a little while. She brought back the greenness of those days when he had been concerned with nothing more important than seeing how many maneuvers it took to get one of those sorority girls in his bed. He even found himself wondering the same thing now with Elizabeth Parkins. He downed the last of his drink. What in the world was he thinking!

He pushed his chair back, stood up, and walked into the living room. He stared out the window for quite a while and watched the black limousine pull into the curb in front of his house. A man stepped from behind the wheel and walked up to the house. "I think your ride is here," he said. His voice was flat, revealing no emotion.

Elizabeth walked into the living room and watched through the window as Walter climbed gingerly up the rickety steps. "My grandmother's chauffeur," she said, but there was no response from Sam. He kept his back to her and walked to the door, opening it before Walter had a chance to knock. "Hello, Walter," Elizabeth said from across the room. "Thank you for coming."

"Hello, Miss Parkins. And you, sir." He barely acknowledged Sam's presence in the room. What Miss Parkins did was her own business. He saw and heard nothing the family didn't want him to see or hear. "Are you ready to go?"

"Yes. Did you take care of the car?"

"Yes, Miss Parkins, a truck has taken it to the garage."

Sam tried not to roll his eyes. The man had said it more like "gare-rage."

Elizabeth extended her hand to Sam. "Well, thank you for the wine."

He hesitated before taking her hand. "I'm the one who owes the thanks. The paint, the plasterer, the hard work." Their hands met and the warmth of their flesh caused both of them to stare at each other. He was looking into her green eyes, but all he was aware of was the heat that surged from her small hand into his, traveling through his body at the speed of light.

Her face flushed at the contact of their fingers. She

wanted to keep hers in his forever, feel their sensual warmth, know their strength. A strange ribbon of fear curled through her and she disengaged her fingers from his grasp. "Good-bye, Sam."

He watched her walk down the steps of his house, leaving his neighborhood, leaving his life. He couldn't let her go! "What about the equipment that's needed for the hospital?" he called out to her. "The floors, the ceilings?" Anything to get her back to this neighborhood.

She stopped in the middle of the sidewalk and stared up at him. "I don't know. I'll. . .I'll let you know. I just don't know," she said as she entered the backseat of the limousine.

Walter closed her door. "Good day, sir," he said to Sam, and walked around to the driver's seat.

Sam stared after the car as it pulled away from the curb and drove down the street. Good day? "Hardly."

Chapter Five

"I don't understand it, Elizabeth Adele. I just don't understand it." Eva readjusted a bronze figurine on the shelf. Elizabeth had relegated it to the back of a far corner of the bookcase, but Eva brought it back to the left and front where it had perched for years.

Elizabeth watched the altercation from a psychologically remote distance. Somehow she had kept those little things from gnawing at her through the years. She had convinced herself that none of it mattered anyway. She glanced over at her mother, seated on the couch. She was hugging a pillow to her chest, a drink in the other hand.

"Nothing to understand, really," Elizabeth said. "I had no idea my car would be vandalized."

"That is not the point, dear. The question is why were you there in the first place?"

"I was painting in the hospital."

Eva turned back from her adjustments at the bookcase. "The one you talked about at the meeting last week?"

"Yes."

"But the committee decided not to forge ahead with that particular project."

"That's right. The committee isn't."

"I see." Eva frowned as she looked at a painting on the wall. "Where did you get this?"

"I bought it last year, Grandmother. In New York."

Eva shook her head. "The Lautrec looked much nicer there. What gave you this absurd notion to do something on your own at the hospital?"

Elizabeth gritted her teeth. "It needs so much. I have so much." She didn't fail to catch the arch of Eva's eyebrow, so she quickly amended her statement. "We have so much."

"That's very benevolent of you, dear, but you must confine yourself to projects that can not only benefit the unfortunates but also yourself. What can you possibly get out of this west side endeavor?"

Elizabeth stared at her grandmother for a long moment, then glanced at her mother, who was draining the last drop of her sherry and debating whether to get up off the couch to pour another. "Self-satisfaction, maybe," she said.

Eva scrutinized her granddaughter carefully. "I understand from. . . through the grapevine that there is a young preacher over there who is in charge of this hospital project. Is that right?"

Elizabeth hesitated for only the slightest of seconds. "Yes."

"I see. And it was his house from where you called, is that correct?"

"It is."

"His name, please."

Elizabeth climbed off the den barstool and walked to the window. She opened the stained wood shutters, buying as much time as possible. She didn't want to talk about Sam Winslow to her grandmother. To anyone. It was like having a prize possession that you wanted to share with no one, wanted to keep wrapped up and bring out only when you were alone, to examine, to study. "His name is Sam Winslow."

"Where is he from?"

"Oak Park."

"I don't know any Winslows in Oak Park. Is he the reason you wanted to continue with the project, Elizabeth?"

Elizabeth turned to glare at her grandmother. And for the first time in her life she allowed the rebellion to foment and grow. She could not repress it this time. "What concern is it of yours, Grandmother Eva?"

The elderly woman blanched and grasped the edge of the bar for support. On the couch, Louise moaned and flung back on the pillows, covering her forehead with the back of her hand as if she would faint.

"Oh, my God, Grandmother!" Elizabeth whispered, shocked beyond belief at her own insolence. "I'm... I'm so sorry! I didn't mean that."

Eva closed her eyes and took a deep breath to recover her sensibilities. "Yes, dear," she whispered with such hurt that Elizabeth cringed, "I know you didn't. It's just that I'm so concerned about your welfare and your safety. That is a dangerous area, Lizzy. I would prefer that you not go there again."

Elizabeth's breath stuck in her lungs. Her voice was only a thin, dry whisper. "But I told him that... There is more that needs to be done."

Eva opened her eyes and stared at her granddaughter. Life had come full circle. Her family had never really had it ("it" being unlimited resources), and yet they had never been without a considerable amount of money. So it had been essential that Eva marry a man who could carry her through life in the manner to which she had been accustomed and to which she had striven since the day she was born.

At eighteen, she had fallen head over heels in love

with a young union organizer who was conducting a rally in front of her father's factory. Passion had flared between the two of them for two short months before her father got wind of the relationship and broke it up. A year later she married Edward Rowen, an already successful and influential railroad magnate with the Illinois Central. Though the passion between them only simmered, without a single flare in the forty-two years that they were married, she could honestly say that she never regretted her father's intervention in her love life. He had known better than she what it would take to make her happy in life and he had been right. Just as she now knew what it would take to make her granddaughter happy in life. Someday Elizabeth would thank her.

"Elizabeth." Eva's emotional wounds had fully cauterized themselves and her autocratic demeanor had returned. "I would prefer that you not."

She stopped and stared at her grandmother. Prefer did not mean prefer. She knew that. What Eva was saying was that Elizabeth was not to do it. Period. But if she didn't do as her grandmother asked, what then? What was the "or else" that was implied in her tone?

She turned to look out the window. Whatever it was, she wasn't ready to find out. Grandmother Eva had given her everything she had ever wanted, done so much for her, carried her right next to her big regal bosom for so many years. Didn't Elizabeth owe her something for it? Couldn't she give in to this one small request?

She looked back at Eva and at her mother, who was now watching her with anxious eyes. "All right, Grandmother Eva, whatever you think best."

Though the bitter aftertaste of the discussion stayed with her long into the evening, she tried to ignore it and push it into the far reaches of her mind. She closed her eyes to better savor the exquisite flavor of the turbot poché, then opened them and smiled at the man across from her. She was delighted that Thomas had picked La Cheminée instead of Maxim's or The Pump Room. It was so much quieter and more intimate with its authentic French countryside charm. She especially needed the quiet atmosphere tonight to help her forget her traumatic session with Eva this afternoon.

Thomas lifted his glass of wine and took a sip, watching Elizabeth over the rim. "I've missed you."

Her laugh was light and gay. "It's only been since Saturday, Thomas."

"A lifetime," he said. "Besides, we had to spend the evening at Chez Paul with all those people you know, and I had to compete for your attentions all night."

She smiled and lifted her glass to join him in a toast. "To a quiet evening without competition, then." She smiled.

"I'll drink to that."

"Did you look at any condominiums today?"

"No, I didn't have time. Melanie's probably ready to boot me out of the house, but I just haven't been able to spare a minute to look for a place."

"Melanie loves having you there. I'm sure she's in no hurry to be rid of you. But if you need help trying to find something, I could help you look."

"That would be wonderful, Liz. I'm pretty good at sales techniques myself, but I have a lot of trouble letting those real estate salesmen and women do their jobs. I keep wanting to do it for them." He reached across the table and took her hand. "Besides that, it would be much more enjoyable having you along."

She smiled and watched his hand squeezing hers. Theirs was an easy relationship, one to which she could probably become very accustomed. In fact, he was the first man to whom she had ever been able to imagine herself married. Easy, steady, pleasant. She couldn't help but notice the looks they received whenever they went anywhere together. With his stylish dark hair as a contrast to her blond, his blue eyes accentuating her green ones, they were truly an elegant couple, complementing each other's best qualities.

"Maybe some week you would like to go back to Virginia with me," he said. "There are some lovely spots I could show you. And the family would love to meet you."

She studied him closely. She wanted to feel something for this man. She really did. But no matter how hard she tried, she could not conjure up the feelings she knew should be there. She would just have to try harder. He was a man she couldn't let slip away. He had too much to offer. She smiled a little too brightly. "Maybe sometime."

As the dessert was brought to the table Elizabeth sat back and looked around the restaurant. A man and a woman were seated at a table across the room, but the man's back was toward Elizabeth. She stared, unable to take her eyes off his back. Sam Winslow's back. Hair the color of wheat, broad shoulders under a dark navy suit coat. Her breath caught and held and her heart started to pound beneath the rose silk of her blouse.

The man stood up and moved around the table to help the lady as she rose from her chair, and Elizabeth got the first glimpse of his face. It was not Sam Winslow. This man had a soft, almost effeminate face, light brown eyes, and a thin, dry smile. No, this man was definitely not Sam Winslow.

She hadn't realized that she was sitting forward in her chair with her hands clutching the edge of the table. Now she sat back and slowly allowed her breath to escape. How could she have been so stupid to assume that it was he? And why should she be so interested anyway?

She let a half smile play on her lips as she thought of

him in a place like this. Now that she knew the other man was not he, it seemed inconceivable that she had thought that. And yet, what would it be like if he were here, in a softly lit, intimate restaurant like this, his hand stretched across the table to meet hers, his eyes warm and seeking, his mouth...

"Is something wrong, Liz?" Thomas leaned his arms upon the table and studied her with quiet appraisal.

Her surprised gaze shot to him and her cheeks suffused with color. "No-no," she stammered. "Nothing is wrong. Why?"

His head was tilted to the side as he watched her and her question went unanswered. He knew the answer already. She had been sitting across from one man and was seeing another. And Thomas Benson had to know that. He was no fool. She had known that from the beginning.

When Thomas took her home later, both were in a quiet, reflective mood, and he did not expect to be asked, nor did she offer, for him to come in for a drink.

It was past midnight when she gripped the phone receiver tightly in her hand and listened to each successive ring. She was holding her breath, waiting to hear the clear, warm voice that would answer. She closed her eyes when she heard the click and then the low, husky quality of sleep that came from his voice.

"Sam?"

There was a long pause while he processed the one-word inflection. "Elizabeth?"

"Yes." She sat on the edge of her bed, holding a pillow tightly in her arm, and her fingers tightened their grip on the lace edge. "I wanted to call you and tell you that—that I can't help anymore...in the hospital."

In the silence that followed, she felt an ache inside of her unlike any she had ever known.

"You really like to drop these little bombshells late at night, don't you?"

There was a hint of laughter in his voice, but it didn't carry over well.

"I'm sorry. I—I didn't realize it was so late."

"That's okay." *More than okay.* "I like hearing from you."

Elizabeth's throat was dry and she had to swallow several times before she could continue. "I hope you will understand that I wanted to do more, but I just can't."

"Do you want to talk about it? About the reasons you can't do more?"

Yes, yes, yes! I want to talk! I want to see you again! I want...I want! "No," she said softly. "I don't think so. I'm sorry. I really am."

"Yes," he said without a hint of the thoughts that were housed behind the words. "So am I."

"Good-bye," she said.

If you ever change your mind, he wanted to say, but all he said was, "Good-bye, Elizabeth."

He dropped the receiver into the wall cradle and stared blindly at the apparatus. He rested his flattened palms on the wall, his arms straight, and let his head hang between them. It was better this way. He knew that. The woman had been on his mind for a week and a half now and he had to steer clear of her. A clean break. She would simply never show up again; she would just fade from existence like a colorful rainbow. He could now get on with life as he had planned it. It was better this way.

With the night sounds floating disjointedly outside the living room window, Sam was aware of a sadness and an emptiness he had not known since before he retired from the Peace Corps and returned from India. He had been so sure of where he was going in life, of what he wanted out of it. Now, like a breath of fresh air that has wafted through an open window, Elizabeth Parkins gave him the sight of something else, something he thought he no longer wanted or needed.

But now she was gone and he wouldn't have to worry about it anymore. He slapped his palm soundly against the wall. "Damn!"

Chapter Six

With the onset of November, the twilight of the year began. As if it happened overnight, fall took wing and flew into the past. The air was still moist, but now cold. The trees, stripped of their leaves, were stark in the sharp wind, and the grass along the parkways was stiff and dry. Even the faces of people along the streets had changed with the advent of winter, hardening in some subtle way in preparation for the long bitter spells ahead, buttressing themselves against the months of cold and snow. Very few now walked with leisure along the lakefront or picnicked in Grant Park. Now everyone hurried from one building to another, rarely stopping to talk to friends or even to look up at the sky.

The most significant difference to be noted in Elizabeth's sphere was in the clothes her friends were now wearing. Lamb's wool sweaters had replaced rayon and crepe de chine blouses, wool Chanel suits were worn instead of linen, camel's hair day coats and full-length evening minks instead of short leather or fox fur jackets.

The Women's Guild had just finished up their annual holiday bazaar, and Elizabeth had, as always, been in charge of everything from handpicking the women who would help customers and restock merchandise to arranging with the Goodwill Industries to cart off all that was left over at the end of the day.

Now she was exhausted. It was Friday night and Thomas had to fly back to Virginia for an important meeting tomorrow, so they had canceled out on the dinner party to which they had received an invitation. But he assured her he would return to Chicago by Sunday afternoon at the very latest.

A quiet Friday night lay before her and she couldn't help but breathe a sigh of relief. Thomas's campaign to win her affections had intensified in the last couple of weeks, and she was left slightly breathless from the onslaught.

Elizabeth enjoyed his company and thought him a most attractive man. And everyone, from her mother to her friends, had assured her that he was the catch of the season. So why, then, did she look forward to his trips back to Virginia? Why had she never committed herself to him in any more than a perfunctorily physical way? And why... why had she never ceased thinking about Sam Winslow, a man she would most likely never see again?

It was a question she had asked herself over and over again these past two weeks, and she still had found no answer. What was it? And why? And when would these strange earthy feelings for him come to an end?

Suddenly the weekend ahead loomed empty. Thomas had taken up the slack, filled the empty space. But now that he was gone, there was nothing left to push aside the thoughts that kept chipping away at her neatly carved existence. There is no room for you, Sam Winslow. Don't you know that? Can't you leave me alone and let me live my own life the way I always have?

It was late into the night before sleep replaced the need for answers to her haunting questions.

Everything always looks brighter in the light of morning, or so her mother had always said. But then, her mother was always too drunk to remember the night before, so what did she know? Elizabeth was sitting at her glass-topped breakfast table, watching the last of the leaves drop from the trees in her backyard. The yard crew was sweeping away the piles that had blown onto the tennis court and around the pool. Beyond her backyard, the terrain dropped off in a sharp incline to the ravine below, the trees now reed thin and brittle along its banks.

She lifted the cup of hot coffee to her lips just as the doorbell rang. She sat still, sipping delicately from the flowered cup that matched her new set of breakfast china. Letti would answer it...God willing that there were no soap operas on television on Saturday mornings!

Within seconds she could hear Adrienne's voice, shrill as always but more agitated than normal. She hurtled through the kitchen door like a whirlwind, her eyes red and puffy and her hands shaking like a leaf that was hanging on to life with only the greatest temerity.

Her lower lip quivered as she plopped down at the kitchen table next to Elizabeth.

"What is it, Adrienne? What on earth is the matter?"

Her friend shook her head and her lips continuously quivered as Elizabeth got up to fix another cup of coffee. After she poured it, she set the cup in front of Adrienne.

"Do you have something stronger to put in this?" Adrienne croaked. "Something...anything, for God's sake!" Elizabeth quickly opened a cabinet and pulled down a bottle of Kahlúa. Adrienne took the bottle, uncorked it, and poured a hefty amount into the cup.

Then, with shaking hands, she lifted it to her mouth and drank it all in one long, hot gulp.

"What is it, Adrienne? What has happened?"

The tears began to fall from her eyes as the alcohol unclogged the emotional dam inside of her. "It's John... He's... Oh, God, I can't even say it!"

"What, Adrienne, what?"

She looked up at Elizabeth with the most devastated eyes she had ever seen. "He's having an affair... with..." She shook her head again and the tears fell anew.

Elizabeth laid her hand on her friend's arm, feeling pity for her and disgust at the husband who would do this to her. "It's going to be all right, Adrienne. Believe me, John loves you. It's only a—"

"With a man."

"What was that?"

"I said... he's having an affair... with another man."

Elizabeth sat perfectly still, moving not a muscle, her hand resting lightly on Adrienne's arm. "You mean he's... he's..."

Adrienne's face hardened with anger. "Can you believe it? After all these years. And I didn't even know it!" She looked at Elizabeth with so much hurt. "How could I not have known, Liz? How could I have lived with that man for seven years and not known?"

Elizabeth shook her head, not knowing what to say, how to react. How could she tell her that everything would be all right, that it was only a transgression that probably meant nothing, that he truly loved her? How could she explain it when she didn't understand it herself?

She had known John as long as Adrienne had. Since they were all young. They had played together, gone to parties together. In the summers they would swim and play tennis and drive fast in their new cars. All of them together. How could she not have known?

"I'm so— Adrienne, I don't know what to say. Are you—" She almost asked her if she was sure. But, of course she was. All she had to do was look at her face to know that she was positive, that whatever proof she had was overwhelming. "I'm sorry."

Adrienne looked around the kitchen with despair written on her face. She spotted the Kahlúa and grabbed the bottle, filling her cup with the liquor. She took a large sip, grimaced at the taste, then set the cup back on the table. "What am I going to do, Liz?" she asked as she stared down into the dark liquid. "How can I possibly face everyone?"

"It won't matter to anyone," Elizabeth said, knowing in her heart that she was lying. Nothing would be the same again.

Adrienne shoved her chair back forcefully, stood up, and hurried toward the kitchen door. Elizabeth was right behind her. "What are you doing, Adrienne? Where are you going?"

She pushed through the swinging door and continued moving at a brisk pace toward the front of the house.

"Adrienne, what are you doing?"

"I'm going to the club, dammit! That's what I'm going to do. I'm going to drink myself into oblivion and then I'm going to find the first available man to take to bed. If I have to pay Stefan Vorga, I'll do it."

Elizabeth's hand clutched her friend's arm. "Don't go, Adrienne. Stay here with me. We'll work this—"

"Don't try to stop me, Liz. I'm going to do it, by God. To hell with John, and his—his damn boyfriend, and you, and the rest of the stinking world." She wrenched her arm away and stalked out the front door. Elizabeth watched her go and, once again, wondered when the world had become so complicated.

Where had the simple life, with no burning questions, with no shocking surprises, with no hurt and no cares, gone? All her life those little problems had simply been taken care of and whisked away. Suddenly, that was no longer the case.

She closed the door and leaned her back against it, wishing Adrienne had not left. Wishing too that she had never come in the first place. She had run off to solve her problems in the only way she knew how, and here Elizabeth was left with nothing but confusion with which to contend.

She had to get out. She had to get away from this place, this neighborhood that could not hold on to what it had, that could not seem to hold her. She was flying apart and there was nothing to hold her together.

She pulled a short wool jacket from a nearby closet and called out to the back of the house. "Letti, I'm going out." She didn't know if the housekeeper had heard her or not, and at this point, she really didn't care. She had to get out!

She drove fast, her grip on the wheel tight and determined, switching lanes, swerving around slower cars, leaving the North Shore and her troubled thoughts far behind.

The gray walls of the city that loomed around her were reassuring. They held her together and gave her a focus and direction. When she left home, she had not realized that the direction was going to lead her to Blackhawk. It had never entered her conscious mind. All she had done was to climb behind the wheel of her car and drive as fast as she could away from her neighborhood.

But like a moth drawn to a warm yellow light, she had flown inexorably toward the west side and toward Sam. She needed to talk, needed someone to put all of this in perspective for her. Who else could she have gone to?

Certainly not her mother or grandmother or any of her friends. They were what she was running from. And Thomas... even if Thomas were in town, there was no way she would feel right talking to him about this. He didn't know John, he hadn't grown up together with them, he didn't know this group of people the way she did. What she couldn't make herself admit was that she simply wouldn't have wanted to see him right now; she wanted to see Sam Winslow.

She parked the car directly in front of his house and stepped out. For a moment she just stood there, looking at the weathered Victorian facade. So much could be done to make it really nice. She glanced at the ones on either side of it. They too were time-worn and in much need of repair. She looked down the street. Several sections of a newspaper were loose in the wind, rising and falling with the gusts as each piece floated separately down the street. She lifted her eyes toward the sky. The sun had been shining up north by the lake, but here it was too hazy to see even a patch of blue.

Elizabeth walked up the sidewalk and very carefully climbed the steps, holding tight to the rail in case the wood gave way. She lifted her hand to the door to knock, but hesitated. Maybe she shouldn't do this; maybe he wouldn't want her here; maybe he had company. She swallowed hard and then knocked. She waited, then knocked again, louder this time. Still no answer.

The anxious vibrato in her chest was gone, replaced now by a heavy weight of disappointment. He wasn't even home. She backed away slowly and turned around. Her eyes landed on the figure standing twenty feet away on the sidewalk. Sam was motionless, his hands thrust into the pockets of his jacket, his eyes regarding her with caution.

He could only stare, not believing that what he was

seeing was anything more than a mirage, a flight of wishful thinking. He had walked down the sidewalk, seen the car at the curb, turned toward his house, and there she was, standing on his front porch!

They both stood this way, unmoving and watchful, for several interminable seconds. Memories, as yet unmade, filled the air between them. Finally, he moved up the sidewalk toward her. He placed a hand on the railing, one foot on the lower step, and again looked up at her. This time he smiled. "Hello, Elizabeth."

"Hello, Sam."

His other foot followed and he climbed to the porch and stood in front of her, looking down into a soft innocent face that held all the doubts and confusion he was now feeling.

She forced herself to speak, but there was a tight lump in her throat that made it extremely difficult. "Am I catching you at a bad time?"

He slowly shook his head and spoke softly. "No, not at all." He was only a foot from her. He could reach out and cup her jaw, lay his hand against the back of her neck beneath her hair. He wanted to touch her so badly that his fingers were stinging as if from high voltage electrical current. But he didn't dare. "I've been trying to organize some VISTA workers this morning. I hope...you haven't been waiting long, have you?"

"No, I just got here a few minutes ago." She looked away self-consciously. She had been standing there in front of him, wishing he would touch her, wishing she could reach out and touch him. But the idea was so ludicrous, it was embarrassing. "This is going to seem strange, but... well, you see, I needed someone to talk to and..." She searched his very still expression and forged ahead. "And I thought of you."

He let out a long, slow breath and nodded. "I'm glad.

Here, let me open the door.'' He pulled out his key and turned the lock. "Come on in.''

As Elizabeth brushed past his chest and shoulder to enter the house, she was aware of a current of heat that surged between them in that briefest of contacts.

He sucked in his breath as she passed him, her closeness burning a path across his body, through his jacket, and leaving behind only the fresh scent of hair and feminine fragrance in her wake.

He started to reach out and help her with her jacket, but she slipped it off by herself. He peeled his off and they both hung them on the coat tree by the door. "It's pretty cool out there today.''

"Yes, it is.'' *God, this is so stupid! I shouldn't even be here!* "Listen, Sam. I don't know why I'm here, really. I mean. . . well, I feel so awkward.''

"Please don't. I'm glad you're here. Let me light a fire and we can fix something to drink. How about some more of the delectable French wine I have?''

"Ah, yes, Monsieur Mogen David.'' She laughed. "I'd love some.''

"Good. Why don't you pour us both a glass and I'll light the fire. The heat in this old house isn't so great, so we'll need it for warmth.''

"Okay.'' She dropped her purse onto a chair and walked into the kitchen. She tried to remember from which cabinet he had pulled the glasses when she was here before, but it took several tries before she found the right one. There were only about six plates and bowls and maybe a dozen glasses in the cabinet. She pulled down two unmatched jelly jars and set them on the counter. Opening the refrigerator, she found the bottle of wine, smiled as she opened the screw-off top, and poured it into the glasses. She placed the bottle back in the refrigerator and carried them into the living room.

Sam was squatting in front of the fireplace, lighting a piece of wadded-up newspaper beneath the log, and after the flame ignited, he stood and closed the screen. "Thanks." He took the wine from her and scanned the room for someplace to sit. He shrugged. "I don't have a couch, just these two old chairs."

"They're fine," she said, sitting in one. "Very comfortable."

"Yeah." He laughed. He went back into the kitchen and grabbed a hard-backed chair from the table, brought it back to the living room, and placed it backward about four feet from hers. He straddled it, resting his arms along the back, and took a sip of his wine.

"How have you been?"

She smiled almost shyly. "Fine. Not so fine." She took another drink. "The strangest thing has happened."

He waited out her silence, knowing when she wanted to talk she would.

"You remember Adrienne? The one who was with me at the hospital that first day?"

He nodded.

"She and I go back a long way together. We have sort of a love-hate relationship between us. Most of the time I don't really like her and yet...she's the best friend I have." She laughed, embarrassed. "This is stupid."

Sam only shook his head and watched her. She slipped off her shoes and tucked one leg under the other on the chair. In the periphery of his mind, he thought about running his hand up the length of those brown suede pants and farther up, past her waist, up the soft lamb's wool beige sweater. These ideas were in the back of his mind, working on his subconscious, while he listened carefully to what she was saying.

"When my mother and I still lived in River Forest and

I used to go up to Winnetka to visit my grandmother, Adrienne and I would play together. Then when we moved up there, the relationship just continued. A few years ago...seven years, it was, she married another friend of ours. John Stebbins. The three of us used to play together when we were young. We really were best friends, inseparable, you might say.''

There was a long pause while she stared at the fireplace, watched the flames licking the logs, circling with their blue and orange tongues. The wood made a hissing sound from the moisture that was still locked inside of it.

"This morning Adrienne came over to my house. She had just found out that her husband...that John was gay and was now having an affair.''

She noticed the slight lift of Sam's eyebrows, but that was the only sign of surprise he showed.

She shook her head. "I don't know what it is that bothers me so much. It's not really the fact that he's gay. It's—I don't know. It's just that I thought I knew him. I thought things would stay the way they were.''

"Change is inevitable," he said when she was silent for several seconds.

Elizabeth studied the strong, handsome face before her, looked into his warm brown eyes, which had seen so much more than she had, things she could not even imagine. "You're right, of course. I just don't understand why it happened or what is going to happen to Adrienne now.''

"How was she taking it?" he asked.

"Badly. She left the house to go to the club—the country club we belong to. And she wanted to get drunk and find a man to—to—" She glanced at Sam and he nodded, relieving her of having to spell it out. "I think she probably doesn't feel like much of a woman right now and she just needs to...to feel that way.''

Sam examined Elizabeth sitting comfortably and at home in his big chair. It was almost as if she were relaxing against his own arms, her shoulders, her back, her hips, resting against him. He breathed deeply. "I think you like Adrienne more than you will admit," he said. "You care about her. It shows."

She sighed. "I don't know. Maybe you're right. I am worried about what everyone—all of our friends—will say about this and how they will treat her. Things won't be the same, I know that."

"You mean because her husband has cheated on her or because he's gay?"

"Oh, everyone cheats on everyone," she said with a marked accent of disgust. "That's nothing new. But this other thing...his being gay. Well, just nobody in our circle of friends would ever admit to such folly."

"In other words, it would be okay if he'd had an affair with...oh, say, his secretary or some other woman?"

Elizabeth glanced up sharply. "I'm not saying it's okay, Sam. I'm just saying that it's accepted. Right or wrong, it is." She suddenly laughed and sucked in her cheeks. "As Grandmother Eva would say, 'Men are a different breed. It is our duty to see that the rigorous demands of society are met. Let the boys play at their little games and believe that they are being so clever.'"

Sam smiled at the imitation. "Seems as if Grandmother Eva doesn't like men very much."

"I'm not so sure she does," she admitted. "I think my grandfather played around, as they say, a lot. Grandmother had to find other things to occupy her time and attention." Elizabeth frowned and looked over at the fire, crackling now under a full blaze. "Maybe she was lonely."

Is that where you are headed, Elizabeth? he asked the question in his own mind. Is that all you have to look forward to, that same kind of quiet desperation? He looked away. He couldn't bear to look at her, thinking those things. He wanted her to always stay the way she was right now. Soft, beautiful, with a kind of insulated innocence that most people—people with less wealth and social security—lose when they are much younger. He refused to admit that she could very easily become another Grandmother Eva or Adrienne someday. And yet, inside, he knew that it was very likely that that was exactly what she would become.

Refuge, in any form, always had its price.

Chapter Seven

"No," Sam said, laughing. "My parents are not at all like me." Elizabeth had slipped on one of Sam's over-sized cable-knit sweaters and the two of them were now sitting on the floor of the front porch, their feet on the top step. The brisk fall air was a welcome change from the warm, almost too intimate interior of the house. "My mother keeps plastic covers on her furniture. Never a thing out of place. She is constantly fluffing up pillows and straightening pictures. She's the type that would keep paper under a cuckoo clock, just in case. She's a character, but I love her."

"And your father?" Elizabeth hugged her knees and smiled up at Sam sitting next to her. The cool air gave a ruddy glow to his face and his eyes sparkled with an inner heat that fascinated her. Everything about this man fascinated her. They had been talking nonstop for two hours, and the afternoon was rushing away from them too quickly. She didn't want this easy togetherness to end. It was the most relaxed she had been in a long, long time.

He shook his head and grinned. "My dad is...well, he's a little more difficult to peg. He is afflicted with the old Puritan work ethic. Early to bed, early to rise—that sort of thing. He's a tightwad too. Jonas used to be able to imitate him perfectly, like you do your grandmother, and we would get hysterical over some of the things he said.'' Sam deepened his voice and scowled down at Elizabeth. '' 'Boys,' my father would say. Then he'd clear his throat a few times. 'Boys, today we begin the planting season.' Keep in mind, we didn't live on a farm. We lived in the middle of the suburbs.'' He went back to his imitation. '' 'Today we will sow our seeds and tomorrow we will reap.' '' He laughed and shook his head. ''The problem was we never got around to reaping. Dad kept telling us it wasn't quite time yet to reap all that bounteous harvest he was always talking about.''

Elizabeth laughed with him. ''He sounds great!''

''Yeah, he is. He went through the Depression and doesn't trust anyone with his money, especially banks.'' He studied Elizabeth for a minute. ''You want to know a deep, dark secret?''

Her eyes glistened. ''Yes, oh, yes!''

He chuckled and leaned close. ''You've heard stories about some of these old geezers who stuff all their money into mattresses?''

''Uh-huh.''

''Well, my father has his 'savings' changed into quarters, then he carefully drops them one by one into a garden hose and buries it in the backyard.''

Elizabeth's mouth dropped open. ''You're not serious!''

Sam held up his hand. ''Scout's honor. The neighbors just think he is a dedicated gardener out there digging in the flower beds week after week.''

''Incredible!'' She laughed, burying her head in her knees. When she looked up, her eyes were streaming with tears of laughter. ''I do believe your family is more of a nut case than mine. I can just see my mother sitting on your mother's couch, spilling dry vermouth all over the plastic cover.''

"Oh, no," he said. "That's another thing. No liquor in my parents' house. Not a drop. Even after we were in college and home on break, Jonas and I would sneak off to a neighbor's house to have a beer. Then we'd each chew a whole pack of gum on the way home to get rid of the evidence."

"Who is Jonas? You've mentioned him several times."

"My brother." Sam's jaw tightened a little, but she didn't notice.

"Where does he live?"

He grew unusually quiet and stared off toward the empty street. "He doesn't. Jonas is dead."

Elizabeth's smile faded. She stared long and hard at him, probing behind the emotional curtain that fell over his eyes. She saw the hurt that lay deep within him and wanted to make it go away. She wanted to talk to him, but couldn't make herself get the words out. She wanted to reach over and lay her hand on his arm and comfort him.

He glanced at her, made note of the concern, and smiled, but it was a labored effort at best. "He died in Vietnam. He would be thirty-seven now." He smiled as the new image formed in his mind. "He would be a lawyer. A slippery son of a bitch, no doubt. He would live in a big house with a four-car garage, drive a Ferrari. Real nouveau riche stuff. He always was a flashy one, throwing his money around everywhere. He had at least a dozen girlfriends at a time and spent a fortune on each of them. You would have loved him."

"I'm sure I would have." She smiled, sad for the loss that was obviously still felt so deeply.

Sam regarded her closely. "And he would have loved you." He could see it now. Jonas would have swept into the house, flashing those pearly white teeth of his, dazzling Elizabeth with his panache, and he would have whisked her away and Sam never would have stood a chance with her. He smiled. "I learned at an early age that if I wanted to keep a girl, I better not introduce her to my brother."

An awkward pall of silence lingered between them as they contemplated each other. It was as if a new door had opened up before them, but neither Sam nor Elizabeth would enter it. She looked away first, watching the gray afternoon fade into a deeper shade of evening. She should go home now. She should leave this man while she still had a chance. He scared her terribly. He and everything about him. His physical strength, his profession, his life-style, his deeply felt emotions, the way he looked at her as if he were touching her...the way she so desperately wanted him to touch her. Yes, she should go.

Sam could no longer deny the electrifying tension that arced into him from her nearness. His hands burned with the need to know her, to have her, to make this beautiful woman his own. *She's all wrong, Sam. She's not the one for you.* There will be others, pretty ones, smart ones, ones that are eager to please. Someone who shares your philosophies, who knows what it is you feel and need and have to do. Someone like you. Not this one. Don't be a fool. Nothing will ever come of this, and you know it. Send her home, back to the lovely gold perch where she belongs, where she will be safe, away from the storm that is a constant in your life. *Send her home, Sam.*

As if she could read his thoughts, she looked at him with eyes so green against the gray sky, so vulnerable and open, and the words he knew he should say would not come. "Are you hungry?" he asked instead.

"A little."

"Would you like to stay for dinner?"

You will be making a big mistake, Elizabeth. Don't do it. "Yes, I'd like that," she answered.

A heavy weight of tension was released from his chest as he stood and took her hand. He helped her up and resisted the urge to pull her against him. Instead, he opened the door and the two of them went inside.

"I don't think I have anything here. Let's take a look and then run down to the market." He led her into the kitchen and opened the almost-empty refrigerator. "Let's see, we have some ham in here, but I'm afraid it's a tad old." He lifted the packet to his nose and smelled. "Whooo," he said and tossed the packet into the trash. "Unless you want American cheese sandwiches and strawberry soda, we'd better go to the market. What sounds good to you?"

"Anything. Don't go to a lot of trouble."

"Listen, I'm a great cook. I need to keep in practice or my culinary skills will atrophy. You don't want that to happen to me, do you?"

"Heavens, no! What do you want to fix, then?"

"My specialty leans toward the more exotic, maybe like...oh, perhaps *un poisson et fromage* casserole."

Elizabeth considered him with a frown. "Fish and cheese casserole?"

"Well, actually tuna and cheese, but I don't know how to say tuna in French."

She made a face. "They probably don't even eat tuna in France."

"If they're smart, they don't. Okay, give me a substitution."

"You mean that's the extent of your cooking abilities?"

"Well, I don't have too many friends in this neighborhood dropping by for chateaubriand, and I can't watch Julia Child without a television, so..."

"I get the point." She laughed. "Why don't we just walk to the market and see what they have?"

He grinned and draped an arm over her shoulder. "My kind of woman."

It grew dark early now in this space between autumn and winter, and the wind was sharp against their faces. Elizabeth huddled deeper into the huge sweater, wishing now that she had worn something a little heavier.

"Cold?" he asked, wrapping his arm about her again. Instantly the chill was gone, replaced by an increasingly restless heat. It was such an easy gesture, without artificiality, and yet the line across her neck and back and shoulder burned as if his arm were a brand, sealing her to him in a permanent bond.

Night people emerged from the dimly lit interiors of crumbling buildings, pouring onto the dark sidewalk, preparing once again to play the street life they knew so well. A couple of people greeted Sam, but most eyed him stonily when they noticed the woman at his side. It only took one glance to know that she didn't belong. Even if she had been dressed as they were, there was a distinct difference, a scent of prosperity that clung to the very rich and insulated them from the real world.

Sam was aware of the antagonistic undercurrent that swirled around them as they made their way to the market. And he knew that Elizabeth noticed it too. He could feel the tightening of her shoulder where it fit so perfectly beneath his arm. He saw the uplift of her chin and made note of the set angle of her mouth.

"Here we are. This is Alfredo's store." He ushered her into the small market where he did most of his shopping. "Wish you could meet the old man himself. You'd like him. That's his son over there. Hey, Paolo. How's it going?"

"*Bene,* Sam. *Molto bene,*" Paolo answered with exaggerated gestures, then eyed Elizabeth appreciatively. "And with you too, I see."

Sam winked at Elizabeth and shrugged. "You know how these Italians are."

"I cannot deny the obvious," Paolo countered good-naturedly. "What you need tonight, Sam? A little eggplant? A little pasta?"

"Excuse me just a minute, Elizabeth." Sam moved away from her and placed an arm around Paolo's shoulder, leading him to another corner of the small market. "How do you make spaghetti, Paolo?"

The young man looked surprised. "Simple, Sam. You cook the pasta in a little boiling salted water."

Sam nodded. "Well, that sounds easy enough. Is that it?"

"That's it. Now, you want sauce too?"

Sam's return look was blank. "Yeah. How do I make it?"

Paolo exhaled with an exaggerated sigh. "You cook a few tomatoes, add a pinch of sugar, lots of garlic, onion, a good amount of oregano, a dash of salt..."

"Paolo?"

"Yes?"

"Forget it." Sam started to walk back to Elizabeth.

"Sam, wait." Paolo called him back. He reached under the counter and pulled out a jar of prepared spaghetti sauce. At Sam's surprised look, Paolo shrugged. "I use it, too. But don't ever tell Mama."

Sam offered a conspirator's true smile. "Wouldn't dream of it. *Grazie,* Paolo."

"Prego."

Sam walked back to Elizabeth, and together they picked out a head of lettuce and an onion. He paid for the vegetables and a bag of spaghetti, but Paolo drew the line at the jar of sauce. "I can't charge you for this, Sam. I'd have to explain the item to Mama, and, well..."

"I owe you one, Paolo."

"Nah, Sam, not you."

Back in Sam's kitchen, Elizabeth took off the heavy sweater, then washed the lettuce and made a salad while Sam cooked the spaghetti and heated the sauce over the stove.

She glanced through the kitchen doorway and noticed that the fire had burned out. "How do you survive winters in this drafty old house?"

"Lots of blankets," he said. "At least I've got a fireplace. Some of these people around here have nothing. The super doesn't pay the gas company and the tenants end up suffering." He shook his head as he thought about it. "Every year we have several old-timers who freeze to death in their sleep."

Elizabeth stopped slicing the onion and held the knife still on the counter. In this country, people freezing in their own homes? Was it possible? Or was Sam just exaggerating? She glanced over at him. No, he wouldn't exaggerate about something like that. But how could that be? This was America! Were people actually allowed to freeze to death?

"Sam?"

"Yes?"

"I was just thinking. Did this dinner... I mean, all this food... will it run you short of money?" She swallowed at the slim space of quiet that followed.

He turned around from the stove and smiled at her. "Whatever it costs, it's worth it. Don't worry about me, kiddo. I'll manage. I always have."

She knew she shouldn't ask. It was really none of her business. Her mother would be horrified if she could hear her now. Well-bred people simply did not discuss personal finances. And yet, she had to know, wanted to understand this man and how he lived. "Did you say you are paid by the church?"

"A small salary," he answered, not at all upset by the question. "And I get a little from the city for running a drug rehabilitation center and setting up some VISTA programs. Nothing great, mind you, but I get by. My needs are small."

"I see. Do you mind if I ask you why you decided to move here and do this rather than take a more conventional position like most ministers do?"

"You can ask me anything, Elizabeth. Of course, I might reciprocate." He grinned and watched for her reaction, but she only shrugged. "There are a lot of people who would never set foot inside a church," he explained. "It just doesn't offer them what they need. So, I thought maybe I could take what faith and optimism and limited knowledge I have to them. I don't make a big difference here, I know that. I may be optimistic, but I'm also a realist. Whatever effects I have accomplished here are small. But the name of the game is to do something. I can't turn my back on it. I have to try."

Elizabeth had never known anyone like Sam Winslow, never known anyone with a commitment to something other than themselves. It was odd in a way how she had never really given any thought that a person like him might exist. And being around him now made her suddenly aware of limitations she never knew she had.

"I've never been a particularly religious person. Oh, I go to church every Sunday, but I guess basically because it is socially the thing to do. It is sort of expected." She paused, frowning at the salad. "Do you have something to make dressing?"

"Yeah. There's some oil in here." He opened a cabinet and rummaged around until he found a bottle of vegetable oil and one of vinegar. "I don't have a lot of seasonings, but just pick out whatever you want.''

Elizabeth made the dressing with what little ingredients he had and poured it on the salad. Sam had already set his mismatched silverware and paper napkins on the table, so she added the salad bowls to the arrangement. ''Did you know when you were young that this was what you would do?''

''No. Here, let's eat our salads while the spaghetti cooks. I'll get the wine.''

They sat at the table and started eating before Sam fully answered the question. ''I was twenty-one and a senior in college. Jonas was away fighting a war that I didn't understand and didn't want to take the time to try and figure out. It was just too far away. I had too many other things to think about. I was involved in a fraternity, and the most important thing on my mind was how to get the girls in the house across the street into my bed. Am I embarrassing you?''

Elizabeth blushed, but stammered a quick no.

''And then we got word that Jonas had been killed, and everything just sort of fell apart for me. My parents, of course, went through hell over their son's death, and whether it was real or not, I felt that a lot of their frustration and anger was directed at me. I was in some way responsible. In a sense, it was my own guilt that made me so paranoid. In my mind, I was guilty. I should have been over there fighting at my brother's side, protecting him, doing anything except worrying about my next sexual conquest. It was as though my apathy was to blame for his death.''

Elizabeth was holding her glass of wine in both hands and staring hard at Sam. ''But you weren't responsible,'' she said.

''Oh, I know that...now. But then, God! It was so...hard. You see, Jonas wasn't just my brother; he was my best friend. And I had let him down. Anyway, after that I became pretty outspoken in the antiwar movement. Not SDS or anything that extreme, but still actively involved in demonstrations. And as you probably know, Madison was sort of the hot seat for some of that activity. A whole shift in my outlook on life occurred at that point."

He finished his salad, then sat back in his chair and watched her.

"Don't watch me while I eat," she said.

"Why not?"

"Because you make me nervous."

He smiled and leaned his elbows on the table, watching her even more closely. "Good. I'm afraid it has been a long time since I've made a woman nervous."

Elizabeth hurriedly finished her salad, then stood and picked up both bowls and set them in the sink. "Is this where you keep the plates?"

She was standing only a foot away from him, facing the cabinets. He stood up behind her. His hands lifted, his fingers slightly spread, and he laid his palms flat against her waist, a couple of fingers touching her sweater, the others resting against the velvety softness of her brown suede pants.

Elizabeth's arm was up as she reached for the plates, but she stopped, her hand caught in midair, frozen by the devastating impact of those hands against her side. Her arm lowered very slowly and she turned around to look at him.

Her lips were parted and her eyes were like damp grass in the morning. But he saw the slight shake of her head. An imperceptible denial of the impetuous elements that flowed between them like a rippling stream, racing toward some unseen ocean into which neither of them was yet ready to dive.

With extreme effort he lowered his hands from her waist and turned to the stove to remove the boiling pan of spaghetti. He took a plate from her hand and served the spaghetti and sauce, then set it on the table.

She handed him the second plate and watched him as he ladled sauce over the spaghetti. She wanted to say something to remove this heavy shroud of sensual tension that draped the room. But she didn't know what to say. If she ignored it, would it go away?

"Why did you back out on the hospital, Elizabeth?"

She sat in her chair and stared up at him where he stood, still holding his plate in his hand. She watched him set the plate on the table and sit down across from her. They both ate a few bites before she answered.

"My grandmother and I discussed it." She shook her head. "Well, not exactly. She discussed it. I listened. Anyway, it was decided that I should not spend any more money or time here."

"Decided."

"Yes."

"By you or by her?"

"Sam, you don't understand. I'm living in my grandmother's house. Oh, she gave it to me, but it's still really hers. I have money of my own, of course, and I have since I was twenty-one. But, well, most of what I am and have is due to my grandmother."

"She owns you, in other words."

Elizabeth slammed her fork to the table. "She doesn't own me! She has given me everything I have ever wanted. I owe her something for that. You don't understand."

"You're right. I don't."

Elizabeth looked down at her plate of half-eaten spaghetti. This wasn't going to work. What did she think she was trying to prove by being here with him? He would never understand her and she could not really understand him. "Sam, I think I should go."

He silently considered her remark. Maybe he should

have tried harder to understand what she was saying. Maybe he could have at least said it differently. But he didn't understand, dammit! And he wasn't going to lie to her. Perhaps there were people who were too different to ever come to terms with each other. Maybe that's the way it was between the two of them.

He threw his napkin onto the table and slammed his chair back as he stood up, but his voice didn't reflect the anger of the physical movements. "Right," he said softly.

He waited for her to stand, but avoided looking at her. She watched him set his plate on the counter, and then she too stood.

"Thank you for the dinner."

He didn't want it to end this way. He knew he should say something—apologize maybe. But all he said was "You're welcome."

She walked through the living room, picking up her purse on the way, and stopped in the foyer to get her jacket. She slipped one arm in, but before she could manage the other one by herself, she felt his hands guiding the jacket onto her shoulders. They stood still for a moment, her back to him, his hands on her shoulders, and then she stepped away and opened the door.

Together they walked onto the porch and into the darkness toward the car. "Well, at least this time you have all your wheels."

Without answering, Elizabeth unlocked the door and started to slide behind the wheel. But the hand on her arm stopped her. She turned to face him and suddenly his mouth was there, warm and sure and insistent. There was no question inherent in the kiss, nothing pleading. But there was a finality about it as if he were a condemned man and this had been his last request. His hands were against her jaw, his fingers were wrapped around the back of her neck under her hair, and his thumbs were against each of her cheekbones.

He stared at her mouth as he stepped back, then looked at her eyes. Slowly she slid down into the car and closed the door. She didn't look back at him as she started the engine and pulled away. She couldn't. If she had, she never would have left. And that was the most frightful revelation about this man and her feelings that she had yet faced.

Chapter Eight

"Come, ye thank-ful peo-ple come, Raise the song of har-vest home: All is safe-ly gath-ered in, Ere the win-ter storms be-gin; God, our Ma-ker, doth pro-vide For our wants to be sup-plied: Come to God's own tem-ple, come, Raise the song of har-vest home."

As soon as the hymnals were closed, the low buzz of idle gossip and a whirlwind of colorful pastel wools accompanied the exodus from the huge beige brick church on the North Shore. Elizabeth was wearing a green La-Roche suit as she towed behind her mother and grandmother. As always, everyone wanted to stop and talk to the three of them and receive their blessings on this bright and clear Sunday morning. Eva, wearing a pink Chanel, waved her gloved hand like the staff of life, rationing her affections to those most deserving of them.

Louise clung close to Elizabeth. She was slightly hung over from last night's binge and was also overwhelmed, as she had always been, by Eva's dominance. "Did you see what Mildred Reitman was wearing?" Louise asked. "My Lord, I have never seen anything so hideous in my life! You would think a woman with her weight problem would wear something besides all those big polkadots."

Edna Wordsworth joined in step with Louise and Elizabeth. "Did you two hear about Rita Morgan's latest fling?"

A small crowd gathered around to cluck and tsk at the latest tidbit of scandal.

"Well, I heard something even better yesterday at the club. It's about . . ."

Adrienne walked up to the crowd as she had done every Sunday for the last seven years, sidling up to hear the latest news. But today there was a difference.

All conversation ceased and eight pairs of eyes shifted anxiously about, looking everywhere but at her.

Elizabeth felt the tension around the group and wished there was something she could do to ease it. Adrienne broke the thick crust of ice by speaking.

"Are you going to the club for lunch, Liz?"

"Yes, would you like to—"

Eva plunged into the crowd and took charge. "Elizabeth, dear, you do remember that we're having lunch with our new minister at the club. So sorry you won't be able to join us, Adrienne."

Adrienne stared at the older woman, then looked at Elizabeth for her reaction. Elizabeth's mouth tightened and she glanced at her friend with uncertainty. Adrienne saw the look, nodded fatalistically, and walked away.

Elizabeth's gaze shifted back to her grandmother, who was now holding court as the group of women gathered around for her opinion on John Stebbins's "problem." As they all moved like a tide to the club, Elizabeth was aware for the first time in her life of a bitter self-loathing.

The country club sat atop a bluff, jutting out over the lake, and surrounding it to the north and west and south was an undulating thirty-six hole golf course, twelve tennis courts, a large pear-shaped pool, and an exercise studio with saunas, steam baths, and the latest in Nautilus equipment. There were also two dining rooms and three bars within the main structure. In the largest dining room a huge buffet was spread each Sunday, and

Elizabeth stood in line behind the minister of their church, who was choosing from the vast array of salads. "Oh, nectarines! How marvelous! I do love them so. And you, Miss Parkins, what will you have?"

Elizabeth stared at the middle-aged man with a blank look, not wanting to respond. Her mood was gray and as brittle as a dry twig. Why had she allowed Adrienne to be excluded from this lunch? And why was she now forced to endure the company of this irritatingly urbane minister?

He was dressed in a smart Pierre Cardin suit that covered his thin continental frame. His hair was short and stylish, his fingers slim and perfectly manicured, and his eyes were filled with the golden display of wealth that now surrounded him.

After serving herself, Elizabeth sat across from him at the round table, Eva to his left, Louise next to her, circling around to include the Bennett family—Roger, Helayne, and little Mitzi.

Elizabeth observed Reverend Hawthorne as he ordered a Scotch on the rocks, and took note of all the ways in which he was different from Sam. He was charming, witty, and well versed on all of the newsworthy topics of the day. He played tennis every afternoon except for Sunday. On that afternoon he played golf. He was well received by all. All, that is, except for Elizabeth.

"We are still so delighted to have you with our church," Eva said. "We need a man who knows the problems of the community and the world and who has a realistic view of life."

"Thank you, Mrs. Rowen. The past two months have been wonderful for me. I'm delighted to be among all of you and I hope that I and the church will serve you well."

Elizabeth felt a surge of hostility for the man. "Have you ever worked with the poor, Reverend Hawthorne?"

"The poor? Oh, I went on a sabbatical once to Africa and visited various tribes. It was a combined study trip and mission that the church sent me on. Why do you ask?"

"What about in this country?" she asked, ignoring his own question to her. "Have you ever worked in the inner city with the poor?"

"No." He laughed easily. "I've been fortunate enough to be assigned to some of the more gracious churches, such as your own." He smiled at Eva, sitting next to him.

Elizabeth watched the exchange with a blank face, then mused aloud. "I wonder whatever happened to the idea of taking religion to the people, into the streets, where it's needed."

The silence settled at once on the table, throbbing in each beat of Elizabeth's pulse. Everyone was staring at her as if she had lost her mind. She glanced at Eva and the expression that met her was carved in stone.

The minister laughed uneasily. "Well, Elizabeth." He laughed again and looked around the table for support. "Times have changed a bit from that. The church has become more sophisticated, more relevant to the needs of contemporary society." His laugh was growing bolder by the minute. "Taking it to the streets, yes, that's an interesting idea, Miss Parkins. Antiquated, I'm afraid, but interesting nonetheless."

With one last warning glare at her granddaughter, Eva shifted her attention to Reverend Hawthorne. "Elizabeth is always coming up with some of the more provocative questions. Always a challenge, that girl. Now, Reverend Hawthorne, have you thought any more about the budget the board has proposed?"

"Liz, you're just too good at this game for me!" Thomas laughed and wiped the sweat from the back of his neck with a towel.

Elizabeth swung her tennis racket, replaying the stroke that had been the deciding blow in their match. She grinned. "I told you I've been taking lessons."

"Yes, I've heard about the kind of lessons Stefan Vorga gives. I certainly hope you've been confining yourself to tennis."

"Wouldn't you like to know," she teased. "Let's go up to the house. I've had about all the exercise I can stand for today."

Thomas draped the towel around her neck and pulled her close. "Not me," he said, planting a persuasive kiss upon her lips.

Elizabeth wiggled from his embrace. "Race you to the house!" She laughed, running up the hill away from him.

Once inside, she went upstairs to change into another warm-up suit. Letti had some coffee made when Elizabeth came down to the study. Thomas was lounging in the brown leather chair, sipping a bourbon and water. He watched Elizabeth as she curled on the couch with a cup of coffee in her hands and he felt real contentment here in this house and with this woman. He wondered if she felt it too.

"I wish you would have gone with me to Virginia this weekend, Liz. The weather was beautiful there. Still autumn, not nearly as cold as it is here."

"That would have been nice, Thomas, but I had so many things to do yesterday." She didn't like the fact that she was lying to him, but how could she tell him that she had spent the day with another man? Even now, as she thought about it, she was frightened by the overwhelming intensity of her body's reactions just at the thought of Sam Winslow. She didn't want to feel this way for him. This was the way it should be with Thomas. He was the right man for her, of her class and background; not this unorthodox preacher living in the slums of west side Chicago.

She looked at Thomas, leaning his head against the high back of the chair, his eyes closed, the glass held loosely in his fingers. It would be so easy to tell this man that she loved him, that she would marry him. She knew that was what he wanted. But she just couldn't. It would be a lie that she could not live with inside herself. She did not love Thomas Benson.

She couldn't admit to herself the reason why. It was there in the image of another man. A collage of sensations. Strong hands, warm eyes, passionate convictions, an insistent mouth against her own. But she could not yet accept what that man meant in her life.

When she and Thomas were in the middle of a light lunch that Letti had prepared for them and brought to the study, the phone rang. It rang a second time.

"Where on earth is Letti now?" Elizabeth asked.

"I'll get it, Liz," Thomas said, getting up from the table to answer the phone. "Hello? Yes, this is the Parkins residence. May I tell her who's calling? Just a minute, please.

"Liz, darling, it's for you." He placed his hand over the receiver then and whispered, "Someone named Sam."

Elizabeth's hand froze where the fork was lifting the ham salad to her mouth. The fork slowly lowered to the plate as she stared at the receiver. She stood and walked to the phone, taking it from his hand. "Thank you. Hello?"

"I'm sorry to bother you, Elizabeth. I can tell you're...busy."

"It's...that's quite all right, Sam."

There was a long span of silence while he tried to think of something to say. He had called to apologize for the things he had said yesterday about her grandmother owning her. But now he couldn't make the words come out. "I needed to ask you a question about the paint you bought for the hospital," he said instead.

"All right."

"The hospital wants to use that same color in the nurses' area between the children's wing and the emergency ward, but they don't know what the color is. You had it mixed, didn't you?"

"Yes, let me think a minute. It was...Canary Smile."

"Canary Smile. Got it. Thank you."

"You're welcome. Is...is that all you wanted?" she asked, her voice cracking under the strain. Thomas was sitting at the table again, but he was watching her closely. She turned her back to him. "I mean, if there was anything else..."

"No," he quickly said. "That was all."

"I see. Well, good-bye, then."

"See you." Sam hung up first, cutting the connection between them with a resounding click.

Elizabeth replaced the receiver and turned back to Thomas. She smiled. "Just a little problem with one of my charity projects."

"All taken care of now?"

"Yes. Finished."

Fifteen miles away, on Blackhawk Street, Sam kept a tight grip on the phone even after he had hung up. The blood was pounding through him like lava jetting up through a volcano. How could he have been so stupid to call her? Why hadn't he known that she would have plenty of other men to occupy her time?

He felt as mad and flustered and confused as a seventeen-year-old who finally got up the nerve to invite the girl of his dreams to the prom, only to find out she already had a date with the star of the football team. What was the matter with him? This wasn't like him at all. He didn't need her in his life, not some rich broad whose only thoughts were what she would wear to some Thanksgiving ball at the damn country club!

He moved away from the phone, grabbed his jacket from the foyer, and stormed out of the house, finding a certain sanctity and release in the desolation that enveloped him on the street.

Elizabeth finished her salad and laid her fork on the plate. "If you'll excuse me, Thomas. I have to run upstairs for a minute." Without waiting for his reply, she left the room and dashed up the stairs, hurrying down the long hallway to her room. She closed the door and locked it, moved to her bedside, and picked up the phone. Opening the drawer in the table, she pulled out the slip of paper with Sam's telephone number. She dialed too quickly and made a mistake. She tried again.

The phone rang and rang and rang, and soon she had counted twenty-five unanswered rings. An indefinable sadness washed over her as she hung up the phone and returned to Thomas's side downstairs.

Chapter Nine

The sunlight made a silver sheen as it reflected on the first snowfall of the year. Elm trees arched silent against the backdrop of white. A few empty birds' nests remained in the high crotches of trees, their occupants having long since migrated south to warmer climates.

Elizabeth stood in front of the gilt-edged mirror that hung over a credenza in the foyer and checked her tan.

Thomas smiled indulgently. "It's still there."

"No, it's fading. I spend a week on Maui and I still look like a paleface." She turned away from the mirror, totally disgruntled. "Oh, woe is me."

He laughed. "You've got a lot to complain about. While you and your little friends were romping along the sand and drinking Singapore Slings, I was stuck here in the cold with my nose to the grindstone."

"Poor baby," she said, patting his arm with distracted sympathy. The whole time she was in Hawaii, her friends had insisted that she was crazy not to commit everything to Thomas Benson. And they were right...from their standpoint. But she couldn't seem to shake this dissatisfied feeling. Something was missing. Call it chemistry, call it genuine caring, call it love. Or call it all three. Something was definitely lacking in the relationship.

She smiled at Thomas. "We did have a wonderful time. I wish it could have gone on forever."

He heard what she said and he also knew what it meant. She had not missed him as much as he had missed her. But he wasn't going to give up. Not yet. She was everything he was looking for in a woman. They had talked enough about their pasts for him to know that there never had been any serious relationships. Surely if it were someone new she had met, he could fight that. Whatever was holding her back couldn't last forever. He would wait it out. It was all he could do for now.

"Look, Balls, I think I know how you feel...."

"How do you know, man? How do you know nothin'?"

"You're right," Sam said. "I don't know, but all these other guys do." He looked around the group for reinforcement. No one volunteered a thing. "My point, Balls, is that you're not alone in this. You have friends here."

As every Friday night, Sam was holding the drug rehabilitation meeting in the high school building. So far, the evening was not going too well. They were all too aware of the empty chair in the circle, the one that had belonged to Chaco, the one that would be Chaco's no more. It was another battle that Sam had fought and lost. Another boy was dead and all he could do now was try and help those who still had a chance to break their drug habit before it was too late.

"I don't need no friends," Balls said. "I need a fix." He finally relaxed his shoulders and snickered. "Or at least a good lay."

"Don't we all." Sam laughed. "Don't we all."

"What happened to that high-class chick I seen you with?" asked Blanco, a tiny albino who had only joined the group about a month before.

"She didn't like his style," one of the boys slurred, his words dripping with sarcasm. "Or was it something else, preach? You ain't got what those upper-class broads need? Heh?"

"Guess not," he said, then looked over at Edgar, the oldest member of the group. "Haven't heard much from you tonight, Edgar. How did it go with you this week?"

To Sam's relief the conversation turned to Edgar's problems instead of his own. He didn't want to talk about Elizabeth with these guys. He didn't even want to think about her himself. He had been that route. He had even broken down and called her a couple of weeks ago, but her housekeeper said she had gone to Hawaii. To Hawaii, for God's sake!

Since then, he had redoubled his efforts to erase her from his mind. He had not succeeded, but he still tried.

"That's good to hear, Edgar," he said when the boy finished talking. He wanted to focus all of his attention on these kids who were rejected by society and left with only drug addiction to give parameters to their lives. "And after Edgar's encouraging news, I think we'd better call it a night. Does anybody have anything else to say?"

As usual, everyone was eager to get out on the streets, so no one had anything else to add. Most of the boys in the group were there by court order anyway, so they shot out of the meetings like prisoners released from a long, torturous sentence.

Sam grabbed his coat, turned out the lights in the schoolroom, and locked the door behind him. He hunched down into his coat, but the wet snow lashed at his face until it was numb.

As he climbed the steps to his house he heard the telephone ringing inside. Hurriedly unlocking the door, he ran into the kitchen and grabbed the receiver off the hook.

"Hello?"

"Sam? It's Eugenia...at the hospital."

"Yes?"

"I...well, I told you I'd call you if there was any change and...well...I'm sorry, but...Daniel died tonight."

Life wasn't fair. He had seen enough in those two years with the Peace Corps in India to know that. He thought he had seen it all. And yet, this one child's suffering—his battered, emaciated body and spirit— had affected Sam more than he thought was possible anymore. He felt diminished.

He stared at the wall in front of him, his attention focused on the hairline crack in the plaster that ran from ceiling to floor. Don't think about what she's saying. Think only about this house, that crack...yeah, it needs to be fixed. Maybe I'll do that tomorrow...or the next day, or the next...

"Thank you for calling," he croaked, hanging up. He stared at the crack, but it suddenly changed shape as his fist flew into the plaster with a sickening crunch, shattering the wall and leaving a raw, gaping hole. He continued to stare at the hole, aware only of the raw, gaping chasm inside his gut.

On Sunday morning it was still snowing and the cold added an icy sheen to the white lawn. Elizabeth, unable to sleep, was up early and was sitting by the window, watching the snow fall, troubled by the ever-tightening circle of her life.

Last night she and Thomas had gone to Judith and Ross Amberson's Thanksgiving party and had not returned home until very late. As she thought about it now she tried to find fault with the party, but there was none to find. It was something else entirely. It was the way everyone had looked at her with Thomas, the way they were treated as a couple. It was the permanence of the thing that scared her. As if they were already married, that's the way people treated them. As if she had no say in the matter at all. And to top it off, Thomas had drunk too much and pressed her harder for a commitment, for some proof that she was his.

Well, she wasn't his, dammit! Not yet, anyway. And she just wished everyone, including Thomas, would stop viewing her that way.

She was startled out of her bad mood by the ringing of the telephone. She walked to the table, checking the clock beside the bed. Seven o'clock. Who in their right mind would call at this hour of the morning? Please don't let it be Thomas! She just wasn't up for his contrite apologies right now.

She answered, expecting the worst. But nothing had prepared her for the bitterness she actually heard.

"Well, well, the butterfly finally comes home to face reality. Oh, ho, reality, what a joke that is, right? You don't know about reality, do you, butterfly?"

"Who is this?. . . Sam? Is that you?"

"She remembers my name!" His voice was harsh and too loud. "Well, maybe she remembers a starving kid... Nah, she's too busy running off to Hawaii to bask in the sun. Get a good tan?" he asked, his voice dripping with sarcasm.

Her heart was pounding, just hearing his voice again, knowing he was still there, just across the wire, across town. But what had she done? Why was he so angry? And what did he mean about a starving kid? Her pulse fluttered erratically. "The little boy in your hospital?"

"What a wonderful memory you have," he slurred, and she had the sudden suspicion that he was drunk.

"What has happened, Sam?"

"He's dead, that's what's happened. Other than that...well, everything's just peachy. But, heck, enough of all that depressing stuff." His accompanying chuckle was low and ugly. "How was your trip to Hawaii? Was the weather nice?"

"Sam." Elizabeth squeezed her eyes shut. She heard the bitterness and the anger. And beyond that, she heard the hurt. Inside, Sam Winslow was crying. "Sam, I'm so sorry. I—I know how you felt about that little boy."

"Oh, you know, do you? Lady, how the hell do you know how I feel about anything?"

"I want to see you. I want to come over there."

"How charitable of you," he sneered. "But you're too late."

She gritted her teeth and closed her eyes again. "Listen to me. I'm coming over there now. I want you to stay put, because I'll be there as soon as I can. Do you hear me?"

He laughed, unkindly. "Oh, I'll be here. Where the hell else would I go? This is where I live."

Forty-five minutes later Elizabeth stepped out of the car in front of Sam's house and stared up at the quiet gray Victorian facade. It was too still here in the early morning. The whole street, in fact, was cloaked in an unreal quiet. This wasn't Blackhawk. Blackhawk was teeming with life, bustling with activity, pulsating with an urgency that was lacking in her part of the city. But then, she had never been here in the early morning before. She didn't realize it could have such an unearthly stillness to it.

She closed and locked the door of her car, not yet accepting the fact that if someone in this neighborhood wanted it badly enough, a little lock would prove no deterrent.

She walked up the stairs, holding her coat tightly

against her torso. She knocked, but there was no answer. Where was he? He knew she was coming. She tried the knob and it turned. The door wasn't even locked.

The foyer was dark and quiet and Sam's coat was lying in a heap on the floor. She bent over and picked it up, dusted it with her hand, and hung it on the coat tree.

She walked into the living room. On the table between the two chairs was a dirty glass and an empty wine bottle. A newspaper was strewn across one of the chairs and the floor. The fireplace was cold. It was obvious no fire had been lit for several hours.

She went into the kitchen. It too was a mess. Plates of uneaten food lay on the counter and another newspaper littered the round table. And then she saw the gaping hole in the wall beside the telephone.

When she walked back into the living room to pick up the glass and the empty bottle, she saw him. He had just come downstairs and was leaning against the opening between the foyer and living room.

"Sam?" She stared with disbelief at the man before her. He only bore a faint resemblance to the man she had been with a few weeks earlier. His face was unshaven, his hair uncombed. He was wearing faded blue jeans and a flannel shirt that hung open.

She took one step toward him. "Sam."

His return stare was self-mocking. "The real me," he said. "Like it?"

She held his stare. "Not really."

He rested his head back against the wall and closed his eyes. "Neither do I."

In a way she was lying. She loved the way he looked. She stared at his chest. Hard, athletic, solid. Her gaze dropped to his waist, and then to the top of his jeans.

"Why aren't you in church?" she asked. "Don't you have to help with the services?"

"I called in sick." He opened his eyes to regard her. "If I had the money, I'd flit off to Hawaii and just forget all that's been happening here."

"I'm sorry that it bothers you so much that I went on a vacation," she said. "But I go somewhere every year at this time."

"How nice," he sneered.

"It is nice, Sam. I enjoy my money. There's no crime in that."

He sniffed derisively, but refrained from commenting.

"I'm sorry about Daniel, Sam. I really am."

He shook his head and squeezed his eyes shut. "I don't want to talk about it."

Elizabeth's heart ached for the man across the room. He was in so much pain, but he wouldn't let her in. She looked about the messy room. "Where is Mary?"

"Don't know. She didn't come here last Wednesday." He frowned. "That's another thing..."

She waited to hear more, but he didn't finish the thought. "Why don't you take a shower, Sam. I'll clean this up."

He looked at her for a long moment. Funny that he could stand so far away from her and yet feel so much sexual tension inside himself. He could smell her, feel her, taste her even from here. And he wanted to climb inside her and wrap her warmth around him like a summer night. "Yeah," he mumbled, tearing his eyes away from her. He slowly climbed back up the stairs.

Elizabeth sighed heavily, then removed her coat and hung it with Sam's in the foyer. The first thing she did was light a fire. It was much too cold in here without it. As the flame took hold and wrapped around the logs, she thought about that day she had come here to talk about Adrienne's problems. He had given so much to her that day, so much emotional support and friendship. She owed him.

As she carried the glass and the wine bottle to the kitchen, she admitted to herself that it was much more than that. She wanted to be here, debt or no debt; wanted to be with him and take care of him. Despite his tough loner exterior, he seemed to need so much. Not like Thomas, who probably didn't need anyone. He could survive without her quite easily, she was sure. But Sam Winslow . . . was it really he that needed so much or she that needed so much? The puzzle was too intricate to solve, and no matter how she arranged them, the pieces didn't seem to fit.

The water in the shower was running through the pipes above her as she washed and dried the dishes. She wiped up the counter and threw away the newspaper, making the room at least a little more presentable now. She opened the refrigerator to see if there was anything to fix him to eat. There wasn't much there at all, but she did find a couple of eggs and another packet of ham.

After a while Sam came downstairs and stopped in the doorway to the kitchen. Elizabeth had cooked breakfast for him and the table was set with knives and forks and spoons and napkins.

They looked at each other across the space of the kitchen, both unsure of what this seemingly innocuous meal could possibly mean.

"This is nice," he finally said, moving to the table and sitting down.

"Welcome to the Parkins Diner." She smiled, pouring two cups of coffee and setting them on the table.

He looked at the plate in front of him. It was heaping with food, while the other plate had only toast. "Did I sit in the wrong place?"

"Shut up and eat." She smiled, sitting down in the chair across from him.

He wasn't about to argue. It had been a couple of days since he had eaten much of anything. He had gone through a couple of bottles of wine, but that could hardly be considered sustenance. He finished his food and set down his fork on the now clean plate at about the same time Elizabeth was lifting her toast to take a second bite.

He sat back, drank his coffee slowly, and watched her.

"I told you before not to do that," she said. "It makes me nervous."

He set the cup down. "Why are you here, Elizabeth?"

"Why do you always ask me that?"

"Because I have to know these things."

She laid her toast on the plate and dabbed at her mouth with a napkin. She spent several seconds on these superfluous activities before she looked at him. "I was worried about you, Sam. You sounded so...different, distraught."

His eyes closed and his mouth was tight. "I—I had such a strong feeling for that...for Daniel. I guess I thought if I loved him enough, he would pull through." He was quiet for several seconds before he continued. "He had so much wrong with him. Inadequate growth development, atrophied liver, edema. He'd gone into shock several times. But still, I thought he was getting better. I guess I just wanted it so. You know what it was that finally did it, what the final straw was that killed him?"

Elizabeth shook her head.

"It was an infection, a staph infection, they called it. Something you can get in hospitals that have unclean equipment or too many germs floating around." He lifted his eyes to stare at Elizabeth. "The one place that should have helped him was unable to. All that technology, all that care, all my love, none of it helped. Another five-year-old dies, and it's all so senseless. The old world just keeps on turning.''

Elizabeth felt the tears pool beneath her eyelids. She swallowed hard several times. ''The fact that my life kept revolving...that really bothers you, doesn't it? You have so much to worry about, and I went off to Hawaii.''

He nodded slowly. ''Yes, and you went to Hawaii.''

The tension between them was tangible, a field of electrical energy so strong, they both felt its magnetic draw pulling them under.

Elizabeth stood and carried the plates to the sink.

Sam managed a weak smile. ''That's a bad habit of yours.''

''What's that?''

''Leaving the scene at the moment of crisis.''

She turned around to face him. He rose from his chair and moved up to the counter a few feet away from her.

''Is this a crisis?'' she asked, her voice as weak as that of a trapped bird.

He leaned his back against the counter and hooked his thumbs in the pockets of his jeans. ''It could be for me,'' he said. ''Who was the man?'' he asked. ''The one who answered your phone that day I called?''

Elizabeth clutched the edge of the counter with her fingers. She tried to look away from him, but his penetrating stare held her captive. ''His name is Thomas.''

Sam nodded, digesting the name. ''Is he someone''— he cleared his throat—''important in your life?''

She felt the lump in her throat move up to the backs of her eyes. Her answer was a frail whisper. ''I don't know. I honestly do not know.''

''Are you sleeping with him? Do you make love?''

The pressure behind her eyes increased. ''Why are

you asking me this?'' Her voice, her eyes, her tense stance all implored him not to delve too deep, not to ask too much of her.

But he had already come too far, delved too deep. He was beyond the stopping point. He studied her beseeching face for a minute, and when he finally spoke, his voice was a low, dry groan. "Because I want to make love with you.''

Elizabeth stared, unable to move or breathe. But the tears began to roll down her cheeks as she stood there silently watching this man who had stated the very thing she had been afraid to admit to herself. She couldn't deny it. She had thought it. Over and over again. The feel of his hands upon her body, the taste of his mouth, the unleashed hunger she sensed was inside of him.

She felt his cool hands against her warm, wet cheeks. Her head fell back into the cup of his fingers. His thumb stroked across her jaw, wiping the tears away. His mouth touched her cheek, moved to her eye, then her temple, and back to her cheek. Slowly her head turned until their lips met and opened, offering themselves an entrance to the sensations they both wanted so desperately to feel.

His hand lowered to cover her breast and her hands lifted to his waist. She could feel the heat from his body traveling into her fingertips, she could taste the hunger that was in him. And she wanted to feed that hunger, wanted to feel him unleash it inside of her. And yet, she knew that with this man it would be so much more than just physical. She was afraid of not having the power to give him the very thing he wanted and needed.

"There are things I wish I could say, Sam.'' Her voice was a soft whimper against his mouth.

Her voice, soft and lovely and warm against him. In his kitchen, in his house, in his arms. "You don't have to say anything, Elizabeth.'' His voice was low and silky against her skin, and his breath was quick and uneven. "There are things I could say too. If you want me to, I will."

"Will you tell me what I want to hear?"

He brushed her lips very gently with his own. "I doubt it. It would be very easy for me to say I love you. Very easy. But what is hard is knowing what to do with that love. This is where I live, Elizabeth. This is who I am."

"I know who you are," she said, but her eyes wavered with the uncertainties.

He shook his head wistfully. "No, you don't, Elizabeth."

"It doesn't matter," she insisted.

He smiled sadly. "It will. Maybe not today, but it will. I want you to realize that."

She pulled her head away and turned her back to him, facing the counter. "I don't understand you," she said softly. "You say you want to make love to me and then you sound like you're trying to talk yourself out of it."

He laid a hand against her side just beneath her breast and ran the fingers of his other hand into her hair. He stepped closer, aligning his body behind hers, and spoke low against her ear. "It's just that I'm not looking for a one-night stand, Elizabeth. If that's all you're offering, I'll take it. I'll take whatever you want to give, but I'm looking for much more. I just need to know from the beginning what to expect. That's the way I am."

She laid her hands on top of the counter and looked down. "I'm scared, Sam. I need time to adjust to all of this. This is the first time I've admitted to myself that...what I feel for you. I need a little time to get used to that."

His breath was ragged against her neck. "I sure hope you're a fast thinker."

She turned around in his arms and smiled almost timidly. "You're terrible," she said softly.

He kissed the corner of her lips and slid his mouth across her cheek and up to her temple. "Me? Hey, I'm a preacher. I'm one of the good guys."

Her laugh was low in her throat. "You sure are the strangest preacher I've ever seen. I didn't think you were supposed to think about things like that."

He moved his hands onto the counter on each side of her body and looked down at her. "Like what?" He smiled. "Lightning won't strike you if you say the word, you know."

"Okay, sex. I didn't think you were supposed to think about sex."

He chuckled. "A monk, I'm not."

"Haven't there been any women in your life? Any relationships?"

"Sure. But recently there have been none that I would, as they say, take home to mother."

She sighed and looked around the room, hesitant as to what she was supposed to do with this fascinating man and her feelings for him. "Well, I just don't know what to say now."

He saw the look in her face and understood it. She was full of questions, doubts, and needs that she was trying desperately to deny. The one thing he didn't want to do was rush her into a relationship she wasn't ready for. If and when she said yes to him, he would know she was giving more than just her body.

He smiled and leaned closer. "Say yes and I'll make up the question."

"Do I dare?" she asked herself in a mumble. "Well, all right . . . yes."

"Good answer. Now for the question. Would you like to go on a picnic?"

Her expression was incredulous. "It's freezing outside! And snowing! And we just ate breakfast!"

"So what?"

"Are you serious?"

"Sure. I've got to get out of here, Elizabeth. I've been cooped up for two days, mourning and...also wallowing in self-pity. And now with your warm body so temptingly close to mine...well, I just need some air."

"But what about your church? If you told them you were sick, won't the other minister or some of the people come to check on you?"

"Are you afraid I'll get in trouble for playing hooky? Look, Elizabeth, even preachers are entitled to an occasional emotional breakdown. I'm only human. Now come on." He moved away from the counter, holding her hand and pulling her with him through the living room. "It'll be fun. You'll see."

He reached for her coat and helped her put it on. His fingers lingered only a second too long on her shoulders, the temptation to touch her again wavering in the air between them.

She slipped on her gloves and raised the hood on her coat. "Shouldn't you wear a hat?" she asked.

He shook his head. "I'm counting on you to keep me warm."

"Rather presumptuous, aren't you?"

"I told you before, I am a very optimistic man."

They headed down the stairs and sidewalk, and she pulled her car keys from her coat pocket. He shook his head and covered her hand with his own. "Let's take the train."

"The train?"

He gave her a patronizing look. "You remember, that big thing that goes clickety-clack along the track."

"I know what it is, wise guy. It's just that...well, is it safe?"

Sam stopped and looked down into her wide-open face, her green eyes sparklingly innocent against the white sky. A snowflake fell against her cheek and melted there. "You are incredible," he whispered with a laugh. "Here you are, in one of the highest crime areas in the city, and you're worried about the safety of the train!"

"Well, I've never ridden the train and I've heard all sorts of horror stories."

"You've never been on the train? Are you kidding?"

She lifted her chin higher. "No, I've never had a reason to ride it before."

He wrapped his arm around her shoulder and pulled her close. "Shtick with me, shweetheart. You are going to get an education today."

"That's what I'm afraid of," she murmured, but swallowing a slight twinge of trepidation, she let Sam lead her down the street. The snow was falling harder now, and she questioned their sanity in going on a picnic in this weather. But he only laughed at her and told her she'd love it.

They stopped at Alfredo's and bought some pastrami, hard rolls, cheese, and a jug of apple cider. After leaving the store they turned the corner and headed across a vacant lot that Sam insisted was a shortcut to the train stop. Two small boys were in the lot, climbing over a huge pile of trash while they took turns kicking at a tin can.

When they reached the platform, Elizabeth held tightly to the stair railing to keep from slipping on the wet wood. "I certainly am glad I wore boots and heavy pants today," she said. "Although, if I had known what you were going to suggest, I would have worn my Nanook of the North snowsuit."

"Stop complaining or I'm going to put a snowball down your back."

"Oh, yeah?" She grabbed a handful of snow from the platform railing and threw it back at him. He ducked, but a good portion of it still smacked him on the cheek.

"Oh, ho, woman, this is war!" He scooped up a handful and shoved it up beneath her jacket and sweater, rubbing his icy hands across her bare back to the accompaniment of her shrieks.

They ran across the platform toward the token booth, laughing hysterically, and they paid no attention to the deadpan stares they received from other passengers waiting for the train. When they reached the window, Sam pulled his money from his pocket and counted it out for the woman in the booth.

"You're ten cents short," the lady said.

"Ooops." Sam checked his pockets again. "Have you got any money, Elizabeth?"

"I left my purse at your place." They looked around for someone who might appear friendly enough to loan them the money to get the tokens. "Oh, goody." She laughed and clapped her hands together. "I have always wanted to say this." She singled out a man who had already gone through the turnstile, and she smiled sweetly at him. "Say, mister, have you got a dime?"

He stared back at her with a frozen expression. "Is that supposed to be some sort of joke?" He turned without another word and walked away.

Sam and Elizabeth stared wide-eyed at each other for a long moment, then fell together in a new round of hysterical laughter. The lady in the cage rolled her eyes and pushed two tokens through the hole in the bottom of the window. Still giggling, they dropped them into the slots in the turnstile.

The train screamed along the track as it drew into the station and pulled to a screeching halt in front of them. Because it was Sunday, there were not many people on the platform, and when the doors slid back, Sam ushered her onto the train and into a seat.

He couldn't take his eyes off her as the train pulled out of the station and rapidly accelerated to fifty miles an hour. She was like a little girl on her first carnival ride, full of wonder and excitement.

She stayed glued to the window, watching the blur of scenery that passed before her eyes. It was a view of the city she had never seen before and it struck her that she didn't know the town she had grown up in nearly as well as she thought she did. This was something new, a wondrous place with homes that lay within only a few feet of the track, second-story windows peering out on nothing but a gray streak of metal flashing by. There were areas decimated by fire, and housing projects where tenants were forced to keep bars on their windows for their own safety. In the distance was the modernistic skyline of the city, the pyramidal shaped Hancock Building, the looming black Sears Tower, the clean, sleek upthrust of the Standard Oil Building. Those were not unknown to her. But all that one must pass through to get there was very, very new.

"This is an eye-opening experience for me," she said only seconds before the track dropped in a coaster slant down under the ground. "What's happening?" she cried, clutching hold of Sam's arm. "It's so dark!"

He laughed, but held her tight. "Easy, love, it's just the subway. This route is above ground part of the way and underground the rest of the way."

The scream of the wheels against the track was almost deafening as the train rounded a curve, the lights inside the car blinking on and off for only seconds at a time. Finally, it ascended through the hole in the ground, rising up above the streets of downtown Chicago. It finally slowed as it drew into a station, and Sam stood, pulling Elizabeth to her shaking legs. "This is where we get off."

"And not a minute too soon," she mumbled shakily.

The snow was falling even heavier now, big wet flakes that clung to everything they hit. But Elizabeth huddled deep inside her coat, determined to brave it out. If Sam could do it, well, then, so could she. They descended the platform in front of the Marshall Field department store.

"I remember when I was a little girl, my mother used to bring me here at Christmastime. It was a kid's dream come true. She would let me play in the toy department while she went shopping." She glanced up at Sam. "Not the safest thing a mother could do, I agree, but back then all the mothers did that. I'd meet my friends there and we would spend hours going through the games and dolls."

He smiled. "When I was young, we used to come here only for very special treats. We never bought anything in the store, of course. My father wasn't ready to reap yet. Anyway"—he laughed—"I remember looking at all the ladies in their gloves and hats. So prim and proper."

"Oh, that's true," Elizabeth agreed. "Back then you didn't come to Marshall Field unless you were in your very best."

At almost the same instant they both noticed an old wino who sat in the protected doorway of the store, shivering inside his threadbare coat. "Times have certainly changed, haven't they?" she commented.

"Oh, I don't know," he said. "There have always been poor people. The difference now is that we could do something about it, but we don't. That's what bothers me the most."

They walked from State Street, across Michigan Avenue, then passed in front of the Art Institute on their way to the park.

"But surely you realize our welfare system doesn't work," she said. "The people who really need the money very rarely get it."

"No, I know it doesn't work that well. But the problem stems from something much deeper. Until people start genuinely caring about each other, no system will ever work.''

She was silent as they walked through the park. The sky was cloudy white, but the air was full of icy excitement and the snow found a home against the bark of bare trees as well as against their clothing. A few blurred footprints dotted the sidewalk that wove through the park, but the vast expanse of white was unbroken by human trespassers. A few squirrels darted out to the ends of tree branches, checked a fallen clump of snow for food, sniffed, tasted, and finding none, darted back into the security of their tree houses.

"Cold?" he asked, wrapping a thick woolen arm around her padded shoulders.

She looked up at him and a snowflake hit her right on the nose. "If I say no, will you dump another snowball down my back?"

His mouth widened into a huge grin. "Trust me."

"I think I just won't answer the question. Now where should we sit?"

"There's a table over there."

They stopped in the path and stared as an old woman, weighted down with yards of woolen coating material wrapped around her, sat down on a bench about thirty yards from them. Very carefully she pulled a brown paper sack from her pocket and grasped the neck of it in her hand. Then with much theatrical display, she stretched up her arm and shook the paper sack as loudly as she could. Seconds later, hundreds of pigeons flocked down to the sidewalk and sat like well-trained soldiers in front of her. She waited until she had their undivided attention and then she furiously rattled the bag at them again. The birds didn't budge. She repeated the procedure several more times before rising from the bench and moving on down the sidewalk. And the birds, like soldiers falling out for weekend leave, dispersed into the sky.

Elizabeth stared at the scene with gaping mouth and moved on toward the picnic table only after Sam tugged on her arm. "What on earth was that?"

"That's the pigeon lady. She's sort of an institution here in Grant Park. You mean to tell me you've never seen her before?"

"No. Why does she do that?"

He shrugged. "Who knows. Maybe the pigeons are the only ones who will pay any attention to her. Or maybe that's just her identity."

"Looked more like insanity to me."

"She probably wouldn't give up that image for anything."

Elizabeth watched the old woman walk up toward Michigan Avenue, disappearing in a cloud of snow as she crossed the busy street. "I guess she's really no different than anyone else. I have to admit I've known a few people who cultivated images almost as bizarre as that."

Sam set the sack of food on the table and pulled out the bread, pastrami, cheese, and the jar of cider.

"How are we supposed to make sandwiches without a knife?" she asked. "And we forgot plates."

"Relax. Let me show you how we uncivilized types do it." He broke off a piece of bread, split it with his fingers, and stuck a handful of pastrami and a hunk of cheese inside, then placed it in Elizabeth's gloved hands. "See? A sandwich."

"Tastes wonderful," she said between bites. "Must be the snow that adds all the flavor."

"I thought you'd say it was the way I laid that piece of cheese in there just so."

"Oh, that too." She watched him unscrew the lid from the jar of apple cider. He held it up to her lips and she drank, then watched him take his turn, lifting the jar to his mouth and drinking deeply.

His hair was turning white from the snow that collected in it, and she reached up to dust it away. "Now I know what you'll look like when your hair turns gray."

"Distinguished, right?"

She paused to dust some more of the snow away. "Gray."

He shrugged. "Oh, well."

"Sam, may I ask you something?"

"Anything," he answered, taking a bite of bread.

"Do you ever want something more out of life?"

He finished chewing. "Like what?"

"Oh, I don't know...a bigger house, a car, trips, things like that."

He rested his elbows on the table and looked at her for a long, studied moment. "Tell me, Elizabeth, have all of those things you mentioned made you a happier person?"

She looked away, flustered. "I—I don't know," she stammered. "It just seems like that's what everyone wants, isn't it?"

He looked out across the park. A month ago, that question would have been such an easy one for him to answer. But that was before he had met Elizabeth Parkins. Still, he had to believe that his basic ideals were right. He had to.

He expelled a quick breath that sounded as if he intended it as a chuckle. "You know, my mother has a nice couch, but like I told you, she keeps it covered with plastic so nothing bad will happen to it, so she won't lose it. She's obsessed with keeping it perfect, unused. I grew up in that house, but I've never been able to relate to that sort of thinking." He looked at her and frowned. "I look at you and I see a woman who has had everything, every advantage, all the material things she ever wanted. But I see it surrounding you, locking you inside, and holding you down. There's a woman in there that I think wants to be free, but all those things keep her a prisoner.''

Her mouth grew tighter with each passing second. ''That's a lot to read in one person. I didn't know you had such powers,'' she added on a snide note. What he had said hurt and her best remedy for that hurt was anger. She looked away toward the lake, unusually calm for this time of year. She felt Sam take her gloved hand in his and she turned back to him.

He slipped his bare fingers between her covered ones, sliding them down until they locked together. ''Elizabeth, you asked the question, remember? I try to always say what I feel. Life's too short to have it any other way.''

She heard what he was saying, but all of her concentration was on the fingers that wove deliberately between hers, the thumb that stroked a sensual path along her thumb, inciting the nerve endings even through the thick wool of her gloves. She wanted to deny all that he said to her. She wanted to believe that her life and her values were intact, set forever. But she didn't know anymore. She just didn't know.

His other hand lifted and slipped inside the hood of her coat. His fingers threaded through her hair and pulled her closer until his elbow was resting on the table, his face only inches from hers. ''Promise me one thing, Elizabeth.''

She swallowed convulsively, afraid to make any promises to this man but, at the same time, wanting to commit something of consequence to him. ''What?'' she whispered.

''Promise that you will be honest with me, that you will always tell me exactly what you feel or what you're thinking. Even if—'' He stopped and his eyes dropped down to their hands. He was only remotely aware that his grip on her fingers had tightened, that he was squeezing her small hand within his larger grasp. His gaze lifted back to her face. "Even if it means that these feelings between us cannot last."

They stared at each other while the snow fell around them, clinging to their food and their coats and the trees above. But inside they stayed warm with the emotional current that ran like a hot spring between them, circulating through their bloodstreams and filtering into the fingers that were joined in much more than a physical bond.

She wanted to promise him everything. She wanted to be able to say that what she felt right now would last forever. But she couldn't. All she could do was promise that she would be honest with him. He deserved much more than that, but it was all she could give him for now. "I promise, Sam."

"Then I'm a very lucky man," he whispered before pressing his lips to hers. "A very lucky man."

Chapter Ten

By the time they arrived back at his house, the sky was a dark purplish gray. The snow had been sporadic for the past hour, but the air was heavy with the weight and scent of more to come. The minute he turned onto the sidewalk leading to his house, he felt a tightening hesitation in Elizabeth's body.

He looked down at her. "Something wrong?"

"I think I'd better go now."

"Why?"

"It, uh, seems the thing to do."

He held both of her shoulders in his grasp and pulled her closer. "What are you afraid of, Elizabeth? Me?"

"No," she scoffed, brushing away the absurdity of the remark. It wasn't him; it was her.

"Then what?" he asked. "Is it this house? The neighborhood?"

"Oh, Sam, I just don't know. I...I'm confused and scared and...maybe I'm afraid that if I stay any longer, I won't be able to leave tonight or tomorrow...or the next day."

"Sounds good to me." He rested his chin on top of her head and closed his arms about her. He wanted to beg her not to go. He wanted to force her to stay. He didn't want this day or this moment to end. Not just yet.

"Would you like to go for a ride...in my car?"

He stood motionless. That was not what he had expected her to say at all. He had thought she was planning to leave...without him. He glanced at her car, now covered with a layer of snow. "Okay." He nodded, walking over to it and brushing away the snow from the windshield. He grinned at Elizabeth. "How can I pass up the opportunity to ride in a Mercedes with a beautiful lady?"

"You can't."

Their ride took them east toward the lake. Elizabeth turned on Lake Shore Drive and they drove north along the Gold Coast, so-called because of the plethora of extravagant condominiums that faced Lake Michigan along the route.

"Do you think you will always stay on the west side?" she asked. "Or will you be moved to another church in a different area?"

"Nothing is permanent in the ministry but, as you can probably guess, there aren't too many ministers clawing for my position. So, I would imagine I'll be there for quite some time."

"I see."

He looked over at her behind the wheel. She had removed her coat and laid it in the small space behind the seats. She brushed her fingers through her long blond hair several times to straighten what the hood of her coat had messed up. His attention focused on her profile, on the soft line of her jaw, the slight upward tilt of her mouth, the long eyelashes that graced those beautiful green eyes. His gaze dropped to her sweater, an expensive jade mohair that clung in all the right places. How many months would he have to work to afford clothes like that? Even her slacks were an uncut corduroy with a designer's name scrawled across the right front pocket.

She glanced at him self-consciously. "What are you looking at?"

"You."

"Why?"

He let his eyes feast upon her for a moment longer. "Because you are beautiful." He smiled at her. "Like a fresh new dawn. Like a morning in May." Although he said it in a teasing voice, he still meant it. For it was true. While everyone else was already longing for the fresh breezes of spring, he had it right here with him. He knew he should feel a bit guilty for enjoying her so much when the people he was supposed to help had so little. But right now, he couldn't help but feel good.

She looked back at him, embarrassed. "Like a morning in May. Don't you think you're going a little bit overboard?"

He shook his head. "I don't think so. And I still say that for these eyes of mine, you are a feast."

She smiled almost shyly and pointed out of her window. "Look over here. This is a beautiful old cemetery."

"Calvary, isn't it?"

"Yes."

"It's been so long since I've been up this far north. I knew quite a few people who went to Northwestern and I used to come up and visit them sometimes, but that was... well, too many years ago to count."

"How old are you, Sam?"

"Thirty-five and counting. You?"

"Thirty."

He studied her a minute. "How come you're not married?"

"Now you sound like my mother," she grumbled.

"Sorry. I'll retract the question."

They were both silent for the next few minutes. The only sound was that of the wheels spinning against the wet pavement beneath them. "I guess I just never found anyone I wanted to spend my life with," she finally said.

He turned away and looked out the window at the passing scenery. He thought about the man she called Thomas, the one who had answered the phone the day he called. Was Thomas the one she would end up spending her life with? He tried to imagine what he must be like. Successful, bright, handsome, exceedingly wealthy, no doubt, and perhaps good in bed. *Dammit, Sam, don't do that to yourself. Don't compare yourself with someone else. There is no point in it. You are who you are.*

But the assertion in his own mind wavered in and out as the car moved through Wilmette and on into Winnetka. Even in the dark, he could note the transformation of houses and large, tree-covered lawns, the stately mansions, the quaint villagelike atmosphere of the downtown shopping district, the sense of money that was everywhere. And he wondered, in only the briefest of seconds, if perhaps he had been taking the wrong road all these years. If he had missed out on something of value along the way.

Night had fallen and with it came new flurries of snow. But the white sky lent a gray light to everything, highlighting the sweeping drives and large estates that they passed.

Elizabeth finally slowed the car and turned it into one of those sweeping pebbled drives. A large red-brick house loomed before them, striking against the grayer background of the night. Sam couldn't make out all of the architectural details, but he noticed the black shutters on the windows, the two wide steps that led up to the white gabled front doors, and the large evergreens that hovered close to the base of the house beneath the first-floor windows.

Elizabeth stopped the car and turned to look at him. "This is my house."

He looked directly at her, but said nothing.

"Would you like to come inside?"

He took a deep breath. "Yes."

They both opened their car doors and climbed out onto the circular drive, now covered with a light film of snow. It was already starting to accumulate on the lawn.

They walked up the steps, and Elizabeth pulled her keys out of her coat pocket and opened the front door.

"No butler?"

She shook her head. "No. I have a housekeeper, but she's off on Sundays. She won't be back until late tonight."

They stepped into the foyer. The walls were papered in a gold brocade, and the architectural moldings divided the room into a series of rectangles. A large walnut credenza sat against one wall, and above it in frames were two silk paintings from the T'ang Dynasty. A sweeping staircase rose dramatically to the second floor.

She watched closely for his reaction, and her pulse fluttered anxiously in her neck. What was he thinking? What would he think of her? Why was she so nervous about this?

Sam looked about the entry, knowing enough from Elizabeth's description of her grandmother to realize this had probably been decorated long before she moved in. But he couldn't be sure. He looked at her and knew she was waiting for some reaction from him. He tried to smile, but he was too nervous to make it seem genuine.

Her stomach turned over. He hated it! He thought it was pretentious, gaudy, fake. She shouldn't have brought him here. But she had to, didn't she? She had to know...what? If he could fit in? How pompous was that! No, it was more that he had shown her how he lived and now she needed to do the same. It was imperative that he know from the beginning what her life was like.

"This house was built in 1937," she began, moving like a tour guide through the rooms. "Some of the houses in the area are much older, but my grandfather had this built when he brought Eva here. It's on three and half acres. There is a swimming pool and two tennis courts and a guest house and—"

"Elizabeth." Sam touched her arm with his hand, shattering the cool reserve she was trying so hard to wrap about herself. "It's a beautiful house."

"You don't really like it."

"I didn't say that."

"But you're not really impressed by all of this, are you?"

He slowly shook his head and smiled. "No, not really."

She was uncertain what to do or say next. She had never felt this anxiety with a man before, this nervous excitement and fear. "Do you want to see the rest of the house?"

Sam's hand never left her arm. He stepped closer and his fingers slid up the furry mohair arm until they reached her neck. His thumb lifted her chin. "I want to see your room."

Her breath caught in her throat. This was the moment she had been dreading and anticipating and wishing fervently for. It was upon her at last. She looked up into those warm brown eyes and at that slow smile and realized that this was most likely the man she had been waiting her whole life to find. This man with hair like a fertile field of wheat she could run her fingers through, with eyes that shone with a glow she had never seen before, with a mouth that promised smiles and laughter and untold pleasures. Whatever differences in life-style there might be between them could be worked out. She had to believe that. All that mattered now was that he wanted the same thing she did, to stay together through the night.

She took his hand in hers and led him back through the house to the foyer. They slowly ascended the stairs and walked together down the long hallway to the suite at the end. Double doors lay open to her bedroom. She flipped on the light.

It was just as he had imagined. White, elegant, full of the satin touches that would fit her so well. He tried to calm the pounding of his heart as his eyes scanned the room and landed on the bed.

He felt as if he had walked into a dreamworld, a world of sight and touch and smell that was so far removed from the world of Blackhawk that he almost could not even picture his own house accurately in his mind. All of his senses were tuned to this one room, this one woman, this one huge white bed.

His eyes moved back to her, and, this time, she knew he was pleased. "I'm so glad you're here, Sam." She stepped up to him and lifted her hand to his face. His skin was warm and a little rough, and the feel of it beneath her fingers sent a flood of heat and anticipation through her bloodstream. She wanted to feel all of his skin beneath her hands, wanted to know the texture of it. Drifting into her mind in a fleeting thought was the hope that he wanted to know her as much as she wanted to know him.

"I'm going to go change."

His hands clamped down on her waist, holding her in front of him. He pulled her up close, letting her feel how much he wanted her now. His eyes were trained on her mouth. "Don't take too long."

She shook her head, breathless with the impact his body had upon her. "No, I won't."

He finally released her and she hurried through her dressing room and into the bathroom. He stood rooted to the spot in the middle of the room for a long minute, until he could finally make his feet move. He walked around slowly, touching everything, absorbing the essence of this room. Everything about it spelled Elizabeth. It was hers. It was where she belonged. Soft, elegant, beautiful.

He unbuttoned his flannel shirt as he walked toward the dressing room. The door to the bathroom was closed, so he looked around the large dressing area. Two silver-backed brushes lay facedown on the table. At the back were several atomizers of perfume, different types—for different moods, perhaps—all in expensive bottles, some with designer names, some with birds' wings spread above the bottle. A basket of cotton balls sat in one corner next to a vase of jonquils. Live jonquils. At this time of year. *Amazing*.

He slipped his shirt from his arms and dropped it onto the chair in front of her dressing table. He then stepped into the huge walk-in closet. Along one wall were clear acrylic boxes with shoes. Hundreds, it seemed. High heels, low heels, open toe, closed toe, every color in the spectrum. Above the shoes were more boxes with hats and purses for every occasion. The other side of the closet was devoted entirely to hanging clothes. One half had double rods for blouses above and skirts below. The other part was dresses and robes.

He touched a long green velveteen robe, running the material through his fingers. He lifted it to his face. It smelled like her, clean and fresh. His body hardened at the thought. What was taking her so long?

He unfastened the buckle of his belt and slipped it through the loops around the waist of his corduroys. His eyes landed on a silky blue nightgown and robe set hanging from the rod. As he unfastened his pants he stepped closer to take a look. He pulled the gown out, away from the other clothes. It was long and had a deep neckline that was open to the waist. He stared at the vee opening and swallowed, imagining Elizabeth's body under the silky material, his mouth following the opening to her abdomen.

The door to the bathroom opened and he glanced up, still holding the blue gown between his fingers. There was a backlight from the bathroom that gave Elizabeth's body an ethereal glow. She stood there watching him. His eyes feasted upon her, unable to believe that for tonight, she was really his. His eyes dropped by inches from her golden hair down her body, draped in oyster satin. The gown had soft lace around the neck and satin-covered buttons from the top all the way to the bottom. And with the light behind her, he could see the silhouette of her body beneath the gown.

He walked over to her and stood a couple of feet away. His eyes fastened on the top button and moved slowly and painstakingly down each one, his eyes alone mentally opening them and revealing the body that lay in wait for his touch. When he reached the bottom, he looked back into the emerald pools of her eyes. "Just as I imagined."

He stepped closer and his hands slowly lifted to each side of her jaw, his thumbs tilting her head back to face him.

The skin on his waist was hot against her hands and she felt her heart beating frantically inside of her, like a bird held in the grasp of a huge hand that was preparing to set it free.

His mouth came down upon hers, ravenous, burning, and exquisitely demanding. His hands still held her face captive, and her fingers clutched the taut skin of his sides. He drank her in, exploring her with his own hunger.

One arm snaked around her, pulling her tight, while the other hand shoved into her hair, holding the back of her head as he absorbed the taste of her mouth, the scent of her neck, the hot energy of her hands rising up his spine.

He pulled back just a little and looked down into her face. Her eyes were closed, but they opened slowly to look at him, offering all, holding back nothing. She was a gift, he knew that. One that he must never defile. One that he must take great pains to care for, protect, caress, and not rush.

His eyes dropped to the top button of her gown. Still maintaining a hold around her waist, his fingers worked at the first button. He felt the trembling inside of her and he urged her up against him.

Her eyes fell closed when she felt the pressure of his body against hers. His warm, shaking fingers moved down the front of her gown, slipping the buttons easily through their openings, his hand grazing her bared skin as it dropped lower and lower.

His finger brushed along the skin of her abdomen. "We promised to be honest with each other, didn't we?"

His voice was so low and husky and filled her with such longings, she could only nod. But her hands tightened against his bare waist.

His eyes moved by inches across her face until they centered on her waiting mouth. "I just want you to know that I have never wanted a woman as much as I want you right now."

Elizabeth's eyes fell closed. The satin dropped over one shoulder and he bent down and burned the spot with his lips.

When he lifted her into his arms and carried her to the bed, she knew that this was what she had been waiting all her life for. This man, this feeling, this utter abandonment to another's touch. Never had she let go like this or known the give and take that can pass between a man and woman who care so much and who want to please each other far beyond their own desires and needs.

His body with hers was at last the precise instrument that unlocked the tightly structured cell she had existed within for so long, replacing her emptiness with the physical and emotional component that had been missing from her life.

Never had she been with a man who gave so much, tirelessly, endlessly, urging her body into places it had never been. Falling into the warm, moist night, she knew she was changed. She would never be the same again.

Chapter Eleven

Sam rested his hand against the wall and stared out the window. The snow had stopped sometime during the night and the sky was now clear and blue. The front lawn below stretched out like a white down quilt, the driveway slicing a clean curve through the middle. A block away was a small park, the snow dimpled by stark trees that arched above it. And beyond that was the lake, shimmering and cold under the morning sun.

He could see why she liked living here. It was really beautiful. He wondered what it would be like to wake up every morning and look out this window and have this view.

He thought about the view out his own window. Blackhawk Street. Across the street from his house was a small vacant clothing mill that had been left to ruin. Next to it was a liquor store and next to that a two-dollar hotel with enough rooms for fifteen transients at the most. A couple of blocks away was the church. His church. The one he had asked for, the one where he had planned to stay for many years.

He turned around and looked over at the bed. The white quilt lay at an angle across Elizabeth's body. Her yellow hair fanned out on the pillow beneath her head and one arm was thrown above it toward the brass headboard. Like the snow under a warm sun, he felt a melting within himself as he watched her sleeping. She was so beautiful. And last night, she had been his.

He had lifted her into his arms and carried her to that big white bed. The bed of his fantasies, the woman of his dreams, the greatest gift of his life. He remembered each electrifying touch of her fingers on him, each languorous sigh, her low cries of "Sam, oh, Sam!"

He let out a quick breath. Had she been his or was it actually the other way around?

He walked into the bathroom, turned on the tap, and splashed cool water on his face. He reached for a towel beside the sink and had a sudden vision of other men here in this bathroom, doing the same thing he was doing now. A male arm reaching for a towel to dry his face after a night of lovemaking... in that bed. Don't think about it! You're being ridiculous. Of course she's had relationships. So have you. She may even be having one now with Thomas Benson. Don't think about it. It doesn't matter. He threw down the towel. *Like hell it doesn't!*

He walked out into the other room and saw that she had turned and her hand was now touching the pillow where he had slept. Watching her, drinking in her quiet beauty, he slipped on his pants and walked into the hallway, taking the sweeping stairway down to the foyer. She had shown him several rooms last night, but the kitchen was not one of them. So he wandered around until he found it, and pushed through the swinging door from the dining room.

A black woman stood at the counter, brewing coffee, her back to him. She half-turned as he entered. "Oh, morning, Mr. Bens— Oh! You're not Mr. Benson."

"No." Sam tried to smile. "I'm not."

Letti gave him the once-over and nodded like a scientist satisfied with a new specimen. "You most certainly aren't." She turned back to the coffee and pulled the pot from beneath the automatic drip spout. "Coffee?"

"Yeah, thanks. I think I'll take a cup to Miss Parkins, also."

Letti pulled down two cups and poured the coffee into them, dumping a packet of Sweet 'n Low into one and stirring it carefully. "Sugar or cream for you, sir?"

"No, thank you." He took the coffee from her hand and leaned against the counter.

Letti noticed his relaxed stance and mentally nodded again. Looked like that girl had a fair amount of good sense, after all.

"I was wondering," he said. "You think I could make some toast or something to take up to Miss Parkins?"

"I have some coffee cake here," Letti said, reaching for it at the back of the counter. "And I can whip up some eggs if you want them."

"What does Miss Parkins usually eat?"

"Not much of anything," Letti drawled disapprovingly. "But I think she'd probably like the coffee cake this morning."

"That's fine, then." He watched her as she cut a couple of pieces of cake and set them on plates. She pulled a tray from a cabinet under the counter and arranged the plates and cups on it. He noticed a bouquet of flowers on the table and carefully pulled a yellow pansy from the arrangement and laid it on the tray. After thanking Letti, he carried the tray out of the kitchen and up the stairs to the room at the end of the long hallway.

In his absence, Elizabeth had awakened. She heard him coming down the hall and propped an extra pillow behind her head. She smiled when she saw the tray in his hands.

"Good morning." He smiled.

"Hello. For me?" She sat up as he set the tray on the bed and sat down beside her.

"Coffee with Sweet 'n Low and coffee cake."

She laughed. "I see you've met Letti. Oooh, this looks wonderful." She looked up with a coy expression. "I think I'll keep you around."

He leaned across the tray and kissed her. Her arm snaked up around his shoulder, holding his mouth prisoner. When she finally released his lips, she kept her hands clasped around his neck. "Mr. Winslow, I'm glad you came into my life."

His breath was shallow as a desperate want for her took over his mind and body once again. "So am I, Miss Parkins. So am I."

She loosened her hold on his neck and propped up against her pillows, waiting for him to hand her a cup of coffee.

He smiled tolerantly. "Madam." He bowed and handed her a cup, then picked up his own.

She took a sip. "I was thinking, today we could drive up north farther or maybe go somewhere for lunch or— Do you play tennis? Our club has indoor courts."

He watched her sweet face, saw the look of happy-go-lucky innocence, and wished he could indulge her forever. He smiled at her, but shook his head. "Elizabeth, I have to get back home. I have things I have to do today."

Her smile faded as she looked at him. "Oh," she said.

"Yes, oh." He laid his hand on her thigh. "I have to help out at the mission today. And tonight at the church we're setting up a study program for some of the little kids in the neighborhood to help them with their schoolwork."

She had turned her head away from him toward the window, while her mind tried to deal with the lifetime of differences that stretched between them. Well, what had she expected? She knew his life was there. But she had

hought...? What had you thought, Elizabeth? You
stupid fool! That he would just jump right into your
world with both feet? It was just going to take time, ad-
ustments, compromise. She would have to give some-
hing too. But they would work it out somehow. They
had to!

"I understand, Sam," she said, looking back at him.
"I...just want you to know that I wish you could
stay."

His hand came up to rest on the side of her neck. "So
do I, Elizabeth. But, as tempting as it is, I have an
obligation, a pledge of sorts. I don't think you or I
would be very proud of me if I let all those people
down."

"When will I see you again?"

"Soon. I promise."

"I'm having a party next Thursday night. Will you
come?"

He regarded her carefully. Her eyes were so bright
and eager, he had trouble resisting. But still he shook his
head. "I can't do that, Elizabeth. I—"

"Please, Sam! Please. I want you here...with me.
I'm not complaining about you going back to Blackhawk today. Can't you give in to me on this?"

He shook his head, amused and confused at the same
time. "I don't know, Elizabeth."

"It's a nineteen forties party. I'm having a band,
everyone will dress in forties style. Oh, Sam, I want you
to come so badly!"

He stared at her, thinking. "Won't I have competition?"

"What do you mean?"

"Thomas Benson."

"He won't even be in town."

"And if he were going to be in town?"

She tilted her head to the side and sighed. "Sam, I've

never felt for Thomas even a quarter of what I feel fo
you." Her voice dropped to a whisper. "I love you
Sam. Please come to my party."

He laid his fingers against her cheek. "I love yo
too." She was a dream, a dream that might fade awa
with the glaring light of morning. But for now he didn'
want to wake up. He wanted it to go on and on forever
He lifted the tray and set it on the floor, then peeled th
covers back from her body. His eyes locked with hers
Then their fingers touched and entwined. With hi
mouth against her parted lips, he slowly followed he
down to the bed. And he knew that whatever it took t
have her, he would do it.

Louise downed her glass of wine in one unladylike gulp
"The service in this place is just not what it used t
be."

Elizabeth looked around, bored by the conversation,
the company, and the lunch itself. And her mother'
criticism irked her, for actually, she liked this restauran
a lot. It was one of the small out-of-the-way places t
which she was always drawn. Small, quiet, unassuming.

"Oh, I don't know, Mother. I think the service has
been fine. How is your salad?"

"The lettuce is wilted, the crabmeat is foul, and this
wine is atrocious. Would you pour me a little more,
dear?"

"Certainly, Mother." Elizabeth sighed and poured
the wine into the glass. "Now what was it you were
starting to say about my new neighbor?"

"Well, do you know who it is?"

"No. I just saw the moving truck there the other day
and—"

"Well, I know." Louise smiled triumphantly. "It's
Suzanne Elliston."

"The author?"

"Yes, apparently she is just leasing the house for a month or so. Doing some sort of research on her next book. I can't imagine what kind of research she could be doing."

"Did you see the film they made of her last novel?"

"No. I have to admit, I'm not a fan of hers. She gives money such a bad name. All those suicides and drug parties and sordid affairs she has in her books. But it is so exciting having her living right next to you. I think it would be a good idea for you to go over and introduce yourself. You can ask her to your party Thursday."

"But the party is only two days away. Don't you think it's too short of a notice?"

"Nonsense. I'm sure she would love to come. Besides, just think how that will look in the society pages. Suzanne Elliston attends Elizabeth Parkins's party. What a coup that would be!"

"I suppose," Elizabeth agreed halfheartedly.

"Suppose! Don't be absurd, Liz. You absolutely must do it. Don't pass up the opportunity."

"All right, Mother. I'm sure you're right."

Louise patted her daughter's hand. "Good girl." She took another hefty slug of wine. "Oh, by the way..." She stopped to play with her salad, debating how best to bring up such a delicate subject. But she absolutely, positively had to know. "When I came to pick you up today, I was talking to Letti for a few minutes and... well, she... mentioned that you had a gentleman visitor the other night."

Elizabeth stared at the salad in front of her, her fork poised in midair. Slowly she set it on her plate. She tried to laugh it off. "Well, you know Letti. Always exaggerating about everything."

"I thought Thomas went back to Virginia on Saturday."

Elizabeth dug back into her salad, concentrating very hard on spearing a piece of crab. "Yes, he did."

"Well, goodness, then, if Thomas wasn't in town... Liz, dear, surely you aren't entertaining gentlemen when—"

Elixabeth's fork clanged against her plate. "What are you suggesting, Mother? That I do that sort of thing for a living?"

"Of course not, dear. I've always tried to mind my own business when it came to your...affairs."

Elizabeth rolled her eyes.

"I just hope you understand how something like that will look if it should get out."

"Well, it won't get out if you and Letti will keep your mouths— Sorry, I didn't mean that."

Louise was staring at her, her mouth open, her glass of wine halfway to her mouth. She looked as if she might faint. "I'm not thinking of myself, Liz. I'm thinking of you, you know. And your grandmother. It would break her heart, Liz, if she heard any tawdry rumors about you."

"I know," Elizabeth said, her mouth tight, a huge lump filling her throat.

"And you know how Thomas Benson adores you. He is perfect for you, Liz. Don't do anything foolish that might anger him. Will he be back in time for the party?"

"No."

"Oh," Louise mourned. "Then you'll be all alone again."

"Well, not exactly," Elizabth said, gritting her teeth for the scene that was about to take place.

"What do you mean, dear?"

"I mean I've invited someone else."

Louise stared, afraid to ask. "Who?"

"Sam Winslow."

Louise took a quick drink of wine to steady her nerves. "Winslow? The man...the preacher from that little neighborhood on the west side?"

"That's right."

Louise slumped down in her chair, picked up her glass of wine, and drained it in one long gulp. "Oh, my God!"

Sam walked down the street, carrying a large bag of groceries. He climbed up a narrow stairway, opening the door at the top that led into a darkened hallway. At the far end was a door with the number four in gold, sticky paper peeling off.

He knocked and waited for several minutes while he listened to the scrape of a foot as it crossed the wood floor. "Yes?" a weak voice asked.

"It's me, Mrs. Romanowski. Sam Winslow."

Slowly the bolt slid back and the door opened. The frail old woman moved aside to let Sam enter. "God bless you, Reverend," she said as he crossed the room and started putting the food in her cabinets and tiny refrigerator.

It was food grocery stores no longer could sell, but it was still wholesome and nutritious for those who could afford nothing better. Sam and a couple of nuns from a nearby church often worked together, collecting and distributing it to the old people in the neighborhood.

Using her crutches, the old woman walked back to her chair, dragging her paralyzed leg behind her. She plopped back down and watched him.

"What's the matter with your sink?"

"Don't know. It's been stopped up like that for three days." Her voice became a dry lament. "It smells so bad, I can hardly stand it. Nobody to help me, landlord doesn't care, nobody cares."

Sam walked over and stooped down in front of her.

"I care about you, Mrs. Romanowski. And I'll try to fix your sink for you, okay?"

She nodded and wiped a stray tear from her eye. Large folds of skin hung from her cheekbones, and as she rubbed her gnarled hand across her face, the skin stretched like putty to the side. "You're the only one who cares, Reverend. Where would I be without you? I would have starved up here and nobody would care... nobody would even know."

He patted her knee and stood up. "You want me to fix you a sandwich before I start on the sink?"

"No, I'd rather you get rid of all that smelly stuff first."

Sam rolled up his shirt sleeves and went to work on the drain, trying not to breathe in the rancid odor that came from the backed-up debris.

An hour later he had unclogged and cleaned the sink and prepared a light lunch for Mrs. Romanowski She had fallen asleep in her chair, so he had to wake her and set the plate in her lap. "You need any help eating that?"

"No, I'll manage." She nodded. "You run on now. God bless you, Reverend."

He smiled at her. "Thank you, Mrs. Romanowski. I'll see you Thursday. We have some new VISTA workers in the neighborhood and one of them may be coming to visit with you in a day or two. Will that be all right?"

"That would be nice. Someone to talk to."

"Well, now, if someone does come, don't you give him a hard time the way you did when I first came here." He grinned at her and watched a smile widen across her face.

She bent her head almost coyly. "Oh, Reverend, I thought you were a mugger."

"You didn't!"

"You're too handsome for a preacher."

He grinned. "Thanks, I think. See you Thursday."

As he left the apartment and headed down the sidewalk toward the mission, his mind once again flitted back, as it had continuously done all morning, to Elizabeth. He wondered what she was doing right now. Was she having lunch with friends? Playing tennis? Having a drink at the club? He tried to picture what she might be wearing, but the only vision that filled his mind was of her in her oyster satin gown, the sleeve falling over one shoulder. He closed his eyes as the taste of that shoulder and her cries of pleasure came back, forming like a tight ball of need within him.

She was like an oasis amidst an arid desert, an emerald island set in the middle of a choppy sea. Compared to the weed-infested area in which he lived, her world was a garden, and she a flower within it.

Suddenly he thought of the flower shop that was about three blocks away. Hurrying so he would not be late to help out at the mission, he ran all the way up to North Avenue and turned left. He rushed breathlessly through the door of the shop and glanced about at the colorful variety of flowers.

"How much are these?" he asked the man behind the counter.

"Twelve dollars."

"Twelve!" Still out of breath, he looked around at some different types. *Twelve dollars. What am I doing? I can't afford twelve dollars for flowers.* He thought of how they might brighten Elizabeth's day. God, he missed her! He wanted to touch her and hold her, hear her laugh and feel her sighs against his throat. This was crazy! Twelve dollars! "I'll take them," he said, wondering how on earth he was going to afford food and his house payment this month. "Can you send them?"

"Where you want 'em to go, bub?"

He pulled a slip of paper from his wallet with her address on it and handed it to the man to copy. "May I sign the card?"

He turned it around and begrudgingly offered Sam a pen, looking as if he thought Sam were sure to run off with it.

"Okay," the man grumbled when he got the card and the pen back. "She'll get 'em."

"When?"

"When she gets 'em!"

Sam cleared his throat. "Right. Thanks." He darted back out into the cold November day and hurried back toward the Blackhawk mission. He never had fixed his watch, so he wasn't sure what time it was, but, as usual, he was probably late. Twelve dollars!

As he headed down a side street he saw a young prostitute hawking her bodily wares to any passersby, and Sam wondered once again what had happened to Mary. He had asked around, but nobody had seen her for a couple of weeks. It wasn't the first time she had run off to hide for one reason or another, so he would give it a few more days. But if she didn't show up soon, he was going to have to pay a visit to Sly. He knew Mary was pregnant, even though she wouldn't admit it. And he hated the fact that she was out there alone, scared, uneducated to the ways of her body. He only hoped she'd seek some help soon.

He turned the last corner and dashed into the steamy kitchen of the mission. But, as luck would have it, he ran right into the open arms of Anna Vinzetti, setting the pace for an even steamier afternoon working under her lascivious stare.

Elizabeth propped up against her pillows and pulled the cover over her thighs. She picked up the phone and dialed Sam's number, grinning as she noticed the time on the clock beside the bed.

"Not calling too late, am I?" She laughed when she heard his groan.

"And you had to wake me during one of the best dreams I've had in a long time."

"Was I in it?"

"You are the main event of them all." His voice was low and gravelly.

"You're a wonderful man, did you know that?"

"You call me at one o'clock in the morning to tell me that?"

"I got the flowers this afternoon."

"Oh...good."

"They're beautiful, Sam. I have them sitting right here beside the bed so I can see them first thing in the morning and last thing at night."

"God, I miss you!"

"And I miss you. I don't think I can wait until Thursday night to see you. You are coming, aren't you?"

Sam hesitated. "If you really want me to."

"I'll pout all night if you don't."

"Well, we can't have that, can we? The beautiful hostess pouting at her own party. No, that would never do. But there is this slight problem."

Elizabeth held her breath. "Yes?"

"I don't have anything to wear that looks like the 1940s. I could run down to the Salvation Army and find plenty, but...well, I'm afraid I'd stick out like a sore thumb."

She laughed, relieved that he was still planning to come. "I'm going to send my grandmother's chauffeur to pick you up. You remember Walter?"

"Yes."

"He will bring you something fortyish to wear, okay?"

"Could you have him drive something other than that tank?"

"How about my car?"

"Still conspicuous, but better than the hearse. Everybody on the street would think I had died. What's he bringing me to wear? Not a zoot suit, I hope."

She leaned back against her pillow and stretched. "No, I keep imagining you in a navy officer's uniform. You've just come home on leave and you are meeting me at the Aragon Ballroom, where we will dance all night to Tommy Dorsey. What do you think?"

"I think you have a very vivid imagination."

"Indulge me, please."

"Will you indulge me?"

His voice had dropped to a huskier level, sending an electrical spark through her body. "How can I do that?"

"What are you wearing?"

"To the party?"

"No. . . right now."

"An old flannel nightgown with a high collar and long sleeves."

"Try again."

"No, it's true!" she insisted. "This is my very favorite gown. And it was so cold out that I wanted to be cozy and warm."

"I'm having trouble picturing that." He chuckled. "But if you insist it's true."

"How about this," she said, and her voice now slid like slick satin through the phone wires. "What if I take it off before I go to bed? I'll have nothing on."

"Do you have any idea what you are doing to me?" he groaned.

She continued in a low whisper. "And then I'll pull

the other pillow into my arms and fall asleep thinking about your hands roaming all over me.''

''I'm going to pay you back for this,'' he growled.

''Oh, I hope that's a promise. This Thursday you can pay me back all night long. I really can't wait, Sam.''

''Neither can I.''

Elizabeth hung up the phone and closed her eyes, knowing that whatever torture her words had put him through, for her they were equally as agonizing. She stood up and, true to her promise, removed her gown, then climbed back into bed and held the pillow close, her dreams of Sam's hands and mouth upon her forming in her mind before she even fell asleep.

Chapter Twelve

Elizabth rang the doorbell several times before the door was opened by her new neighbor. "Hi. I'm Elizabeth Parkins. I live next door."

Suzanne Elliston tried to hide her irritation as she pulled the door open wider for Elizabeth to enter. She was dressed in a baggy sweat suit, her short brown hair curled about her head in disarray, and her face bare of makeup. "I wasn't expecting visitors," she explained when she noticed Elizabeth's eyes flicking over her in assessment. "I usually work until noon every day."

"I'm sorry to bother you, then," Elizabeth said. "I just thought I should come over and meet you and let you know that if there is anything you need or—"

Suzanne sighed in resignation. "Come on in. I was at a pretty good stopping point anyway. Did you say your name was Elizabeth?"

"Yes. Parkins."

She led her into the large den. "Haven't I read about you in the society pages?"

"Probably." She shrugged. "My family has been around this area for quite a number of years and... well, I've sort of been adopted into the inner circle."

Suzanne observed her quietly for a moment, but Elizabeth felt a trace of cynicism in the perusal. "Have a seat. Would you care for a beer?"

"No, thank you." She sat in a large crewel chair. "What do you think of Chicago?"

Suzanne walked behind the bar and opened the small refrigerator, pulled out a beer, popped the top, and drank it straight from the can. "I come from humbler beginnings," she explained, raising the can in a toast to Elizabeth. "I've never developed some of the more refined tastes." She walked around the bar and headed toward the couch. "What do I think of Chicago?" she mused aloud. "Full of electricity, dynamic political struggles, terrible weather, nice people. It's a little fast-paced to suit me, but I'm interested in learning everything I can about the city."

"Will it jinx the book if I ask what you are working on?"

"It won't unless you know Norman Mailer and rush out and tell him what I'm working on." She shook her head and laughed. "Of course, he's too busy hobnobbing with the jet-setters and pleading causes of criminal injustice to be interested in mine." She grinned at Elizabeth. "I'm indulging in a little professional jealousy. Hope you don't mind."

"Not at all." Elizabeth laughed. "It's much more interesting than most of the forms of jealousy I hear about."

Suzanne regarded her closely for a minute, sizing up the woman sitting in the wing-back chair across from her. Elizabeth squirmed internally from the inspection.

"The book," she finally said. "It's a novel about a family living in Winnetka. The father is a famous attorney, the mother a social achiever, the teen-age daughter an anorexic, and the nine-year-old son is a manic-depressive. Doesn't that sound cheery?"

Elizabeth's eyes widened. "Wow, when you hit, you hit hard!"

"It's a family that's been living in my head for a long time. I'm sick and tired of all their depressing ramblings and I just want to get them out of there."

"Why did you pick Winnetka?"

"It had the ambience I was looking for. The societal emphasis, the kept wives, the spoiled children. Need I go on?"

Elizabeth looked uncomfortable. "You don't like us much, do you?"

Suzanne shrugged. "I suppose it seems that way. I'm just looking at it from a different perspective, that's all. Are you married?"

"No. You?"

"I was."

Elizabeth waited for further elaboration, but none came. Suzanne Elliston was obviously a woman who said what she wanted to say and no more.

"That's very surprising that you're not," she said, narrowing her eyes as she probed further into Elizabeth. "May I ask why?"

"I don't know. It always seemed like more trouble than it was worth. I just never found anyone worth all that trouble." There was a quiet, thoughtful moment between them before she again spoke. "Listen, I'm having a party Thursday night at my house. Why don't you come? You'll meet a lot of people, and it might help with your research of all us debauched, wealthy society types."

Suzanne laughed. "I like you."

"Thank you. But I have to admit something. My mother thinks it would be a great idea to have you there because it would make me look good in the society pages."

"You're very honest, aren't you?"

Elizabeth smiled weakly and glanced toward the window. "I'm learning."

She nodded. "All right, I'll come. For the research, not for your standing in the society column."

Elizabeth smiled at her. "Fair enough."

Sam pulled on the white trousers and buttoned the fly front. He didn't have a full-length mirror, so he had no idea what they looked like on him. But he felt like an idiot. He lifted the shirt from the bed and walked to the window, glancing down toward the sidewalk. Walter stood beside the Mercedes, with that superior pursed-mouth look, as if he had just finished sucking a lemon. He kept glancing anxiously toward the house now and then, and it was obvious how uncomfortable he was with the neighborhood.

Sam's eyes lifted to follow the line of Blackhawk. Billy Hawkins was standing over a trash can in the vacant lot between the liquor store and Wilbertson's old haberdashery. With great care, he held up a cup and poured the liquid remains of five or six different cans into his cup. When it was full, he drank the contents down.

Sam turned away, sickened by the scene, and stared at the spit-polished shoes he was to wear with his uniform. Why was he going to a party like this? What in heaven's name did he think he was doing?

He pivoted and looked back out the window, his eyes lifting to the northern horizon. His body churned with the need to see Elizabeth while his mind revolted at his own defection from this neighborhood.

He raised the window and continued to stare into the wintry twilight while a too-loud radio on the street below blared out the sounds of "Funky Town."

The strains of Dorsey and Miller and Kaye and Goodman mingled with the chords of easy laughter. Elizabeth greeted another guest and then anxiously glanced toward the door one more time. Where was he? Why didn't he hurry and get here? What was taking him so long?

She smiled at the couple who had just arrived. "So glad you could come, Eunice. Milton, it is wonderful to see you, as always." She kissed each of their cheeks and followed them into the other room.

The band at the far end of the room was playing "It Started All Over Again" as Elizabeth glided around making sure that everyone was well taken care of. The caterers had laid out a huge buffet of oysters imperial, caviar, stuffed artichokes, baked pears in port, shrimp croquettes, and rack of lamb. A huge rotating glass ball, reminiscent of the great ballrooms of the forties, had been hung from the cathedral ceiling and was now turning and casting phosphoric sparkles upon the walls.

"Don't you look divine," someone said to Elizabeth as she breezed by, but she didn't hear. All of her attention was focused on the foyer, where Sam was now standing. She stopped and stared, mesmerized by the sight of him. He was dressed in the white naval uniform, his hat held in the grip of one hand, his hair casually styled, his legs slightly parted as he surveyed the room.

His gaze circled the room until it landed on Elizabeth standing apart, watching him. He drew in a sharp breath as he stared at her. She was dressed in a strapless green velvet gown, her hair crimped and pulled back at the sides in an old-fashioned style. He tried to smile, but his mouth would not move. He didn't think he had ever seen a more beautiful woman in his life. He had thought about her all week, wanted her, remembered the taste and feel of her. But nothing had prepared him for the overwhelming desire he had for her right now.

She walked toward him and held out her hand. "Hey, sailor."

Sam lifted his hand to hers and wrapped his fingers around her palm. Slowly he lifted it to his mouth, kissing the back of her hand, but never taking his eyes from her face. He didn't let her fingers loose. "It's been the longest week of my life," he whispered.

A shiver of longing rippled through her body. "For me too," she whispered back, looping her arm through his. "Come on, sailor. Let's get you something to drink and eat."

She led him into the living room and over toward the buffet table. A bar was set up to the left of it and several bartenders were kept busy mixing drinks. Champagne was carried on silver trays throughout the room by other waiters. Elizabeth took a couple of glasses from a passing tray and handed one to Sam.

"What shall we toast to, Sam?"

He looked around the room, dismissing the party, the opulence, the people. He looked back at her, her eyes as transparent as glass. "To us."

"Yes." She smiled. "To us." They took a sip of the champagne and he lowered his glass.

"You look beautiful tonight."

"Thank you. And you are just as I imagined in that uniform. Would you like something to eat?"

He looked at the vast array of food, some of the delicacies he had never even seen before. "I'll wait a little while. I'm not that hungry."

"Then come on, I'll introduce you to some of my friends."

"Is that Adrienne over there?" he asked.

Elizabeth rolled her eyes. "Yes, can you believe how she's dressed? Ever since John dumped her for his boyfriend, she has gone off the deep end."

Sam looked at the woman across the room and chuckled. She was wearing a gold lamé one-piece outfit that was pulled up between her legs like a diaper. And on her head was a fire-engine red headband. Good for Adrienne, he thought to himself. If this was her way of coping, more power to her.

"Let me introduce you to my mother." She pulled him over to a group of people standing beside the French doors that led to the patio. "Mother, this is Sam Winslow. Sam, my mother, Louise Banning." Elizabeth's body was tense as she made the introduction, knowing she had no control over what her mother might say or do. And when she glanced up and saw some new guests arriving at the door, her anxiety increased. "Oh, dear," she sighed, "I'm going to have to leave you here."

Sam touched her arm gently, a gesture that did not go unnoticed by Louise. "Don't worry, we'll be fine."

With a final warning glare at her mother, she moved away toward the foyer.

He watched her go, then turned back to Louise. He smiled politely. "This is a beautiful house."

Louise snapped angrily at a waiter who almost bypassed her without handing her more champagne. She brightened when she finally had a full glass in her hands. She stared into his eyes. "So, you are the man to whom Elizabeth has lost her head."

He laughed lightly. "I don't think you have to worry about Elizabeth losing her head to anyone. She's a very independent woman."

"And maybe very susceptible to a revolutionary way of life," Louise mumbled, taking a loud sip of her champagne.

The quick lift of his eyebrows was his only answer.

"Would you look at that," Louise drawled in disgust as they watched Adrienne walk by. "Look at those shoes."

He glanced down at the Miss Piggy tennis shoes Adrienne had on her feet as she walked past them. He chuckled, but wiped the smile off his face when Louise frowned at him.

"Elizabeth has always had a weak spot for the down-trodden, Mr. Winslow . . . or is it Reverend?"

"Sam would be fine."

"Take Adrienne, for example. I told Liz not to invite her. She has become such a tramp since this horrid episode with her husband. But my daughter insisted. Refused to ignore her. And then look at the way the woman pays her back. Comes to the party dressed like something out of a Hollywood horror picture." She held up her glass as she stared at Sam. "And you? How are you going to repay my daughter for her attentions?"

He looked directly at her, not in the least intimidated by her probing questions. "I love your daughter, Mrs. Banning. I don't have any money, so my love is all I have to give her."

"Did you also know that she is practically engaged to another man? It just happens that he's out of town tonight."

He hid the flinch that tightened his body. "You're referring to Thomas Benson?"

Louise couldn't hide her surprise. "You know about him?"

"Elizabeth and I are very open with each other."

"Well, let me be very open with you also. If Elizabeth persists in this rebellious charade—you do realize that that is what her relationship with you is all about? An act of rebellion against all that her grandmother and I have done for her. And if she does persist, her grandmother will most likely give her an ultimatum—you or money. Are you willing to be responsible for that?"

"You're saying her grandmother will cut her off if she doesn't stop seeing me?"

"It would eventually come down to that, I'm quite sure."

He didn't try to hide his disgust. "What Elizabeth decides to do with her life is her business. Not mine, not yours, and not her grandmother's. Why don't you give her the chance to grow up and be who she wants to be? Now if you will excuse me, please," he snapped, moving away from a stunned Louise.

He found his way through the crowd, moving as far away from all of these strangers as he could. He didn't have to put up with this. What was he doing here anyway? He should be back on Blackhawk, where he belonged. At least there, reality existed; not some fantasy world created by whatever money could buy. He opened the door to the room that enclosed Elizabeth's private bar and stepped inside, wanting a moment of peace and quiet away from the madding crowd.

Letti glanced up at him, surprised and embarrassed. She was in the process of pouring the Chivas Regal into a large flask that she held in the crook of her arm. "Ah, Mr. Winslow, you're not gonna tell Miss Elizabeth or me, are you?"

He laughed conspiratorially. "No way. Take whatever you want. You like that stuff?" He grimaced.

"It's for my friends. On my day off, we meet to play poker down at Waldo's place in Evanston. And, well, I bring the refreshments." She looked at Sam long and hard. "You're a good man, Mr. Winslow. I just hope Miss Elizabeth knows how damned lucky she is."

"You got any tips on how I can get along with her mother and grandmother?"

"Oh, Lawdy! Those two is a pair. With Miss Louise, the trick is to keep her juiced up. As long as she's got a drink in her hand, she's as happy as a mutt with a bone. Now, Miss Eva, whooo, she's a picture! I've known that woman since I was eighteen and I never have figured her out. Watch your step with her, 'cause she's a woolly bear."

"I'll remember that." Sam smiled. "Take care, Letti."

"You too, Mr. Winslow. Waldo and the rest of the gang is sure gonna appreciate this."

He closed the door behind him and stepped back into the living room. Elizabeth hurried over to him. "Where have you been? I was worried about you."

"Just wandering around," he said, wrapping his arms around her waist and pulling her close. "Just biding my time until I can have you all to myself. What are we doing here, anyway? I don't want to share you with all of these people."

"Why, sailor, I think you've been out to sea too long," she teased. "But I want you to know that I plan on making your R and R quite memorable."

"I'm going to hold you to that," he murmured next to her ear.

"How did Mother treat you?"

"Like I'm Quasimodo come to abduct her daughter."

"Well, don't pay much attention to her. She's relatively harmless. Grandmother Eva is the one we will have to contend with."

"Is she here?"

"No, thank goodness. She's in the Holy Land with some friends of hers." Elizabeth smiled brightly. "So you missed her."

"What a shame." He grinned. "Uh-oh, looks like someone needs you." An elderly woman was signaling to Elizabeth to come over to a group of people that was waiting to be blessed by her charms.

"Oh, dear," she moaned under her breath. "Here I go again. Will you be all right?"

"Of course."

"Why don't you go over and introduce yourself to that man in the blue suit there. He's the minister of our church."

He watched her walk away, then he walked toward the man, now engaged in conversation with an older couple. He stood back and listened.

"No, no," the minister was saying. "I really do like it here. It's quite different from southern California, of course. My last church was in Beverly Hills, a lovely setting for worship." His eyes had a dreamy quality as he stared off into the distance, reminiscing about the warm nights, the afternoons in the swimming pool, tennis with various members of his congregation. "Yes, Chicago is quite, quite different. But lovely all the same."

The small group dispersed, and the minister was eyeing the buffet table.

"Excuse me." Sam stepped up to him. "My name is Sam Winslow. Reverend Sam Winslow. And you are the minister of Elizabeth's church?"

The minister had a surprised gleam in his eyes. "Yes...I am." He regained his composure and extended his hand. "Ralph Dudley Hawthorne." He shook a finger at Sam. "So you are the one who called me about some hospital in your area that needed help."

"Yes, I did. Thank you for mentioning it to the Women's Guild. Elizabeth helped with the painting and now we've got a pretty good start on finishing the rest."

"Splendid!" He smiled, but his attention was obviously on another thought. "Aren't you also the man that Eva Rowen mentioned to me?"

Now it was Sam's turn to be surprised. "I don't know. Am I?"

"Are you the one who has been filling Elizabeth with these rather unorthodox ideas about theology? You see," Reverend Hawthorne hurried to explain, "one day at the country club, Elizabeth started rambling with some antiquated nonsense about taking the message to the street or to the people or something. It was really quite distasteful, considering the setting, and Eva Rowen was concerned. She thought I should talk to Elizabeth about this. We feel that she has been...misguided.''

"Is that right?" Sam's face and body were rigid, and it took all of his efforts to hold in the anger he was now feeling. This man, this apathy, this urbane view of society and religion, nauseated him. And to label Elizabeth as misguided! His hands remained clenched at his sides. If he were on Blackhawk...

"It's the people on the street who need it most," he answered through tight lips. "They're the ones who need the most hope, who could use a little faith in themselves and in their fellow man. I thought that was what we were supposed to do. Teach some human dignity, understanding, patience."

Reverend Hawthorne's expression was smug. "But you must move with the times, Mr. Winslow."

"*Reverend* Winslow," Sam said in a low, threatening voice.

The minister's eyes grew wary. He wasn't used to these street ministers. He didn't know how to deal with them. They were influenced too much by the rabble. "All I'm saying is that the tide has changed. To keep young, sophisticated, intelligent people involved in the church, we must follow their lead for a change, discuss the problems that concern them—"

"And what about the thousands of people in this city who are old, unsophisticated, uneducated! What about a little concern for them?"

Reverend Hawthorne cleared his throat. "Please, Mr...uh, Reverend Winslow. This is a party. A festive occasion. Surely we can leave our work behind for one evening and enjoy ourselves."

Sam stared at the minister for a long, hard minute. "Maybe you can, but I sure as hell can't." He turned away abruptly, angrily glaring around the room in search of Elizabeth. He had had it! He had tried, he really had. But this wasn't the place for him. He could try to fit in, but he didn't want to. He had to get out.

With a growing sense of claustrophobia, he looked through the crowd for an escape. It was the clear low voice beside him that filtered through his fog of anger, lending him a thread of rationality that had been rapidly unraveling within him.

"Why don't you come outside for a little while and get some fresh air." It was the emphasis on the word *fresh* that made him turn toward the woman beside him.

He looked at her, knowing she was familiar, but he couldn't quite place the face.

She extended her hand. "My name is Suzanne Elliston. I couldn't help but overhear your conversation with that minister."

Sam nodded. So that was where he knew the face. She was a well-known author and her book had been on *The New York Times* Best Seller List for the last year. Her photograph had accompanied numerous articles.

"Sam Winslow," he offered, still tense from the encounter with Hawthorne.

"Would you like to come outside with me for that... fresher air?"

He let loose a quick breath of tension and smiled. "Sure."

They opened the French doors and stepped out onto the patio. The night air was cold, but the sky was clear, and it felt like he was taking his first clean breath after years of nothing but stale air. He breathed deeply and sat down on the raised brick well around a large elm.

"I admired what you said in there," Suzanne said. "It was...let's just say different from most of the remarks I've heard tonight."

"Just a difference of philosophy," he mumbled, not wanting to get into another argument.

"That's what interested me." Suzanne watched him closely as she too sat on the brick wall. "Where do you preach?"

"West side Chicago."

"I don't know much about Chicago, but I do know that's a far cry from this area. Why are you here tonight?"

He glanced at her quickly, then looked away again. "Elizabeth invited me."

"Oh, you are a good friend of Elizabeth Parkins?"

"Yes."

Suzanne was a very perceptive judge of people and character. It was one of the things that had made her such an excellent writer. She could read people from a smile, a tone of voice, a twitch of the eye. And she could read Sam Winslow from the sound of his yes. He was in love with Elizabeth Parkins, but he wasn't really sure that he should be.

"Do you think Elizabeth Parkins will give up all of this for love?"

He glanced sharply at her, surprised that she had guessed the situation and had gone right to the heart of it. "You're very blunt, aren't you?"

"There simply isn't time to be anything else."

He studied her closely and finally shrugged. "I can't answer for Elizabeth. She'll do what she can do."

"You must have lots of faith in people's ability to make the right decisions. Surely this has caused you to have some terrible disappointments in your life."

"Elizabeth knows what she's doing. She's a grown woman."

Suzanne smiled as she watched him. "So, tell me about Sam Winslow?"

"Is this an interview?"

"Don't worry. I promise not to put you in my next book. Maybe the one after that."

He chuckled. "Not much to tell. What you see is what you get."

"I see quite a lot."

"Yeah?"

"You want to know what I see?"

"I'm almost afraid to ask."

"I see a man who is dedicated to something that few people can understand. But I would say you're not as patient as you would like to be. You have a temper that you can't always keep under control. You have a lot of confidence in yourself. You're one of a rare breed who knows where he's going in life. But. . .I would say, just by the fact that you are here tonight, you are having some doubts about all of those convictions."

He was staring at her, his eyes riveted on her dark brown eyes. Finally he shook his head in disbelief. "How do you do that!"

"I've had lots of practice." She laughed. "I figure if I can't sell any more books, I can always open up a fortune-telling salon. Madam Elliston, Spiritual Reader and Adviser. I'd probably make more money than I do now and I wouldn't have to do all those god-awful promotional tours."

"Okay." He smiled. "Turnabout's fair play. You know everything there is to know about me. Now, how about you. Who is Suzanne Elliston?"

"Does this social repartee mean you're going to stick around the party for a while longer?"

"What do you mean?"

"Just referring to the way you looked in there awhile ago. Like a caged animal. You wanted out bad. Elizabeth might be awfully disappointed if you left her party."

He chuckled at the way he must have looked in there

after talking to Reverend Hawthorne. And he thought of Elizabeth. He wouldn't leave her. "Yeah, I guess I'm going to stay."

Inside, Elizabeth was searching the living room for Sam, wishing she could spend more time with him. It was a good party, a successful one, but all she wanted was to be alone with him. She didn't want to be around all these people with their same dreary remarks. She wanted something different. She wanted Sam.

Her gaze was drawn to the windows and she could see him out on the patio, sitting beside Suzanne Elliston. They were sitting on the low brick wall, his black military shoe propped up over his other knee. He threw his head back and laughed at some remark Suzanne was making. A swift spasm of jealousy convulsed through Elizabeth as she watched the two of them so easy in each other's company. She didn't really blame either of them. They were both outsiders here and that alone would inevitably draw them together.

She opened the door and stepped out into the cold night air. They both looked up. "Aren't you two freezing out here?" Elizabeth asked, always the perfect hostess. "Suzanne, I could get you a heavier wrap if you'd like."

"No, that's all right. I'm going to go back inside to mingle. I've enjoyed talking with you, Sam." She looked up at Elizabeth. "You are one lucky woman."

Elizabeth smiled and shifted her eyes to him. "I'm aware of that."

Suzanne walked past her toward the house. She turned around before entering. "Shall I close the drapes when I go in?" She grinned.

"Just turn off the outside light." Elizabeth smiled, never taking her eyes from Sam. "The switch is on the wall by the door."

She kept her eyes trained on him as the light went out.

The cold white moon gave a glow to his hair and eyes as he watched her. The music from the living room filtered through the curtains and glass wall as the band played the final stanzas of "Melancholy Serenade."

"Here, you'll get cold." He stood, slipped his jacket off, and wrapped it around her shoulders. He held on to the lapels and pulled her close, looking down at the expanse of pale skin that was exposed above the line of her dress. His finger brushed across the scalloped top of it.

"I'm afraid my sailor is not having much fun," she said, looking up at him.

"I am now."

Her breath was drawn in as his finger lowered to stroke her breast over the thick velvet material. "Hear that?" she whispered. " 'Moonlight in Vermont.' It's my favorite piece."

"Then why don't we dance?"

"I thought you'd never ask."

His arm snaked inside the coat, his fingers pressing against the small of her back. Her hand lifted to his shoulder and her other was held in the palm of his hand. They began to move to the warm, lacy sounds of saxophone, trombone, and brushed drums. Her body was pressed against his, fitting perfectly, the two halves notched together in one smooth bodily flow. "You dance very well," she said. "I like us this way."

He moved his mouth across her temple. "Just like Fred and Ginger," he murmured. "You feel so good next to me, in the cold air, under the moonlight." He lifted both of her hands to his neck and one arm wrapped around the outside of the coat, holding it against her for warmth. His lips touched her cheek, her neck, her hair.

As the music swelled, so did her body, the fluttering wild need within her rising with the orchestra's crescendo. Sam held her tight and she clung to him, loving the feel of his arms and his warm breath against her cheek and his hand moving across her hips beneath the coat. Her breath was rapid, the vibrating pulse within her reaching up and out for his touch. "Come up to my room."

"Now?" he whispered, but his breath too was quick and short.

"Yes. I'll sneak away. You can follow me."

His mouth glided across her neck and his tongue touched the quivering pulse in the hollow of her throat. "Yes." His lips traveled up her chin and onto her mouth, urgently parting her lips and teeth with his tongue.

She knew the desire in his body as he pressed against her and she wanted it. She wanted everything to disappear except for the two of them, together, their bodies as one being, their differences superseded by their need to be as one.

She tore away from him, her breath ragged and her eyes brilliant with desire. She handed his jacket back to him. "Please, Sam! Please follow me up there."

"I will. I'll be right there." He closed his eyes, forcing his body to relax. He couldn't walk through her living room full of people, not in the state he was in. He turned toward the yard and stared out into the darkness, taking huge gulps of air into his lungs. The darkness was a comfort that made him forget where he was for now. Forget all that awaited his attention on Blackhawk. Right now, the only thing that mattered was his driving need for that golden woman of his fantasies. Tomorrow he would think about reality. For now he was going to let the night live on.

Chapter Thirteen

The zipper lowered, stopping a couple of inches below her waist. His arm was around her and his hand dipped inside the opening, his fingers splayed across her hips, pulling her tightly against the spread of his legs. Her hands were on his face, and her mouth was open under his probing tongue.

He pulled the dress from her shoulder while her fingers fumbled with the buttons on his shirt. "Hurry," she begged, and his hands became more insistent in response.

The dress fell to her waist and her bare breasts were flattened against the stiff white cotton of his shirt.

"Elizaaaabeth!" Elizabeth froze, staring up at him. That wasn't him singing her name. It was too high pitched. It came again. "Liiizzzz, dear."

"Oh, my God, it's my mother!"

Sam leaned back against the wall, his breath heaving like after round four of a boxing match. "Are you kidding me? I'm thirty-five years old and I've got to contend with your mother catching us!"

Elizabeth buried her head in his chest, wanting to cry and laugh at the same time. "Help me, hurry!" Together they lifted her dress back onto her shoulders. He turned her around and raised up the zipper, and she straightened the bodice with her hands. He was just tucking his shirt back into the waistband of his slacks when the door opened and Louise Banning stepped into the room, turning on the light.

"Oh, dear," she gurgled, shrinking against the wall as if she might faint.

Sam's hand froze inside the waistband of his pants. Slowly he resumed the task of aligning his shirt, then slipped his jacket back onto his shoulders.

"Mother, have you ever thought of knocking?" Elizabeth snapped impatiently.

Louise's face turned righteous. "If I had known I was going to stumble upon an orgy, I would have."

Sam stepped forward, hoping to effect a calm settlement to this. "Mrs. Banning. . ."

She glared at him and interrupted hotly, switching her gaze back to Elizabeth. "Reminds me of the time when you were seventeen and your stepfather caught you up here with one of your little boyfriends from high school. Did you tell him about that, Liz? Does he know all about your past love affairs?"

Elizabeth had gone stark white, unable to believe her mother would resort to this type of attack.

"Is that supposed to matter to me?" Sam asked, anger rising like a barometer inside of him.

"It should. It seems to me a preacher would want someone a little more virtuous, a virgin, perhaps, someone who could fit the image of hearth and home and ministerly things."

"I'm not looking to fill some sort of image," he said. "I don't need that. I love your daughter and she loves me. If you can't accept that, I'm very sorry. But I wish you would let her grow up to pave her own way in life."

"Enough of this!" Elizabeth cried, tears forming in her eyes. "I will not have this!" She stamped her foot in a childish display of temper. "Both of you just go away and leave me alone!'' She turned and stalked away to the bathroom, slamming the door behind her.

Sam's eyes followed her until the door was shut, then he looked back at Louise.

Her expression was one of victory. ''You see what my daughter is made of? Give up, Reverend Winslow. She will never be what you want her to be.'' Then she too turned and walked out of the bedroom, leaving him alone to contend with the bewildering wake both women had left him in.

Suzanne Elliston was right. He had had a lot of disappointments in his life. And right now his faith in people's ability to make the right decisions was teetering on the edge. Perhaps now he was on the downhill side of that too-perfect dream. Morning was waiting at the bottom.

Elizabeth rang the doorbell and shuddered beneath her black wool jacket. Finally, the door opened.

''Elizabeth, come in.'' Suzanne Elliston stood back and held the door wide for her. ''When you called a few minutes ago, I was just fixing to have a beer, but instead I've put on a pot of tea. Sound all right?''

''Sounds wonderful. I don't want to keep you long from your work. I know you probably have deadlines and all that.''

''Only the ones I set for myself. And I never keep those. Makes for lots of guilt and self-recriminations. A shrink would have a field day with me.''

The two women walked together into the kitchen and Suzanne poured them both some tea. ''Lemon or sugar?''

''A little Sweet 'n Low if you have it.''

''I don't.''

Elizabeth laughed and shrugged. ''Then plain, please.''

"Thank you for inviting me to your party the other night. It was quite entertaining."

"I know there is some cynical sidebar in that statement"—she smiled—"but I'm not sure I want to know what it is."

"Well, some of the people aren't"—she raised her cup in toast—"exactly my cup of tea, if you'll excuse the pun. But I must say I got some great material for my book."

"Good, you can dedicate it to me."

"Your Sam Winslow is an interesting man."

Elizabeth sighed and looked out the breakfast room window. "That's sort of what I wanted to talk to you about."

"Sam?"

"Yes."

"You aren't upset that we were talking out on the patio, are you?"

"Oh, no!" Elizabeth hurried to assure. "Although, I have to admit, my eyes turned a tad greener than normal when I first saw you two out there. No, what I was wondering was if he said anything..." She puffed out her cheeks and expelled a tired breath. "I don't know what I want to know. I guess I am just wondering what he's willing to give."

"Why are you asking me?"

She shook her head. "I don't know. I just thought maybe he might have said something that would give you a clue."

"Are you expecting him to give up his way of life for you?"

She contemplated both Suzanne and the question for a minute. "No, not really. I admire him so. I respect what he does. It's just that I don't know if I could give up my way of life for him."

"It is not a question of if you could; it's a question of whether you want to."

"It's funny...no, it's really quite sad, but I've never before had to examine what I wanted out of life. I just assumed that I would follow in my mother's and grandmother's footsteps. My little world was so self-contained until Sam came along. There wasn't time for all this crazy self-reflection."

"I don't envy you your decision. It can't be an easy one. The life you would live with Sam would be very different. More interesting, perhaps, but not easy. On the other hand, if that is your only choice and you decide not to change to fit with him, I suppose you would have to learn to live without him." Suzanne shrugged and took a sip of tea. "Nope, I don't envy that one little bit."

Elizabeth bit her lower lip in thought. "In other words, it is either I change or I don't get the prize."

Suzanne studied the frown upon her face. "I don't know Sam, except for that one brief conversation, but I'd say that if he tried to change for you, he would end up losing everything that mattered. He's a man with a mission. There aren't many people who have that anymore. I'm not so sure he could live without it. It's his life. He and it seem to be one and the same."

"Look, Sam, all we need is someone to sit in the office each day. We have everything else. We've got the building, the people to run the sessions, now we just need an office person."

Sam regarded the young woman volunteer in front of him. Her jeans were faded and her braless torso was covered in a tight T-shirt with the words "The Doors Live On" spelled out in fluorescent lettering across the front. "Do you mean out of all the volunteers I've rounded up for the Youth Excellence Service, not one of them can work the office?"

The girl shifted hesitantly and shoved her hands into

the back pockets of her jeans. "It's just that, well...
like, we're all social psychology majors and, I mean, it's
just sort of beneath... What I mean is, we're not, you
know, like secretaries."

Sam's impatience began to rise, but he worked hard
at keeping it down. Heaven help any of these armchair
social psychologists if they had to do anything that was
beneath their station in life! No, they all wanted
something that spelled glamour, something snappy to
put on their résumés when they finally went looking for
a "real" job. It was a constant problem with any project. People volunteered only for what they thought
would be fun. To heck with the nonglitzy work that had
to be done each day. They couldn't be bothered with
that.

"All I know, Sharon, is that as many wonderful
moderators and counselors as we have for the sessions,
YES will not get off the ground until I find someone to
work in the office."

The girl had no answer for that one, so Sam nodded a
quick good-bye and left the building. He slipped his
arms into his suit jacket and hurried the few blocks to
the train stop. Out of habit he checked his wrist for the
time, but he had stopped wearing his watch, since it
didn't work anyway. He wondered how late he would be
for this engagement.

He boarded the elevated train and found a seat in the
back of the car as it sped off toward downtown. Once
seated, he watched through the windows, looking down
at the world he was leaving behind. No, he wouldn't
look at it that way. All he was doing was seeing some
old friends. No crime in that. But he stared at the
disintegrating neighborhood below him and the meager
rationalization burned into his mind like a slow trickle
of acid. He was copping out.

Thirty minutes later he rounded the corner of Wells

and Madison on foot. The restaurant was dim and dark, an old-world retreat, full of the smell of money and success and weighty financial decisions. Halfway between Wells and LaSalle, it catered to those who made the financial decisions, the fortunes, the economics waves. And to the lawyers who volleyed for justice amidst class action litigations and the most sensational crimes.

He walked in the front entrance, and the doorman greeted him with a "Good to see you today, sir," as if he ate there everyday. Sam only hoped he had enough cash on him to pay for the meal. Flowers last week and an expensive lunch this week; he would be lucky if he could pay his house payment next month!

The maître'd politely asked him if he had a reservation.

"I'm meeting friends. I think the reservation was in the name of Updike."

"Yes. You must be Mr. Winslow. Right this way, please." He led the way to the table where his friends were waiting for him.

"Sam, hey, great to see you!" The round of greetings began and he found himself clasped, slapped on the back, hugged, and fired upon with questions. "Where you been hiding out the last ten years? Married? Why the hell aren't you working as my partner?"

There was hardly time to answer the questions or even catch his breath. A waiter came and took drink orders and finally the joyful reunion faded to a warm glow of camaraderie and reminiscence around the table. They had all gone to school together in Madison. Fraternity brothers. Best buddies.

Adam Updike was a partner in the prestigious law firm of Aglestone, Martin, and Updike. David McCormick was a commodities broker who worked on the floor of the Exchange. And Eric Booker was an engineering consultant who worked with some of the major oil and chemical companies all over the Midwest.

"Well, what is it exactly that you're doing right now, Sam?" they all wanted to know.

"I'm a minister in a church on the near west side. Blackhawk Street."

The round of silence that greeted him was palpable.

"Sam Winslow a preacher!" Eric finally exclaimed. "Wow! That really is a mind blower. How the heck did that come about?"

How could he explain it to these guys? As close as they all used to be, they had never talked about anything serious. It was always girls, sex, booze, parties, war, sex, a little homework, sex. Never where they were going in life, what they felt about things. Never the pain or the doubts; those were not allowed to escape. Life was one big party. "It's a long story," he finally said. "It was just something I wanted to do."

"You were in the Peace Corps too, weren't you?"

"Yeah."

"Bangladesh? Venezuela?"

"India."

"You still boxing?"

"Not really. Oh, I occasionally go down to the gym, just to keep in shape. But I tell you, most of those guys that hang around down there are better than I ever was. It's a different sport nowadays."

"I'll drink to that." David laughed. "In more ways than one."

They all lifted their glasses in a toast. "To the good old days!" Sam toasted along with them, but he wondered to what good old days they were referring. What were the good old days? Days without responsibility? Had they forgotten that during all those blindly delirious days of college there had also been a bloody, irrational war going on, and on the home front racial tension was at the breaking point, and even the

Democratic National Convention right here in Chicago had been the backdrop for more bloodshed between police and youth? Yeah, the good old days.

Talk shifted then to contemporary problems in the economy, to political campaigns and international crises. Lunch was served and from there the conversation digressed into things the other three men had in common. Parties they all attended, clients they all knew.

"How come you never married, Sam?" one of them finally asked.

"Guess it just hasn't been in the cards."

"Hey," Adam cried. "Remember that chick...what was her name? Betsy..."

"Betsy 'Easy Rider' Walkins!" David said. "Yeah, old Sambo and Easy Rider. What a pair!"

Sam groaned. "Don't remind me. What an education I got from that girl."

They all laughed. "I remember the night campus security caught you two down in the steam tunnels with your pants down."

Sam clicked his tongue between his teeth. "Believe me, for all the trouble we were in, it was worth it! I learned more about meaningful dialogue in that one night than in four years of political science courses."

"Listen." Eric laughed. "I'm having a party before Christmas. The eighteenth. Why don't you come, Sam? Dave and Adam are coming and bringing their wives. You could bring a date. What do you say?"

Sam regarded the three friends around the table. It had been so easy to slip into the old dialogue with them, the old ways. It would be so easy to keep on slipping. After all, that's what he had called Adam for and the reason he had come to this lunch gathering. He wanted to see for himself what he had been missing. He had to find out if he had taken the wrong route. He had to know.

But as he looked at his friends, all of them waiting for his answer, he knew this was not what he wanted. Whatever they had that he had missed, it didn't matter. He didn't have all of the answers he had come for, but he had enough to know this was not the path for him.

"I'll have to let you know, Eric," he said, putting off the answer he knew he would give. "I have to see what's going on in the neighborhood and in the church."

"Sure. Let me know."

"Yeah. I will."

"And listen," Adam said, "let's do this again real soon. You've been out in the boonies too long, Sambo. We've got to get you back in where the action is. So you give me a call and we'll meet for lunch again."

"Sounds great," he lied, knowing that he would not call. He had come to find out, and now he knew.

Chapter Fourteen

As soon as the train sliced its path across Halsted and rose up from the tunnel, angling over Division Street, Sam breathed easier. He was almost home. The familiarity pierced him with a sense of belonging. This was where he should be.

The fact that he wanted and needed Elizabeth in his life was something he did not know how to reconcile. All he knew was that he did want her, despite all of her mother's dire warnings and Elizabeth's own bewildering cry of "Leave me alone!" Despite their vast differences in philosophy and life-style, he wanted her in a way he had never wanted anyone or anything in his life. And the desperateness of that want scared the hell out of him.

He was thirty-five years old! He was supposed to have his life together and under control by now. And he had until that cool day in October when she stepped out of her car onto Blackhawk Street.

He had at first tried to erase her image from his mind. When that proved futile and he knew that he loved her, he tried to diminish her importance to him. But that too was a failure. She was there with him every minute of every day, and there she would stay. He would just have to find a way to make it work. This was where he belonged and he didn't want to sacrifice that. But neither could he sacrifice what he felt for her. He would work it out.

As he left the train and walked the few blocks toward his house, he knew that this was where he wanted to be. This was what he wanted out of life.

He climbed the steps to his front porch and stopped, staring down at a box set against the door. He squatted on his heels beside it.

It was a cardboard box filled with a stack of newspapers. But from beneath the newspapers a small gurgle reached his ears. He peeled back the layers of paper and underneath them was a tiny baby, sucking on a still-warm bottle of milk that was propped up by a wadded ball of newspapers.

Stunned, Sam continued to stare down at the infant wrapped in a worn sleeper, oblivious to the cold air that surrounded it. He reached out and tentatively touched the tiny brown fingers that clutched blindly at the air.

He stood up and looked down the street. Someone had left the baby only moments before. That was obvious by the still-warm skin and milk. But who? He scanned the street in both directions, but didn't see anyone who might have left a newborn infant.

He turned back and unlocked the door, then picked up the box and carried it inside. He laid it in the living room on the area rug and hurriedly built a fire in the fireplace. Once a strong blaze was flaring, he turned back to the baby, who was now sucking at nothing but air. He tilted the bottle higher so that the liquid in the bottom moved to the nipple.

He stared in bewilderment at the tiny thing. A baby. Why would anyone bring a baby here? It happened frequently in this part of town that mothers would abandon their infants. But usually the end result was a tragedy both for the child and the mother. But someone had brought it here.

And then it hit him. Of course! It had to be! Mary. But could she have had it already? He noticed how tiny the baby was. Maybe it was born early. But that had to be who it belonged to.

Under the baby's foot he noticed a folded piece of paper. He gingerly lifted its leg and slipped the paper out, opening it up to read.

Mister Sam. please kepe my baby. I be comin for her. I am. But I got to work sum things out furst. you watch her for me, mister sam. She is a good baby. she is not sik. i took her to a doctir. please. mary. I calls her Adeline.

He sat back on his heels and stared at the note. A hiccuping whimper from the baby drew his attention. The bottle had fallen out of her mouth and she wanted it back. He picked it up, but there was no milk left. What was he supposed to do now?

He reached into the box, gently sliding his hands beneath the tiny body. One hand automatically went behind the neck and head and he lifted, grimacing as he did it, wondering if he was going to snap the little thing in half. How could anything be so small!

A large wail bounded off the walls of the living room and Sam immediately set the bundle back down and stared in absolute horror. Where did that horrendous noise come from? Surely not from such a minute creature! He had been around babies before in the hospital and in India. But always before, someone else had been taking care of them; a mother would hold an infant while he administered a polio vaccination, or a nurse would change a diaper at the hospital while he looked on. But never, ever had he been left alone with one of them. What on earth was he supposed to do now?

The crying hadn't stopped, but had increased in intensity and magnification. He removed his suit jacket, wiped his sweaty palms on his trousers, and attempted once again to lift the baby. Weren't you supposed to burp them or something after they ate? Yeah, that was it. That was all that was the matter. He gritted his teeth and lifted the bundle onto his shoulder, administering easy little pats to her back while he tried to keep the bobbing head from wobbling off her neck.

That didn't help. She was still screaming at the top of her lungs. His neighbors would probably think he was trying to murder someone! Out of sheer panic, he began to walk, bouncing about the room in a frantic dance that had begun the moment in history when fathers first took it in their minds to hold their own babies.

The most uninfantlike noise suddenly came from the baby's mouth, followed by half the contents of her stomach, which ran down the back of his shirt. So much for bouncing, he thought ruefully. Since the baby was still hollering, he decided to lay her down for a minute until he could figure out what to do. The box was too small and confining, but he didn't want to set her on the rug, in case it wasn't clean enough. He took his suit coat from the back of the couch and spread it out on the rug, then set her down on top of it. It was only when he sat back on his knees that he noticed the warm wet circle on the front of his good white shirt, his only good white shirt. And as he looked down he could see the moisture spreading onto his suit jacket.

In a glazed stupor of one who has absolutely no idea what he is doing, he set about the task of changing her diaper. "Adeline." He tried the name a few times. "Adeline, that's a good name," he said, not having even the faintest clue how you were supposed to talk to a baby, but figuring any talk was better than none. "You've got to tell me what's wrong, though. I'm not too good at this sort of thing. Now, what we've got to do is find you something dry to put on. You stay right here and I'll be back. Don't go away, now.''

From the moment he began talking, the baby stopped crying and was staring at him with a penetrating gaze that made him feel like a blathering idiot. But at least she wasn't crying. He ran upstairs, taking them two at a time, and searched through his drawers for something that could serve as a diaper. He found some handkerchiefs, but decided they probably wouldn't be thick enough. He opened his closet and pulled down his second set of sheets. Using the diaper that had been on her as a guide, he cut about fifteen pieces of sheet the same size. He also grabbed the blanket from his bed and wet a washcloth in the bathroom, then ran back downstairs with his arms full of material.

But as he looked down at sweet, innocent little Adeline, he realized it had been a mistake to leave her unclothed. His suit coat was now not only wet, but also soiled. Adeline gurgled pleasantly and raised a leg in a playful kick as Sam, with the diaper material still clutched in his arms, stared with blank eyes down at her.

''You're trying to make this difficult for me, aren't you?'' he gently scolded and knelt down to remove the coat from beneath her. He tried to keep a pleasant expression on his face as he pulled it out from underneath her, but it was exceedingly difficult. He folded up the blanket from his bed and slipped it beneath her, then used the washcloth to wash off her bottom.

''Now, let's see.'' He looked at the pieces of cloth and then at her body, trying to figure out the best way to approach the maneuver. Deciding he had better not wait too much longer or he'd have to repeat the whole cleaning procedure, he took two pieces of cloth and put them together, then laid them under her and brought them up between her legs. He picked up one of the pins that had been in her diaper and turned it different ways, trying to figure out how he was going to get it fastened without puncturing her tummy. Finally he put his fingers between the material and her skin and gently inserted the pin. "Dammit!" He quickly fastened the pin, then pulled out his finger and stared at the red dot of blood that appeared.

With the next pin he was more careful, but as he examined the overall work, he noticed how baggy the diaper hung on her. "Well, kiddo, that is going to have to do." He shook a teasing finger at her. "And you'd better not make me go through that again very soon."

He raised himself to the chair, flopped into it, and closed his eyes. He was exhausted. What on earth was he going to do with this baby? Mary said she'd come back for her, but when? He didn't want to take her to the hospital, because they might give Mary trouble over getting her back. But what was he going to do?

He sat up quickly, his eyes wide. Elizabeth! He'd call her and she could come take care of the baby. Of course! What a great idea. Women always knew how to handle this sort of thing. "I'll be right back," he whispered to the now sleeping baby and tiptoed off to the kitchen.

Elizabeth pushed through the swinging door into the kitchen and hesitated for a moment before walking over to the counter where Letti was putting the dishes into the dishwasher. "Letti?"

"Yes, Miss Elizabeth."

"I need to ask you a question."

Letti never stopped rinsing the dishes and bending to put them into the machine.

"I was wondering. . . well, is there some special way to take care of a black baby?"

Letti finally turned off the water and stared at her

with wide eyes. "What on earth are you talking about, child?"

"I just received a phone call from my friend, Mr. Winslow."

"Oh." Letti smiled. "I remember that looker, and if you were smart, he'd be more than just a friend."

Elizabeth pursed her lips. She was used to Letti's blunt observations on the family's personal lives. "An abandoned baby was left on his porch this afternoon. He says it belongs to a pros—" Elizabeth cleared her throat. She simply couldn't say the word to Letti. "She's a girl that he knows, and he wants me to come help him take care of it. I thought maybe there might be something I should know."

"The mama's black?"

"Yes."

Letti shook her head in mild rebuke. "Oh, Miss Elizabeth," she said. "There ain't no difference in a white baby or a black baby. They all need the same thing."

"What's that?" Elizabeth asked excitedly, wondering if perhaps she should get a piece of paper to write the instructions down.

"Why, love, Miss Elizabeth! Love!"

"Oh." Elizabeth stared at the maid, waiting to hear if there wasn't something else. "That's all?"

"That's all. Oh, you got to change their diapers and feed them and all that. But that isn't nearly as important as the other."

Elizabeth frowned and nodded her head slowly. "Okay." She had never been around babies before, and she didn't want to look like a complete fool in front of Sam. "Well," she began, absently thinking of all the things she might need, "I guess I could stop and buy some of those disposable diapers. And milk, and—"

"How old is the baby?"

"He said it was a newborn."

"Oh, Miss Elizabeth! You don't want to be giving a newly born babe regular milk. You buy you some of that formula they sell in the store. Don't you buy regular milk."

"Oh, God! I'm never going to make it. I'll probably end up killing the kid through some stupid mistake like giving it whole milk."

"You're gonna do fine, Miss Lizzy," Letti said, not even realizing she was calling Elizabeth the same name she had called her when she was a little girl. "Just get you some of that formula, some diapers, and maybe something warm to wear, and that little babe'll be fine and dandy."

What Elizabeth finally ended up with after her trek to the nearest department store was a fifty-dollar infant basket with a calico lining, three cotton blankets and a down comforter with matching pillow, six boxes of disposable diapers, three sleepers and two gowns, some socks, and a stuffed pink Humpty Dumpty with a bell inside. After stopping at the grocery store and buying a case of already prepared formula in cans and a set of bottles with disposable liners to go with it, she was on her way.

She pulled in to the curb in front of Sam's house and parked the car. She opened the trunk and lugged two sacks out and up the sidewalk. Through the walls of the house, she could hear a high-pitched wail and she stopped, dreadfully afraid to go inside and face her own incompetence. She took a deep breath and doggedly climbed the stoop and knocked on the door with her foot.

Sam opened it, but she couldn't see his face. A huge blanket was covering most of it and a tiny furry head bobbed beside his ear, screaming her little lungs out. "Thank God!" Sam said, but the sound was muffled behind the blanket. Elizabeth set the sacks on the floor and hurried back out the door. "Where are you going?" he cried, panic inherent in each syllable.

"I have some more things in the car. I'll be right back."

"Well, hurry!"

She grabbed the other two sacks, closed the trunk, and ran back up the sidewalk. She knew the noise must be drawing attention all the way down the street. Once inside, she closed and locked the door, then began pulling everything out of the sacks, trying to organize it all on the floor.

"What are you doing? What is all of that?"

She looked up at Sam with the identical panic that was registered in his eyes. "I didn't know what to bring. I have no idea what babies need."

"Could you take her for a minute? Just hold her. There—no, watch her head and neck. You're going to let her head fall. Watch it now. No, put your hand under—"

"Would you stop giving me so many damn orders!" Elizabeth snapped. "If you're such an expert, you can do this all by yourself."

"I'm sorry, Elizabeth," Sam said, plopping into the chair with one leg thrown across the armrest. "I'm a wreck."

"Oh, my," she said, noticing for the first time how ragged he looked. "You are a wreck. Here, spread that new quilt out over here."

"You mean I have to get up again?" he asked weakly.

"Would you please hurry up."

With great force he managed to push himself from the chair and brought all of the equipment into the living room. He laid the quilt out on the rug and Elizabeth very carefully set the squalling baby down.

"They ought to capture this sound and use it for

burglar alarms," she said. "It would scare anybody off."

"I can't hear it anymore. My ears are numb."

"Well, look at this, no wonder she's crying. Her clothes are soaked."

"They are?" Sam was stunned by this revelation. "But I've changed her diaper three times in the last two hours."

"Well, she's wet, Sam." Elizabeth's chin lifted with the superiority of one who has discovered that a problem has such a simple solution.

"Don't look at me like you've done this all your life," he snapped. "You don't know any more about it than I do."

"Maternal instinct," she drawled with that superior lilt.

"Bull."

Elizabeth unsnapped the wet sleeper and pulled it off, then started to unfasten the pins in the ill-fitting diaper.

"Wait, you have to put your hand under the diaper so the pin doesn't stick her."

"I knew that." She gingerly slipped her hands into the soggy diaper, hoping she didn't gore her own finger. "Oooh, ick."

"Don't tell me," Sam said as he leaned his head back and closed his eyes for a moment of rest. "Tell her. Her name is Adeline."

Elizabeth slipped the diaper out from under the baby. "Okay. Oooh, ick, Adeline. Now, I brought you some fresh, new diapers and they are going to feel sooo good."

Sam opened his eyes halfway and smiled, then let them close again.

She dressed Adeline in a new diaper and gown and slipped the heavy socks onto her feet. Already the crying had stopped, and only a few wimpering whines were emitted every few minutes. Elizabeth took this time to go to the kitchen and pour the formula into the bottles. It was only after she opened the package that she realized it was not going to be as simple as all that. She tried several times to make the plastic liners fit the rim of the bottle, but two tore before she could get them on and another dropped to the floor.

"I can see you need an expert here," Sam boasted from the doorway, eagerly drinking in the sight of her working at this task in his kitchen. Her head was bent over in concentration, her pale yellow hair washed by the light from the ceiling, her slim fingers holding the white plastic bottle so tightly. It was a beautiful sight.

"Okay, hotshot. Get over here and do this." She watched him stretch the plastic liner over the edge of the bottle, executing the task perfectly the first time. Disgruntled, she reached for it, but he caught her hand in his.

"I don't think I said a very proper hello awhile ago." He kissed her lightly on the lips. He smiled and something in her melted as those warm brown eyes moved across her face. Even under fatigue, he was the most handsome man she had ever known. There was a strength about his looks that defied definition. It was simply there in his smile, in his eyes, in the secure grip of his hand. And she wanted to lose herself in it one more time.

But he handed her the bottle and she turned back to the counter to fill it up with the formula.

"Aren't we supposed to sterilize these?" he asked, holding up the nipples.

"Oh, yes, I guess we are." She glanced out at the temporarily happy baby lying on the quilt. "How quickly can you do it?"

He followed her gaze to the living room. "In record time."

Within five minutes the nipple was sterilized and the bottle was ready to go. "Maybe you'd better get a bunch of those linings ready to go. Just in case we need them later."

"Right," he said, going to work on the bottles while she took the full one out to the living room.

She sat down on the rug and, for the first time, really examined the tiny baby in front of her. Her fists were balled and one was stuck in her mouth as she sucked on it. Her eyes were puffy from crying, but the dark centers were clear and bright. "Hi, there, little one," Elizabeth said, and took the fist in her hand. She stroked her finger across the back of the knuckles, marveling at the softness. Adeline's cheeks were fat and her hair was dark and thick and curled loosely around her ears.

The fist fell from her mouth, but the lips kept moving in the same sucking motion. Elizabeth very slowly and carefully picked her up and laid her across the length of one forearm, curved against her body. She leaned back against the lower part of the chair and picked up the bottle. Within seconds some inner radar alerted the baby that food was near and her head turned in the direction of the nipple. Elizabeth smiled and watched her as she sucked on the bottle with almost fierce intensity.

She looked up at Sam, who was now standing over her, and smiled. "She's really something, isn't she?"

He watched her for a minute. "So are you."

Elizabeth smiled at him again, feeling a closeness she had never known with anyone before.

"Are you hungry?"

She looked down at the baby in her arms. Adeline's eyes were closed, but her mouth still moved rhythmically against the bottle. "Not really."

"Well, the lady next door brought me some soup this

morning, so I'll heat it up in case you want it in a little while.''

"Uh-hmmm," she answered distractedly, placing her finger in the curve of the baby's fist. This was a new experience for her, one she had never dreamed she would enjoy. From the friends she knew who had children, she assumed they were merely some playthings you dressed in pretty little clothes to show off to your friends, or that you shipped off to summer camp, or that you worried yourself sick about getting into the best schools. She had never held a baby in her arms before and she had not realized what a nice feeling it would be.

After Adeline finished her bottle, Elizabeth laid her in the basket she had bought and covered her with a blanket. She was sound asleep when Elizabeth left her to join Sam in the kitchen.

"Asleep?"

"Yes." She smiled softly and wrapped her arms around his back. "She's fun to hold."

"Yeah, she is." He turned to enclose Elizabeth in his arms. "When she's not squalling like a stuck pig."

She struck his chest with her fist. "You're awful." It was the descent of his mouth that took all teasing from her smile, and she parted her lips to meet his. His mouth was gentle, but decisive, wanting to claim all that she was, all that she could give him. Her arms looped around his neck and she arched her back, pressing her abdomen against him. He pulled her closer and ran his hands across her snug cream wool pants. She tilted her head as his lips blazed a heated trail down the side of her neck.

"Don't you hate me for what happened at the party?" she breathed, wanting to know, but not wanting him to cease the delicious meanderings of his mouth.

"Yes," he murmured, moving back to her mouth,

while his hands wrapped all the way around her and his thumbs began to stroke the swell of her breasts.

"Please don't hate me," she sighed against his mouth only a second before his tongue slid in to take control again. A bellow shook the air around them as Adeline once again made her presence known. They jumped and turned to look at her in the basket, but she had already fallen back asleep.

Sam's gaze returned to Elizabeth, and he held her face between his flattened palms. "How could I ever hate you? I know how difficult this is for you. It's not an easy relationship. It's not for me either. But we'll make it work because we want it to."

She nodded and stepped out of his arms. "I didn't mean to run away from you the other night. It was a horrible thing to do. But all of a sudden I felt so much pressure and...I don't know, I just don't want that in our relationship."

"But there will always be problems, Elizabeth." He hesitated at her startled look. "That's the way life is. But if two people love each other enough, those problems can be worked out."

"I know you're right. But I've only seen firsthand the way it worked for my mother. Every time there was a little problem, she got a divorce. If that's the way it would be for me, I don't ever want to get married."

He reached for a couple of bowls in the cabinet and ladled some soup into them. "It wouldn't have to be. You just have to believe that."

"I wish I had your faith in things," she said as he set the bowl of soup in front of her. "Thank you."

He said nothing, but only watched her as she dipped the spoon into her soup and lifted it to her mouth. If she didn't have enough faith in herself, he would simply have to help her gain it. He would wait. If it took forever, he would wait.

"Why do you suppose Mary left the baby?" she asked between bites.

"She probably didn't want anyone to know she had one. Especially Sly."

"Oh, you mean her...pimp." The word was pulled hesitantly from her mouth.

"He knew she was pregnant and he has been pushing her to work the streets anyway. Now that the baby is here, he would have her back in action immediately. I forgot to offer you anything to drink. What would you like?"

"I hadn't even thought about it. Maybe just some water. You mean that Sly would make her work even if she didn't want to?"

Sam nodded. "You see, he thinks he owns his ladies. They are his property. He tries to keep them on birth control, although you see how well it worked in this case. He buys them clothes, gives them an identity, bails them out of jail, and in return they give him everything they make and their undying devotion. Mary's first crime, in his eyes, was that she got pregnant in the first place. And he was angry because she didn't come to him when she found out. He doesn't want his ladies to have kids to distract them. He wants them on the street making money. So he would probably try to take the baby away from her. And if she is hiding out from him, no telling what he'll do when he finds her."

"That is sick," she said, pushing her bowl away. "Why would Mary live that way?"

He shrugged. "The American Dream. A piece of the pie. I guess she didn't see any other way of having anything. Little girls grow up fast on this street, and from a young age they see these fancy ladies in their slick clothes being picked up by men who will pay good money to be with them. It looks pretty enticing to a girl who knows nothing but poverty and who is still too young to know all that is physically involved in those relationships.''

"I guess I have really lived a sheltered life. I just had no idea that all of this existed. Of course, you see it in movies and television, but it's not real life. You think of it as pure fantasy. Hollywood magic.''

"Fantasy it's not. This is the real world.''

Elizabeth took a deep breath and expelled it slowly. "I'm not sure I'm ready to face that much reality. I'm not sure that I can.''

Once again, Sam wondered if he was making a mistake, a terrible mistake. Not for himself, but for her. Was it better to let her go back to her world, untouched, innocence intact? It wasn't too late. He could still let the butterfly go free. Couldn't he?

Chapter Fifteen

By nine o'clock they had changed Adeline two more times and fed her once more. Now they assumed, as most first-time parents do, that the baby was ready for a long night's sleep.

Sam carried her in the basket up to his room and laid it on the floor beside the bed. To his great relief, she didn't make a sound. He flopped down on the bed and laid his forearm across his eyes. "If I were wearing my hat," he mumbled tiredly, "it would go off to all the mothers of the world."

He opened his eyes and looked up at Elizabeth standing beside the bed. "Come here." She laid her hand in his and he pulled her down on top of him, spreading his legs enough to nestle her body between them.

His hand slid beneath her hair and his fingers wrapped around the back of her neck, kneading the stiffness away. She dropped her head onto his chest and closed her eyes, but her fingers trailed languorously down his side.

"Sam, do you ever wonder where this relationship will lead us?" She kept her head turned toward the wall, her cheek resting on his chest. She was afraid to see if there were any doubts in his eyes.

One of his hands was on her back, the other in her hair, and she felt the increased pressure in the tips of his fingers. "I try to just be thankful that we have the chance to see where it will lead. Very few people are as lucky as we are."

She raised her head to look at him, sliding her body up higher into the junction of his legs. Her voice was soft and full of wonder. "Do you really feel lucky?"

His hand gripped her hips, holding her tight against him. And the other hand grasped the back of her head, his fingers wrapping tightly in the fine cords of her hair, as he brought her down to his mouth. "I'm the luckiest man alive."

Morning came early, in fact, Elizabeth felt as if she had been asleep for only a few minutes. She opened her eyes at the uncustomary noise and realized it was still dark. It wasn't morning at all. And that noise! What was that horrible racket? She tried to sit up, but Sam's arm was thrown across her waist, pinning her to the mattress. She pushed the cover back, then lifted his arm off her.

She knew now what the noise was; it was Adeline screaming her little lungs out. Elizabeth shook the heavy fog of sleep from her mind and leaned across Sam's body to turn on the light by the bed. She shivered as the cold air in the room first touched her naked skin. "Oh, you poor baby," she crooned. "No wonder you're crying. It's absolutely freezing in here!"

Before picking Adeline up, she changed her soggy diaper and sleeper, then wrapped her in the blankets and picked her up. But the crying had not stopped.

"What's going on?" Sam groaned and raised up on one elbow, trying to force his eyes open. "Who's being tortured?" He sat up farther, the cover thrown across his legs, and stared at Elizabeth bouncing around the room with the baby in her arms.

"I think she's hungry, Sam." The now familiar panic was trilling in her throat.

"Okay, I'll get the bottle." He climbed out of bed and slipped into his jeans, then hurried downstairs to pour the formula. When the bottle was warm, he ran back upstairs and handed it to Elizabeth. "Aren't you cold?"

"Freezing."

"Here, come sit in bed with her. There." He helped her into the bed, then wrapped the blanket around her Indian style. He sat down beside them and watched as the baby clutched on to the bottle for dear life. Elizabeth laid Adeline on the bed and held the bottle while she and Sam reclined on their elbows on either side of her. He adjusted the blanket so it covered them to the waist. "I guess they don't sleep through the night yet." He yawned.

"I guess not. Don't you fall asleep now," she scolded. "You'll smother her."

"I'm not going to sleep. I wouldn't miss watching you like this for anything in the world. You'd make a good mother."

"One day of baby-sitting does not ensure good mothering."

"I know, but I can tell these things." He yawned again.

"Oh, sure." She laughed. "Right now, you probably couldn't even tell me your own name. Do you remember it?"

His hand reached over to caress her hip through the blanket. "No, but I remember you. Every moment, every touch."

Her eyes dropped shut for a second, then opened to look at him. "I remember too."

Adeline spit out the bottle and stretched her arms and legs, kicking a few times at the mattress beneath her. "I think she's settling in for the night," he said.

Elizabeth smirked. "Oh, yeah? Well, where are you going to sleep, then?"

"Very funny," he retorted. "I would suggest we all sleep here together, but I really am afraid we would smother her. Besides, I'm not giving up this golden opportunity to have you sleep in my bed."

"Stingy." She looked back down at Adeline, her arms thrown to the sides of her head, her legs stretched wide. She was sound asleep. "It must be hard for Mary not to be with her baby."

He glanced up quickly at Elizabeth. "I'm sure it is. I'm going to try to find her tomorrow and talk to her. As much as I like little Adeline, I think Mary should take her and try to make some kind of home for her."

She ran a finger along the backs of the baby's knuckles. "Will she grow up like Mary?"

"You mean will she become a prostitute?"

"Yes."

He looked down at the baby sleeping without a care in the world and shook his head. "Hard to say. We all start out pretty much the same way, but there are so many factors that make us who we are."

On an impulse, Elizabeth leaned over and planted a delicate kiss on Adeline's head. "Maybe you'd better put her back to bed."

Sam watched her closely, amazed at the constant surprises and secrets he found in her. "Yeah, I suppose we'd better get some sleep too. Who knows how long this peace and quiet will last."

He picked the infant up as gently as possible, hoping that she would stay asleep, and laid her in the basket, covering her legs, but keeping the blanket away from her head. Then he removed his jeans, crawled back into bed, and pulled his own covers up. He looked over at

Elizabeth, who was curled on her side, her eyes closed. She was already asleep. He pulled the cover up over her shoulders and lay back on his pillow, his hands hooked behind his head.

He had had some important things taken away from him in his life. Things and people he hated to lose. He glanced briefly at Elizabeth. But he had also been given much, and this woman sleeping beside him was the best present of all. The corners of his mouth turned up in a slight smile. "Thank you," he said to the warm dark night.

It was in the early hours of morning when Elizabeth finally awakened. She heard a muffled conversation coming from the bottom of the stairs.

She leaned over the edge of the bed and looked into Adeline's basket, but the baby was not in there. Figuring Sam must have taken her downstairs with him, she climbed out of bed and dashed across the cold floor to the bathroom.

When she was dressed in the same clothes she had worn yesterday, with a few of Adeline's gifts now adorning her sweater, she went downstairs.

She stopped halfway down when she saw Sam standing in the foyer, talking to a young man and a woman. Adeline was in his arms. The couple looked up at Elizabeth in surprise. Sam smiled and motioned for her to come on down.

He reached around her with his free arm and kissed her lightly on the temple. "Elizabeth, this is Tony and Barbara. They're students from the university and they're helping me on a special project here." They all greeted each other, the two students still with that same surprised look on their faces at seeing her here. Elizabeth wasn't sure if it was she with whom they were surprised or the fact that Sam had a woman spend the night.

"Do you want me to take Adeline?" She reached for the baby and he handed her over.

"She's already eaten," he said, then turned back to the students. "Look, I've made it as clear as I can, you guys. We are not going to start the center until we have someone to work as a secretary. If none of you is going to volunteer, then we'll just have to wait until I can find someone."

Elizabeth carried the baby into the living room. Adeline was wide awake and staring with clear eyes at everything that passed within her line of vision. She walked her, but she was listening to the conversation in the foyer. She was surprised at Sam's tone with the students. He seemed unusually short and unbending. Barbara and Tony shifted rebelliously on their feet before him, but finally seemed to accept his demands. They mumbled a quick good-bye to Elizabeth and left the house.

He closed the door behind him and shook his head in exasperation. "Those kids can't get it through their heads that organization is the key to a successful project. They want to just jump in headfirst without any plan and then expect it to work." He walked over to her and wrapped his arms around her and the baby. "Sorry. Not a very pleasant way for you to wake up." He planted a firm kiss on her mouth.

"Good morning to you too." She smiled, standing on her tiptoes to kiss him again, but this time, Adeline squirmed impatiently between them. Elizabeth resumed her stroll about the room. "What kind of project is it?"

"It's called YES—Youth Excellence Service. It's a program to help juvenile offenders keep themselves out of trouble. It's meant as a supplement to their parole. They may only see the parole officer once a week or once a month, depending on their sentence, but they are required to come to YES meetings one day every week.''

"So what is the problem with the program? Why can't you start it?''

"Well, we first need someone to work in the office, to keep up with all the paperwork, answer the phone, organize the sessions and so on, but none of the volunteers is willing to do that.''

"Why not?''

"Because they don't realize that with every program like this there are little jobs that, while not as much fun or as glamorous as others, still have to be done.''

Elizabeth had stopped by the front window and was silent for a long while. Adeline swatted distractedly at the curtains. She turned back to Sam. "Why couldn't I work in the office?''

He stared at her blankly. "What?''

"I said I could work in the office. That's all you need, isn't it? Just someone... anyone, right? And stop looking at me like I just escaped from the zoo.''

That was exactly the way he was looking at her, or rather as if she were stark-raving mad. "Elizabeth.'' He chuckled, unaware that her mouth was hardening at the patronizing tone. "I appreciate the offer.'' He chuckled again. "But it isn't necessary for you to do that.''

"But you need someone to do it. Why not me?''

"Look.'' He walked over to her and laid his palm on her cheek. "I know you want to help, but this wouldn't be a very good job for you.''

"You don't think I could do it, do you?'' Her lips tightened at the corners.

"It's not that.''

"It is. You think I wouldn't be able to handle it.''

"Elizabeth, I don't think you understand what is involved. It would not be a safe job.''

"Well, why is it safe for somebody else but not for me?''

"I'll find someone who has worked with juvenile offenders before."

"I have."

He was very still as he watched her intently. "What do you mean?"

"I mean I've worked with juvenile offenders before. When I first joined the Junior League, that was one of the things we initiates had to do. My job was to counsel juveniles who were on parole. I had to meet with them twice a week."

Sam studied her closely. Her chin was tilted up and she had a self-satisfied expression on her face. He couldn't help but smile. "What kind of offenses had they committed?"

"Different things. Truancy, shoplifting, things like that."

He nodded slowly and this time did not smile. "Do you know what offenses these kids have committed?"

She shook her head.

"Well, I'll tell you. There's rape, armed robbery, assault with a deadly weapon, drug dealing, arson... need I go on?"

"They're still kids, Sam. They need the same thing."

"I know that, but it takes a different approach."

"An approach I couldn't handle, in other words." Anger was clearly marked in the tone of her voice now.

"Elizabeth, I don't want to fight about this. I appreciate your offer, but the answer is no. We have some things to work out between us, but this isn't the way." He brushed his hand down the side of her hair and let it rest on the back of her neck. "Okay?"

Her chin tilted higher. She would let it drop... for now. There was too much to do today with Adeline to cause a fight now. But she wasn't going to forget about it. Once Elizabeth Parkins's mind was set on something, she didn't let it go. Persuasion was her forte. So she did not answer okay to Sam. She simple nodded and turned away. "I'll fix us some breakfast."

He took the baby and watched Elizabeth walk into the kitchen. He was frowning in her wake. Something about that conversation did not sit well with him. It wasn't exactly that he had been defeated and overruled. It was something more subtle. It was more like he had been quietly dismissed as though he were an errant child.

He narrowed his eyes on her back and a half smile played about his mouth. Elizabeth Parkins was full of surprises.

Chapter Sixteen

"Where is she, Lola?"

"I ain't supposed to tell, Sam."

"I want to see her."

The young prostitute shifted nervously on her feet. "If Sly finds her, he'll...no telling what he'll do," she whispered.

"I just want to find her before he does."

"How can you help her, Sam? No matter where she goes, that man will find her."

The two of them stood together and studied each other quietly. Finally, Lola looked away and spoke softly. "Oh, hell, she's at Sawanee's. But so help me, Sam, if you tell her I said it..."

"Thanks, Lola. You're doing the right thing."

"Yeah, well, I ain't so sure about that," she mumbled as he hurried away. "I ain't so sure."

Sam took the side streets and alleys, walking as quickly as possible through the melting brown slush left over from the early morning snowfall. Tonight, it would probably freeze and then tomorrow the reheating process would begin all over again until the streets were caked in a hard brown crust that would not disappear until spring.

He quickened his pace toward Sawanee's combined house and business establishment. The seventy-five-year-old woman was a self-proclaimed entrepreneur, dabbling in a variety of trades from bookmaking to fencing of stolen goods. She had started out in the nineteen twenties as a young bootlegging partner with her father, Waldo Grant Hayes. From there, she branched into her own pursuits, managing a bar for a while until it was closed down by the local police because of the numbers-running operation in the back.

Everyone in the area knew or at least had a passing knowledge of Sawanee Hayes. She had become a semilegend in her own time. She had made her mark on the area and it would remain long after the woman herself had gone.

Sam reached the front door of her house and knocked. After a couple of minutes a bolt lock slowly slid back and Sawanee stuck her head out the slim opening. Her way was to say nothing, just stare until the other person spoke first. Sam knew this. He and Sawanee had sized each other up several times in the past five years and had finally arrived at a plateau of mutual respect and understanding.

"I came to talk to Mary."

Sawanee cast her gaze off into the distance behind his head. "Don't think I knows any gal named Mary."

He smiled wistfully. He knew the game. He and Sawanee had played it many times. "She's got a responsibility now," he said. "There's something she's got to take care of."

"That so?"

He nodded. "I know she's scared, but I want to help."

"Wantin' and doin' ain't the same thing."

"I know that, but I want to try."

She narrowed her age-rimmed eyes on Sam in critical speculation. "You're a man of your word," she finally admitted. Sawanee wasn't generous with praise of any kind, but she had just given the best judgment she could ever give another person. "She's inside."

"Thank you," he said, as she opened the door for him.

Once inside, he was led down a dark narrow hallway to a rough wooden door at the other end. He tapped on it and after about twenty seconds the door opened.

"Hello, Mary."

Her expression was cautious. "Mr. Sam." She stepped back into the small room so that he could enter. "Where's my baby?"

"Adeline is with a friend of mine. Do you remember Elizabeth Parkins? She was at my—"

"I 'member her," she answered sharply. Her mouth turned down into a frozen frown and she clenched her fists at her sides. "Why ain't you watching her, Mr. Sam? I give her to you."

"She's being taken care of, Mary. Elizabeth is treating her fine."

"Don't need no prissy white woman taking care of my baby. I wanted you to do it."

"I have things to do, Mary. I have my own work. I certainly can't leave her alone in the house. She needs constant attention."

She moved over to the bed and sat on its edge. Sam took a seat in a hard-backed chair and leaned his elbow on the desk. "That's why I came to talk to you, Mary. You need to take your baby. Adeline needs you."

She glanced briefly at Sawanee. "I can't have my baby here, Mr. Sam. Sly is gonna find me sooner or later and make me go back on the street. He's gonna be mad, real mad."

"You can come stay at my place."

"No, he would find me there. I can't go to my mama's neither. He's sure to find me no matter where I go."

"Then I'll help find a place for you. A place where you and Adeline will be safe. But she needs you and I think you need her too."

Mary sat on the bed, looking down at her hands, a sullen expression on her face. "When you want me to go with you?"

"I'll come get you tomorrow, okay?"

She only shrugged, but after a moment she looked up with a more hopeful expression in her eyes. "Will you bring my baby with you?"

He smiled. "I'll bring her, Mary. I promise."

Louise breezed through Elizabeth's kitchen door, filling the room with a cloud of heavy perfume. Letti turned from her post at the sink. "Morning, Miss Louise."

"Hello, Letti. Where's Liz?"

"She was pretty tired, Miss Louise. She's upstairs resting on her bed."

"In the middle of the day? That doesn't sound like her. She must be coming down with something. She was supposed to be at the Symphony League meeting this morning, but she never showed up. I'm sure she must be ill. I think I'll go check on her."

"Well, she's been pretty busy," Letti drawled in her slow, easy way as Louise headed for the door to the dining room. "What with the baby and all."

Louise stopped with her hand poised on the swinging door and looked back at the maid. "Baby?"

Letti nodded toward the basket that was sitting in the middle of the glass-topped table in the breakfast room. Louise hesitated, then walked over to the table and peered down at the sleeping bundle nestled between the calico lining. "Why, Letti!" Louise smiled with the polite interest of employer toward employee. "I didn't know you had a grandchild. Isn't she...sweet, though." Louise really had no time for small things like pets or children, but she knew that others found something endearing about them.

"Oh, it isn't mine, Miss Louise. Miss Elizabeth brought her home."

"Brought her home?" Louise felt stuffy all of a sudden and unconsciously loosened the silk tie at the neck of her blouse. "I'm afraid I don't understand."

"She and Mr. Winslow have been taking care of her. The poor little thing was left on his doorstep."

Louise stared at Letti in shock. Her hand rested on the back of a chair and she kept her head perfectly aligned so that she would not have to look back into the basket. "Oh, my God!" she whispered.

"Oh, nothing to worry about, Miss Louise," Letti answered with protracted syllables. "The babe's got a mama. But, being a prostitute, she's got a few things to work out before she can take her little one back. Miss Louise? Miss Louise?"

Louise shrank into a chair and her hand began waving uselessly in front of her. "Get me a drink, Letti," she croaked. "Get me a drink!"

Elizabeth realized her unfortunate timing as soon as she walked through the kitchen door. She had been aware of voices down here, but in her exhausted state, she had not recognized one of them as her mother's. Now, with one look at her mother's face, she knew she should have stayed in bed.

"Good morning, Mother." She tiptoed gingerly across the floor in her bare feet, as if her own gentle steps might temper the trauma of the moment.

Louise took a hefty slug of the sherry Letti set in front of her and stared at her daughter. "What is the meaning of this?"

Elizabeth pulled down a cup from the cupboard and poured some coffee into it. She dumped in the sweetener and stirred it very slowly. As she walked over to join her mother, her eyes were lit with beguiling innocence. "Oh, I know I missed the meeting this morning, Mother, and I'm sorry, but I was so tired, and—"

"I am not talking about the meeting."

"Oh?"

"I am referring to this...this..."

"The word is *baby*, Mother. Ba-by." At Adeline's first stirrings, Elizabeth stood and reached into the basket, pulling her into her arms as she sat back down.

"The child of a strumpet!" Louise whispered with a hiss. "A common, streetwalking trollop. What on earth are you thinking about, Liz!"

"I'm thinking about this little baby, Mother. Right now, she holds priority over my time."

"Why did you bring it home? Why doesn't that—that man Winslow take care of it? Why did he involve you in this unsavory situation?"

"First of all," Elizabeth stated calmly, "the baby is not an 'it.' She is a girl. Her name is Adeline. Second of all, Sam is trying to locate the mother this morning, so I am watching Adeline until then. Third, I am involved in this...unsavory situation, as you call it, because I am involved in his life. And I intend to remain involved in his life."

"You can't possibly be serious, Liz."

"Deadly serious."

"Deadly is right. This will kill your grandmother. Are you willing to drive her to an early grave because of this man...this gold digger? Your own grandmother!"

"Spare me that, please," Elizabeth groaned. "Grandmother Eva will weather this with the same staid posture that she weathered the death of her first child, the philandering of her husband for forty years, your drinking, my disinterest in marriage...need I go on? Grandmother Eva is a survivor. And she will survive this just fine."

Louise shuddered in her chair at the uncustomary insolence coming from her daughter. "And what about me?" she whispered. "Do you not even care what I think about all of this?"

Elizabeth stared at her mother long and hard. "I just want you to love me for who and what I am, Mother. That's all I've ever wanted."

Louise shifted uneasily in her chair, uncomfortable with sentimentality in any form. Adeline took that moment to relieve her of her acute embarrassment by bellowing for her lunch.

Elizabeth turned toward the stove. "Letti, would you heat her bottle?"

"I have it ready here, Miss Lizzy," she said, handing it over to her.

After another loud cry, Adeline found the nipple and went to work at easing the hunger pains in her tiny stomach.

Elizabeth glanced up. The moment for closeness and honesty was gone. She knew her mother would not pick it up again, so she didn't bother, either.

"Isn't Thomas in town?" Louise asked haughtily, hoping to climb back on top of the situation once again.

Elizabeth looked down at the baby and then toward the back windows. "Yes," she said quietly. "I think he wants to come by tonight."

"How cozy," Louise drawled. "It will be just you and Thomas and...the baby of a streetwalker. I certainly hope Thomas is an understanding man."

"It really doesn't matter one way or the other."

Louise looked startled. "Liz, surely you are not planning on doing or saying anything stupid.... I mean, you mustn't close doors, if you know what I mean."

Elizabeth regarded her for a long moment. "No, I don't know what you mean."

Louise sighed impatiently. "Have your fling, if you

must, with this street minister. But do not ruin your chances with Thomas Benson. There is no reason for him to know about Mr. Winslow, you know. You needn't look so pious, dear, there is nothing really dishonest about what I'm saying. All you would be doing is keeping your options open. All intelligent women do that, Liz.''

Elizabeth pulled the empty bottle from Adeline's mouth and lifted her up onto her shoulder while she patted her back. These few seconds gave her the time to process what her mother was saying to her, to think about it, weigh it, pass judgment on the statement without passing judgment on her. Finally, she looked back at her.

''Then, Mother, I guess I am just not a very intelligent woman.''

Later that night Elizabeth hovered nervously at Thomas's side, wishing she had some means to buffer him from the shock. ''Are you sure you don't want a drink?''

He dismissed her solicitations with a listless wave. ''No, it's all right.'' He looked once again into the calico basket that lay in front of him on the floor. ''I don't think I want a drink right now.''

''I know all of this is sort of a shock, but...well...''

He glanced up at Elizabeth. ''How long will you be keeping the baby?''

''Probably only until tomorrow. I think Sa—my friend wants me to bring her back to his house tomorrow morning.''

''Where does this friend live?''

''On the near west side of town. I couldn't ignore the child, Thomas. She has no one to care for her right now.''

''She has a mother?''

"Yes, but...she...needed some help for a few days." Elizabeth shifted her attention to the paintings on the wall, hoping the lie by omission would not show on her face.

She was aware that Thomas was watching her closely, scrutinizing the line of her profile, but she did not turn back to him. After a few minutes he stepped up beside her and laid his hand against her waist. "I think you're a very special lady to help out your friend this way." He laughed shortly. "I admit I was taken aback by the sight of a baby in your care, but...well, I admire you for it, Liz."

She hoped her smile didn't look as sick as she felt inside. He admired her now, but what would he think when she told him the whole story about her friend? No doubt his admiration would dwindle somewhat after that.

Unaware of the inner rumblings of her conscience, he pulled her close and murmured against her temple. "I'm so happy to see you again. I've missed you."

"You have been away quite a lot lately," she admitted evasively.

"Yes, but I have remedied that," he said with triumph resplendent in his voice and eyes. He held her at arm's length and grinned down at her. "I have wonderful news. I've found a condominium...finally, and I'll be moving in on Saturday. I picked up several new clients in the city, so it looks like I will be staying here for at least the next year."

Elizabeth knew he was waiting for her reaction, so she tried to muster up an appropriate one. "That's...that is just wonderful, Thomas. I'm very happy for you."

He waited for more, but nothing more was forthcoming. "Happy for me?" he asked, his tone reflecting a slight bewilderment. "I was hoping that you would be happy for you too."

"Oh, Well, I am, Thomas, I really am." She stepped back and his hands fell to his sides. She turned and walked across the room at a leisurely stroll, casually picking up and replacing items on the shelves as she moved. "I've enjoyed your company very much the last few months and—" She turned around and saw the package in his hand. "What is that?"

He was holding it out to her and his smile held a hint of mischievousness. She had never seen him look this way before and it both intrigued and worried her.

"I was planning to save this for Christmas," he said, "but I don't think I can wait that long. I want you to have it now."

She remained rooted to the spot in the room where she had stopped. She stared at the tiny box in his hands, dreading what she already knew was implicit in the gift. She didn't want this from him. Not now. Maybe not ever.

She had hesitated long enough while Thomas held it out to her, so she slowly crossed the room and took the package from his hands. She stared at it for a long moment before she began to unwrap it. She glanced up at him only once, for the unadulterated look of eager anticipation cut through her with sharp-edged pain. The wrapping paper fell to the floor and she lifted the lid on the cardboard box. She pulled out a smaller felt-covered box and opened the hinged lid.

"Merry Christmas, Liz." She heard the low voice beside her, but she could not look up. Tears were forming beneath her lower lids, blurring the vision of the sparkling diamond in its spiraled gold setting. "I would like for you to marry me."

She had never meant to hurt him. That had never been her intention. God, what had she done! She finally forced her eyes to meet his. "Thomas, I don't know what to say."

He saw the tears and wondered if they were tears of happiness. But some vague, fleeting doubt told him that they were not. "Say yes, Liz."

Her gaze dropped to the floor between them and she shook her head. "I wish I could, Thomas, but I can't."

He was silent for several agonizing seconds. "Why?"

She walked over to the couch and sat down, taking one last look at the diamond before she closed the lid and set it on the coffee table in front of her. He hesitated for a moment, then joined her, sitting on the edge of the couch with his wrist resting along its back.

"Thomas, I think you're a wonderful man. I really do. You're handsome and intelligent and fun to be with..." Her voice trailed off into the space between them.

He tried to laugh. "I sound too good to be true. So, what's the problem?"

She looked up at him. "The problem is that I don't think I love you. Not the way I should if I were to marry you. It wouldn't be fair to you."

He moved his hand to her shoulder. "Why don't you let me be the judge of that. I love you, Liz. I want to take care of you."

"I know that. And maybe I'm a fool if I don't let you take care of me. But I have to figure out what I want out of life before I make a step like that. I'm not even sure I know who I am anymore. Everything is so mixed up."

"Everyone goes through these growing pains, Liz. There is nothing unusual about that. Maybe you should get away for a little while, go on a trip, or—"

"There's more to it than that." She clenched her hands in her lap. "I've met another man."

His body went rigid and his thoughts were temporarily suspended in the split seconds of unreality. He wasn't a vain man, but he had assumed that there was no competition from any other man in her life. He obviously had assumed wrong. "I see," he finally said.

"Looking at it from the outside, it's kind of bizarre. He's nothing like you. He doesn't have any money. He doesn't care at all about having a refined life."

"What does he do? I mean for a living?"

Elizabeth took note of the effort he was making to remain calm and rational about all of this and she gave him a small smile of thanks. "He's a preacher on the west side of the city."

"Your friend," he said, but there was dejection in his tone. "The one you're helping out with the baby?"

"Yes. He lives in a very bad section of town, seedy, run-down, crime-ridden. And I don't think he has any intention of leaving it for me or anyone else."

Thomas breathed a quick sigh of relief. As he rapidly synthesized all that she was saying to him, he formed a composite of this man who had captured Elizabeth's interest. Suddenly, he was no longer quite as worried. It was a transition period for her, a phase. Nothing more. She would get over it, and he would wait it out.

"How long have you known him?"

"About two months."

"You never mentioned him before. I didn't realize that all this time I've had competition."

"You have never had competition, Thomas. You are who you are and Sam is a totally different kind of person. It's just that he has made me see things from a different perspective. I even view myself differently now."

"There is nothing wrong with that, Liz. We all need a friend, whether it's a male or a female, to help us see things more clearly. That is very important. And I would never presume to tell you who to be friends with. If we were married, you could see anyone you—"

"I love him, Thomas."

He stared at her, hoping the words would simply disappear in the air, never to be heard again. But they played over and over again in his mind. "Maybe you just think you do," he whispered and cleared his throat several times. "You can love your friends and still—"

"I've been to bed with him." She flinched as she watched the effect of her own words on him.

He pushed from the couch and walked over to the bar, leaning his elbow against it for support. "All this time there has been another man? You've been making love to someone else?"

"Not the whole time," she said. "I only... we...became serious about two weeks ago. I'm sorry, Thomas. I really am. I never meant to hurt you."

He shook his head roughly to dismiss the idea and cast his eyes about the room. "Liz, think about this for a minute! What can this man offer you? What would your life be like with him? Have you thought of these things? Have you?"

"Yes," she answered slowly and carefully. "I have thought about them. I just don't know the answers to them yet. But don't you see?" she pleaded, standing and walking over to him. "I have to try to find them."

His eyes lifted over her head and he sighed. "I suppose you do. But what am I supposed to do in the meantime?"

She cocked her head and regarded him quizzically. "What do you mean?"

With a sudden thrust he reached out and grasped her upper arms, holding her tight in front of him. "Don't you know how much I love you? Don't you understand? I'm willing to wait for you, Elizabeth. I really believe that you will find this man's way of life is not for you. You are going to want to come home. I have a lot of confidence in that belief. And I'm going to wait for you."

Somewhere in the back of her mind she knew she

should tell him not to wait. She should deny the fact that she would ever want out of Sam Winslow's life. She had told her mother only this morning that she was not one of the intelligent ones. She did not care about options or leaving doors open. And yet within her there was a thing too ambiguous and potent to fight, like some disembodied turnkey, that kept the denial locked deep inside of her, caged and fettered, as yet reluctant to set her free.

Chapter Seventeen

"I'll only be a minute, Sam." William O'Conner walked slowly over to the kitchen counter in his tiny efficiency apartment and began the long, intricate process of brewing his Earl Grey tea.

Sam leaned back into the couch and smiled to himself. How many times had he heard that from William? *I'll only be a minute.* Just one short minute, while he brewed tea or finished reading an article or watched the last rays of the sunset grace the lower sky. Was it from this man that he had learned what little patience he had? Along with so many other lessons in life.

For ten years now, William O'Conner had been Sam's mentor, counselor, and confidant. He had served as Chairman of Theology at one of the oldest and most controversial institutions of its kind. Obstinately impudent in its teaching methods and in its doctrines, it was referred to in some of the more astringent theology circles as "Hooligan House." And William O'Conner, as its head, was considered to be a crusty old heretic who was unleashing a pack of undisciplined ruffians into the religious community. To Sam, William was the most brilliant, kind, and reverent individual he had ever known.

"All right," he sighed, sitting down in his soft easy chair across from Sam. All around them in the small room were floor-to-ceiling shelves lined with books and torn-out magazine articles and stacks of bound dissertations. "Now, what seems to be the problem?"

"No problem," Sam said. "I just wanted to visit with you."

William peered over the tops of his glasses at him. "The last time you came all the way down to Hyde Park to see me was in March. Nine months ago. Let me see, at the time you wanted to discuss the position of that friend of yours... what was his name?"

"Jackson."

"Yes, that was it. Noel Jackson. Uh-huh. And now you have come back... nine months later... to visit." Once again he stabbed Sam with his piercing gaze. "Now why don't you just get on with it, tell me what the problem is, and save yourself a great deal of misery."

Sam's laugh was self-mocking. "Is it that obvious?"

William took a drink of his tea and closed his eyes as the liquid flowed down his throat. "You forget, I knew you when..." He paused and regarded him carefully. "When you looked about the same way you do now. When you first came back from India, you were a very troubled young man. Angry, bitter, full of self-doubts. You have come a long way from that same young man. But your general posture now tells me that perhaps distance in terms of self-growth is more of an abstract wish than a realistic, reachable goal, and also more mercurial than we might like. So, I'm waiting. What is it?"

"I've met a woman."

"Such is the fate of man."

He regarded William with a pensive smile. "This one is different."

"Different from what or whom?"

He shook his head and laughed. "You are not making this any easier, you know."

"If I taught you nothing else, Sam, I hope it was to

make yourself understood, to say what you mean, and to stop using these artfully euphemistic expressions that say absolutely nothing.''

"What I'm trying to say, William, is that I love her. I'm actually like a lovesick hound. I think about her constantly, shirk some of my responsibilities so that I can be with her...God, you'd think I was seventeen instead of thirty-five!" He rose from the couch and started pacing the room like a caged animal. He stopped after several minutes to lean against the windowsill and look out over Jackson Park in the distance.

After a few minutes he spoke again, but he did not turn away from the window. "The problem is that I know inside that she could never adjust to my way of life, and I don't know whether I can give up mine for hers. She has money, social prestige, an existence so far removed from what I am doing that it's almost unbelievable that we were ever even attracted to each other. I'm not sure I should take her from the life she has lived for thirty years and that is so indelibly imprinted in her genes. But, at the same time, I simply can't let her go.''

He breathed deeply and massaged the back of his neck, then turned back to William, who was still sipping his tea and watching Sam with his steady gaze. "I'm walking a tightrope. I don't know what in the hell I want anymore. I want Elizabeth, and it scares me to want her that much. How far do I go? How much do I give and still keep a sense of direction? Tell me what to do, William!"

"Sit down, Sam." William rose and walked into the kitchen to pour himself another cup of tea, giving Sam enough time to collect himself and relax once again into the couch. When he resettled himself in his own chair, he spoke. "Let me ask you something, Sam. Why do you stay in that neighborhood? For what reason do you do the things you are now doing?"

"I like to take care of people."

"Yes," William mused, nodding his head slowly. "I suppose it is easier to take care of other people's emptiness than to take care of your own."

Sam was silent for a long minute while he tried to decide whether to ignore that remark or not. "I need to give."

William scoffed at that. "Why? The world is full of takers. Why should you not be one of them? Why should you be any different?"

"I think I'm afraid of complacency."

"Why? What could be more easy or enjoyable than a complacent life?"

"You lose too much when you become complacent," he argued. "People are taken away from you, things that matter are lost."

"Oh, I see. And when you give and care and fight for all of these just causes, you don't lose anything? Is that what you're saying? Since you've been working on Blackhawk Street, you haven't lost people or things that are important to you?"

Sam leaned his head back and closed his eyes, thinking of Daniel, of Chaco, of the countless people and causes that had simply slipped through his fingers no matter how tightly he clutched on to them, no matter how much he cared. "Yeah, I've lost a lot. But I guess the difference is that when you give your all and still lose those who mean so much to you, you can't blame yourself."

"Ah, so that is what it all comes down to in the end, isn't it, Sam? That is what you have been doing for so many years. Blaming yourself."

"For what?"

William studied him carefully. "For your brother's death."

His face froze and his eyes did not waver from William's.

"So now," William continued, "you've taken on the world's burden of care and you will never be found guilty again. You still feel like a man who has been tried and convicted, don't you?"

"No!" Sam shouted, glaring at the older man across from him. His gaze dropped to the floor. "Sometimes." He sighed heavily. "But, dammit, William, it's more than that. What I feel is more than guilt. I know it is!"

William considered the statement and the man for several long seconds, then nodded. "I wouldn't have wasted my time and energy on you all these years if I didn't believe that. And I also know that a lesser man would have rationalized away his guilt a long time ago."

"Then why did you ask me if that was my only motivation?"

"Because you need to face it, Sam. It is still with you, just like it was when I first met you after you came back from India. You have to know it is there, face it, and put it in its proper perspective. That's all. Just don't hide the truth from yourself."

Sam stared at his fists clenched so tightly on his knees. "You're right about that, I know. Jonas is with me every day. I still have a long way to go. But assuaging my own personal guilt doesn't help me with Elizabeth Parkins. I still don't know what I should do."

"Maybe you should let yourself care about this woman for a while and care about yourself too. You have given so much, Sam. More than most people ever do. Maybe it is time to step back and give something to yourself."

"But there's still so much more that I want to do. Don't you see? There is more that has to be done."

William took a drink of his tea and let the moment settle slowly upon him. "Then I would say, Sam, that you have answered your own question."

A half hour later Sam walked down the stairs of the

train platform, zipped up his leather jacket, and raised
the collar to cover his neck against the cold wind. He
still had an hour before he was to be at the hospital, so
he decided to walk for a while. With his hands buried in
the pockets of his jacket, he strolled up one street and
down another, covering a six-block area that surrounded Blackhawk, past the high school, turning the corner
at Immaculate Virgin Catholic Church, following the
block that contained a languishing government-
subsidized housing development known only as "the
project," across a small park where the loose sections of
a newspaper were held by the wind against the rusted
poles of some playground equipment, past the 16th in-
fantry division armory building, then along the Turning
Basin for the Chicago River, and then back to Blackhawk.

The walk took almost an hour, and in that time he
came to the conclusion that William was right. It was
there all the time and he had answered his own question.
There was still so much to do here and he could not walk
away from it. Not just yet. He had the drug rehabilitation meetings, the YES program, the hospital, the old
people who counted on him for food. So many projects
and programs and friends to help. Mary's problem had
been solved, at least temporarily, when he sent her to
some friends in Gary. But out of all the things he'd
started, there were very few that were finished, wrapped
up neatly where he could say yes, I've done it, now I can
move on. There was still too much that he needed to do
here. It was more than guilt, more than self-righteous
absolution of his own built-in complacency. This was
what he wanted to do, and this was where he would
stay.

As he rounded the corner to walk the last block to the
hospital, he realized with a sense of clarity that the
problem was probably not going to disappear that easily.

He suspected that the next time he saw Elizabeth, the next time he touched her and watched her smile, he would once again be lost. All of this wonderful, new-found sense of direction would slip away and he would have to start all over again at square one.

Elizabeth took the last of the shiny balls from the box and, standing on tiptoe, hung it up high on the tree, then stepped back to admire her handiwork. Every year she followed the same rituals of decorating her house for Christmas, although she rarely spent much time in the house during this season. She was always at parties, or at the club, or vacationing with friends. But this year would be different. Tonight Sam was coming up here to be with her, and she wanted everything to look absolutely perfect.

The tree was alive with color and lights and on the mantel above the fireplace were four fat red candles with holly and pine cones and garland draped around them. As she was closing up the boxes of decorations and setting them aside for Letti to put back in the closet where they belonged, the doorbell rang.

She glanced up with surprise as Suzanne Elliston walked into the den. "Hi, Suzanne! I thought you had already left for New York or Hollywood or wherever it is you're off to now." She stood and greeted her friend with a hug.

"Are you kidding! Without saying good-bye to you? And besides, I don't leave for a couple of hours, so I wanted to come by and drop off something for you."

"Aren't you sweet!" Elizabeth smiled and clapped her hands together with delight. "Christmas is such fun! And I have something for you too. Let me run get it."

"Okay." Suzanne set the package on the couch and walked over to the tree to examine a couple of carved wooden ornaments. "Must have been all that strict upbringing when I was a kid,'' she explained when Elizabeth came back into the room. "But now that I'm an adult, I can't go near a Christmas tree without touching everything on it."

Elizabeth laughed. "Go ahead and touch. That's part of Christmas. I have a friend who puts her tree in a playpen so her little kid can't get to it. Can you imagine that? A Christmas tree in a playpen!''

"Why doesn't she just put the kid in the pen instead?''

"Beats me. I get the impression she has read too many of those parenting books for her own good. The little boy is only four, but he already looks and acts like he's going to be a terrorist when he grows up."

"There may be a story in there somewhere,'' Suzanne mused. "But I think I'd better store it away in my mental file for a while. I've got too much else going on. Is that for me?''

"It most certainly is.'' Elizabeth smiled and held out a package to her. "You open yours first."

"Gladly. I always throw a tantrum if I don't get to go first.'' Suzanne tore into the bright wrapping paper and flipped the lid off the top of the box. Inside were two pewter beer mugs. "Great!'' she cried. "I'll use these every day, you can rest assured."

"Spoken like a true beer guzzler." Elizabeth laughed. "Now, I get to open mine."

"Right,'' Suzanne said, but her smile became almost wistful.

Elizabeth carefully peeled away the wrapping paper. "It's so big!'' She lifted the lid on the box and folded back the tissue paper, then pulled out a dull olive green flight jacket. She looked it over carefully, then glanced with a quizzical expression back at Suzanne.

"I know it's not exactly haute couture, but... well, hell, Elizabeth, I'm going to go all serious on you for a minute." She reached out and touched the jacket reverently. "This belonged to my father. He was an aviator in World War Two. From information I learned from my mother and from some of his wartime buddies, his division was involved in some island-hopping operations in the Pacific, where they were trying to force the retreat of Japanese forces. The enemy had been doing some pretty heavy artillery shelling on the allied land forces and the troops were going to be overrun if my father's division didn't go in and bomb the Japanese artillery positions.

"He was leading the mission and they were taking lots of fire from below. Several planes had already gone down, and my father had to make the decision to cancel the mission. He radioed back to the other pilots, ordering them to return to the base. But he didn't turn back. He flew on in, trying for a direct hit on the artillery line. He hit it but, in the process, his plane was hit too. He bailed out at the last minute before the plane crashed, but...it was too late. He was killed."

Suzanne sat on the arm of the chair and stared at the jacket in Elizabeth's hands. "I never knew my father. I was only one year old when he flew that final mission. His act of heroism saved thousands of lives and helped the allies' position. His courage paid off. He received, posthumously, a Congressional Medal, and this jacket was sent home, with some of his other effects, to my mother."

She looked up at Elizabeth and smiled. "The point of this long, dramatic tale is not that you should become a kamikaze pilot. But this jacket has always meant something special to me. It symbolizes not only my father's bravery and heroism, but it symbolizes courage in general. Whenever I have been particularly afraid to tackle something new, I've worn it. When I decided to write my first novel, I had no encouragement from anyone but myself, so I wore this jacket every day when I sat at the typewriter, and then I wore it again to the Post Office when I mailed off the manuscript. And there have been other times, equally as important, when I have used it to give me the courage that I didn't think I had. I know you have some big decisions ahead of you and I think you could use a little of that courage right now."

Elizabeth glanced down at the jacket, then back to her. "But, Suzanne, I can't take something that means so much to you. It was your father's and it has—"

She laid her hand on Elizabeth's arm. "I want you to have it. I want you to have the courage to do what's best for you. I like you a lot and I want you to have the best life possible. Please take it and wear it if it will help you make the right choices."

"I don't know what to say, Suzanne. I have. . . well, I've never had a friend like you before." A small smile lifted the corners of her mouth. "I'm not sure I deserve you."

Suzanne closed the gap between them and gave her a quick hug. "Go get 'em, kid. Give 'em hell." Then she picked up her box with the beer mugs and walked toward the door. "Have a great Christmas," she called back from the doorway. "I'll call or write in January."

"Okay. You have a wonderful Christmas too and sell a million copies of your new book." Elizabeth watched her go, then held the jacket up in front of her. She slipped her arms into the sleeves and adjusted it in front. She sat down on the couch and wrapped her arms around her torso, holding it closed around her. Courage? Is that what it would take to be with Sam? She had thought that love would be enough, but maybe Suzanne knew more than she did. Maybe it would take much, much more.

That evening she took the first step in finding out

what it would take to be with him. The logs made a loud popping sound and sparks of fire shot up toward the chimney. Sam and Elizabeth were sitting on the rug in front of the couch, watching the blaze. Each held a glass of red wine, and a full bottle was on the table in front of them. The only light in the room came from the firelight reflecting off the colorful bulbs on the Christmas tree.

Sam looked down and admired his Christmas present again. "I love my watch." He played with the complex set of buttons on it, checking the time in Paris and Cairo and Sri Lanka. "The only problem is now I don't have any excuse to be late for appointments."

"Unless you mistake London time for Chicago time."

"True," he said, pushing a couple more buttons to try and get it back to central time, U.S.A. "Guess I'll have to watch that. Do you like your photograph?"

She glanced at the framed picture of an empty Chicago street in the early hours of morning, when a faint mist still hung in the air. "I love it, Sam. Your friend does beautiful work."

They were both quiet for a few moments as they watched the fire. Sam leaned over and picked up the check from the coffee table. "This...this is the best present of all." He looked at her. "You are really something, you know that?"

She smiled and looked down at her glass. "Will the hospital be able to buy enough with that?"

"This will pay for a dialysis machine, toys for the children's wing, probably much more."

"I still want us to do some more painting in some of the other wings, okay?"

"We will. We'll do it together." She laid her hand in his and they both leaned back and watched the fire for several more minutes.

He set his glass on the table and laid his arm along the

couch behind her. "Earlier tonight you were awfully quiet. Is everything okay?"

She took a sip of wine, then held the glass between her clasped hands. She nodded. "I've just been thinking about...things."

"What kinds of things?"

Her smile was impish. "Like what I'm going to do with you."

He returned the same playful smile. "Is that right? And what, may I ask, have you decided?"

"Well, for one thing, I think you've been living alone for too long. You're getting too set in your bachelor ways. I think you need some company, some female company."

"Hmmm." He smiled. "Interesting proposition. I think you may be right."

"So what would you think if I were to come visit you for a week or so?"

His hand moved to the back of her head and his fingers grasped a handful of hair. "Nice," he said, guiding her face toward his.

"Only nice?" Her breath caught and her pulse accelerated with every inch their mouths moved closer. "You can kick me out anytime you—"

His mouth clamped down on hers in one swooping descent of raw hunger, an eagle capturing and devouring its prey. The wineglass was lifted from her hands and set on the table in front of them, and he lowered her to the soft pile of the rug. He moved one leg over her and held her face between his hands as her fingers wove through his hair. His heart was pounding in unison with hers and he urged her thighs apart with his knee. But suddenly, he stopped, his face only inches above her, his breath quick and warm against her mouth, his eyes closed.

"Sam? What is it?"

His eyes remained closed and she watched him start to speak several times before the words actually came. "We have to talk, Elizabeth."

"Okay," she whispered. Her hands moved from his hair to his shoulders, and after a minute he opened his eyes and looked down at her.

His thumb stroked the high plane of her cheek. "What about Thomas Benson?"

"I've already told him about you."

He watched her carefully, looking for the truth, hoping that it was there in her eyes and in her voice. "And?"

"He was very understanding."

A slight frown creased Sam's brow. "What exactly did you tell him?"

"I told him that I had been to bed with you." Her fingers began kneading the material of his shirt at the shoulders. "And that I love you." She felt the tensing beneath her hands as he watched her.

He rested his weight upon his elbow and ran his fingers across her face, stroking her lips, caressing her brow, brushing aside a stray lock of hair. "You told him that?" he asked, his voice full of wonder.

"Yes."

"And he was understanding?"

She paused, wondering if she should mention what Thomas said about waiting for her. But there would be no point in that, would there? What purpose could it possibly serve? She wouldn't even bring it up. "Yes, he was understanding."

The thumb that traced the outline of her lips was replaced by his mouth, a slow kiss that drank in all of the gifts that she was giving him in this moment. His mouth touched her cheek and her nose, then dipped down to her ear. "What about your mother and grandmother?"

She tilted her head upward, giving his warm, insistent mouth access to her neck. "It's my life, Sam."

He lifted up to look at her. "But do you have any idea what you might be getting into? What kind of life it would be?"

"That's what I have to find out."

"Yeah, both of us, I guess."

"Are you sure you want me?" she asked.

He lifted his face upward toward the ceiling and closed his eyes. "It's not a question of whether I want you." He looked back down at her. "It's a question of whether I can have you. Of whether it will work."

She lifted her fingers to his temples and let them follow the curves and angles of his face. Her voice was a whispering rush of wind through his mind, stirring up all the needs and hopes he had for them. "I thought you had all the answers, Sam Winslow."

His chuckle held little laughter. He shook his head solemnly. "I don't even understand half of the questions."

She watched him for a long moment while her fingers trailed down his neck and onto his shirt. "Well, how about this one?" She shifted her body beneath him and smiled coyly. "And this one?" She unbuttoned the top button of his shirt and her mouth trailed across his chest. "And this?"

His breath was no more than a short burst. Slowly he lowered himself, pressing into her, holding her beneath him as he lowered his mouth to hers. "That one I think I can answer."

Chapter Eighteen

"I still don't like it, Elizabeth. I don't like it at all."

"Sam, would you relax. Everything is going to be fine. Is this where I sit?"

He dusted off the chair for her and she sat down behind the desk. "You don't know what you're getting into," he said, frowning.

"You are a worrywart. I told you, I've worked with juvenile offenders before."

"But not like these. There are other things you could do here in the neighborhood. There are elderly shut-ins you could visit. You could help at the mission."

"I can do those things too, Sam. You said this would only take about twenty hours a week. Now what time does the meeting start?"

He shook his head. Damn, but she was a determined woman. They had been arguing about this all weekend. She insisted that she wanted to work in the YES office and nothing he said would deter her enthusiasm. "The volunteers should be here any minute." He leaned over her. "Did you know you are the stubbornest woman this side of the Great Lakes?"

"I could comment on that"—she smiled—"but I won't." She had won this round and she didn't want to press her luck. Sam Winslow had his own strong-willed, stubborn streak, and she didn't want to see it exercised over her. "So," she said, adding brisk efficiency to her tone. "All I do is answer the phone, field questions, talk to the parole officers, schedule counseling sessions, type a few letters, right?"

"Right. And also make sure this outside door is locked tightly each night. The clinic keeps medicine and some petty cash in that part of the office over there."

She snapped her fingers. "Piece of cake."

She was saved from his reply when one of the student counselors came through the door into the office for the meeting. Only four of the eight volunteers made it on time. The others were at least a half hour late.

Sam's opening remarks to the group were cool and to the point. "We're lucky the clinic is providing this space in their building for us to use for this program. Now the most important thing is for everyone to be on time for their counseling sessions. If we don't show these kids that we can be responsible, how can we expect them to be responsible? I know everyone has tight schedules, but if you're going to work here, you've got to be on time."

While he talked Elizabeth looked around at the volunteers and saw the respect in their eyes. They knew that as far as this project went, he was the boss and that what he said was law, but they also realized that he was a fair man, and any suggestions or comments they had would be considered important.

"Now, I know all of you have taken lots of sociology and psychology courses," he said. "But so have I. And most of what I've learned has not been in the classroom. It's been right here on the street. I know some of you won't agree with me on all my theories, and that's okay. I'd worry if you agreed blindly with everything I said. But I'm going to air my opinion anyway. The way I see it is that these kids we're going to work with cannot function normally in a society that is competitive and that strains their abilities to make decisions each and every day. So our major task is to help them learn how to cope in this aggressive society without being overly aggressive themselves. They made the conscious choice to commit a crime, and we have to help them learn how to make the right choices from now on.''

"That's ridiculous," one young man blurted out. "Conscious choice...that's absurd! Their environment controlled their destiny from the moment they were born. They had no choice but to commit the crimes they did. Our job, as I see it, is to ride herd over these kids until their parole period is over so that they're not sent to prison and thus punished more for their only crime— that being that they are poor.''

A girl in a pink leather jacket sat up straight and spoke loudly. "Everyone who walks through this door is responsible for his or her actions. You won't do these offenders any good if you justify their behavior with one of your bleeding-heart, left-wing maxims.''

"Yeah?" the young man countered. "What the hell do you know about it? You grew up in your pasty-faced, hoity-toity neighborhood and you have no idea what the real world is like.''

"All right, you guys." Sam stood to intervene. "This isn't really meant to be a discussion of our philosophies. This is a meeting to set certain standards for the YES program. And since I'm in charge of the project here..." He grinned to show that he didn't take himself as seriously as he sounded. "I feel I should lay down a few guidelines. Regardless of your own personal feelings about free will or not, I want these kids to come away with a feeling that they do have control, that they can change their situation if they want. This is to be a positive experience for them. If it is for you too, that's great. But first priority are the kids. This is their program. It's for them, not us. So, let's just make sure that they know that and that they benefit from it in a positive way. Any questions?''

"How do we know what our schedules are to be?" someone asked.

"That's what Elizabeth is here for. She will let each of you know when your sessions are to be. If you have any questions or problems, call and talk to her."

Both Sam and Elizabeth were aware of the curious and somewhat suspect looks she received. She was too old and well dressed to be a student and she was far too glamorous to live in this neighborhood. Only the two volunteers who had seen her at Sam's house knew that she was here only because of her relationship with him.

Sam gave her a reassuring nod and concluded. "Now, unless somebody has something else to discuss, I think we'll wrap this up."

As soon as the students left the building Elizabeth went over to her desk and ran her hand across the wood surface. A sense of excitement and accomplishment surged through her. She had volunteered for hundreds of projects and served as chairman of many committees. But never before had she been involved in a project that was not based on societal standing or how much money a person donated. YES was going to be carried out on a shoestring budget from the meager funds of the Council of Churches and was based on nothing more than dedication and hard work.

It was a surprisingly good feeling.

That evening Elizabeth was bending over, checking the progress of the food in the oven, and she didn't hear Sam come into the house. When his arms closed around her from behind, she jumped and let out a small scream.

"Sam, what are you doing? You scared me half to death!"

Still holding her from behind, he kissed the back of her neck. "Couldn't resist. Such an inviting position."

She leaned back against him while his hands moved across the front of her body. "It's going to burn," she said, but there was no concern in her voice. She closed her eyes and thought of nothing but the feel of his hands as they moved.

"It smells delicious," he whispered against her neck. "What is it?"

"What is what?"

"In the oven."

She opened her arms and reluctantly pulled away, grabbing the potholder off the counter. *"Coq au vin."* She bent over once again and lifted the dish from the oven.

Behind her, Sam slipped on his baseball cap and washed his hands at the sink. "Sounds great, whatever it is."

"Why don't you make a salad," she suggested. "Hey, you didn't tell me what you thought."

"About what?"

"Didn't you notice anything different in the house?"

He looked around. "Hmmm, different. No, I don't think so."

She huffed loudly. How could he not have noticed? She stared at him for a moment until she saw the gleam in his eyes. "You devil! You saw those new curtains I put up."

Sam tossed the towel on the counter, pulled her up next to him, then lifted her to the counter and slipped his cap on her head. He stood between the spread of her legs with his hands on each side of her. "Shhh. You're going to have to watch what you call a preacher, woman."

"Devil, devil, devil. You are, you know." She looped her hands around the back of his neck. "Aren't you even going to tell me what you think about them?"

"The curtains?"

She huffed again. "Yes, the curtains."

He glanced through the doorway at the living room

windows. "Very nice. But don't start putting up anything too fancy. I don't want it to look like I run a bor-
dello."

"Those are perfectly tasteful curtains and you know
it. And I have lots of other ideas in mind for the
house."

He shook his head and moved in closer, lifting the
hem of her sweater up. His mouth lowered to her breast,
making it perfectly clear what ideas he had in mind for
her.

"The *coq au vin* is going to get cold," she whispered,
closing her eyes as she bent her head over him.

She felt the curve of his lips as he smiled against her.
"Doggone it," he breathed into her skin and her fingers
clamped more tightly around the back of his head.

The next morning she had settled into her work at the
clinic and at noon, when Sam walked up to her desk, she
was hard at work typing a letter with her two index fingers. "How am I doing?"

"Beautiful." He sat on the edge of the desk and lightly pulled a strand of her hair. "Boy, do you brighten up
this place! And, I might add, my entire day."

She stood up and draped her arms around his neck.
The past few days with him had been almost too good to
be true. There was an easy sensuality between them, a
familiarity and, at the same time, a constant undercurrent of sexual tension. Even now the feel of his neck beneath her hand and the slight upward curve of his
mouth sent a hot spark shooting through her.

He rested his hands on her waist and pulled her close,
grinning as he held her imprisoned within his arms.
"You had better stop me before I get carried away."

"I'd rather not," she breathed lazily.

"How much more work do you have to do here?"

"Quite a bit, actually. Maybe I'll come back this

afternoon and finish up. I have a luncheon engagement with some friends.''

He contemplated her expression and the statement for a minute, then expelled an uneven breath. ''I see.''

''It's with Adrienne and Jennifer and Paula. We meet every first Monday of the month for lunch and have for the past three years. You don't mind, do you?'' She anxiously searched the veil that had dropped over his eyes. ''You're not angry, are you?''

He shook his head. ''Angry? No.'' He cleared his throat and stood up, slipping on his jacket. ''What time are you going?''

She glanced at her watch and grimaced. ''Now. I'm going to be late as it is. Since I left my car in Winnetka, I guess I'll have to take the train.''

He chuckled at her indignant tone. ''Gosh, but life is tough.''

''Don't you make fun of me,'' she warned with a laugh. ''I have no idea where to get off of the damn thing. I might end up in Calumet City.''

He wrapped his arm around her shoulder. ''You'll do fine. Where are you going to eat?''

''Water Tower Place.''

''Okay. Get off at the Lake Street stop. Take a bus or subway to—''

''I think I'll take a cab from there.''

''Okay, but the buses are really easy to—''

''No, I'll take a taxi.''

He paused, watching her closely. ''Sure.'' He helped her with her coat and walked her to the door. ''Guess I'll see you at home this evening.''

She turned and wrapped her woolen arms around his waist, laying her head against his chest. ''That has such a nice sound to it, doesn't it?''

His arms came around her back. ''It certainly does.'' He kissed the top of her head, then held the door for her as she hurried out into the cold January air, leaving Blackhawk for Water Tower Place, leaving his life for her own. He breathed in the cold air and looked up at the sky. He had known this was the way it would be—known there would be compromise and adjustments. But it was worth the risk. And he had known. Hadn't he?

"I just don't understand, Liz! What on earth has happened to you?" Jennifer cried. "We're all so worried about you!"

"Nothing has happened to me," Elizabeth answered haughtily. She considered all three women at the table with her. Adrienne in a canary-yellow sweat shirt, miniskirt, and L.L. Bean hiking shoes; Paula Ayers wearing her green egg-shaped glasses and silk shirtwaist; and Jennifer in a tailored Norell suit, as always. They were all gawking at her as if she had lost her mind.

"But who is this guy you're living with?" Paula asked. "We have heard so many stories, I don't know what to believe."

"His name is Sam Winslow. He's a minister. He—"

"A minister!" they all cried, and Adrienne's expression quickly changed to one of sudden comprehension and amazement.

"You don't mean. . .not the. . .surely not, Liz. . .the minister who gave us the tour of that awful west side hospital!" Her voice was incredulous.

"Yes." Elizabeth's chin tilted higher, daring her to say anything more. Surprisingly, Adrienne became unusually quiet and sat back in her chair, watching her friend with newfound interest.

"Why are you living with him, Liz?" Jennifer asked.

She stared at the three women as if they were all daft. Didn't they get it? Didn't they understand anything? "Because," she said, "I love him."

The baffled look that was exchanged between the three women at the table was the only comment she received.

Three hours later she zipped up her fox fur jacket and stepped off the train onto the platform. The wind was not quite as fierce here as it was downtown near the lake. But it was still a very cold day. She shivered and hurried down the stairs to start the five-block walk to Sam's house.

She had gone a block and was crossing the alley between the Second Hand Rose thrift shop and a Mexican café, when a tall shadow fell across her path. Her eyes lifted and locked with those of Stripes while her peripheral vision included four of his loyal disciples.

"Hey, hey," he said, strutting around her with a heavier than normal Chicano accent and his typically superior swagger. "If it isn't our newest angel of mercy."

Elizabeth tensed and remained silent as she took in the hostile glares from each pair of eyes that was directed toward her. The hot greasy smell from the café drifted out onto the sidewalk and she felt a quick spasm of nausea. But whether from the smell of the food or from fear, she didn't know.

Stripes reached out to finger the luxurious gray-blue fur collar on her jacket.

"How much you suppose that coat is worth to her?" one of the boys asked.

"Hey, Angelina! *Esa chaqueta para su vida, no?*"

Her eyes flashed from one to the other. "What did he say?" she demanded of Stripes.

He grinned menacingly. "He said, 'That jacket for your life.' "

She swallowed a lump of fear. "You have jackets," she huffed indignantly. "Filthy as they are. And you have no right to talk to me this way."

"Whooo!" He laughed mockingly. "A little righteous indignation she shows. Tough, lady, very tough."

"Look who thinks he's tough," she countered. "I know all about you and you're nothing but a coward."

A slim space of silence opened and sparked between them. Then the angry rumblings of his apprentices demanded that he do something about her, that he not let the insult pass.

Stripes stared at her for a long moment, debating the best course of action. If it were anyone else, he would have cut her up in a minute. But he knew who this one was and who she belonged to. And he wasn't sure that teaching this broad a lesson would be worth Sam Winslow's revenge. Maybe some other day.

Elizabeth backed against the brick wall of the café as Stripes hovered over her with an expression full of hate and thwarted vengeance. "You throw any more of that rich-bitch *mierda* at me, gringa, and you won't live very long here. Now, me and my friends here are stopping to pass the time of day with you, and you are going to show a little respect."

"Right!" his followers cried in support. *"Respeto!"*

The memory of the knife that had flashed in his hand once before filled her mind with terror. She saw the look of violence and the need for power mirrored in each boy's face, and she knew this was not something she could fight.

She swallowed hard and nodded slowly, aware immediately of the victorious light that flared in Stripes's eyes. He had won. And that was all that mattered to him. His power and the respect of his peers was intact. He had saved face.

He leaned closer, his face only inches from hers as he gave her one last warning glare. "Don't forget it next time, gringa." He pushed away from the wall and seconds later they were gone.

Elizabeth's hands were flattened against the brick wall and she didn't move. She tried desperately to find her breath, but the smell of grease from the café filled her lungs. A huge lump of fear was lodged in her throat and her vision was blocked by a thick film of tears.

After a minute she sniffed, dabbing her nose with the back of her shaking hand, and stood straighter, determined to pull herself together. They were gone. They did not hurt her. They didn't even take her jacket. She sniffed again and wiped the corners of her eyes. She was all right.

With one last wary glance around her she started walking, moving almost mechanically in the most direct route possible toward the house. But as she drew nearer her quick steps slowed. She didn't want Sam to see her this upset. She wasn't sure he should even know about what happened. What if he went after Stripes? What if, in the process, he was seriously hurt? And after all, they had only scared her. They did no physical harm, so it was logical to assume that they would not hurt her any other time either. But if they knew that she told Sam, they might not be so lenient.

She took a deep breath and expelled it slowly. No, she was not going to tell him. It would only cause more problems, add more strain, and she was afraid to see how much tension this relationship could withstand. Despite the love and easy familiarity, they both felt the vast differences that yawned like a deep chasm between them. They were walking a thin, tight line across it as it was. One hard tug in the wrong direction might break the fragile bond that held them together. That was a gamble she did not want to take.

Sam leaned forward in the chair and rested his forearms on his knees, his hands clasped in front of him. "Why do you think you reacted that way, Blanco?"

"What the hell was I supposed to do, man, just let him walk away?"

Sam regarded the young man for a minute, aware that all of the others in the room were waiting to hear what he had to say. "What would be so wrong with that? What would be wrong with just letting him walk away? So he insulted your sister. You know inside that what he said isn't true. So who gives a damn what he thinks? It's what you know and think that matters."

"He would have looked like a wimp," one of the other boys said.

"Maybe the guy just wanted to get a reaction out of you," Sam suggested. "And you played right into his hands. If you had ignored him, he would have gotten no satisfaction at all."

Blanco shrugged with disinterest.

"And tell me this," he continued. "If you hadn't been taking quaaludes at the time, would you have gone after him with that lead pipe?"

Blanco snorted disdainfully. "That's what you just don't get, man. The 'ludes, the meth, the downers and uppers...makes no difference. I ain't ever gonna stop, 'cause it ain't no big deal. Every judge in the county can send me here time and time again for these bullshit sessions, but it ain't gonna make no damn difference!"

Sam contemplated the boy, who thrived from sunup to sundown on amphetamines and hallucinogens and barbiturates, and he hoped Blanco wasn't right about the sessions making no difference. He had only been coming to the meetings for about two months and he still had five months to go on his sentence. Surely, in the time remaining, something would get through to him. Sam's deeply embedded optimism told him that he would somehow get through to the boy. He would have to.

"I think the problem with the preach is that he's gone all soft on us since his squeeze came back."

Sam's gaze swept around the tittering circle. "You think so?"

"Soft!" one of the boys snickered. "Are you kidding? With that broad around you think he's gonna go soft?"

"Real funny, guys. Now, let's get on with the session."

"I want to ask a question first," Raul said.

"Okay."

"What is it you see in that chick, preach? Is it her money?"

"Money!" Johnny Johnson interrupted with a laugh. "It's her body, you ass."

Sam's smile was strained but tolerant. "I happen to love her."

The room exploded with hoots of laughter, and he could do nothing but wait it out. How could he expect these kids to be comfortable with the word *love* when they had never known it before?

"I also like her very much," he added when the laughter finally died down. "She's a very special person."

"What's so special about her except for her money? She's loaded, isn't she?"

"Money has nothing to do with it."

"Well, I don't like her," Blanco challenged. "I don't like any of those rich whores. And I don't think she belongs here."

Sam stared long and hard at him. He knew what the boy was doing. He was trying to get him riled, trying to see if his theory of letting someone walk away was all talk or if he really meant it.

He shifted his gaze to encompass all of the boys in the room. "I want to get something straight with you guys. I have a personal life. And that personal life is not going to be up for open discussion every Friday night. If you have a pertinent question you want to ask, that's fine. But I won't put up with insults or slurs about my personal affairs. And as for Elizabeth Parkins, it doesn't really matter to me if you like her or not, or if you think she belongs here or not. What it boils down to is this: If you accept me, you have to accept her. That's the bottom line. Now, are there any more pertinent questions? Rooster, you got something you want to say?''

"My old lady and man was talking the other night and they said you're a sinner."

"Is that right?"

"Yeah, 'cause you're living with whatsername."

"Elizabeth."

"Yeah, her."

"Well, I'm sorry they feel that way about it."

"You gonna marry the broad? I mean, Elizabeth?"

"If and when the time is right."

"So for now, you're just gonna go right on sinnin'?"

Sam thought of how Elizabeth looked this morning when she first woke up, fresh and seductive, the way her fingers felt against his bare chest and then her lips as they followed the line of her hands, her smile so innocent yet so knowing.

Sam looked back at Rooster and took a deep breath before he answered. "Yep. Right on sinning."

It was cold as he walked back to the house, and he hunched down into his heavy jacket and kept the collar raised against the back of his neck.

A light was on in the living room as he walked up the sidewalk to his house, and the warmth of it flowed like a welcoming current through his bloodstream. He hurried up the steps, careful to avoid the danger zone, and used his key in the front door.

All was quiet, but a fire still burned in the grate. "Elizabeth?" he called softly but was not answered.

He walked into the living room and found her asleep

in his big easy chair. She was curled up in it, her feet covered by long woolen gray-striped socks, her body wrapped in a pink floor-length terry cloth robe. On the floor beside her was the bound copy of his Ph.D. dissertation. He chuckled silently. No wonder she was asleep. No doubt it had bored her as much to read it as it had him to write it.

He knelt down beside her and rested his elbows on the arm of the chair, watching her sleep. He remembered the day she had come here to talk about her friend Adrienne. He had watched her curve her feet up into this very chair, had wanted to run his hand up the length of her suede pants. And now she was here, asleep in his chair, a hint of thigh exposed behind the veil of robe.

His thoughts slipped back to a couple of days ago when they had taken the train downtown and had gone for a long walk along the peninsula toward Adler Planetarium, visiting the Field Museum and Shedd Aquarium. He remembered the way the cold air heightened the color of her skin as they stood on the boulders at the water's edge and looked back at the view of the city across the breakwater. He had opened his coat and, shivering, she slipped her arms around his waist and huddled close for warmth. After visiting all the museums, they sat for a long while on the rocks and watched the huge cargo ships that skimmed across the horizon. The day, the woman, the feelings he had for her. It was a day that would remain with him forever.

He smiled as he watched her sleeping so peacefully in the chair. It was still so hard to believe she was actually here, living with him, sleeping with him every night, eating breakfast with him in the mornings. He had seen too much over the years to believe that life could suddenly become a bed of roses, but this woman made it very easy to believe in almost anything. Miracles really did seem to exist.

Her eyes fluttered open and she started to jump when she saw the figure that knelt beside her. But the reassuring warmth of his hand upon her thigh quickly subdued the impulse to run. She smiled sleepily, and he leaned over to kiss her warm mouth. Her hand lifted to the back of his head, holding the heat of his mouth against her own. "It's been such a long day without you," she murmured against his face, sliding her lips back to his. "When are you going to take me to bed?"

His low moan was the only response she received before he once again claimed her mouth with his own. With one hand under her arms and the other behind her knees, he lifted her in his arms and carried her up the stairs to the small bed they shared.

In his arms she was ever new, always fresh, like the very first time. The thrill came from her hands where they touched him, her legs entwined with his, her eyes closing in ecstasy, her mouth so warm and moist, her low moans in his ear, her hips and thighs and breasts and neck. All his to caress and taste.

And then, finally, his name on her lips, a lingering sigh in the dark of the night.

Chapter Nineteen

The heating system was on the fritz so the congregation of the little church huddled inside their coats to keep warm. But no one really seemed to mind. Their attention was directed on Sam, who was filling in for the regular minister this Sunday, and he gave them little space to reflect on the cold.

Elizabeth was sitting in the back row while she listened to him and watched the people who seemed so captivated by his words. Though his voice was low and even, there was an eloquence there that was riveting.

"We're afraid to believe that good things can happen to us. We're afraid to look up and laugh, and to love and live. And I guess it's because we are afraid that it might not last."

How could he know so much about human nature? Elizabeth wondered. How could he know that those were the things she was afraid of? She held back so much love that she wanted to give to him, because she was afraid. Afraid to give it all and then lose it in the end. He was so good, the best thing that had ever happened to her. And yet, she could not take full advantage of it. Something still held her back and would not allow her to be completely free.

"We have to face reality. But we also must have hope. That is the foundation of everything that is worthwhile. We have to aspire to be something greater than what we are now. It's the American Dream to aspire for something beyond our reach. And it's available to all of us. All of us—no matter what neighborhood we live in, what type of families we come from, the clothes we wear, who we know, how much money we have. Those things don't mean anything when it comes to achievement. All we need is lots of faith in ourselves and lots of hard work.''

Elizabeth held her coat tightly against her as a cool blast of air blew through a broken windowpane. The walls of the church were plaster and the floor was a rich dark hardwood in need of a good wax job. There were ten rows of chairs, ten in each row, but the room was only half-filled with people. Sam had told her before how poor the attendance was, and with such a poor heating system, she could certainly see why.

Not long ago she had contrasted Sam with the minister of her church on the North Shore, and now she was comparing the structures as well. Her church had stained glass windows, a forty-voice choir, crystal chandeliers, and plush blue carpeting. And the congregation was always dressed in perfect accord with the elegant surroundings. Today she was wearing a pearl-gray wool dress, but most of the people in this church were dressed in jeans or suits purchased from the Goodwill Industries.

Elizabeth glanced at the slim gold watch on her wrist, and her thoughts kept filtering back to her other world. In less than an hour all of her friends would pour out onto the church lawn for a few minutes of gossip before heading off to the club for lunch. Her mother and grandmother would hold center court as always, and the hungry geese would flock around them. On this day would they ask about Elizabeth? Would they miss her or would they simply be curious about the outrageous scandal she was causing?

She tried to take a deep breath, but she couldn't pull in enough air. Did she miss all of those people or their conversations or the lavish spread of food and gossip at the country club? No, she was just thinking about them, that's all. She didn't miss them a bit.

A sudden feeling of claustrophobia washed over her and she had to loosen her coat and let in the cold air to keep from fainting. She looked up at Sam and their eyes caught and held for a long minute. He looked away first, but his voice felt like a soothing balm against her troubled thoughts. The airless moment passed and she studied him standing up there, optimism radiating from him like a warm light. And she knew in that moment that no matter what happened, no matter which way their paths took them, she would never love anyone as much as she loved him.

"Some of us are drifting," he was saying. "And we've been drifting long enough. We have to care enough to stop the aimless wanderings, care enough to start actively doing and giving to each other. Without that, we are all nothing. We're going to eventually pass on, and to the world we leave behind, it will not matter one little bit. It makes no difference in the scheme of things. That is unless we actively choose to believe in all of the possibilities of reality, see who we are and what we can be. Unless we have faith in ourselves and in our fellow man. And unless we honestly choose to care and love each other. If we don't, then nothing matters. If not, then we don't have to worry about losing self-esteem. We've already lost it."

While the congregation dispersed Elizabeth remained seated. Several people glanced her way and smiled as they walked out into the cold sunlit day, but a few eyed her with a mixture of suspicion and disapproval. Over the last week she had heard some of the hushed remarks about Reverend Winslow and that woman who was living with him. And now she saw the same thoughts reflected in several pairs of eyes.

But beyond them all she saw Sam gathering up his coat. Then he turned to her and smiled, and all of her doubts and all of the thoughts of her other life floated out the door and into the wind.

While he organized his papers Elizabeth waited outside on the sidewalk. She was talking to Father Stanislavski, who was walking home from his church, and she didn't see Sam come out and lean against the wall of the building, listening to them.

"Why, Father Stanislavski, I think a block party is a splendid idea!" Elizabeth looped her arm through the old priest's. "I'll mention it to Sam tonight. I know he'll think it's a wonderful idea too."

"I may have mentioned it to him once or twice." The old man frowned as he tried to remember if he had or not. "It worked so well in the old neighborhood. Lots of dishes from the homelands."

Elizabeth was consumed with excitement for the idea. "Oh, yes! And we could block off the street and set up tables in the middle. Everyone would come, I'm sure. Oh, it sounds like such fun."

Sam walked up and shook hands with the man. "Hello, Andrew."

The priest nodded. "Samuel. Miss Parkins and I were just discussing the possibilities of a block party."

Elizabeth laid her hand on Sam's arm. "Isn't that a great idea? It would be so much fun."

Sam looked from one to the other, both hardly able to contain their excitement. He cleared his throat. "Well, it...I suppose we could...well, consider it." He cleared his throat again and looked at Elizabeth.

"But right now, we need to get you over to Zelma Worlitzer's."

"That's right." She looked at the priest. "I promised her I would have lunch with her today."

"How is she doing?" Father Stanislavski asked.

"She hasn't been feeling very well, I'm afraid. If only I could talk her into going to the doctor, but..."

"She is an old woman, Miss Parkins. It is hard sometimes to change the old patterns."

Elizabeth watched the priest walk away and she thought about what he had said. It was as if he were talking about himself, or maybe he was talking about life in general. Young or old, it was awfully hard to change the old patterns.

She shrugged and turned back to Sam, hooking her arm in his as they walked down the sidewalk. "So what do you think?"

"About what?"

"About a block party. Don't you think that is a great idea?"

Sam smiled down at the sidewalk as they walked. "Elizabeth, I don't want to put a damper on your enthusiasm, but Andrew and I have talked about that I don't know how many times. It wouldn't work."

"Why not?"

"It would mean nothing to the kids in this neighborhood. You have to reach them on their level. This isn't your typical smiling suburb." He smiled down at her. "Or maybe you haven't noticed."

They stopped in front of Mrs. Worlitzer's building, and Elizabeth thrust out her chin. "Oh, I've noticed, all right. And I've noticed a few other things too." She started to climb the narrow stairway, but Sam stopped her.

His eyebrows were raised and his hands were in the pockets of his coat as he looked up at her. "What other things have you noticed?"

Her smile was smug and superior. "Only that you don't have the answers for everything." She smiled again and turned away, climbing the stairs that led up to The Traveler's Hotel, an old, run-down establishment that now catered only to full-time residents and a few winos who graced the hallways at night.

At the top of the steps she turned around to look at Sam still standing on the sidewalk below. His eyes were narrowed and his forehead was creased into a frown as he contemplated her remark. She smiled again and walked through the doorway.

She stepped around one of the hallway boarders as she hurried to Mrs. Worlitzer's apartment. A rat scurried into the shadows a few feet ahead of her and she shuddered. But more than anything else, it was the awful smells of these old unclean buildings that got to her. Every time she came here, she almost gagged from the overpowering odor.

Mrs. Worlitzer peeked through the slim opening of the door. "Hurry and get in here." She tugged at Elizabeth's arm. "Two defenseless women alone with that wild animal out there."

Elizabeth looked back down the hall at the drunken old man asleep with his head resting on an empty wine bottle. "Him?"

"Hurry up!" Mrs. Worlitzer pulled her into the apartment and slammed the door behind her. "Oh, my, oh, my, oh, my!" She laid the back of her hand against her forehead and swooned. "Never has my reputation been so compromised. Not since that time when that producer expected me to...well, compromise myself...just so I would star in his moving picture. Well, I told him I wouldn't dream of being seen in such an amateurish enterprise. Besides, I had promised Samuel Goldwyn to give him first option on my talents and—

Did I ever show you that photograph I have of Mr. Goldwyn?''

"Yes, you did, but I would love to see it again.'' Elizabeth hid her sigh as she followed the old woman into her bedroom to look at the photo album for the hundredth time, and at the picture of a man who was no more Samuel Goldwyn than that wino in the hall was.

Zelma Worlitzer had played the part of Juliet in The West Chicago Repertory Company's production of *Romeo and Juliet* in 1928. After a mysterious scandal of some sort that Elizabeth could not quite determine, Zelma was dropped from the performance, never to be seen on the stage again. But in her own mind she had built a dazzling career as a stage and screen star from that moment on, and nothing or no one had been able to convince her that she was nothing more than a simple, ordinary mortal.

A thin, dry woman with only a few strands of hair that stuck straight out from her head as if she were in a perpetual state of shock therapy, the woman never set foot outside her apartment. All of her groceries and supplies were delivered to her door, and she truly believed that if she ever set foot beyond her doorstep, she would perish.

Sam had suggested that Elizabeth go see her because he thought that if anyone could help her, it would be someone who had actually experienced the glamour that Zelma Worlitzer knew only inside her own mind. And so, Elizabeth had come to visit her and had been coming several times a week now for over three weeks.

"Did I do that right, dear?'' Zelma swept her hand at the dining table she had set for their lunch.

"It looks lovely, Zelma. But the spoon goes on the right.''

"Oh, I knew that, of course. But I was in such a rush. My schedule is so full now that I hardly have time to know if I'm coming or going. I'm sure you know what I mean, dear. Tell me again about that charity ball you sponsored last summer."

So, once again, Elizabeth told in minute detail about the people and the clothes and the music and the night, adding to Zelma's repertoire of dreams and aging fantasies.

Two hours later they had finished their lunch and rehashed the events of Zelma's resplendent Hollywood career. Elizabeth had also been trying to convince her for three weeks to go see a doctor. She had been complaining of a stomachache since she'd met her. But nothing Elizabeth said would convince the woman to leave her apartment.

It was time for Elizabeth to go. She had done all that she could do for today. And this afternoon she and Sam were going to try to get away for a while and go to Lincoln Park. Except for the nights, they had so little time together, and they desperately needed some quiet moments just for the two of them.

"Well, I'll see you on Thursday, okay?" Elizabeth walked to the door and unlatched the lock, but Zelma's question stopped her. She turned around sharply to stare at the old woman. "What did you say?"

Zelma repeated the question. "I said, is he good to you?"

"Who?"

"Your young man. Reverend Winslow. Is he good to you?"

Elizabeth smiled. "Yes, he is."

"And are you good to him?"

"I try to be."

She smiled. "That's a good start. But, more importantly, are you good for him?"

Elizabeth frowned. "I don't know what you mean."

Zelma dropped into the Queen Anne chair with the faded brocade seat cover and looked through Elizabeth, seeing something far beyond. Her voice had taken on a dreamy quality. "When people have nothing but dreams to live with, everything that makes them what they are disappears. And all that is left is a hollow, faint vision of what could have been. Beyond that fantasy, nothing is left." Her eyes focused on Elizabeth's face. "These are more than the ramblings of an old crazy woman, you know. I know from whence I speak. Be good *for* your Mr. Winslow or else set him free."

Elizabeth's hand slowly lifted to the doorknob, but she could not make her eyes look away from Zelma Worlitzer. All eternity was wrapped in that one tight moment, her fate sealed like a prisoner behind glass doors, yet exposed in glaring detail for her to view and examine. She had never thought of it that way before. She loved Sam. But was she good for him?

She smiled weakly at Zelma, surprised that there was more behind her facade than a fading image of herself as a star. She stepped through the door, closing it tightly behind her, then slipped by the old man sleeping in the hallway and descended out onto the street.

It was the end of January and it seemed as if winter was going to last forever. Every morning was greeted by a gray overcast sky, temperatures hovering around ten degrees, and occasionally a flurry or two of snow that added to the glaze of ice that clung to the pavement.

Elizabeth carefully picked her way down the sidewalk as she headed for Sam's house. She tried to shove Zelma's well-meaning advice to the back of her mind. Well, of course she was good for Sam. But whether she was or not, she didn't want to think about that right now. She just wanted to go home to him, lean against him, and feel the strength of his arms around her. She wanted love, not doubts. Why were there always so many doubts!

As she neared the house she saw the sleek black limousine hugging the sidewalk in front. Walter was behind the wheel, wrapped in his overcoat to keep warm. Elizabeth glanced up at the house. A dark, crouching fear, not unlike that of a child who knows that some rule has been broken and that punishment awaits her return, darted through her. Her stride slowed with impending dread.

Cautiously she climbed the stairs and opened the front door. As soon as she stepped into the foyer, Sam was beside her, helping her to take off her coat and hang it on the coat rack. "Your grandmother is here." He whispered the warning, then stood back to let Elizabeth lead the way into the living room.

"Grandmother Eva! What on earth—"

"Hello, Elizabeth."

"This is such a surprise!" She turned quickly to Sam. "You've met—"

"We've met," Eva stated flatly.

Sam cleared his throat. "Listen, I think I'll run down to the church office for a few minutes. I left some papers down there. If you'll excuse me." He directed his gaze to Eva. "It was a pleasure meeting you, Mrs. Rowen."

Eva nodded without looking at him, then frowned as she watched Elizabeth walk to the door with him.

Stepping out onto the porch, he turned back to her. "Don't worry," he whispered, and kissed her forehead. But he knew it was as much a word of advice to himself as to her. The minute Eva Rowen walked into his house, he had begun to worry. But he smiled encouragingly at Elizabeth.

With one last touch of his fingers against her cheek, he was gone. She closed the door and went back inside. She was grateful that Sam had a fire going in the fireplace. At least the lack of proper heat in the house would not be quite so obvious.

"Sit down, Grandmother."

"No, thank you, dear. I'm not going to be staying that long."

The muscles in Elizabeth's legs went slack and she dropped into the overstuffed chair and stared at her. Her grandmother had not even removed her camel leather gloves.

"Reverend Winslow is a very attractive man," she said as she looked down the bridge of her nose at Elizabeth. "And very nice. I can see why you are enamored of him."

Elizabeth sat up straighter, smiling at the unexpected remark. "Yes, I was hoping you would meet him. I knew you would see what a wonderful—"

"This charade must end."

"I beg your pardon?"

"You heard me, Elizabeth Adele. You must stop your little charade with this man."

She was confused. "Charade? I don't know what you mean, Grandmother. And I thought you said you liked him?"

"I do." Eva brushed her gloved hands together as if wiping away some unseen but irritating dust that had dared to land on her. "But I will not tolerate a grandchild of mine living with him or marrying him. Did you really assume I would cast my blessings on such a union?"

"I thought you might." Elizabeth looked around the room. "At least after you saw how happy I was with him."

"Happy!" Eva's disgusted laugh followed. "When have you ever known anything but happiness, child?"

"I'm not a child, Grandmother. And I'm not sure I ever have been happy until now."

Eva's mouth went rigid and a quiet moan escaped her lips. "What have I done to deserve this?" she hissed. "I gave you everything you ever wanted, sent you to the best schools, gave you riding and tennis and skiing lessons, bought you clothes, introduced you to all the right people—"

"Did you ever think of giving me freedom?"

Eva did not like to be interrupted and it took her a few seconds to get over this rude affront before she could respond to Elizabeth's question. "Freedom is for the bourgeoisie, Elizabeth. Not for you or me. We are bound by rules and they must not be broken, or else we will find ourselves overrun by the masses. It is our job to set an example for the rest of society, to give guidelines for proper behavior. I thought you understood all of this."

Elizabeth's hands were clenched tightly in her lap as she tried to buttress herself against her grandmother's power.

"In the same way that the British need their queen, the middle class in this country needs a ruling class, an elite sector that can give some definition and polish to our nation's existence. And whether you like it or not, Elizabeth, you are bound by those same rules. You cannot escape who and what you are. You were born to this class and you will always remain a part of it. The sooner you learn to stop fighting that and just accept who you are and what you must do in life, the better off you will be."

Eva let loose a fatalistic sigh. "I suppose it was inevitable that you would have your moment of rebellion against our way of life. Almost everyone does at some time or another. But as long as you realize that that is what this is, you will be all right. And as long as you also realize that I have my limits. I am trying to be fair and give you time to come to your senses, but I will not wait forever. Soon, very soon, you will have to make a choice between this man and this way of life... forever...and the life that you were destined to live. You cannot have both. Do I make myself clear, Elizabeth?''

Elizabeth stared back at Eva for an intense moment before she nodded. ''As a bell, Grandmother. Clear as a bell.''

Sam leaned against the rusted pole of the swing set and watched Elizabeth moving slowly back and forth on the swing, her eyes focused on the hard gray ground at her feet. As soon as Eva left, Sam had returned and seen the anguish on her face. He knew he had to get her out of the house for a little while, so they had walked the three blocks to a small neglected park and talked as the evening closed around them.

''That's absurd, Elizabeth. You are free to choose to be who and what you want.'' He watched her draw a design in the dirt with her foot. ''No matter where you come from or what you were supposedly destined to be or do, you can change that. You can be the person you want to be.''

She slid the bottom of her shoe across the design, wiping it away. ''Sometimes I'm not even sure who I want to be.'' She looked up at him. ''I wish I were more like you, Sam. You are so sure of what you want and where you're going. How do you do it? How do you always know that you're doing the right thing?''

He stepped over and knelt in front of her, gripping the swing chain in his hand. ''I don't always know that I'm doing the right thing. Sometimes I think I'm a hundred and eighty degrees off from where I should be. Nobody can be sure of things all the time.''

''But you know that this way of life is right for you and—''

A brisk current of air swirled around them, blowing her hair across her face. ''I've had my doubts,'' he said, brushing the hair back from her temples.

''When?''

''After I met you.''

Their eyes locked and held, and one of his hands slid down the chain and stopped to rest on the top of her thigh.

''I wanted you so badly,'' he whispered, and the pressure of his fingers against her leg increased. ''I still do.'' He was watching her closely and she was searching his face for answers he couldn't give her. ''Important decisions never come easy,'' he said. ''And I know that yours cannot be an easy one. Sometimes, like right now, I look at you and I—'' His voice broke on the words and his hand tightened on the top of her leg. ''I want to scream at you and hold you and shake you and love you until I force you to make a decision. Force you to say yes, you'll take the risk, you'll leave your world for mine.''

Elizabeth's hands lifted to the sides of his face. ''But I have, Sam. I'm here with you now.''

''Yes,'' he sighed. ''But you are also there. Half of you is still in a world in which I cannot live. I cannot live in a big brick house on the lake and drive a new Mercedes or Maserati or Rolls-Royce and indulge in social repartee with your friends. Not while there are people here who need so much. Sometimes, like now, when I look at you and wonder if that is the only way I can have you, I wish I could live that way. But I can't, Elizabeth. You have to understand that. And you cannot live both lives, either. You have to choose one or the other. It won't work any other way. You cannot have both."

You cannot have both. The same words Grandmother Eva had used. They played over and over in her head as they walked back to the house in thoughtful silence. Sam and Grandmother Eva both saw it, knew it, and were warning her. Why was she the only one who had failed to see it? She had never realized the permanence of her choices. She had assumed...what? That she could have both? But Sam knew. And Grandmother Eva knew. And now she knew. She would have to make a choice. But what would that choice be? She couldn't imagine not having Sam in her life. And yet, she could not imagine not having something other than this hand-to-mouth existence. Yes, she would make a decision. But not just yet. She needed awhile longer. Just a little longer.

By the time she went to bed that night her emotions were coiled tightly inside her, a cylindrical core of fear and confusion. Lying in bed, the tears began to fall and she couldn't stop them. Not even Sam's whispers of "Don't cry, Elizabeth. We'll work it out. I love you, that's all that matters..." would make the tears stop.

He held her so tightly in his arms, and her hands clutched on to him for dear life. His mouth moved across her neck, up her face, kissing away the tears as they fell.

"Sam." She whispered his name and felt the electricity surge through her body as his mouth moved. He raised up a little so that he could look down at her. The pain and confusion were plainly written on her face. She spoke, but her voice was only a tiny, frail whisper. "Sam, please tell me, what's going to happen to us?"

The question pierced through him again and again. He had asked himself that many times, but to hear it on her lips gave it a power he didn't want to acknowledge. He stared at her eyes, and then her mouth, and with great effort the answer finally came from his lips. "I wish I knew, Elizabeth. I wish to God I knew."

In a blinding rush of burning need they clung to each other in almost violent desperation, their hands and fingers, and hips and legs, and lips and teeth forming an urgent bond that would seal them together forever, defying all the external forces that they both knew deep inside would eventually pull them apart.

Chapter Twenty

Elizabeth planted her hands on her waist and stood over the old woman. "Zelma, you must be reasonable. That nice young doctor came here to examine you only out of a favor to Sam. But he will not perform surgery on you in this apartment. You are going to have to go to the hospital. That's all there is to it."

"Stop trying to bully me," Zelma Worlitzer groaned. "I haven't left this house for ten years and I don't intend to leave it until I die."

"Which will be very soon if you don't have that surgery done."

"Surgery, my foot! Those quacks want to experiment on me. I know exactly what they're up to. They want to dig into my brain and do some sort of genetic experiments on me. I read in the *National Enquirer* that they did it with Einstein and with a whole group of famous people. That's what they want me for, I just know it."

Elizabeth scoffed. "That's ridiculous. You have a tumor in your stomach. They are not going to be anywhere near your brain."

Zelma continued to rock vigorously back and forth in her rocking chair. "Tumor, hah! What do they know about it?"

Elizabeth let out a deep sigh. She had been battling her for over a week now about this surgery, with little success. She now squatted down in front of her and laid her hands on the woman's knees. "Zelma, listen to me, please. They need to do a biopsy on that tumor. They need to find out if it is malignant or not."

"So what if they find out? That's not going to tell me anything I don't already know. I'm either going to live awhile longer or I'm not. I already know that."

"If it is malignant, they can operate. They might be able to remove the cancer if it is there. You have to give them the chance to do that."

Zelma slowed the rocker and stared across the room above her head. She was silent for so long, Elizabeth wondered if she had forgotten what they had even been discussing. "There's no chance involved," Zelma said. "It is cut and dried. If I leave this apartment, if I go to that hospital, I will die. Sure as the world is round, I will never come home again."

Elizabeth saw the tears that hovered near the surface of the old woman's eyes. She had never seen her like this, never seen her show an ounce of real emotion or fear. "Zelma, you have nothing to be afraid of. If you want, I will go with you to the hospital."

At that, Zelma straightened in her chair and lifted her chin. "I have never been afraid a day in my life. But if it would make you feel better to come with me..."

Elizabeth folded her fingers around the old woman's hand. "Thank you, Zelma. It would make me feel much better."

Sam draped his arm around her shoulder. "I can't believe you talked her into leaving that apartment! You are amazing, did you know that?"

Elizabeth grinned. "So you keep telling me."

"When does she go into the hospital?"

"On Friday. I'll take her over there in the afternoon, and the biopsy is scheduled for the next morning."

"She wouldn't go if you weren't going with her."

"I know. She was so scared, Sam. I've never seen that kind of fear in anyone before."

"There are all kinds of fear in this world."

She shivered involuntarily at the thought of where she and Sam were going today. "But probably none so great as what I am feeling right now."

He grinned at her and pulled her closer. "You've got nothing to be afraid of. They're going to love you." He had been trying to convince her of that ever since they got on the train thirty minutes ago. But they were almost to the station at Oak Park and she was not yet convinced.

"Am I dressed all right?"

"Have you ever not been dressed right?" he teased.

She wiped her sweaty palms together. "We're not talking about *Town and Country*. We're talking about your mother and father. And what do they think about us living together without being married?"

"I'm a big boy, remember? They haven't tried to tell me what to do for a long time. Relax, they're only human."

Elizabeth looked dubious, but refrained from further comment. She watched out the window at the rapid change from inner city slum to quaint suburbia.

Oak Park was one of the older residential areas around Chicago. It was composed mostly of homes built in the late teens and early nineteen twenties, and it was also the home and proving ground of Frank Lloyd Wright; several houses in the neighborhood still reflected the originality and sleek artistry of his style. But, despite its charm, Elizabeth had not been here for years and she wasn't at all sure she wanted to be here now.

"There is my father's car," Sam said as they climbed down the stairs of the platform. "Here." He laughed. "Hold my hand. You're shaking like a leaf."

She laid her hand in his and felt the warmth of his fingers as they wrapped around hers. Why was she so nervous? She had met thousands of people—important people—in her lifetime and always carried it off with style and confidence. But for some strange reason she was scared to death to meet his parents. She wasn't really worried that they wouldn't like her as much as she wanted so badly to please Sam.

Lately she had found herself trying almost too hard to please him—and everyone else. Everyone said she couldn't combine both lives effectively, but she had. She had done it! She had combined them with perfect ease. She kept the YES office running smoothly, visited with Zelma and aided Sam in his projects, helped the North Shore Women's Guild plan its annual orphanage drive, met for lunch once a week with friends, wrote petitions in support of the new candidate for the mayoral election, attended church services with Sam, and still got away once or twice a week for outings alone with him.

She had done it! But, in the process, something vital had drained out of her. Sam noticed it and worried about it, but wasn't sure what he should do about it. She had lost weight and her skin had paled more than as a normal consequence of winter. And she was always so tired.

Only when the two of them got away together did she ever feel alive and whole again. They would go for walks in the park, or window-shop along North Michigan Avenue, or scour old antique shops for quaint little odds and ends that intrigued Elizabeth and, for reasons she couldn't figure out, amused Sam. In those hours she would have no doubts, no cares other than to bring joy to him the way he brought so much love and joy to her.

A tall man stepped out of his 1974 Chevrolet and stood solemnly straight as they walked up. Sam smiled first and shook his father's hand. "Dad, this is Elizabeth Parkins. Elizabeth, this is my father, Arthur Winslow."

"Mr. Winslow, it's a pleasure to meet you." Elizabeth extended her hand and smiled with the outward confidence and skill of a woman who has been introduced to high-ranking public officials, celebrities, and royalty all her life.

His glasses had slipped to the end of his nose so, without letting go of her hand, he tilted his head back at an angle to look at her through them. He then glanced at Sam. "You didn't tell me she was so beautiful."

Sam smiled. "I figured you would see that for yourself."

"Hmmm, yes," he said, letting go of her hand and ushering them into the car. "Secretive as ever, I see."

Sam let the remark slide right off him as he climbed into the front seat of the car after Elizabeth. His father scooted in behind the wheel and started the engine.

"I see it's still running like new," Sam said.

"If you take care of something, it will last forever," his father replied. "That's been my motto for sixty years, Elizabeth. And it still holds true. Had a forty-nine Buick that lasted eighteen years. Never should have gotten rid of that car, but Sam's mother had her eye on one of those new-fangled Chevrolets, so I gave in." Arthur Winslow eased the car into traffic. "Never should have done that," he mumbled, and Elizabeth did her best not to look at Sam. She knew he was grinning and she was trying very hard not to laugh. So she kept her eyes straight ahead on the road as the car inched at a snail's pace down the elm-lined streets of large brick homes and deep front yards.

Mr. Winslow pulled the car into the narrow drive beside a two-story brown brick house with a large front porch. Elizabeth could see a tiny woman standing behind the screen door, watching as the three of them stepped out of the car.

Mrs. Winslow opened the screen door and called his name as Sam climbed up the front steps and gave her a big hug. Her voice was as tiny and soft as her stature, and her big brown eyes constantly searched out her husband's face as if seeking approval for her every remark. "Less than ten miles away, and you don't come to see us for months. This must be Elizabeth." She held out her hand and Elizabeth took it.

"It is so nice to meet you, Mrs. Winslow."

"Come in, come in."

Sam's hand on her back propelled her into the foyer and left into the front room. The furniture was formal, the curtains drawn, the air thick with a closed-in smell. And he had not been kidding; there was plastic covering everything. Plastic over the French provincial sofa, over the two Queen Anne chairs, over the lampshades. Even the candles were still in their original wrappers.

She glanced first at Sam and he turned away to hide his grin, then she looked at Mrs. Winslow, who was beaming with pride over her "parlor."

"This is . . . lovely," Elizabeth said.

"Please do sit down. Oh, not there, dear. Here, if you don't mind."

Elizabeth stepped away from the chair and sat instead on the sofa, where the plastic made a crackling noise beneath her. "Oh, I'm sorry." She grimaced and inched forward as Mrs. Winslow fluffed up the pillow behind her.

"No problem, dear. Make yourself comfortable."

This time Sam didn't hide his grin as he leaned back on the sofa and draped his arm across the back. Obviously used to this house and these people, he had decided the best way to deal with them was to ignore their rules.

"Didn't you make lemonade?" Arthur gruffly inquired of his wife.

"Oh, my, I forgot!" She jumped up with an apologetic look at her husband and scurried into the kitchen to make the drink.

Arthur cleared his throat and pulled a pipe from the front pocket of his shirt. He spent a full minute stuffing the bowl with tobacco and then lighting it. Elizabeth, sitting ramrod straight on the front edge of the love seat, was aware of nothing but the rhythmic ticking of the grandfather clock against the wall and that infernal grin on Sam's face.

"Are you still living in that hellhole, Sam?" Arthur Winslow finally looked at his son.

He seemed unperturbed. "You know I am, Dad."

"Hmmm, yes. Ah, here's your mother with the lemonade."

Elizabeth glanced at Sam and her eyes widened with a million questions. Was this what it had been like for him growing up with these people? She couldn't imagine how he could possibly have survived it.

Mrs. Winslow giggled nervously as she poured the lemonade into their glasses. Elizabeth was scared to death she was going to spill a drop on the plastic. What on earth would they do then!

"Isn't this nice," Mrs. Winslow cooed. "Sam tells us you were born in River Forest."

"Yes, on Franklin Avenue."

"Well, we were almost neighbors, then. Isn't that wonderful, Arthur?"

Arthur puffed a few times on his pipe before answering. "Prices are too high in River Forest. Never could see the point in that. All you need is a roof over your head. Who needs all those fancy mansions and swimming pools? Nope, never could see the use in that."

Elizabeth downed her lemonade in one large gulp.

Mrs. Winslow passed over her husband's remark and spoke again. "But you live in Winnetka now, don't you?" She giggled nervously. "I mean, when you're not at...at Sam's." She giggled again.

Arthur took in a long draw from his pipe. "Last time we were in Winnetka was when we took that trip up to the Wisconsin Dells. You remember that?"

His wife smiled. "Oh, yes, dear. The fall of 1966."

His back went rigid. "It was not 1966. It was '67."

"Oh, well, you may be right, dear, but I was just thinking it was 1966 because it was Sam's first year in college. Anyway, it was such a lovely trip, and we stayed in that little alpine motel, and—"

"It was not alpine, it was built like a Scottish castle."

"No, dear, the Scottish castle was the year we took the trip to Iowa. This one was an alpine motel."

Elizabeth tried her best to smother a yawn and looked to Sam for help.

"Well, if you'll excuse us..." He patted her knee and set his glass down on the table. His mother immediately jumped up, whisked the glasses away, and carried them to the kitchen. "I'm going to give Elizabeth a tour," he said, pulling her up beside him. "Ah, Dad, did you hear me?"

Arthur turned back from his reflections out the window and stared at his son as if he had never seen him before. He was still trying to solve the question of Scottish castle or alpine motel. After a moment he nodded. "Yes, yes, you two go right ahead. Mother and I will be down here. Think I'll go out into the yard."

Sam led her out of the room and leaned close to her ear. "He's probably going to go count his quarters in the garden hose."

Elizabeth laughed softly and elbowed him in the side. He held her hand and led her up the freshly polished stairs to the second floor and down a short hallway, where he opened the door to one of the bedrooms. Inside, the furnishings and wall decorations were those of an adolescent boy, and when she turned to him with a questioning look, he only shrugged.

"They left it just the way it was when I was in high school. If you think this is bad, you ought to see the shrine."

"The shrine?"

He cocked his thumb toward the room next door. "Jonas's room."

"Why are they like that? How could you live—"

Sam leaned against the wall of his old bedroom and crossed his arms. "I've learned to develop a lot of tolerance for other people, Elizabeth. My parents are really good people, loony as can be, I admit, but still good. Of course, now you can see why I don't come to visit more often. We really don't have too much to say to each other."

She shook her head and sighed. "To be quite honest, I thought I was never going to get out of that room."

He pulled her against him and nipped at her neck. "You may never get out of this room."

She laced her fingers around his neck and smiled. "I may hold you to that promise. But first I want to see what you were like as a little boy." She stepped out of his arms and walked slowly around the room, looked into an egg container full of assorted rocks, picked up a pair of burgundy boxing gloves, and examined a row of books on a shelf. *The Catcher in the Rye,* a set of Ian Fleming spy thrillers, a history of American baseball, and a large hardbound copy of *Boxing Basics*. On the wall were posters of Floyd Patterson and Sonny Liston.

"I was the tidy one," he explained as she opened the closets and drawers. "Jonas's room was always a wreck. I can't figure out how he got that way. Must have been some sort of rebellion."

"I wish I had known you then," she said. "Wouldn't that have been fun?"

He studied her from across the room. "I don't know," he hedged. "You would have run around with that snooty cheerleading crowd and never given me a second glance. And thinking about you all the time would have made me even more frustrated than I already was. Being an adolescent was hard enough without you."

Elizabeth smiled coyly and crossed the room to him. She looped her arms around his neck and pouted. "Are you saying you wouldn't have liked me?"

His answer was a low groan. He sat on the bed and pulled her on top of him as he lay back against the pillow. His hands rested on her hips. "Do you have any idea how many nights I dreamed about having a girl in bed with me? Wondered what it would be like? And that was just normal girls. If I had had to think about you..." He edged her between his legs.

She moved her lips down his throat. "Would you have thought about kissing me?"

His reply was a low chuckle. "Nothing quite so innocent or honorable."

"No? Then what?"

He rolled over and lay on top of her. "I could tell you, but I'd much rather show you."

She lifted her mouth to his. "Sounds wonderful to me. But what will your parents think?"

His fingers began hastily opening the buttons on her blouse, and his breath was short and quick. "My father is out in the back counting his money, remember? And my mother is probably dusting the back of the water heater. So, don't worry. Indulge me. Make all of those adolescent fantasies of mine come true."

Her blouse lay open and his fingers were trailing down onto her breast.

She lifted her eyes to his. "I can think of nothing I would rather do."

Friday morning Elizabeth woke up later than usual. Sam had left early to go downtown and sit in on a city council meeting. A public debate was being held on the issue of funding allocations for the city's parks and he wanted to make sure some of those funds were distributed to this area of town.

Elizabeth stretched beneath the covers and relaxed back into the pillow that she and Sam shared. It was the first morning she could remember in quite a while that she had not had to rush out of the house to work on some project or another. She had been asked once again this year to head up the Junior League Spring Banquet in Winnetka and, like a fool, she had agreed to do it. But with all of the projects she had going on here, how was she ever going to fit it all in? There was just no way she could do it all. Something was going to have to be dropped. Something had to give. But what?

She closed her eyes and wished that all of the responsibilities would simply fly away, vanish into thin air. She needed a break from all of the projects. She needed to reevaluate what was happening in her life and where she was going.

Before the beginnings of a decision could even formulate in her mind, she fell asleep again. The ringing of the telephone woke her an hour later.

She crawled out of bed and ran downstairs to the kitchen to answer it. "Hello, Mother." Elizabeth leaned against the kitchen wall and yawned. "What day is it? What time is it?"

"Much too late for you to still be asleep, Liz, darling. Now, I want you to get dressed and meet me at Stanley Korshak's. There is a gown there that I am dying to have and I want your opinion on it."

Elizabeth's eyes widened. "You want my opinion!"

"Of course, dear. You have such a knack for this sort of thing. And I need accessories to go with it and... well, I'll just never be able to do it all on my own."

"All right, Mother. Give me a couple of hours to get ready and I'll meet you there at eleven thirty."

"I'm—I'm looking forward to seeing you, honey."

Elizabeth pulled the receiver away from her ear and stared at it for a long moment, frowning. She finally responded. "Me too, Mother."

As soon as she hung up the telephone she ran back upstairs and started to get ready. The morning was clear and sunny and almost warm in comparison to the cold days and nights that lay behind them. The official start of spring was still two weeks away, but from all appearances, the balmier days were here to stay.

After she showered she put on a linen skirt and jacket, fixed her hair and makeup, jotted a quick note to Sam, telling him where she would be, and then she was gone. The thoughts that filled her head on this bright March morning were no longer those of projects and responsibilities. They were of the latest designer fashions; with a lunch at Jacques's of Dover sole, wild rice, and sherry; and with the sheer delight of shopping and dining among bubbling fountains, garden greenery, sunshine, and lots of personal attention.

As she stepped from the taxi along North Michigan Avenue, all of the fatigue of the last few weeks drained from her. This was the kind of lift her spirits had been needing. This was what her emotional self had been craving. It never occurred to her that what she had been wanting to escape for so long was the very thing she was now running back to find.

Louise greeted her prodigal daughter at the door of Stanley Korshak's and together, with anticipation gleaming in their eyes, they entered the world of high fashion and self-indulgence.

The saleswoman greeted them both with familiarity and delight over being able to help them in their selections. She brought over to them the Oscar de la Renta gown that Louise had been admiring. "Don't you just love this, Liz? But tell me honestly, what do you think? Would I look like a cow in it?"

"The color is perfect for you, Mother. And the style too. Try it on and then I can tell more."

After thirty minutes a decision had been reached. Louise would buy the gown. Then all she needed was a pair of shoes and an evening bag, which they found down the street at Gucci's, and a new emerald pin from Tiffany's that she had been debating whether to buy for over a week.

"All that shopping makes me sooo hungry," Louise crooned. "Why wouldn't you let me buy you that suede jacket, Liz?"

"I really don't need it." Elizabeth stopped, startled by her own choice of words. She glanced at her mother to see if she had noticed. She had.

Louise was staring at her daughter as if she had lost her mind. "Liz, darling, I think you have been hiding out in the boonies for too long."

Elizabeth tried to laugh, but it was a weak attempt. Need? Since when had she been concerned only with her needs? What about her desires and wishes and wants and whims? She had the money to indulge them all without worry. Had her weeks on Blackhawk had that kind of effect on her? And did she really want to change all that much?

"Let's go eat lunch," she said, hoping to push all of the uncertainties away. All the doubts, all the confusion, when would it ever end? She didn't want to think about it right now. She just wanted to have an enjoyable day without any concerns other than what she would order for lunch.

They backtracked to Jacques's and entered the summer-drenched garden, taking a seat at one of the tables surrounded by lush greenery and a sparkling fountain.

Louise was on her second martini before she could broach the subject that lay like a wedge between them. "Liz, darling, I've been thinking. Have you, well, you know, made any decision about what you are going to do?"

Elizabeth dabbed the corner of her mouth with her napkin, then laid it back in her lap. She looked up at her mother. "Are you asking for yourself or for Grandmother?"

"For myself. Your grandmother doesn't even know I'm with you today."

Elizabeth sat back in her chair and let out a slow breath. She stared at the centerpiece on the table, but she wasn't seeing it. She was trying to find an answer for her mother and, at the same time, an answer for herself.

"I don't know, Mother. I just don't know what to do anymore."

"Why don't you come home to Winnetka. Take a trip somewhere. Go to the Bahamas. Be with your friends. Liz..." In a moment of unguarded motherly concern Louise grabbed Elizabeth's hand. "Please give up this man and this life-style and come home to us. Please!"

Elizabeth's gaze was fastened on their entwined hands, and the tears threatened to break loose. "But I love him, Mother!"

"I've been in love too, Liz, several times. But I've also been able to see that it doesn't always work out. No matter how much you might want it to work, sometimes two people just cannot be together."

"He needs me," she said softly. "And I need him."

"You need security, Liz. You need someone to give you the things that you are accustomed to having. Imagine what your life would be like if you could never go shopping like this, or eat at places like this. No more trips to St. Croix, no more catered parties, no more designer clothes. What would you do, Liz? Your life would be a series of dishes to wash, beds to make, meals to prepare, windows, for heaven's sake, to wash! Could you live that way? Is that all you want out of life?"

"But surely I can have both. I've adapted quite well to living in both worlds. I live with Sam, whom I love very much. And I still have time for you and my friends and shopping and—"

"It will end, Liz. Your grandmother will see to that."

"Oh, honestly, she wasn't serious. I mean, she wouldn't really cut me off from the family funds... would she?"

Louise snapped her fingers. "Just like that."

"But—but why?"

Louise took a hefty swig of the new drink the waiter had set in front of her before she spoke. "Because she is ruthless, that is why. You don't know her like I do, Liz. You didn't have to grow up in the same house with her." Her mother's voice lowered to a whisper. "Why in the hell do you think I drink too much? Because it's the only way I can deal with my own mother."

"But she has always given me anything I wanted."

"That's because it was what she wanted. Your grandmother Eva gets what she wants. She always has and she always will. You have been spared from seeing to what lengths she will go to get what she wants and, believe me, you don't want to see that."

"But why would she want to cut off my access to the money?"

"Because she does not want you with this man. She

has plans for you," Louise sneered. "She has had plans for you since the moment you were born. You were always more her child than mine. She took you under her wing and I never even had a chance with you."

Elizabeth stared at her mother, aware for the first time of a bitterness and a frustration inside the woman that she had never guessed might exist. "I never knew that, Mother. I always thought that—"

"That I was too busy for you?"

"Well, you were always jetting off to Europe with one or another of your husbands," she countered with her own bitterness. "Always leaving me behind."

Louise closed her eyes and sighed. "Your grandmother pushed me so hard, encouraged me to go, not to worry, she would take care of little Lizzy, her little princess. And I suppose I wanted to go. You always looked to her for anything you wanted, so there wasn't much point in me hanging around."

Elizabeth took a drink of her wine and pulled her hand back into her lap. She stared down at the plate in front of her. "Why is it that our lives make no sense except in retrospect? Why can't we ever understand what is happening when it's happening?"

Louise held her glass tight between her hands and studied the liquid inside. "Liz, please don't let Eva push you further away from me. If you persist in staying with this man, she can and will make your life outside that little neighborhood miserable. You will have nothing. And I will have lost my chance to do the things for you that I have always wanted to do, as your mother. Come home. Please!"

Elizabeth's eyes were fixed on her mother's face. *Home.* The word had such a nice sound. And yet Sam's house was home now. In his arms was home. But her mother was offering her a home too. She had always wanted that, always searched for the key to her mother's love. And now she had found it. All she had to do was go home to Winnetka and she would have her mother's love. It would be so simple.

So simple except for Sam Winslow. If she left him, she would leave her heart behind also. And what good would her mother's love do, or anyone else's, for that matter, if her heart could not be touched?

"I need more time, Mother. I simply need more time."

Chapter Twenty-one

The contrast was always startling to her when she returned to Blackhawk Street. No matter how many times she had gone into the city or to Winnetka and then returned to Sam's house, the transformation from one world to the other was always a shock.

The late afternoon sun was just dipping below the rim as she stepped off the train and walked down the stairs of the platform. The March evenings were still cool and she pulled together the lapels of her linen jacket to keep the cold wind away from her body as she walked the five blocks to Sam's house.

Despite the nagging doubts and still uncertain decisions that had assailed her all afternoon, it had been a lovely day. She and her mother had never had a more enjoyable time together. Something finite and solid had changed in their relationship, and for the first time ever, Elizabeth had been relaxed in her presence.

But she was also glad to come home to Sam. It was always this way. The need for the world she had always known and an equally fierce need to return to Sam and his world.

As she walked up the sidewalk to the porch she saw that the lights were on in the living room and a lazy curl of smoke rose steadily from the chimney. She hurried up the steps and opened the front door.

But a new contrast struck her as she crossed the threshold. The greeting she had expected—the happy smile, the warm embrace—was not there. Instead, he stood in the middle of the living room and watched her silently. His hand was resting on the back of the easy chair and his other arm hung loosely at his side. The fire in the hearth made a warm glow on the walls, but his eyes were hard and cold.

"Well, well," he said. "She returns."

She stood in the doorway to the living room and frowned at the unexpected harshness of his tone. She glanced at her slim gold watch. "It's only five thirty. Didn't you just get home yourself?"

"Oh, yes, I just came home." He reached over to the table beside the chair and picked up the note she had left him this morning. "Came home and found this."

She stepped farther into the room and frowned again. "Is there some problem with me going shopping, Sam?"

"No problem," he growled. "Why shouldn't you just flit off to indulge yourself all day? Why should you have any responsibilities to worry your pretty little head about?"

She planted her hands on her waist. "I don't know what your problem is, but I'm having a little trouble following this conversation."

"My problem is that I had to pick an old woman up off the floor of her apartment today because she collapsed with a heart attack." His voice was harder now. "You want to know why she had a heart attack? Because she was so frightened! She was afraid to leave her apartment and go to the hospital by herself, even though she had been convinced by her very best friend in the world that it was essential that she go. A matter of life or death, in fact, that's what she had been told. But also assured by that same friend that she would not have to go alone."

Elizabeth felt the icy chill run through her blood-stream and an unfamiliar weakness flooded into her knees. "Zelma?" she whispered. "Oh, my God!"

Sam closed his eyes and sniffed with scorn.

"Today is Friday," she said, her voice almost too weak to carry across the room to him. "I was supposed to take her to the hospital." She clamped her hand over her mouth and squeezed her eyes shut as the tears began to fall. "I forgot all about... Oh, Sam, no..." Her eyes opened wide and she stared at him. "Is she...?"

He caught the look of utter panic on her face and he realized that no matter how angry he was at the situation, he could not remain angry with her. She was a fish out of water; and she could not adapt to dry land. "She's alive," he said, and turned away from her to face the fire.

Slowly she walked over to him and laid a hand against his back. But he did not look at her. His hands were pushed into the front pockets of his jeans and his face in profile was grim and tired. There was a strained tautness in the muscles of his shoulders.

She leaned her cheek against the side of his arm. "Sam, I'm so sorry."

He neither removed his hands from his pockets nor looked at her. "I know that." He sighed and stepped away from her, still staring at the fire. "I'm sorry too."

She wiped the tears from her cheeks. "Is she going to be all right?"

"She's in intensive care. Critical, the doctor said. We'll know more in the morning."

She shook her head. "I can't believe I forgot what day it was. I guess I just didn't realize how much she depended on me."

Sam spun around and stared at her. "Don't you realize that everyone you come in contact with here depends on you? Don't you realize that I depend on you?"

She straightened up and her chin shot forward. "I don't think you have any reason to use that self-righteous tone of voice with me, Sam Winslow. And don't try to make me feel like I'm carrying the weight of all the world's problems like you are. I'm not like you," she snapped. "You're so damn responsible and saintly all the time and I'm not. We can't all be as virtuous as you are."

He glared at her for a long minute, then reached out and yanked her to him. "Virtuous?" he growled. "You think I'm virtuous!"

"You're hurting my arms, Sam."

His grip tightened. "I just thought you'd like to see how lacking in virtue I really am." He began pulling her across the room and dragged her behind him up the stairs.

"Let go of me, dammit! Sam, stop it!"

They reached the top of the stairs and he still didn't let go. Without loosening his hold on her arm, he shoved her into the bedroom and pushed her onto the bed. She lay on her back and stared up at this new, undisciplined, uncontrolled man. This man she didn't know. There was a fury inside of him that wanted to blow, that needed an outlet.

She began to cry again as he ripped off his shirt, letting go of her wrist only long enough to remove the sleeve. He stretched out on top of her and grabbed the other wrist. "I have never in my life been virtuous. I have never been a saint. If I were a saint, I would never have wanted you."

She wiggled beneath him and tried to escape his

weight and grasp. But it was hopeless. He only tightened his grip.

"Every second I'm with you, every time I think of you, I'm aware that I am anything but saintly. I am a man." He wedged between her legs and she closed her eyes. "Open your eyes, Elizabeth, and look at me. Don't try to imagine that you're somewhere else. That you're in that big white bed of yours on the North Shore. You are here with me and you are going to face that fact head-on."

She opened her eyes and stared up at him. His breath was warm against her face and his low, angry voice vibrated through her mind.

"Since the moment I've met you, all I've wanted to do is wrench you from that damn gold perch of yours and bring you down to my level. This is me, Elizabeth. This is where I live, who I am, what I do. I want you like I've never wanted anyone in my life. But I don't want only half of you. I've got to have it all."

"You have all of my love, Sam!"

With alarming suddenness he released one of her wrists and slammed his fist against the pillow beside her head. "Dammit, Elizabeth! Don't you realize that this will not work?"

Her chest was rising and falling with each sob, but she couldn't take her eyes off his face. "No!" she cried. "No, I don't realize that!"

He shook his head angrily. "I can't live with you running back and forth to all of your wealthy friends and shopping sprees and gala events. I can't live with that, Elizabeth!"

"But my life has not stopped because I'm with you, Sam. I can't just slam the door on it and give it all up. You say this is who you are, well, that is who I am."

He stared at her for a long agonizing moment, then loosened his hold on her. He sat up on the edge of the bed and cupped his head in his hands. His voice was low and drawn. "I know that, Elizabeth. I've known it all along, but I just didn't want to face it. That's why it will never work between us. We're two different people who live in two very different worlds."

She sat up behind him and wrapped her arms around his waist. "But we love each other, Sam. I've never loved anyone the way I love you."

He turned around and held her face between his hands. "I know that. And I will always, always love you. But . . . sometimes it takes more than that. It takes a commitment to the same ideals, the same goals." His gaze took in the moist green of her eyes, the shape of her nose, the curve of her cheeks and lips. "We don't have that, Elizabeth. No matter how hard we try or how badly we want it, it doesn't change that fact. We don't have the courage that it takes to make this relationship work."

She leaned toward him and pressed her forehead against his chest. "Please, let me try harder, Sam. Please try with me. Don't end it yet."

His arms wrapped around her and held her tightly, encompassing the warmth of her body as they clung to each other. His chin rested on top of her head and the flowery fragrance of her perfume lifted upward, filling his nose with the scent of her. Very slowly he laid her back on the bed and lowered his mouth to hers. And the taste of her poured through him like full-bodied wine on a summer evening.

Elizabeth waited in the hallway until the nurse had finished with her elaborate mechanical ministrations of the patient. When she was given the go-ahead, she walked through the doorway and into the room.

Zelma Worlitzer was little more than a ghostly etching against the white sheets. Her body seemed much smaller than before as she lay all tangled amidst plastic intravenous cords, heart monitoring gadgets, and a tube extending from her nose and mouth.

Elizabeth stepped tentatively over to the side of the bed, and it was several seconds before Zelma opened her eyes and noticed her standing there.

Elizabeth opened her mouth to speak, but nothing would pass the blockage of tears in her throat. She reached out and took Zelma's limp hand in hers and held it for a long, silent time. Finally she was able to speak. "I am so sorry," she said. "I let you down, Zelma, and I'll never forgive myself for that."

With great effort Zelma shook her head and waved her hand at the chair two feet away. Elizabeth pulled it next to the bed, sat down, and rested her arms on the mattress beside the old woman. Zelma grabbed her arm and pulled her closer for a faint whisper.

"Do I look all right, dear? My hair? My makeup?"

Elizabeth tried to swallow the painful lump. "You look lovely, Zelma. Samuel Goldwyn would be very proud of you."

Mrs. Worlitzer leaned back against the pillow and closed her eyes, smiling. "Yes, I suppose he would." She began speaking again, but Elizabeth had to lean much closer to hear her. "Don't feel bad for not being with me," she was saying. "Reverend Winslow may not understand, but I do. Our status demands certain things of us. There are more important things for members of our caste to worry about."

"But, Zelma, you are important to me. And Sam is important to me. There is no one who is more important than you."

Zelma turned her head to gaze upon her with her tired, yellowed eyes. "Do not try to be what you are not, Elizabeth. I know what I'm talking about." She turned her head back and stared up at the ceiling. "To thine own self be true," she mumbled. "And it must follow, as the night the day..."

Elizabeth stayed beside her, waiting, listening, but Zelma Worlitzer said nothing more. She had fallen asleep.

Chapter Twenty-two

Elizabeth only had three more phone calls to make and then she could go home. Two of the counseling volunteers had scheduling problems and another was sick, so their sessions had to be changed to another time. She checked the calendar on her desk and then called the counselors and the parole officers with the new times.

She had been working in the office of the Youth Excellence Service for two months now and she had seen firsthand how well the project was going. Sam had planned everything so carefully before he would allow it to begin, and now it was running as smoothly as something of this type could be expected to run. The young juvenile offenders showed up regularly for their counseling sessions and the volunteers were all happy, for the most part, with the response and cooperation they were getting from the parole officers.

Elizabeth felt a glow of confidence and accomplishment for her own part in the endeavor. Sam had praised her over and over for how smoothly and efficiently everything was running, and even with all the work, she still had time to visit Zelma at the hospital and help him with some of his other projects. Yesterday they had even gotten away for a few hours by themselves.

They had taken a long walk west toward Wicker Park. Once, not so long ago, it had looked about the same as Sam's neighborhood. But now young couples were moving in and fixing up the old Victorian houses, building up the economic base, and bringing in some pride and much-needed capital to the area. They walked along, admiring the brightly painted houses, the new shutters, the stained glass hanging in the windows.

"We could do that," Elizabeth said. "I like that color, don't you?"

"Yeah, it's nice. I like what they did with their porch."

"Oh, this makes me so excited to get started on ours!"

Sam watched her closely and she looked up at him, surprise registered in her eyes. "I said ours, didn't I?"

He nodded, and she knew he was afraid to say anything that might put too much emphasis on her remark. She knew him so well now, and she realized his thoughts were a reflection of her own. They were both afraid to hope for too much. And so the moment and the remark passed as they headed back east toward Blackhawk.

She cleared some of the papers off her desk, locking her work and her thoughts away tightly in the drawer. She wasn't going to have any doubts right now. She simply wasn't going to think about it. No, instead she would think about what Sam would find when he came home today. Every day he found something new in the decor of the house. New curtains, a new throw rug, colorful floor pillows, a vase with flowers. And always, he would shake his head in amazement, smile, and then sweep her up in his arms with an embrace that left her breathless. Today he would find an antique bird cage with a fern inside. She laughed to herself as she imagined his reaction over that one.

She closed and locked her drawers, donned her cardigan sweater, then locked the front door of the clinic tightly. The evening was soft and balmy, with only a light breeze wafting around her.

She was halfway to the house when she stopped. She had left the book she was reading back at the office on her desk. She was hoping to finish it tonight, but she wasn't really sure she wanted to read it badly enough to walk the three blocks back to the office. With an exasperated sigh she turned around and headed back down the street toward the clinic. Alfredo waved to her from his shop as she walked by and when she passed Billy, scrounging with determination through a trash can, she pulled the untouched portion of the sandwich she had packed for lunch from her coat pocket and handed it to him.

She still found it difficult not to be totally revulsed by the sight of a human being foraging through garbage for something to eat, but she was now at least able to face the fact that it did exist and that if nothing else, she could help by giving him something of her own.

Back at the clinic, she inserted her key in the door. There was no clicking sound. She was sure she had locked it when she left. Positive of it, in fact. But now it was unlocked.

She slowly pushed it open and stared into the darkened space of the YES office. Across the room was another door that led into the main part of the clinic, but she couldn't see that far. She could see nothing beyond the light from the open door. The wall switch was several steps away and she had to move from the door to get to it. She took a couple of steps and then froze as she heard a heavier footstep fall behind her.

She pivoted sharply and whispered into the dark. "Who's there?"

The only answer was the decisive click of the lock on the office door behind her.

A split second later Elizabeth's shock dulled all but

he excruciating pain of her arm being wrenched behind
er back. A huge hand covered her mouth and its fin-
ers dug into her cheeks. She could hear two young men
alking, but the words were garbled by her fear. She
vas shoved across the darkened room and felt a sharp
ab of pain when she fell against the desk. And then the
rms were once again holding her and pushing her far-
her back into the building. She could hear one of the
nen as he worked at the lock of the door that led into
he main part of the clinic.

"What do you want?" she tried to say, but her head
vas suddenly knocked back with the force of a hand
hat struck her face. The reverberations in her ears and
he explosion behind her eyes blocked out all other sen-
ations for interminable seconds.

She was aware of mumbled curses, of drawers being
opened and their contents dumped on the floor, of
breaking glass and cabinets being ransacked. The pain
n her arm came back to her and she cried out, but the
arm holding her only increased the upward pressure.

"Hurry up," the one behind her said.

"Got it," the other whispered.

"Then let's get the hell out of here."

"What about her? She's seen us!"

"No!" She shook her head frantically, but they
didn't seem to notice or hear her. She hadn't really been
able to see their faces that well, only vague shadowy
outlines. She felt a dull pain in her back as she was
thrown onto the floor.

"Out...no...care...her." The words they spoke
sounded foreign and so far away. The only thing she
was aware of was the tearing of material and the blinding pain against her face once again.

And then there was nothing.

Her mind couldn't catalog the events that followed.
Although a dull, throbbing pain seemed to rack every

square inch of her body, she was somehow certain that the one who had been hitting her was no longer there. She thought she heard shuffling and groaning, then a low cry. She tried to sit up, but her body would not respond. Suddenly the light was turned on, blinding her, and there was a pair of hands beneath her arms, lifting her.

She stared up into the sweaty brown face she had learned to fear on that November day so long ago. Stripes. The knife was in his hands, the cold shaft of metal that flashed brilliant under the fluorescent light from the ceiling. She cried out. "No!" She tried to get away, but he held her too tightly. Oh, God, not him. She didn't want to know that he and his gang were responsible for this. She didn't want to see his face. It was too real, too dangerous, too deadly. He had warned her that she wouldn't live long. He had told her.

In a fleeting moment of panic she tried to struggle out of his reach. But his grip on her was too strong. He did not try to lift her again, but he still held her down where she could not move. She saw a dark streak of blood on his neck and forearm and wondered remotely if it was her blood. She didn't want to know. He hated her and he was probably going to kill her. She was the one who was going to end up paying for the physical and social lashings that had been inflicted on him all his life. Somehow she was going to pay. That much she did know.

Another one of his followers ran into the room and listened to some order that he shouted in Spanish. Then the boy ran out again. She thought she recognized Sam's name, but she couldn't be sure.

It seemed that she would black out for minutes at a time and then awaken to see Stripes's hard, blank stare. And then she heard Sam's voice, felt his hand against her face, and then a low angry curse. But all she knew

was a blessed relief. He had come to help her, to take
her away from these angry voices, these hard brutal
faces, and these painful hands.

She clung to him and cried while he tried to comfort
her. And then she was lifted onto a stretcher and carried
out the door. A blast of cool air hit her face and the
tears ran like ice down her swollen jaw.

Moments later, it seemed, she was on a table, beneath
a bright light, and a young doctor was pressing on her
face with a cold, smelly cloth.

"Hello." He smiled brightly.

Her eyes slowly focused on the man's face. And her
first thought was to wonder what in the hell he was so
happy about. "Doctors aren't supposed to have
beards," she mumbled, then winced as he touched a
particularly sensitive spot beneath her eye.

"Says who?"

She watched the images fade to a blur, then return
again to clarity. She frowned up at the doctor. "Hip-
pocrates," she answered, not realizing five minutes had
passed since he asked the question.

He chuckled and shook his head. "Nope. I think he
had a beard. All those ancient Greek scholars did,
didn't they?"

"I wouldn't know," she groaned. "I'm only thirty."
She fixed her serious gaze on him. "Am I going to live
to be thirty-one?"

"I think you might," he said. "Can you sit up now?"

"No."

"Sure you can. Come on, that's a girl."

She groaned at the effort it took to sit. "What's the
matter with my wrist?"

"Oh, nothing. It's just cracked."

She stared at the cast that covered her hand and wrist,
then lifted her bewildered eyes to the doctor. "You call
that nothing? What kind of a doctor are you?"

His back was facing her as he reached into a cabinet for some supplies. "I'm a big toe doctor," he replied in all seriousness. "But nobody had any big toe problems, so they called me in to see if I could Super Glue you back together."

A wave of dizziness passed over her and she thought she might fall off the table. She glared at him when he returned to her. How could he act so casual when she was falling apart? "I think you left a piece of me lying over there on the floor," she snapped.

"I should have left your mouth over there. Now would you please be quiet and hold still while I wash this cut?"

She winced at the touch of the cloth on her face. "Where is Sam?"

"He's out in the waiting room, pacing like a wild cat."

"Did they catch the men—" Her voice broke on the memory.

"I think so."

She nodded, wanting to taste the sweet revenge of knowing that Stripes and his gang were behind bars, staring with their cold, cruel eyes at nothing but a cold, gray wall. But her own pain held the vindictive pleasure at bay.

The doctor helped her off the table and walked with her to the door. "You're doing fine. Just take it slow and easy for a few days."

"How long do I have to wear this thing on my arm?"

"We'll x-ray it again in two weeks. Until then, don't move it."

She resented his casual attitude toward her and her injuries, and she scowled at him once more. "And what happens if I do move it?"

He opened the door for her and handed her over to

Sam. "It will hurt," he said, then disappeared behind the swinging door of the emergency room.

An hour later she lay in Sam's bed and he sat on the edge beside her, holding out a glass of water and two pain pills. "Come on, Elizabeth, take them. You'll feel much better."

"What I'd rather have is a glass of wine. Does my voice sound funny?"

"You're a little hoarse, that's all. I'll get you some wine."

He hurried downstairs and she closed her eyes. But they immediately flew open again. All she wanted to do was sleep and forget, but every time she closed her eyes, the images of pain and hard voices came back to her.

She tried to smile at Sam as he handed her a glass of wine, but instead the tears began to fall. He was instantly down beside her, holding her in his arms, his voice low and warm and very soothing.

"Why did they do it, Sam?" Her words were broken by sobs. "Why does he hate me so much?"

He held her head against his chest and frowned. "No one hates you, Elizabeth. You were just in the wrong place at the wrong time." He closed his eyes and gritted his teeth. *Wrong time, wrong place, like hell!* This was all his fault. He had known not to let her work there. He had known that something like this could happen. She had been so innocent, so beautiful and carefree, and because of his own selfish desire to have her here, he had forced her into a reality for which she was not prepared.

When he realized how tightly he was holding her, he laid her back down on the pillow. His fingers brushed at the tears on her cheeks and he tried to check the self-loathing that continuously threatened to rise up within him.

"What would I have done if you hadn't come to save

me? What would have happened to me?'' She swallowed the cry and made a hiccuping sound.

He ran his fingers through her hair. ''It wasn't me.''

''I don't remember anyone else being there. Everything is so mixed up in my head. First one guy was pushing me to the floor and hitting me and then next it was Stripes and then you were there and I was in the hospital and...oh, Sam!'' With her free hand she clutched on to his shirt sleeve. ''I should have told you about the other time. I should have told you about his threats, but I was so afraid you would go to him and get hurt and I just didn't know what to do!''

''Elizabeth.'' He was bending over her, holding her still and trying to calm her down. ''You're just upset...''

''No! I know what I'm talking about. He and his friends stopped me on the street one day...about a month ago. They threatened me and told me I had better show them some respect and—''

''Who are you talking about?'' He was still leaning over her, his voice gentle, his expression dubious as to her lucidity at this moment.

She sighed with fatigue and sagged back into the mattress. It was so much effort to talk and to make anyone understand anything. ''Stripes,'' she whispered weakly.

Sam frowned as he tried to piece it all together. ''Stripes threatened you?''

''Yes. He told me I had better show him some respect or I wouldn't live very long.''

His jaw tightened at the thought of the barbarity he had forced her to confront in living here. ''That's very typical of him,'' he said, wishing he could pull the verbal and physical abuse away from her where it couldn't touch her anymore.

She just stared at him with a bewildered and painful expression. Her throat was really too sore to talk, but she whispered the bitter words anyway. "Then I suppose you'll brush off this last little attack of his as very typical too."

The lines in Sam's forehead deepened as he looked down at her. "I don't understand, Elizabeth. I'm trying to, but I don't. What little attack do you mean?"

She wanted to scream at him, to lash out and strike him and hurt him the way she had been hurt, but nothing would move except for her tears. Finally the words poured out. "I'm talking about what he did to me today, Sam!" Her shoulders began to shake with each cry. "I'm talking about the way he kept hitting me, and hurting me, and—"

"Elizabeth!" Sam stretched out beside her and pulled her head onto his shoulder, his arms looped around her back and chest. "Stripes didn't hit you. He's the one who saved you!"

Elizabeth choked back another sob and lay very, very still. A new form of shock began to spread through her as his statement settled upon her brain. No, he still didn't understand. He had it all wrong. How could that be? Stripes was there and he was holding her under her arms. She could still feel the grip of his hands. And then...

A sense of wonder slowly crept along her arms and neck and face, filling her body with a sense of reality that went far beyond what one read in books, or saw in the movies, or learned in school. This finally was real life. The naked reality. The incomprehensible.

Reality, then, was a boy who was emotionally forty years older than he should be; who had watched the murder of his mother by his father; who had lived by the sword and would probably die by the sword; who had adopted his own form of feudal, ruthless power to defy his own powerlessness against a society he thought would manipulate him; who hated Elizabeth and all the things she represented to him that he would never know.

He was all of these things. And yet, he had saved her life.

She closed her eyes and spoke softly. "I want to go home, Sam."

The words thrust into him with the driving force of a large knife. "I know you do, Elizabeth," he whispered. "I know you do."

"Just for a few days," she said, looking up at him, but he would not look back at her. The lines around his eyes seemed more pronounced tonight, the angles of his face sharper. "Will you hold me until I fall asleep?"

He blinked very slowly and swallowed hard. "For as long as you want me to."

"There is still so much to do," she mumbled sleepily and curled against him. "So much...I have to help Zelma Worlitzer get well...I mustn't forget to reschedule Virginia Willis's counseling session." Her words were becoming more garbled as she drifted in and out of sleep. "Mustn't forget to call Adrienne. We're going to St. Croix...Mother wants me there..."

And then she was asleep and Sam was left with only a dreadful hollow ache. He knew for a fact that it was going to be with him for a long, long time.

When Elizabeth woke up the next morning, her body hurt all over. Her wrist throbbed and every joint and muscle was sore. Some of the puffiness on her face had subsided, but the hollows beneath her eyes were dark and there was a large purple bruise on her lower left jaw.

"I feel like I've been through a meat grinder," she groaned as Sam lifted the pillows behind her and helped her to sit up.

"Do you need a pain pill?" he asked, pulling the covers up over her.

"I don't think I could even swallow one. My throat is very sore. I think . . . he tried to choke me . . ."

"It's okay, babe. Later you'll be able to talk about this and think about it a little easier." He sat on the edge of the bed beside her. "I called your housekeeper this morning and told her what happened. She was going to notify your mother and grandmother and then send Walter to get you."

She looked startled for a minute until she remembered that she was the one who had mentioned going home. But now, for some inexplicable reason, the idea of it terrified her. Wasn't it like taking a step backward? Flying back to the nest when the world proved to be too cold and hostile?

"It will only be for a few days," she said, hoping to convince both Sam and herself of that fact.

He only nodded and ran his hand in a slow caress down the side of her hair. "You just get lots of rest and let them take care of you."

"And what about you, Sam? Who will take care of you?"

Inside, he wanted to hold her and beg her to stay, because he knew what her going would mean. But he only smiled weakly. "I've been taking care of myself for a long time. I'll be all right. You want some breakfast now?"

She reached out and laid her hand on his thigh. "I honestly don't know what I would do without you, Sam."

Every muscle in his body seemed to freeze and his blood felt as if it were congealing. Couldn't she see it? Didn't she have any idea what was happening? It was more than the fact that she wanted to go home for a few days. That was a perfectly normal response, considering what she had been through. But it was much more than that. It was the fact that she had been subjected to the violent reality of this neighborhood, and she wasn't going to get over that very quickly, if ever. Right now she really believed that she would go home for a few days, rest and recuperate, and then come back and find everything the same as before.

Only he knew that nothing would ever be the same again. They could playact for a while. But he now realized that he had made a big mistake, not in loving her, but in trying to make her exist in a place where she did not belong. He should have sent her home last week. But she had begged him to let her stay and try again. He had selfishly wanted her to stay beyond all sense of what was best for her.

He had forced her to exist where she did not belong. It was as absurd as trying to force a fish to live on land, or a deer to live in the desert. He had captured the butterfly and then put her in a jar where she could not breathe. It was time to remove the lid and let her fly away again, back to where she belonged.

Chapter Twenty-three

The dream was back. Leering faces, hard voices, and painful hands. Like the Cheshire cat, Billy Hawkins's face loomed in front of her, then disappeared except for his toothless grin. She was a little girl again, wearing a pink smock and pedal pushers. She was running down a tree-lined street, elms arching over the wide avenue. And then there were three of them. Hurry, Adrienne, hurry, Johnny! She yelled back at them, but they wouldn't keep up. Suddenly there was a car bearing down on all three of them. Closer, closer, forcing them to dive off the park cliff into the lake. She looked up and at the edge of the cliff was the car. A red Mercedes. Her car. She floated for a while on top of the cool water until rough hands wrenched her from it and twisted her arm behind her back. She screamed and cried out for Sam.

Immediately arms enveloped her, warm and tender, but the voice was different. It was all wrong. It was not Sam's voice.

"It's all right, Liz. Everything is all right now. I'm here with you."

She opened her eyes and stared up into Thomas Benson's face. He brushed stray hairs back from her sweat-drenched forehead.

"It was the same dream again, wasn't it?"

She nodded weakly. "I didn't know you were here. How long have you been up here?"

"About an hour. Your housekeeper let me in. I just didn't want you to have to wake up alone this morning. I thought you might need me."

She started to smile, but closed her eyes instead. Why was he here? Why was he being so nice to her? She wanted to be left alone. Her dreams were full of Sam and her reality was full of Thomas. When would she ever have a moment to herself?

She opened her eyes again and he poured her a cup of tea. "Do you need anything for your wrist? A pain pill or anything?"

She sat up slowly and propped the pillows behind her. "No. I'm fine. What time is it?"

"Only eight thirty. If you want to sleep some more, go ahead."

Elizabeth shook her head and took the cup of tea from him. "I need to get up and move about. I can't stand lying in bed another day."

"You had quite a shock and you needed the rest. I want you to go see an orthopedic surgeon about your wrist. Maybe you'll feel like it today or tomorrow."

She glanced down at the sling tied from her arm to her neck. "I suppose. It doesn't hurt much anymore. Maybe they'll take this thing off."

"You need a specialist to look at it. No telling what kind of quack it was in that hospital they took you to."

She looked into her cup. "He was a big toe doctor."

"What?"

She smiled. "Well, at least that's what he told me."

Thomas shook his head in disgust. "He probably wasn't even a real doctor."

She shrugged. "Is my face still bruised?"

He reached over to touch her cheek, his fingers warm from the cup he had been holding. "Just a little. It looks much better than it did when you came home yesterday morning.''

"Everything is still so fuzzy to me. I remember being hurt, but I have trouble picturing the faces. I keep seeing—''

"Liz.'' Thomas laid his hand on her leg. "You mustn't talk about it. You must forget it ever happened. It will go away if you don't think about it.''

Will it? She wondered about that. Maybe he was right, but it just seemed to her that she would never get rid of it if she couldn't get it outside herself. It was all locked away in her stomach and in her chest and in her mind. She wanted it out. She wanted the dreams to go away and those sudden attacks of shakes that she would get in the middle of a conversation with her mother or grandmother or Thomas. If she could tell someone about it, maybe they would take it away from her. But then, perhaps Thomas knew better.

"I just want you to know,'' he was saying, "that from now on I'm going to take care of you. Nothing will ever, ever happen to you again, Liz. I promise you that. You're home now, and I'm going to take care of you.''

She stared at him and tried with all her might to keep the cup from shaking out of her grasp. *Nothing will ever happen to you again.* Didn't he know that was exactly what she was afraid of? With Thomas Benson she would be taken care of. Everything good and bad that could happen to her happened with Sam. With Thomas all that remained was nothing.

She handed the cup over to him and slipped back down into the covers. "I think I'll sleep just a little longer. I guess I'm more tired than I realized.''

He pulled the bedclothes up over her and sat in the chair beside the bed. "That's a girl. You get some more rest. But if you should have the dream again, I'll be here right beside you.''

She turned over, facing the opposite direction, and fell asleep. Only this time the dream was not the same. This time she was in a cave. Dark and damp. Someone turned on a light and she could see that the walls of the cave were papered in gold brocade. Outside the entrance it was snowing and she wanted to go out and play in it, but the walls were slowly closing in, moving closer and closer, lowering over her. She did not cry out. In her sleep she gritted her teeth and clenched her fists, but she did not cry out. She would not let them know that she was frightened. They would never understand it.

"Thank you, Letti. That was a wonderful lunch."

Letti mumbled some sort of disapproving remark, which Elizabeth did her best to ignore, and then removed the tray and took it back downstairs. She stared again at the newspaper spread open before her, and shook her head. She was still reading it when her mother walked into the room.

Elizabeth glared at her. "What is the meaning of this?"

Louise dropped an armload of boxes on the bed and walked over to admire a new arrangement of flowers that had just arrived. "Aren't these lovely. Oh, they're from the Vectors, isn't that nice. And don't you look better today!" She turned to face Elizabeth's stony countenance. "I brought you some lovely things from Mathews. I know they are going to look great on you."

Elizabeth slapped her hand against the newspaper. "Mother, I want to know about this. You did this, didn't you?"

"Well, dear, now you know how those bitchy columnists are. And Helena Shaw is the worst of the bunch. She had been snooping around, asking questions about you for days and I didn't want to see what she would actually print about this 'unfortunate incident' of yours. All I wanted to do was set the record straight.''

"Is this what you call setting the record straight? And I quote dear Miss Shaw: 'Our very own Liz Parkins was viciously and brutally attacked while performing a charitable service on the near west side of town. Miss Parkins is well-known for her philanthropic endeavors with this city's tired and poor. But it gives one pause when one's altruism and selfless devotion to a needy cause is rewarded in such a primitive fashion.' '' She looked up at Louise. "How could you, Mother!"

"I did not lie," Louise said, sitting at the foot of the bed. "Everything that was said there was the truth."

Elizabeth forced herself from the bed and walked to the window. Spring morning. She had seen this view countless times from this window, yet she never tired of it. New buds sprouting on the trees in the park, birds lighting, plucking a loose twig or leaf from a branch, then flying off again. The blue of the lake beyond. Tranquil this morning, without a breeze stirring up its surface. A few sails from boats in the distance.

She turned back to her room, white and lacy and clean. Pure. "Distortion of the truth, Mother. You deliberately distorted the facts. I was not there on some mercy mission. I was there because I was living with Sam. Because I wanted to be there."

"I know that, dear. But, well, we all have these little chapters in our lives that come to an end. We finish them and then... well, we just move ahead in life." Louise watched her daughter staring for so long out the window. "It is a finished chapter, isn't it, Liz?"

She didn't turn around. She kept her back to the room. Finished? She supposed it was. But weren't there those chapters or those books that you carried around with you all your life, that you never forgot? Moving

portraits of people who became like friends, eloquent
tales that you always kept nearby on the bookcase, that
you would open and re-read again and again, finding
the same magic that you found the very first time you
read them?

Oh, but what was the point? Was any of it worth it in
the end? She had taken the trouble to care, and look
where it got her.

Elizabeth looked back at her mother, who quickly
cast her worried gaze down toward the packages on the
bed, then picked one up and started opening it.
"Mother, Thomas thinks I shouldn't talk about what
happened to me on Blackhawk Street. About the—"

"The incident?" Louise quickly inserted, looking
even more worried.

"Yes. What do you think?"

"I think he is absolutely right, dear. You must put it
behind you now and forge ahead. You have so many
wonderful things in store for you and it wouldn't do to
dwell on anything too painful."

Well, maybe they were right. What did she know? She
had made such a mess of her life, she was no longer in
any position to answer for herself. She would just let
everyone else take over that job for her.

She nodded and slowly walked over to the bed, where
her mother was sitting. She looked down at the packages and tried to smile. "Why don't you show me the
things you bought me?"

She had been dreading it almost as much as she had
been longing for it. Every time the phone rang, she held
her breath, wondering if it would be him. Even now, she
reached for the phone on the first ring. "Hello?"

"Elizabeth? It's Sam."

Her breath caught and held in the space between her
throat and lungs. *Sam.* She wanted to say his name over

and over, but she couldn't make that or anything else come out.

"How are you?" he asked, filling in the silence. "Are you feeling all right?"

"Yes, I'm feeling fine."

"That's good." He chose his words carefully, making sure he didn't impart too much. "I've been worried about you, hoping you were getting plenty of rest."

There was so much she wanted to say. So many ways she could tell him that she missed him. But he was trying hard to sound casual, and she knew how difficult for him it must have been to call at all. She would have to try equally as hard.

She brought a lightness to her voice she wasn't feeling. "There is no need to worry. Everyone is taking such good care of me. Mother, Grandmother Eva..."

"Thomas Benson?"

Her heart began to thud hard in her chest and she felt it all the way up to her temples. "Yes."

Sam leaned back, one foot propped against the kitchen wall behind him. He closed his eyes and pinched the bridge of his nose tightly between his thumb and forefinger. Well, hell, he had known how it would be. He was sure if he was to check some astrology chart, it would clearly show that he and Elizabeth were totally incompatible and that she and Thomas were destined to be together throughout eternity like a pair of binary stars. Maybe if he believed in all that nonsense, he could have saved himself a lot of trouble.

"How is Zelma?" she asked.

"What was that?"

"Zelma. Is she better?"

"Ah, yes. Doing much better."

"And the YES program?"

"It's coming along. No one can handle the paperwork nearly as well as you, but we're surviving."

"That's good." Oh, God, why were they doing this to each other! Why didn't they talk it out? There was so much that needed to be said, so many still-unanswered questions and unsolved problems. "Sam, I don't know if you happened to see this morning's *Tribune,* but—"

"Yes, I saw it." He glanced over at the still-open paper lying on the table.

"I didn't have anything to do with that. I hope you know that. I never thought of it that way."

"I know that, Elizabeth."

"The time I spent with you was the best time of my life. Oh, Sam, there is so much I want to say! But I just don't even know what I think or feel anymore."

"You need time. I understand that." The understanding he had was now manifest in the hand that held the receiver in a death grip and in the tight pain that throbbed behind his eyes.

"Adrienne came by yesterday."

"Is she getting along better?"

"Oh, yes, much. She—she wants me to go on a trip with her as soon as my wrist is better. The Virgin Islands, I think."

"Are you going?"

"Yes, I think I will."

His silence was more telling than words could ever be. When he spoke, his voice was labored, but he was again making a supreme effort to remain in control. "That's good, Elizabeth. I really mean that. You probably need a complete change of scene."

"Yes, that's what I was thinking. I sit around thinking too much about what happened to me and I need to think about something else for a change."

"Are you having problems sleeping at night? Are you scared?"

"Just some bad dreams, that's all."

"Do you want to talk about them?"

She closed her eyes. *Yes, yes, yes!* She wanted to talk about them. She wanted to talk about the whole thing, but everyone seemed to think it was best that she push it farther and farther down from the surface. Thomas didn't think she should talk about it. Her mother didn't think she should talk about it. Only Sam thought she should talk about it; only he was willing to listen. But who was she to believe anymore?

"No, I'm having them less and less. I'm sure they'll go away soon."

"Well, if you need to talk . . . or if you want anything, you know I'll be here. No matter how late you want to call."

"I know that." She choked on the lump in her throat. "Thank you."

A lull of silence hung between them and they both knew that there was nothing more to say.

"Good-bye, Elizabeth."

"Good-bye, Sam."

Chapter Twenty-four

The fire spread quickly through the abandoned warehouse. White-hot flames licking like tongues at the walls and ceiling, windows popping out of their casings, and glass shattering from the sustained heat. A swift April wind arose during the night, caught the sparks in its breath, and carried them to adjacent buildings. Within thirty minutes half of the block was on fire and, within an hour, Blackhawk Street became a lurid inferno.

Fire fighters worked through the long night to extinguish the blaze, but in the early dawn hours it was apparent that the fire had taken a heavy toll. The warehouse had caved in entirely, and the two buildings on each side of it were nothing more than charred shells.

Billy Hawkins ambled slowly down the street, carrying a large bundle in his arms. He picked his way through the smoldering ruins, searching diligently for a new place to call home. His corner of the world had been beside the east wall of Marston Metalworks. But that home was gone now. He would have to move on.

Mama Vinzetti moved her soup kitchen to the street, serving hot chicken broth to anyone who was now homeless, had lost a business, or was just plain hungry.

Father Stanislavski organized a group of youngsters to help various shop owners with their cleanup, and everyone on the street pitched in to help turn the disaster area back into a neighborhood.

Sam wiped his forearm across his forehead, removing several layers of sweat and grime. The sleeves of his white oxford shirt were rolled to the elbows and his jeans were covered with dirt and ash. He had been raking through the debris since early this morning, trying to help his neighbors locate some of their personal belongings amidst the rubble.

He looked down the street and shook his head. So much was lost in the fire that it would be weeks before the actual damage tally could be figured. Alfredo had suffered a big loss in his market; The Windy City Pawn Shop had lots of water damage; The Traveler's Hotel was all but decimated; the liquor store, the haberdashery, the hospital annex where the clinic was, and the three factories on the opposite side of the street were all damaged to one degree or another.

The fire chief's car and the police squad cars were still lined up on the street at this hour, trying to keep order and, by their presence, forcing the youth gangs to remain underground and quiet for the time being. But already there had been considerable looting in any shop or apartment that had an opening to the intruders.

Sam pulled a shiny object up from the debris with his rake and bent over to pick it up. It was an ornate brass candle holder that he had seen in Mrs. Romanowski's apartment. He dropped it into the duffel bag beside him with all of the other personal effects he had found. Later he would take the bag to the mission and the owners could claim the items.

The job of raking through the charred wood and ashes was a tedious, solitary one and it gave his mind too much free rein to think. He had tried to keep busy over the past few weeks, hoping to keep his mind so occupied that he would not have time to think about his life. What he had with Elizabeth, what he no longer had. But that had proved to be a futile attempt at best. No matter where he was or what he was doing, he wanted her with him. He would imagine how she might look, what she would say, the tiny gestures she would make with her hands, her eyes, her smile...

And at night the process repeated itself all over again. Only then it was with more intensity and much, much more intimacy. He would imagine the scent of her hair, the taste of her skin, the touch of her fingers upon him. And the need for her would scream through him until he would fall asleep from sheer exhaustion.

He pulled the rake harder and faster through the rubble, doubling his efforts to concentrate on anything but her. She was gone; he had to accept that. In fact, right now she was probably in the Virgin Islands with her friend Adrienne. About as far gone as she could be. All right, so fine. He had to get over her and get on with his life. Theirs was a relationship that simply was not meant to be. He didn't fit in her world and she didn't fit in his.

So think of something else, dammit! Aha, here was a child's toy. Bend over, pick it up. Yes, put it in the bag. Concentrate on the task at hand or think of all the work you have to do, all of the projects that need to be started. Or, better yet, think of someone else's problems. Everybody on this street had problems much worse than his own. He at least still had a place to call home. That was more than could be said for a lot of these people. Why didn't he think about Mrs. Romanowski, or the Lichenburgs, or old Mr. Kaiser. Alfredo was going to have to do a major overhaul on his store. Lola was in the hospital being treated for smoke inhalation. He was at least glad that Mary and her baby weren't around when this happened.

He had received a letter from her a few days ago, the

first one she had written since she moved to Gary. In her cryptic style of writing he had interpreted that she and Adeline were living with a friend who was very nice to them both. Her letter didn't mention the name of the friend, but it sounded as if he were treating her and her baby all right.

She wrote that she was now working part-time cleaning houses, but Sam sensed an undercurrent that was not written so much in the words themselves but was evident somewhere between the lines. There was a feeling of restlessness in her words, a hint of impatience with the life she was now leading. And it was only a matter of time, he supposed, until she was back on the street again. It was always possible that Adeline's presence would help her decide to find a more solid line of work. But it was highly unlikely. The ways of the street were indelibly ingrained at a very young age and they were ways that were not easy to change. He couldn't help but wonder if he had done all that he could do.

Sam remembered clearly that day when he found the tiny bundle wrapped in newspapers on his porch. As the scenes formed in his mind he pictured Elizabeth standing in his doorway with her arms full of quilts and diapers and clothes for the baby. He could see her holding Adeline in her arms, then bending to kiss the tiny brown cheek. He recalled every moment of that dark night, with Adeline asleep in the basket beside the bed. And he could still hear Elizabeth's soft moans against his throat and chest.

He stopped raking and leaned his arm and forehead on the handle of the tool. The smell of ashes filled his nose and lungs and rivulets of sweat ran down his chest. But his mind spiraled like a fire out of control with memories that he could not seem to erase, no matter how hard he tried.

He raised his head and looked down the street at the gray haze that hung beneath the clear spring day. A wasteland. Eliot had been right; April *was* the cruelest month.

The sun beat down, drenching the white sand and their bodies in a delicious sweat. The sky was azure blue with only wisps of cirrus clouds high above them. The gentle breezes off the Caribbean blew ever so lightly over their golden flesh.

Adrienne rolled over onto her back and stretched. "I'm in heaven. This is almost better than sex, isn't it?"

Elizabeth lifted her head from the crook of her arm and blinked her eyes. "Are you speaking to me?"

"The sun, the waves, the exquisite feel of this sand on my body. This place is better than Capri, don't you agree?"

Elizabeth pretended to be annoyed. She sighed and sat up, wrapping her arms around her knees. "If you insist on chattering away at me, I suppose I ought to contribute something to this conversation. And yes, I do like this better than Capri. Too many rocks there and too little beach to suit me."

"Oh, but we had some good times there." Adrienne lifted her face to the sun. "Remember that day when we took the boat over to the blue grotto and met those two boys from Yugoslavia? What were their names?"

Elizabeth laughed at the memory. "I can't remember. Seems like we kept calling them Yagreb and Sagreb or something like that."

"They were actually convinced that we were going to pay them for sex!" Adrienne laughed. "What a riot that was! 'But you are rich American women,' they kept saying."

Elizabeth rested her arms on her bent knees and

looked out across the water, watching the gentle blue waves wash up onto the beach. "Part of their sexless socialist upbringing, no doubt."

Adrienne snapped her fingers. "Maybe that was my mistake. Maybe if I had paid John all those years to make it with me, he would have found it too profitable to look elsewhere. Maybe there's something in the Communist Manifesto about that. Some secret key to dealing with debauched, capitalistic men." She sighed wistfully. "Those were the days, weren't they, Liz?"

Elizabeth turned her head toward her and smiled. "They were much simpler times, I'll say that."

"Remember how it was? Four or five of us girls would take off for the summer to the wine country of France or the Greek Islands or we'd just traipse across the Netherlands. I wish we could go back and start all over again."

Elizabeth's mouth was pressed against her crossed arms, now resting on her knees. "Can't, though."

"It all changed after most of us married. I guess things are not all that different for you, are they? I mean you never really had to grow up, did you?"

Elizabeth closed her eyes, trying to block the pain. *Don't think about it and it will go away.* "Nothing is the same anymore, Adrienne."

Their ensuing silence filled the air and mingled with the warm sunlight that filtered down on them. It was Adrienne who first broke the quiet.

"If you could start all over again, would you do things differently?"

"Like what?"

"Your life. Would you live it the same way?"

"I don't know. I always thought of myself as happy. Everything was so. . .easy."

Adrienne stretched her legs out in front of her and ran

her hands down her calves to her toes. "Yes, it was easy, wasn't it?"

"Do you realize I have never had to make a single important decision in my life?" Elizabeth sat up straighter. "Think about it, Adrienne. Not a single decision. Not one. Everything has always been decided for me. My life has been planned and scheduled and arranged and I've moved through it like a zombie. I always thought the world was a safe place. But it's not. I was just so insulated from the real world that I didn't realize what was actually out there."

"Oh, Liz, come on. You're just reacting to that horrible experience you went through a few weeks ago. And see, there was a decision you made on your own. You chose to go over there and live. No one forced you to do it. So you have no one to blame but yourself."

Elizabeth's mouth hardened and she turned her eyes toward the sea. "I wasn't blaming anyone. And I'm not sure it was much of a decision."

"What do you mean?"

She frowned and wrapped her arms more tightly about her legs, resting her chin on her knees. "It was more like I had to try it out or something. I never said, 'This is where I'm going to live.' I never committed that much...and I let my grandmother's threats pull me back home." She shook her head. "Maybe I don't have the ability to make any decisions. Maybe people like us don't have that capability."

Adrienne sighed. "Well, one thing I learned in my marriage to John was that nothing is as it seems. And you'd better live for the moment, because tomorrow everything might just crash in on you."

Elizabeth smiled. "I think you've survived it all splendidly. You've done much better than I probably would have. Better than I'm surviving now," she mumbled.

Adrienne glanced over at her. "So, is it over?"

She raised her head. "Is what over?"

"Your relationship with that preacher?"

She stared out over the water and was filled with the maddening, but now familiar, ache that gripped her whenever she thought of Sam. How could a relationship that took so much from her and that at the same time gave her so much ever be considered over? The feelings she had for him would go on and on forever. And yet, he was there, secure in his niche in the world, and she was here, well ensconced in the world she had always known. That was the way it should be; the way it would always be.

She glanced at Adrienne. "Yes, it's over."

Adrienne's eyes narrowed on her friend's grim profile. She had known Elizabeth too long and she wasn't fooled by her now. *Like hell it was over.* "So," Adrienne said, yawning, mustering up as much casual indifference as she could. "How is Thomas Benson? I understand that some interesting plans are in the works for you two."

She nodded. "So it seems."

"What is that supposed to mean? Surely you have some say in all of this. Are you serious about him or not?"

Elizabeth closed her eyes and repeated the word slowly. "Serious. God, I wish I knew what that word is supposed to mean."

"It usually means do you love him?"

She pushed her toes into the sand. "Thomas is a very kind, sensitive, interesting man."

"That was a hedge if I ever heard one. You did not answer my question, Liz."

She smiled wistfully. "So I didn't."

"As much as you probably don't want to hear this, I'm going to say it anyway. Thomas Benson is an incredible catch. You will never be lacking for anything you want. He obviously adores you. And besides, it will get Mummy and Grammy off your back.''

"Hmmm, now, that last one is the most interesting advantage of all.''

"Well, what is it? Did he ask you to marry him?''

"Yes.''

"And are you going to?''

The weariness washed through her and she was aware of a throbbing headache behind her eyes. She looked at the space of bleached sand between Adrienne and herself and spoke almost too softly to be heard. "I suppose I will.''

She lifted her gaze toward the sea. It was as though her life had become like a rock at the water's edge; continuously pounded by the surf, over and over again, until it was nothing but a fragmented pile of sand, each granule too insignificant to even merit one's concern.

All of the little truths, and hopes, and facets that had comprised Elizabeth Parkins were now gone. And it didn't matter to anyone; it didn't even seem to matter to her anymore.

"What is today?'' she asked.

Adrienne thought for a minute. "April thirtieth. Tomorrow is the first of May. Why?''

Even his words would not leave her alone. She remembered all of them. The old world just keeps on turning, he had said. Another five-year-old dies, another relationship ends, something dies within. *And the old world just keeps on turning. Life moves on.* "No reason,'' she said. "I just wondered.''

It was close to midnight and Mr. Benson had gone home when Letti climbed the stairs and carried the clean linens down the hallway to the closet. But the sound coming from behind Elizabeth's door made her stop and listen. At the hiccuping sobs that reached her ears, she shook her head, thinking, "That girl had better stop and take a good hard look at herself or she's going to end up just like her mama." The crying followed her all the way down the hall. She continuously shook her head as she stacked the sheets and towels in the closet. "Just a crying shame to see a grown woman who's nothing more than a little girl inside. Ain't never had the chance to grow up, that's her problem." She clicked her tongue in disapproval over the family's present state of affairs. "And it doesn't look like she ever will, neither."

Elizabeth sat on the edge of her bed, rocking back and forth as she sobbed. Back and forth, but the tears would not stop falling. *Things are going to work out beautifully.* Thomas had tried to convince her of that through their entire dinner. "The wedding, the marriage, our lives together. I love you, Liz, and I know that, in time, you will love me too." His hands on hers had felt as cold as ice. "Believe me, everything is going to work out perfectly."

And what had she said to him? "I know that, Thomas." Why in heaven's name had she said that? She didn't believe it for a minute.

Do you know that I love you? And that I'll take good care of you? She rocked back and forth on the bed, trying not to let the panic rise within her. He was going to take care of her, and she was going to be kept in a hermetically sealed jar. But she mustn't let the panic show. No one must know about her fears.

She reached out for the phone and began to dial Sam's number. She had to hear his voice. Just once more. She had to talk to him. He was the only one who could help her.

"Hello," the groggy voice answered.

The sound of his voice echoed deep within her. How could she tell him? How could she expect him to change what she could not even change?

"Hello?" he said again.

He was there, standing in his kitchen, his skin still warm from sleep. And she could not speak. The pain ripped through her, forcing another sob upward and out. She quickly dropped the receiver back into its holder and clutched a pillow to her face, her anguish buried in the night where no one could hear it.

It was an odd obsession to say the least, but it was a compulsion he could not control. For the fifth day in a row Sam bought the *Tribune* and, ignoring for now the front page news, quickly flipped over to the society pages.

"Sam? Sam?" Alfredo cleared his throat. "Listen, Sam, if you're a little short on cash right now . . ."

"What? Oh, yeah, sorry, here it is." He pulled the money from his pocket and handed it over to the grocer. "Things are looking pretty good around here."

"Yes, thanks to you and all my other friends, the store is going to be even better than before. You see, we have moved the fruit bin over to here and the meat over there. What you think?"

Sam's eyes zeroed in on the far right column on the page. Elizabeth Adele Parkins to wed Thomas Longworth Benson. "What? Oh, yes, *molto bene,* Alfredo. *Molto . . .*" His attention moved back to the paper and he tried to catch his breath. Suddenly his heart was pounding so hard, he couldn't even breathe. Married. She was getting married.

"The whole street is looking better than it did a couple of weeks ago," Alfredo was saying. "But we still have much to go, no?"

Sam nodded distractedly and swallowed hard. She

was actually getting married. The possibilities were gone. The dreams were being ripped from him. She was really leaving his life for good.

"I know with much work we will get there, Sam. We have much strength in this neighborhood. We will start anew."

Sam looked up from the paper and stared at the grocer, acceptance pushing hard against the dismay. It was over and he had to accept it now. He took a deep breath to calm his pulse. "Yes, Alfredo, we will all start anew."

He left the shop and walked down the sidewalk with the folded paper tucked beneath his arm. His brain did not seem to be controlling his feet. They were moving at a steady pace down the street. He turned left at the park, walking another two blocks, turning again, and then crossing the threshold of a dark, sweltering gymnasium.

In the periphery of his mind he heard the thudding sound of padded leather mittens against suspended punching bags, saw the liquid gleam of sweat that clung to well-toned bodies. He walked straight toward the ring at the back of the large room.

"Hey, Sam," one of the older trainers called out to him. "Haven't seen you around in ages. Time enough for you to grow soft on us."

Sam stopped in front of him and stared vacantly. He pulled the newspaper from beneath his arm and slapped it against his open palm. "Get me some gloves and shoes, Ozzie."

The trainer saw the hard glint of anger in his eyes and knew that Sam was here today for more than an easy sparring match. "What you gonna do with gloves today, Sam? You ain't in good enough shape to fight any of these dudes. They're animals, man."

"Just get me the equipment, dammit!"

Ozzie Morton was far beyond his prime, but in his heyday he had been one hell of a fighter. He had sparred with some of the best welterweights in the country. Ray Robinson, Marty Servo, Kid Gavilan. And he knew what that look in Sam's eyes meant. He was way beyond the sporting stage. But he also knew that if he tried to take on any of the guys who practiced in this gym, he was asking for big trouble. Ozzie studied him carefully for a minute and then nodded. "I see what you want now, Sam. Come on. I haven't had a good fight in a long time."

Showing no surprise or awareness over who he would be fighting, Sam yanked off his shirt as they walked into the locker room. They stripped to their shorts, then Ozzie tossed him a pair of gloves and shoes. Sam pulled on the shoes and laced them up, then methodically wrapped his palms with tape. He slipped on one of the mittens and pulled the laces tight. He used his teeth to help pull on the other glove and tied it around his wrist.

Ozzie tossed him a head guard. "Wear it. You ready?"

Sam took a deep breath and nodded. Without talking, they walked back into the main room and climbed the stairs to the canvas. Sam shook his arms out and took in several quick breaths. He and Ozzie circled.

His jaw was set tight and his eyes, though looking straight at the older man, were seeing something altogether different. He was not going to hold it in any longer. He had tried to make the need for her go away, but he had failed. So all right, dammit, she was getting married.

His arm shot out with a quick jab to Ozzie's face, but the older man dodged the blow and followed with an upward thrust of his left hand into Sam's stomach. Sam grimaced and danced back and to the side. They stalked each other in a circle again before Sam led with his right and caught Ozzie square on the nose.

The older man dabbed it with the back of his mitten and stepped back, collecting his wits. He looked up and saw that the fire had not lessened in Sam's eyes. If anything, it had intensified. With the force of a small bull, Ozzie slammed into him with all his might.

Sam lost his balance and fell against the ropes, but he missed the next blow by rolling to the side. The two men went after each other with a vengeance, one trying to prove that he was still good enough to fight a man twenty years younger, the other no longer able to control the eruption of anger and frustration and hurt that he had held inside for too long.

The sharp blow to the side of his head sent Sam reeling backward, and he slammed into the padded turnbuckles. But he was back on the offensive within seconds. Outside the ring, hands reached up to stop the sway of punching bags and the sounds of exercise were suspended for the next few minutes. All eyes were now directed on the two men in the ring, where the race of adrenaline and a streak of stubborn tenacity were the only things that kept bringing them out of their corners time and time again.

Elizabeth had always hated the formal parlor in this house, but never quite so much as this morning. Grandmother Eva was sitting straight and square in a burgundy Louis XIV chair, while Elizabeth tried to make herself comfortable on the rigid, stiff-backed sofa.

"Love is such a mawkish ideal," Eva was saying. "Awash with foolish sentimentality. Promises to love, honor, and cherish are easily made and easily broken. That is why realistic and practical women look for something more out of life."

Elizabeth stared at her own hands clenched tightly in her lap. She was afraid to look directly at her grandmother, afraid that the hostility she was now feeling would show in her eyes. She couldn't do that. No one must know how she felt. Not now, not ever.

"After you marry Thomas Benson, you will be a very wealthy woman, Elizabeth. My needs are much smaller now than they used to be, so I have made arrangements with our attorneys for most of the stocks, municipal bonds, real estate, and cash to be transferred to you."

Elizabeth finally looked up and stared with surprise at her grandmother.

"Yes." Eva smiled. "I thought that would please you. That is why I hope you will set aside these silly schoolgirl notions you have been harboring about love, and simply marry your Mr. Benson."

Elizabeth turned her eyes toward the windows. The front lawn looked cool and green under the morning sun. One of the gardeners was meticulously combing the grass for stray weeds while another plunged a huge syringe into the ground, making circles around all the trees to feed them their balanced diet. Notions about love. What were her notions about it? The only love she had ever harbored had been for Sam Winslow. But that was no schoolgirl notion. She looked back at Eva. "What about your marriage to Grandfather? Surely there was something. . . some emotional bond that held you two together."

Eva leaned forward in her seat and impaled her granddaughter with her steel-gray eyes. "Elizabeth, your grandfather was the most boring man that ever walked the face of the earth." She leaned back a bit and smiled. "But he was rich. Infinitely more satisfying than any love he could have offered."

Elizabeth tried not to be sickened by this revelation.

Who was she to judge? After all, wasn't that a big part of the reason for marrying Thomas Benson?

"I must tell you, dear, I have always been disappointed in your mother." Eva's hands were folded primly in her lap. "Louise is a frivolous, spineless, simpering child who has jumped from one marriage to another in search of this elusive thing called love. And in the process she is drinking herself into an early grave."

Elizabeth swallowed hard. Her own mother. Could she let her grandmother talk about her that way? "Maybe she has had too much pressure put on her," she suggested, but there was little conviction or support behind the words. "Maybe she has been striving all these years to be like you and...well, she isn't you at all."

Eva turned her head toward the Monet canvas of wild poppies that dominated one wall. She sat silent and unmoving. Sunlight spilled through the small lead panes of the windows and cut a clear white path across the Oriental rug. Elizabeth explored the marblelike profile of her grandmother and wondered what it would take to avoid becoming like her.

Eva's attention switched back to her. "Enough about your mother. It is you I am concerned about. I hope we have reached an understanding on this. That understanding being that you will marry Thomas Benson, you will carry on with the traditions this family has inspired, and you will do nothing to embarrass the rest of us or to besmirch the family name. After you marry Thomas, there will be no tawdry affair with Mr. Winslow. Now, are we in accord?"

Elizabeth closed her mind to what was happening, tried to blank it out. She was going to marry Thomas Benson. She was never going to see Sam again. The chapter was finished. A new page was turning. Thomas, no Sam. Mrs. Thomas Benson.

She took a deep breath, sat up straighter, and looked directly at the older woman sitting so erect in her chair. She even managed a small smile. "Yes, Grandmother, we are in accord."

Chapter Twenty-five

The last time Elizabeth had seen so many flowers, it had been at the funeral of a national political figure. Funny that she should make the connection between this elaborate grandstand effect and a funeral. But then, one way of looking at her upcoming marriage to Thomas Benson was as a death of sorts. Death of Chicago society's princess. Death of freedom. All of her dreams and desires and the last shred of her self-esteem were being piled on top of the funeral pyre. She had sold herself to the highest bidder and Thomas had won the price.

She looked about her in a panic. She couldn't breathe. She needed to open the door. She moved through the house while the florists and the caterers fluttered around her as if she didn't exist. Even they had noticed. She was no longer among the living. Another group of men was in the living room, setting up the chairs and instruments for the orchestra. An orchestra! Playing a funeral dirge perhaps?

"No, not there!" Louise snapped at an unfortunate young man who was removing a large arrangement of drooping tropicana roses from the room, making space for the fresh flowers that would arrive tomorrow. "Now look at that, you spilled water on the piano. Letti! Oh, dear, how will I ever survive this?" she mumbled to herself. "Put it over here," she ordered the boy.

"And please be more careful. Letti! Oh, there you are. There is water on the piano and fetch me a sherry, will you?"

"Yes, Miss Louise."

Elizabeth hurried to the sliding door and flung it open. She couldn't breathe! She needed some air! She quickly stepped out onto the patio and took in a deep breath, filling her lungs with the fullness of the spring air.

June had burst upon them with its sun-drenched days and warm, starlit nights. And it was a perfect time for a wedding. A June bride was what she would be. Perfect in every way, except that she was marrying the wrong man.

She breathed in deeply and tilted her head back, her eyes closed. Imagine if it were Sam she were going to marry. How he would look, the way he would hold her hand, how much meaning those vows would have for them both. Walking through life arm in arm. She opened her eyes and lowered her head. What a joke! They would have to have awfully long arms to reach from his world to hers.

His world. At one point she had thought that it could be hers too. Those had been good days with him. There had been such a feeling of accomplishment with what she was doing there. Working with the YES program, visiting patients with Sam at the hospital, making friends with Zelma Worlitzer, Father Stanislavski, Alfredo Poleri, Billy the Mole, Maggie Moon... The names and faces filled her mind with memories, nice ones, ones she wanted to keep with her forever. Mama Vinzetti, Paolo, the student counselors with the youth program. Voices, smiles, eccentricities, and divergent life-styles. Yes, those times on Blackhawk had been very good times.

And with Sam she had always felt so warm and safe

and loved. Why couldn't she just have been happy with that? Why could she not have been more like him and simply walked away from the life she had known for thirty years?

She turned and walked over to the swimming pool and stared down into the clear water. Her eyes lifted to the waterfall and the tennis courts beyond. Did he still need her? Did any of those people on Blackhawk really need her there? Or was she just one more superfluous body taking up space in an already overcrowded neighborhood?

Oh, well, it was all water under the bridge at this point anyway. She was marrying Thomas Benson tomorrow. She was fulfilling some destiny under which she was supposedly born. Everyone would be delighted. Her mother, her grandmother, her friends, Thomas.

Everyone but her. And perhaps Sam.

Sam rode the Chicago and northwestern train to Winnetka and walked the few blocks to Elizabeth's house. It was a warm morning, but not nearly as warm as in the city where he lived. Up here, the breezes off the lake were cool and refreshing, and they stirred up the scent of lilac, rose of Sharon, and spirea bushes that surrounded the large estates.

At the entrance to her driveway he stopped, reevaluating for the hundredth time his reasons for coming here. He had to see her one more time. He had to make sure that this was what she really wanted to do with her life. Who was he kidding? He wanted to make her change her mind. He didn't want to lose what little chance they might have of being together.

He shoved his hands into his pockets and walked along the curving drive to the front entrance. He knocked and Letti opened the door.

"Why, Mr. Winslow," she whispered. "I was wondering if you were going to give it your best shot."

"Hello, Letti. Is Elizabeth home?"

"She sure isn't, and you better not come in, 'cause Miss Eva is here and, Lawdy, would it start hitting the fan if she knew you were here."

The voice behind her made her blanch. "Is there someone to see me, Letti?" Eva walked up to her side and flung open the door. "Reverend Winslow. What... an interesting surprise. Letti, don't be rude, let's invite our guest inside."

Sam hesitated for a moment, glancing quickly at Letti's wary expression, then stepped into the foyer. "Thank you, Mrs. Rowen. I hope you don't mind if I wait for Elizabeth to return."

Eva's return look was carved in stone. "Why don't you come with me into the parlor. Letti, bring us some tea. This way, Reverend."

He reluctantly followed her into the parlor and took a seat on the sofa. The room was cold and hard, like the woman before him, and he knew that she had more in store for him than a hospitable cup of tea.

"So, why are you here, Reverend Winslow? Is there something I can help you with? More charity work that needs to be done in your area of the city?"

He stared at her sitting so erect in the chair across from him and debated over the best way to handle her. "I think you know why I'm here, Mrs. Rowen. I came to see Elizabeth, and it has nothing to do with charity work."

"I see. Well, actually, I'm not surprised. I'm sure that for a man like you it must be very difficult to accept the inevitable in a case like this. But you see, my granddaughter is getting married tomorrow."

"Where is she, Mrs. Rowen? What time will she be back home?"

Eva waved her hand in front of her. "Oh, very late,

I'm afraid. She's doing some last-minute shopping. All those little things a new bride needs, you know.''

They were both silent for a long minute, studying each other carefully. Sam was the first to break the impasse. ''I can't believe that she is certain about what she's doing. I think you have influenced her unfairly.''

''Is that so? And what about you, Reverend Winslow? Aren't you here to try and influence her also? We all do that, you realize. Everyone tries to influence the people who mean something special to them.''

''But you are trying to make her like you,'' he argued. ''And she's not. She was happy on Blackhawk Street, Mrs. Rowen. I know that. She was just afraid to take the final step and say yes, this was what she wanted to do with her life.''

''Ah, here is the tea. Thank you, Letti. No, just leave that. I'll serve Reverend Winslow's. Sugar or lemon?''

He clenched his jaw tightly in a futile attempt to calm the racing of his pulse. ''No, thank you.''

She poured a cup for him and handed it over. ''Now, you were talking about Elizabeth's happiness, I believe.'' She took a sip and set her saucer down on the table in front of her. ''You have known my granddaughter for only a few short months, Reverend. I have known her all of her life. I know what makes her happy now, and I know what will make her happy in the years to come. Marrying Thomas Benson is what will make her happy.''

He set his cup and saucer down without taking a drink. ''I'd like to hear that from her, if you don't mind.''

''I do mind, Reverend Winslow. I mind very, very much. I'm afraid that you will not be able to stay here any longer. We have so many things to do today and... well, I believe you will have to go.''

"Why did you invite me inside in the first place?"

"I wanted to get a few things straight with you, that's all. It is time we came to an understanding, for Elizabeth's sake, don't you agree?"

"She will know I was here today," he said.

"How? I'm certainly not going to tell her. Oh, you're referring to Letti, of course." Eva shook her head sadly. "I'm afraid you are going to be disappointed there, Reverend. Letti is too old to start looking for another job. She will not tell Elizabeth."

He glanced around the room and expelled a slow breath, then looked back at Eva. "You're afraid that if I stay, if I see her, I'll be able to talk her out of marrying him, aren't you?"

Eva smiled and stood up from her chair. "Reverend Winslow, I am afraid of nothing." She walked over to the window and looked out across the front lawn and drive. It was the same spot where she had been standing a few minutes earlier and had watched Sam Winslow stop at the end of the driveway and then, making his decision, walk up to the front of the house. She turned back to him now. "Would you like to know why I am not afraid, Reverend?"

"I'm sure you're going to tell me whether I want to hear it or not," he said.

She smiled again. "It is because I always win. Always. So you see, there is absolutely nothing at all for me to fear."

He closed his eyes for a moment, then opened them and stood to leave. She was still standing by the window, her smile as cold as ice, when he turned to leave the room and the house.

"Oh, by the way, Reverend," she called out behind him. "I've already explained to Elizabeth that any cheap little goings-on between you two after she is married will be out of the question. I will tolerate no scandal in my family or in my granddaughter's marriage.''

As he turned to stare at Eva, he could no longer hide the utter disgust he felt for her. He could not even find the words to express to her what he was now feeling. He could only stare.

''I told you, Reverend Winslow, I always win.''

Elizabeth carried the packages up to her room and dumped them on the bed. Her mother had insisted that she buy some new outfits to wear on her honeymoon, so they had spent the afternoon combing Michigan Avenue for just the right things.

She plopped down on the bed beside the packages and let out a tired sigh. This was absurd! Why was she doing this to herself? If only she could become numb to it all and anesthetize herself to what was happening, then she could deal with it. She would smile and go through the motions and no one would ever suspect that she was just a shell.

She grinned at the idea and, with her fingers, slowly inched the packages to the edge of the bed. Then, in one short thrust, she shoved them over the side and to the floor in a pile.

Sitting up, she reached for the stack of mail that Letti had set beside the bed. She thumbed through it with disinterest until one of the letters caught her attention. The postmark was from California. She smiled and slipped it out of the stack, sitting back against her pillows. So Suzanne Elliston was back in Los Angeles. The envelope was hastily ripped open and dropped onto the floor beside the bed. Unfolding the pages, she began to read.

Elizabeth,
Well, here I am in tinsel town. (Heaven help me!) But at least this time I'm doing it right. Percentage

of the gross and final approval on any changes in the script. They say power corrupts. Well, maybe so, but I love it!

It's a crazy place here. The city is built with mirrors. If I see one more pretty-boy actor run his fingers through his blow-dried hair, I think I'll throw up.

Elizabeth laughed and reached over to the table for a lemon drop. After popping it in her mouth, she turned the page over.

How are you getting along? I think I heard that you were getting married to our dashing Mr. Thomas Benson, but I wasn't sure whether to believe it or not. The last I heard from you, you were redecorating west side Chicago and loving every minute of it.

I hope it was your decision alone to come home and marry Thomas Benson. Just remember, choice. That's all there is in life. One after another. It's not important whether you make the right ones or the wrong ones, as long as you make them yourself.

I don't know if you've needed the flight jacket I gave you or not. But before you do anything too rash, you might just put it on. Don't do it for me. Do it for yourself. And let me know how everything turns out.

Say hello to Granny Eva for me, won't you? I know I've put her down a lot in the past, but I'm sure she's really a sweet old gal who has lots of wonderful traits. I understand Attila the Hun even had a few.

I'll be in L.A. for a couple of months, then I'm heading northeast. There is a very wealthy, very

corrupt family living on Martha's Vineyard and in
my next book I plan to expose all of the molding
skeletons in their closets.

Remember, Elizabeth, Choice with a capital C.
You're the only one who should make this one
about marriage. Have courage! It goes hand in
hand with any big decision.

                                                    Suz

Elizabeth stared at the pieces of typing paper in her
hands for a long time. *Choice. Courage.* Words that
didn't even belong in her vocabulary. She had never
made an important decision in her life. She had never
chosen anything. Everything had always just been given
to her, decided for her. And courage, what a laugh! She
didn't have an ounce of it in her body. Who needed
courage when you had money instead?

She closed her eyes tightly. If she was to make the
choice, what would it be? To marry Thomas and never
have a moment of insecurity? Or to run to Sam and
never know anything but insecurity, and have only what
the two of them could give each other? Obviously she
had already made the choice; tomorrow morning she
was going to marry Thomas.

Courage and choice go hand in hand, Suzanne said.
But there had been anything but courage involved in this
decision.

Elizabeth sighed wearily and stood up. Suzanne
shouldn't have wasted that jacket on her. Where had
she put it, anyway? She should just box it up and send it
back to its rightful owner.

She walked through the dressing room into the closet,
at first casually glancing about without much interest in
finding it. Then suddenly she began to rummage
through boxes and shelves, searching in earnest for the
one that held the jacket.

She found it. It was on the top shelf at the back. Standing on her dressing table chair, she was just able to reach the box and pull it down. After setting the package on the floor, she opened the lid and pulled the jacket out of the folds of tissue paper. She held it up in front of her. One arm slipped into a sleeve. Then the other. She adjusted it carefully in the front so that it hung straight, and then she turned to face the full-length mirror on the wall of her dressing room.

Minutes ticked away while she stared at her reflection, hating what she saw. Impotence wrapped in a symbol of power and courage. Weakness. Fear. The self-loathing expanded and rose to a screaming pitch within her and finally some inner wall began to crack. She leaned against the wall and slid to the floor as tears began to cascade down her cheeks. This time she didn't even try to hold them in. *Don't do it. Don't do this to yourself!*

Huddled on the floor against the dressing room wall, she could still see her reflection in the full-length mirror. Pale skin, puffy eyelids, mascara streaks down both cheeks. "God, but you are a pathetic woman!" she cried. "Pathetic and worthless!"

Her eyes closed so that she wouldn't have to look at herself anymore. Time slipped by while she tried to make her mind blank, tried not to think or feel anything. White noise, that was what she needed. Something to drown out the distractions.

Outside, the sun slowly lowered until it hung suspended just over the last hurdle. She ran her hand down the front of the jacket, feeling the cool, smooth leather beneath her fingers. Courage. Did she have any? Had she ever had any? If so, did she have enough within her to say no to all those florists, caterers, musicians, and friends? She squeezed her eyes shut. Even more importantly did she have the courage to say no to her mother, her grandmother, to Thomas... the money?

She wiped her cheeks and nose with the back of her hand and stood up, still watching herself in the mirror. Could she say yes to Sam?

She swallowed hard, then walked into the bathroom, reaching for a band to tie back her hair. She leaned over the sink and splashed cool water on her face. Grabbing a towel, she wiped her face and stared at her reflection once again. *Be good for your Mr. Winslow, or else set him free.* Who had said that to her? Oh, yes, Zelma Worlitzer. Well, what about herself, dammit? All her life she had been what people expected her to be. Be a good girl, Lizzy, and do what your mother or grandmother says. Be good for Thomas. Be good for Sam.

She ripped the band from her hair, picked up her brush, and pulled it hard through the strands. It was high time she started being good to and for herself. To hell with what everybody else expected.

She took note of all the things on her dressing table, the silver-backed brushes, the bottles of perfume. Her gaze swung to the closet, where evening gowns of inordinate cost hung in a long row. There were shoes to go with every outfit; purses to match the shoes; hats for occasional fancies; and countless numbers of skirts, jackets, pants, and blouses.

Funny that she could own so much and have so little. She turned around to leave the closet and there before her hung the dress in which she was to be married. A simple white silk Charmeuse, very elegant, very expensive. She touched the material lightly, then let it drop from her fingers. She would not be wearing it tomorrow. She would not be wearing it at all. It was a dress for a little girl's fantasy world, and there was one thing she could finally accept and admit to herself. Elizabeth Parkins was no longer a little girl.

For the first time in a very long time she was able to honestly smile.

Chapter Twenty-six

A few homemade streamers hung from the awnings of shops. Two old black men sat on stools in the middle of the street and played the harmonica and guitar. At each end of the block sawhorses were set up to keep any traffic away. Four tables, covered with print cloths and set in the middle of the street, held bowls of food. There were some tamales and a couple of corned beef briskets, a few dozen bratwurst, and a large pot of spaghetti. A large bowl of gumbo dominated another table. Cabbages, tomatoes, and potatoes accompanied the varied dishes. Many people on the street had contributed to the fare, for this was a celebration.

Everyone had worked hard over the past two months to build back the neighborhood after the fire. And now the shops were all operating once more and the homeless had new places to live. Everyone was back in the business of life.

Billy Hawkins eyed the feast with hungry eyes, but nibbled on something he had picked up on the street corner. Tiny children wove in and out of the tables while their older brothers and sisters played in the spray from an open fire hydrant.

Sam poured a few glasses of wine and handed them over the table, while a young woman beside him poured Kool-Aid for the kids.

It was in a rare moment of quiet, when everyone had their plates and glasses filled and had moved to the sidelines to eat, that he looked up and saw it. It was a flash of red in the periphery of his eye. And when he turned and looked down the street into the next block, he saw that it was her car.

He continued watching as she pulled it to the curb and switched off the engine. She was a block away, but he knew the minute she opened the door and set her foot onto the street that it was really she. This was no trick of the imagination. She was here.

He followed her every movement as she locked the door of the car and adjusted the strap of her purse over her shoulder. Then she started walking down the street toward him. He waited until she reached the sawhorses at the end of the block and then he began to slowly move in her direction.

She was wearing tan cotton slacks and an olive-colored flight jacket. He could tell it was old and that in itself surprised him. He had never seen her wear anything more than once. But he liked what he saw. She looked different somehow and more approachable.

She was standing in front of him and neither had spoken. His eyes were taking in everything about her while she drank in the very sight of him.

He finally spoke, but it was not much above a husky whisper. "I approve of your tailor."

She glanced down self-consciously at her clothes and then smiled at him. "The new me. What do you think?"

"I can't say it in public." He grinned. "You'd blush too much if I told you. What are you doing here?"

She smiled nervously. "Looking for my backbone, among other things."

"Did you leave it here?"

"I never had one."

He shook his head and looked at her. "I don't believe that for a minute."

"It's true, Sam."

"What else are you looking for?"

She smiled and looked down at the street between them. "For you."

He took a deep breath and stuck his hands in his pockets. She lifted her gaze to the street behind him. "It looks different here. What happened?"

"We had a fire in April, but we're slowly getting it back together again."

She held her breath. "Your house. . . did it burn?"

"No, the fire didn't go any farther than Alfredo's on this side of the street."

She exhaled slowly and looked around her, taking in the sights and sounds and smells of this place that had come to mean so much to her and that had ingrained itself so indelibly on her mind. Mama Vinzetti was mounding pasta onto a plate and covering it with several ounces of tomato sauce. She handed it to Anna, who then smiled invitingly at the man who took it from her. A couple of drunks staggered by with their arms around each other, singing a ballad about a redheaded lass they once knew in the Highlands, while old Father Stanislavski huffed and sweated through a rigorous game of basketball being played at the end of the block.

"I see you finally let Father Stanislavski talk you into a block party."

Sam chuckled. "Yeah, can you believe it? And what's really amazing is it's working. Guess I have a few things to learn after all." His grin was wide and lazy. "You want to go somewhere. . . for a walk or something?"

She pointed to the concrete stoop in front of the high school. "Why don't we just sit over there? I feel like I've been away on a long trip and I've just come home.

I'd like to stick around for a few minutes, if that's okay."

He took her hand and his heart did a quick drumroll inside his chest. "As long as you like, Elizabeth." They started walking over toward the school. "I came to your house yesterday, did you know that?"

"Yes. Letti told me."

"Wasn't she afraid of being fired?"

She took a seat on the top step and looked down at her knees. "She said it was worth the risk. You see..." She paused, then slowly lifted her eyes to Sam. "Everyone has been willing to risk everything...except me."

Sam swallowed hard, afraid to say anything, afraid even to think. He didn't want to hope too much. He had been that road and found it to be a very rough one. He rested his forearms on his knees and clasped his hands in front of him. "I've taken up a new hobby," he said.

She tilted her head, watching him. He was facing the sun, making him squint against the brightness, and little lines branched out from the corners of his eyes. He had never looked better to her. His hair was soft and gleaming with highlights under the summer sun and his eyes were a warm brown like newly turned soil in a fertile field.

"What kind of hobby?"

"Reading the society pages in the newspaper."

"Oh." She stared at him for a long frozen moment. "And you saw, of course, that I was to be married."

He nodded slowly, afraid to speak, afraid to know if that was precisely what she had come to tell him.

She moved her head from side to side. "Not anymore, Sam." She tilted her head back and closed her eyes. "You know what it was? When I was living here with you, I never really closed off my other options. I kept them open...just in case. I always knew I had Thomas Benson and my house and my friends to fall back on. I never had to make a commitment or a firm choice about what I wanted." She kept her head back and her eyes remained shut in the space that followed. Finally she lowered her head and looked back at him. "I can't marry him, Sam."

His eyes dropped shut and he expelled the breath he didn't even know he had been holding. He laid his hand on her thigh and the shape of her leg against his palm shot a hot spark of need throughout his body. "What—" He cleared his throat and tried again. "What made you change your mind?"

"It was several things. First of all, I didn't love him." Her laugh was humorless. "But that didn't seem to be enough to keep me from marrying him." She took a deep breath. "And then there was you. It was the thought of never seeing you again." She looked out over the street. "But beyond both of those reasons, it was the fact that if I did this thing... if I married him, I would lose all chance of finding out what I want out of life. I would be doing only what everyone wanted me to do and expected me to do."

"Not everyone wanted you to get married." He smiled at her when he caught her eye.

"Oh, Sam, there were so many times when I wanted you to come get me, just whisk me away and force me to stay with you, and forbid me to marry him."

His hand began a slow massage against her thigh and his eyes dropped to watch the movements of his fingers. "There were many times when I was tempted. I wish it would have been that easy, but I knew it had to be your decision." His other hand lifted to her neck, and his thumb stroked across the plane of her cheek. "But I have missed you so much, Elizabeth. Every day, every night, you've always been here in my thoughts."

"Were you angry that I went home after my accident?"

He slowly shook his head. "Not with you. Only with myself. The fact that I had put you in a position where you could be hurt was something I had a hard time forgiving in myself."

"But it wasn't your fault! I'm the one who insisted on working there. And like you said, I just happened to be in the wrong place at the wrong time."

He studied her face carefully, searching the angles and tiny lines that revealed her every emotion. "Are you still frightened by it? Do you still have the dreams?"

"Only occasionally. I really think I'm over it. I've been able to push it way, way back."

"Were you able to talk to anyone about it?"

"No, not really." She looked up and grinned. "Hey, maybe someday you'll listen to my long tearful tale, right?"

"Anytime you want, Elizabeth. I mean that. I feel so responsible for what happened to you. And I care about what you're feeling. If you're hurting inside, then so am I."

She reached up to touch his hair and her fingers slid through the soft strands. "Did you ever think...that I wasn't very good for you? That I wasn't quite right for your life?"

He grasped her wrist and held it tight. "Elizabeth, you were the best thing that ever happened to me. The very best."

"But I wasn't always the way you expected or wanted me to be."

He frowned. "So what? I'm sure I wasn't everything you expected or wanted, either. Listen, if you build a relationship on expectations alone, you're always going to end up being disappointed. I didn't do that with you." He laughed and shook his head. "Hell, Elizabeth, I never knew what to expect with you."

He released her wrist and she wove her fingers

through his. "What am I going to do with you, Sam Winslow?"

He shrugged and smiled. "Love me. And let me love you."

She sighed. "Like you told me before, that's the easy part. I've never stopped loving you. Even when I knew I'd never see you again, I still realized I would never love anyone as much as I do you."

"You know I want you to marry me, Elizabeth. I want that more than anything."

She looked down and tightened the grip of her fingers on his hand. "Yes. But I never realized until yesterday that I've been nothing more than a puppet for thirty years. Dangling along while life slipped beneath me. My grandmother has held the strings my whole life." She looked up at him. "I am breaking those strings now. Do you understand what I'm saying?"

He nodded. "It's a big step for you."

"A very big step. And as easy as it would be for me to say that I would marry you now, I know that there are some things that I must sort out before I do that. I have to figure out what I want out of life first. Does that make any sense to you?"

He watched the fire of life that glowed in the center of her emerald eyes and he smiled, cupping her cheek in his hand. "Yes, I do. Remember I told you I had to do the same thing when I came back from India. I just did it a few years earlier than you, that's all. Everybody has to make their own way. But if I can help you in...in any way..."

"Yes, you can help me. I don't even know where to begin. That's why I came to you. I want to be with you and love you and help you. I'm willing to try to make our relationship work. But I also want to try to find myself before I commit to marriage. I don't want to follow the patterns my mother set with marriage."

His eyes grew more serious. "If we try again, it might not work. You know that, don't you? There will be times when it will be very rough. Even for people who are so much alike, it's hard. But you and I...we have a long way to go to reach a middle ground. I want you to realize that. We might not make it, Elizabeth."

"I thought you were an optimist." She smiled, wrapping her hand around the back of his head.

"I am. But I'm also a realist. How do you feel about that?"

She looked down at only the slim space that remained between them. "Scared to death. But at the same time I know you're right, Sam. It might not work. But the difference this time is that I know it's worth the risk. I'm not leaving any other doors open to fall back into. And I want to learn more of the things you've already taught me. Honesty, loyalty, purpose. Love. Will you let me try?"

He looked at her for a long moment, then pulled her close. He held her face between his hands and his mouth closed over hers, sealing the bond that he would fight to protect. Together they would try to make it work. That was all he could hope for, all he could expect. But that alone was a gift from heaven.

He pulled back and looked down into her face. "Did that answer your question?"

She tried to catch her breath and smiled shakily. "I love you, Sam Winslow."

"I love you, Elizabeth Parkins."

She looked back down the street when she felt the tears pressing against her eyelids. Someone waved to them from behind one of the tables. "Is that Mama Vinzetti waving?"

Sam followed her gaze to the tables. "Yeah." He squinted to see what she was signaling for. "Shall we go see what she wants?"

Elizabeth stood up and wiped the stray tears from her cheek. "Sure." She put her hand in his and together they walked down the center of the street.

"Come, Sam, come, Elizabeth! Join the festivities. Please, have some food. Have some wine."

Sam turned to Elizabeth. "Want some wine?"

She laughed. "Need you ask?"

He reached for a couple of Welches jelly glasses and Anna poured the wine into each. He handed one to Elizabeth and shrugged. "My contribution to the party. As you can see, I never have gotten around to buying any wine glasses."

Elizabeth tilted her head and regarded him closely for a long, penetrating moment. Then, with a decisive clink of her glass against his, she smiled. "Who needs them."

An exciting romantic saga
destined to become
the most talked-about book
of the decade

By all-time bestselling
Harlequin author Charlotte Lamb—
writing as Sheila Holland

Secrets
Sheila Holland

Sophia was torn between the love of two men—two
brothers who were part of a great and noble family. As
different as fire and ice, they were rivals whose hatred
for each other was powerful and destructive. Their
legacy to Sophia was a life of passion and regret, and
secrets that must never be told...

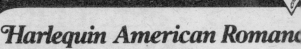

Harlequin American Roman

An exciting series of sensuous and
emotional love stories—contemporary,
engrossing and uniquely American. Long,
satisfying novels of conflict and challenge,
stories of modern men and women dealing with
life and love in today's changing world.